Molly Fish

Jack McMasters

Clink
Street

London | New York

Published by Clink Street Publishing 2017

Copyright © 2017

First edition.

ISBN:
978-1-911525-69-1 paperback
978-1-911525-70-7 ebook

Chapter One

Stumbling once more on the uneven, rocky ground and gasping for air, Arthur wiped at the perspiration stinging his eyes with his damp sleeve. His legs, and his lungs, were screaming for another rest, but he was only too aware that it had been no more than minutes earlier that Rani had urged him to his feet. He remembered her calm encouragement.

'Just put one foot in front of the other; just think about one step at a time.'

'Not much further,' Rani said softly, as if reading his mind, and at the same time pointing to an escarpment above them. 'Once we're over that ridge, it's all downhill.'

'Yes, but a climb down can be about as bad as a climb up, and we've been climbing for hours.'

'No, no, you mustn't think like that. I know you're tired, but stop being negative. It's a gentle path down. Really, it's not that far now. We should be there in another half-hour,' she said, offering the near-empty plastic bottle. 'Have a sip of water.'

It seemed pointless now to wish he had opted for the journey to her village by jeep. She had said it would take at least two days over incredibly rough roads and the prospect of camping overnight in the jungle hadn't appealed to him.

'This would only be a couple of hours of a gentle climb through incredibly beautiful mountain scenery.'

He knew when he'd been had.

From the village where the last bus had deposited them the walk had initially been an easy climb. The path ran alongside a stream that at first had flowed gently, but as the gradient increased the water was rippling noisily over the rocky outcrops. As the climb grew steeper still and the rocky sides of the narrow gorge came closer together the water pounded and roared, frequently drenching them with its spray. At times the path had disappeared completely and they had been forced to wade through the stream itself. Then, after what had seemed like hours, though he was unable to tell, he had *lost* his watch along with his mobile while they were asleep on the bus the previous night, the path became a serious climb and left the stream far below.

During the less steep parts of the climb he had found himself distracted by the way Rani's buttocks swelled against the soft material of the long, loose skirt she was wearing and, not giving enough attention to where he was stepping, he had fallen painfully. Now, with the path only inches away from the cliff face and the faint sound of waterfalls from far below reminding him just how high up they were, he watched every step carefully, knowing his life depended upon it. Still, it was difficult to ignore the long brown legs revealed where she had tucked the hem of her skirt into the waistband of her underwear.

As they continued upwards for the remaining portion of the climb, the absurdity of this holiday struck him. He considered himself to be in quite good shape, at least for someone his age. It took little effort to hold his stomach in while he admired himself in the mirror and there was only a tiny amount of visible flab. Hell, if he stood just right, it almost looked as if he had a six-pack. After all, he was over sixty. No, he thought, be honest for a change, seventy was looming far too close to be comfortable. Perhaps it wasn't so embarrassing that he needed an occasional rest, or wouldn't be if Rani didn't make the climb look so ridiculously easy.

He had flown to India with her after only a very short acquaintance and it had been necessary to satisfy Ester by inventing a last-minute invitation to an interesting dig. Along with an excuse that one of the other members of his "Architectural Society", as she persisted in calling it, confusing his former occupation with his current interest, had been unable to go. He was, he assured her, only making up the numbers for the good of the club.

To be honest, he thought, he had met Rani when he was attending a meeting of his archaeological group. Rani had been staying in the same hotel having met, she later told him, a series of buyers for the products she exported. He had noticed her sitting alone in the bar, dressed in a smart business suit, making notes on her laptop and it was a matter of habit that he attempted feeble flirtations on such occasions. He expected to be rebuffed; he was more often than not rebuffed, but she had surprised him by accepting his offer of a drink. He had found her a surprisingly amenable companion for the evening and conversation had flowed easily between them. He was, he found, attracted to her unexpected sense of humour. After dinner together, and perhaps a little too much to drink on his part, they had ended up in her room.

When they landed at Goa, she had changed to more casual attire, so different but just as striking in appearance to her beautifully cut business suits, for the daylong journey by train. After a further night and a morning's ride, sandwiched between the local natives and various animals on an ancient bus that rattled and shook them constantly, they had finally arrived in the last village. He felt as if he hadn't shaved or bathed for a week and the strange and frequently unfamiliar odours surrounding them seemed permanently ingrained in his body. The khaki-coloured trousers and expensive shirt Ester had insisted on buying for his journey were sweat stained and looked fit only for a dustbin.

Rani, in contrast, still looked as if she was about to step out for a day's shopping. Her apparel of good quality linen was only slightly creased and looked as if it had been designed for her. She had momentarily shaken her long, dark hair from the bun it was in and after briefly running a comb through it, had deftly pulled it back into place. A quick dab at her face with a scented wipe had removed any trace of tiredness and revealed her total lack of make-up. Six hours later, as they finally reached the last ridge and stopped to rest once more before descending, she looked remarkably unchanged, with only a few wisps of hair out of place.

The valley she had described earlier lay before them, surrounded by mountains as far as he could see. A lake in the far distance sparkled in the light of the setting sun and a similar reflection traced the path of a river that meandered through a varied, rolling landscape, past lush fields and small villages. The trail leading towards the nearer villages appeared to be as gentle as Rani had described and after a short rest and draining the last of their water, they set off once again on this final leg of their journey. The exhaustion that had overwhelmed Arthur earlier began to ease with the easier pace and was gradually replaced with a growing excitement; after all, he was on a promise.

Her proposition had been so completely unexpected and so unlike anything he had ever experienced, he kept telling himself that there had to be some catch. She was, after all an attractive, relatively young woman. No, let's face it, she was a beautiful woman, early forties at the most he thought, with incredible poise and a dress sense that flattered a still slim figure. Okay, he wasn't bad looking for someone his age. He made sure he exercised regularly, even though he couldn't stand the boredom of a gym. He looked after his teeth meticulously and chose his clothes carefully, but his hair was seriously thinning and had long lost all but the faintest hint of its former colour.

Thinking about their first conversations, it seemed her interest had increased when he mentioned his holiday earlier in the year to India. He had broken his rule of never mentioning Ester when talking to another woman and told of his disappointment in missing so much of the tour because of her illness, adding how much he wanted to return.

She had ignored his reference to Ester, but started asking more questions. Had he enjoyed the holiday? Did he have problems with tummy bugs? Was his visa still valid? They had conversed easily all evening; she was knowledgeable on a wide range of subjects and for once he had remembered to ask questions of someone instead of trying to impress them with the extent of his own experience. He'd had the distinct impression that her attitude had changed abruptly and it must have been about then that she had suggested having a nightcap in her room. Once they were there, her manner seemed to have changed once again. She had become openly flirtatious, amorously brushing against him as he poured drinks from the minibar.

At the time and already under the influence of the larger half of a bottle of wine, he had assumed it was his irrepressible charm, but later he realized she had been in control all the time. She had kissed the nape of his neck while stroking his back, hip and buttocks. In response, he had turned to her and they had immediately embraced. They had held each other like that for a long time, swaying gently back and forth as if dancing. She had allowed him to unbutton her blouse and kiss her breasts, but each time he had tried to kiss her lips she had turned her head slightly. The last time he had tried, after a series of little kisses up one side of her throat, he had just barely brushed the corner of her lips and it was as if a firework had exploded in his head.

It was then that she had pulled away slightly, looked him directly in the eyes, and asked if he would accompany her on her return to India. She could promise him two weeks of the greatest sex he had ever had, she had said, adding that not only would it take years off him, but that all women would then find him irresistible for the rest of his life. He was tempted to make a joke; to say he had always assumed that such was the case, but he took her earnest gaze as an indication that this was one time he should refrain from stupid remarks.

Their arrangement had been so straightforward and so business-like. They had met for lunch two days later to discuss preparations. He had confirmed that his visa was still acceptable to the Indian authorities and that he had invented a sufficiently credible excuse to satisfy Ester. On his need of Ester's complete approval, Rani had been strangely insistent. His suspicious side kept waiting to be asked for something, perhaps to invest his life savings in some project that 'couldn't fail to double his investment', but nothing like that was ever voiced. She had already purchased his ticket and even stubbornly refused his offer to pay. The following morning they were on the plane.

By the time they reached the outskirts of her village, dusk had turned into actual darkness; Arthur had forgotten how quickly the transition occurred this close to the equator. The streets were dimly lit by strategically placed torches held in sconces projecting from corners of the buildings. Arthur wondered momentarily whose job it was to maintain these; some old fashioned lamplighter as depicted in nineteenth-century prints perhaps, lugging around a ladder and the long-handled device for snuffing the flames out at a predetermined time. Or, were they lit by individuals living nearby and allowed to simply burn themselves out each night?

In the dim flickering light, the buildings had a surprisingly Mediterranean appearance, even some Venetian influence, with tiled roofs and walls rendered in warm earthen colours. They soon encountered small groups, usually in two or threes, but occasionally more, of colourfully dressed women. All seemed to be moving towards the sounds of music and laughter and the flickering light of what Arthur assumed to be a large bonfire a few streets away. They invariably exchanged what sounded like friendly greetings and some good-natured banter with Rani, in an unfamiliar-sounding language.

She continued to lead him into a quieter area where the houses were larger, many with full-length verandas and large mature trees in their front gardens. Rani turned into the path leading to one of these and Arthur watched as she ascended a short flight of stairs to the veranda. At the top, she stopped and embraced a young woman standing in the shadows. In the dim light, Arthur hadn't noticed her and her greeting to Rani momentarily startled him. After they had exchanged a few excited words Rani turned and beckoned for Arthur to follow.

'This is Arthur,' she said with a note of pride. 'Isn't he beautiful? He's going to be staying with us for a while.'

Embarrassed as a child might be at hearing himself described as "beautiful", he awkwardly went to shake the extended hand, too late realizing that she was offering to take his shoulder bag. In his confusion he didn't hear her name as Rani introduced her, but meekly allowed her to remove his bag, take both his hands and pull him closer to her. He could feel her warm breath on his face and was aware of the closeness of her body as she softly kissed him on both cheeks, then continuing to hold both of his hands, she exchanged a few more words with Rani. Abruptly, she released him and disappeared in the direction he had seen the other women take.

'She was late for the gathering,' Rani explained, leading him into the house, 'but she has prepared us a supper. Shall we eat first?'

Her question reminded Arthur that he had last eaten many hours ago and that his stomach had been growling for the last half of their descent from the mountains.

'I think…' he paused, then despite his fatigue and the urgent desire

10

for a shower or bath, the appeal of food took an upper hand and he continued with an enthusiastic, 'Yes, please.'

Rani led him through a large entrance hall dimly lit with a few candles, into a smaller, more brightly lighted room. A low table was nearly covered with assorted small dishes and strategically placed candles reflected from the polished surfaces of the table and the tiled floor. She gestured for him to sit on one of the cushions placed either side of the table, then as if to show by example, neatly tucked her legs under her and knelt on the one closest. Arthur stood awkwardly, not knowing whether to kneel or squat and not sure that his knees, suffering from the afternoon's climb would survive either position for long.

'I should have asked you to leave your shoes at the door,' Rani said, 'you'll be much more comfortable without them'.

Arthur saw that she had slipped her own off at the doorway. Stooping to unlace and remove his sturdy, thick-soled shoes, he placed them alongside hers. As he returned he was all too aware that his socks were damp with sweat and were leaving faint footprints on the polished tile floor. He prayed that there was no discernible smell from them as he followed Rani's lead and carefully lowered himself onto the remaining cushion.

The array of small dishes spread out on the table was at first confusing until Arthur remembered once having enjoyed a thali in a vegetarian Indian restaurant. Rani told him the names and explained each of the dishes as she passed them to him. He recognized a few of them, but found that most were things he had never heard of. The dhal was wonderfully flavourful and still warm, as was the naan and Arthur wondered how the young woman had managed to predict the time of their arrival. He hadn't seen Rani use her mobile or go near a phone booth at any time since their plane had landed. He resolved to ask her, but quickly forgot as he lost himself in the profusion of flavours and textures. In his hunger, he ate far more quickly than he normally would, but listened attentively as Rani kept a running commentary of how and from what the individual dishes were made. With his mouth full, Arthur could only nod and make appreciative noises. When they had finished eating, Rani filled two small glasses from a white china jug and placed one in front of him.

'Try this,' she said. 'I think you'll like it.'

Arthur raised the glass to his lips, surprised to feel it too was quite warm, but finding the aroma very pleasant. At first he couldn't remember what it reminded him of. It was like a mixture of apple blossom and cedar wood, with something strangely familiar that he couldn't quite identify, thrown in. The taste was quite unlike the smell; a mixture of fruit juices with, he guessed from the tingle in his inner cheeks, a fairly high percentage of alcohol. Although the consistency was thicker than he was expecting, it was indeed very pleasant and he drained the cup far more quickly than he had intended.

Rani smiled at him across the table, slowly sipping at her own cup.

'I think perhaps I was right,' she laughed. 'Did you enjoy that?'

'I'm sorry if I wolfed my food,' Arthur apologized, his shoulders slumping as he relaxed more comfortably onto the cushion, 'I hadn't realized just how hungry I was. Did you get enough, or did I pig most of it?'

'Oh, I think I got my fair share,' Rani replied. 'But now it's time we got you cleaned up and ready for bed.'

She rose and reaching over the table, helped him to his feet. His hunger agreeably sated, but racked with fatigue, Arthur allowed her to lead him to an adjacent hallway and up the flight of stairs, hoping there was no hidden meaning in her last remark.

More appropriately placed candles gave ample light for Arthur to see, at the top of the stairs, a long balcony overlooking the large hallway. Along one side there were several doorways; Rani gestured at one, telling him that it was to be his room while he was staying, before leading him through another that was obviously a bathroom.

The fixtures in gleaming cream-coloured china were of such an unusual design that Arthur was unsure of their workings, but he found them intriguing nevertheless. In the centre of the room was a shallow, saucer-shaped tub, over two meters in diameter and a similarly large, showerhead hung from the ceiling directly above. A freestanding basin stood to one side echoing the shape of the tub, but its slender stem and large circular base made him think of a classical champagne glass. Partly screened on the opposite side, a shorter, lidded version without the stem appeared to be a toilet. From the curved lips of the basin and tub projected single gracefully turned handles. Arthur was unable to see anything else in the way of taps.

Sensing his bewilderment, Rani demonstrated the usage of each, pushing the handle one way, then another, saying, 'Hot, cold, open, closed,' as water flowed from under the lip, partly filling the basin and then disappearing.

'I had these made in Japan' she said, unable to hide a note of satisfaction, 'Zanli, one of Ashri's friends created the design and I couldn't resist having them made.'

'They're absolutely beautiful. I've never seen anything like them,' Arthur replied, wondering who Ashri was, 'I've always loved designing rooms and especially bathrooms, but I've never had fixtures like these to work with.'

'Sorry, but we're not going to use them tonight,' Rani said. 'Tomorrow night Ashri has something special planned for you and she doesn't want, shall we say, the edge taken off.' She opened a tall cupboard and withdrew a thick mat, spread it on the floor and turned to leave adding, 'Come, get out of those filthy clothes, I'll be right back.'

Wistfully looking at the huge tub, Arthur slowly removed his clothes, indecisive about his last item of underwear. He neatly folded the smelly, wrinkled items and looking about for a somewhere to put them, decided that the floor was the most appropriate.

'I meant everything,' Rani said, as she re-entered with an armful of towels and carrying a large basin and jug, 'and kneel here on the mat'.

Arthur did as he was instructed, grateful for the dimness of the candlelight. He noticed as she knelt opposite him, that Rani had changed into a pale-coloured dressing gown belted at the waist. She filled the basin from the jug and using a combination of her fingers, a comb and a washcloth, began carefully cleaning his hair.

He found the gentle action of her massaging his scalp, stroking with the comb, rubbing with the wet cloth and the warm, iridescent water that smelled of citrus completely hypnotic. Dropping the comb, Rani continued to work down his neck and shoulders using little circular movements of the wet cloth, ringing it out frequently to mop up the excess water. She continued to cleanse his face, arms and torso, paying particular attention to his hands and each finger.

The soft candlelight, the aroma of the water and the sensations of her gentle massage would have been enough, under normal circumstances, to create unbearable desire in Arthur, but he was so tired from his journey and at the same time relaxed from Rani's efforts, that when she asked him to stand, he was barely able to struggle to his feet. When he had finally managed that task, he merely stood meekly as Rani continued to wash and massage his legs and feet.

When she had finished, he followed her instruction to turn around and sit down, letting her pull him over backwards and cradle his head in her lap. Unaware of what was about to happen, he wallowed in the softness of the inner thighs that supported his shoulders. Trying not to think of what was immediately beneath his neck, he felt the unmistakeable rush of arousal until a gleam of candlelight reflected from the cutthroat razor she was holding and panicking, struggled to sit up.

'Relax, I'm only going to shave you,' she laughed, dipping the blade into the basin. 'What did you think I was going to do?'

Arthur remembered with sudden apprehension, his early attempts at using his father's razor on his first few half-developed whiskers. He could still feel the pull of the blade on the skin, the sharp sting and remembered the jibing from his friends about the multitude of small scars.

'Relax,' she repeated, stroking his forehead to pull his head deeper into her lap. 'I promise it won't hurt. I have done this before.'

Wetting his face again from the basin, she proceeded to shave him. Wetting, dipping, gently pulling the skin to tighten, turning his head first one way, then another for the best angle, her fingers flew over his face as a pianist's over a keyboard. Arthur was scarcely aware of feeling the blade. Finally, she dried his face with a towel and rubbed a spicy smelling cream into the skin. Lifting his head slightly from her lap she bent over and kissed the top of his forehead.

'All done,' she announced. 'Now let's get you into bed.'

His earlier feeling of a draining fatigue was replaced with one of relaxation. Arthur gratefully let her lead him to the bed where she pulled a light covering over him, and was vaguely aware of her telling him of the folded duvet at the foot of the bed; there in case it turned chilly through the night. Although his eyes were already closed, he heard her remove the jug, basin and shaving paraphernalia; by the time she returned to blow out the candles, he was fast asleep.

Chapter Two

Arthur awoke to find Rani bending over him, her eyes smiling down inquisitively. She was sitting sideways on his bed, one knee against his chest. Behind her, mottled sunlight flooded the room, filtered through the leaves of a tree outside his window. The air coming in was pleasantly cool and smelled of blossom.

'Come on, sleepyhead,' she teased, 'you can't sleep all day. There are things to do, people to meet. And perhaps more importantly, breakfast to eat.'

'What time is it?' Arthur asked, stretching luxuriantly, 'How long have I been sleeping?'

'Oh, it's not late. Mid-morning. I thought you might want to get out and see some things before it gets too hot. You can have a nap this afternoon, if you like. I've brought you something to wear.'

Arthur looked to where she was pointing; at folded items of clothing on a low table next to his bedside table. He worried briefly about the pile of dirty clothing he had left on the bathroom floor the night before, but just as quickly his concern disappeared.

'I'll let you get dressed,' she said, running her fingers through his hair, as a mother straightening a schoolboy son's.

Arthur sat up and putting one arm around her waist, pulled her towards him, but she pushed at him with one hand, laughing.

'You must have had a good night's sleep. But not yet my little tiger, I'm afraid you'll have to wait until tonight.'

She looked him directly in the eyes, her nose two inches from his and lowering her voice until scarcely audible. 'Be patient. I promise it will be worthwhile.' She brushed his hair with one hand again, then leaned forward and kissed him on the forehead.

Turning her hand so the knuckles were against his skin, she slowly drew them down his temple and, lingeringly, across his cheek.

'You're so beautiful,' she whispered softly, her eyes dilating. The change from turquoise to sudden darkness was startling. Arthur couldn't remember having ever seen such a rapid transformation on anyone. It reminded him of a cat he had seen once, concentrating on a toy bird waved in front of it.

Rani raised one forefinger to her mouth, kissed it and then brushed it lightly against his lips. The sensation of a blinding explosion within his head was the same as when, a few nights earlier, he had tried to kiss her. He found himself momentarily unable to breathe. The room swirled around him drunkenly and he seemed to see the room from several different viewpoints at the same time. When he could see clearly again, she had disappeared.

He sat up, stretched again, swung his legs out of the bed and stood up. The expected protests from muscles about the previous day's climb failed to appear and he couldn't remember when he had felt so well. He examined the clothing she had left. White boxer shorts, loose, creamy-coloured cotton trousers with a drawstring waist and a long sleeved, unlined cotton jacket that buttoned to the neck.

'Oh well,' he thought, quickly starting to dress, 'when in India'.

A grumbling from his stomach, despite the quantity he had eaten the night before, reminded him that breakfast was waiting for him. He found his way down the stairs and to the room where the previous evening's meal had taken place.

In the daylight, the room had a completely different feel. It was light and airy with a minimalist theme. Pale walls and two modern paintings, one small and one larger, in contrasting colours, drew Arthur's eye into the room as he entered. Near the adjacent wall was a small table on which stood a tall vase with a simple arrangement of fresh flowers. The dining table, now laid for three, held a collection of white china dishes, some filled with assorted fruit and pastries.

Rani was seated as before. Sunlight through the window behind created a halo of her hair. The effect was stunning.

'You look a proper Indian gentleman,' she said, looking up and smiling.

'I feel like I'm wearing pyjamas,' he replied, 'but they're very comfortable. '

'They are pyjamas,' she teased. 'We can't help it if you silly English choose to only use them for sleeping.'

The young woman that Arthur had met the night before came into the room carrying a tray loaded with a teapot and cups. She carefully placed them on the table, leaving the tray to one side, before sitting down beside Rani.

'You remember Ashri? From last night?' Rani asked, reminding him of her name. Arthur could only nod in agreement, astonished with the similarity of the two.

From the resemblance, he assumed that Ashri must be Rani's daughter. Perhaps she had told him that last night when he was exhausted. He couldn't remember. He took the cushion opposite them and tried to listen as Rani explained the breakfast items, but he was unable to take his eyes from the pair of them long enough to concentrate on what she was saying.

They were dressed quite differently, Rani in a conservative white blouse and dark skirt, as if she were to spend the day in an office and Ashri in more traditional Indian attire. She wore a long, colourfully patterned skirt; were they called saris he wondered, and a short, tightly fitting top that showed a generous amount of bare midriff. The two women's hairstyles were very different too, but of the same dark reddish-brown colour and they both had the same startling, dark turquoise eyes. He sat fascinated, observing mannerisms in the younger, which were identical to the older of the two. He could only assume that this is exactly what Rani must have looked like twenty or twenty-five years earlier.

'Sorry?' he said, suddenly aware that Rani was waiting for an answer to a question.

'I asked if you wanted some tea,' she said, holding the teapot poised above his cup. 'You were miles away.'

'Oh, yes please. I'm afraid I was daydreaming.'

'It's English breakfast, in your honour. I hope you like it'

The two of them appeared to be competing in offering him items from the breakfast menu. Rani filled his cup as Ashri spooned chunks of pineapple, mango and several sorts of melon onto his plate from the beautifully prepared fruit salad. Rani offered a strange mixture that looked like muesli, or porridge, mixed with orange juice. He refused at first, then at her insistence tried a spoonful and found it strange, totally unlike he had expected it to taste, and surprisingly delicious. He found a generous helping being thrust at him.

'You must try these,' Ashri pleaded, lifting a chafing dish from a low flame. It was filled with what looked to be miniature pancakes and she waved it in front of him, 'Rani makes them herself.'

'I'll try one, they look like something I've had in Amsterdam, I can't remember the name, though.'

'Poffertjes?' Rani suggested.

'Yes, that's it. I remember, God, it's years ago. It was in a little café in the big park, uh, Vondlepark? You could have them with chocolate or marron sauce, or marmalade.'

'That's where I learned to make them. Amsterdam, that is, not the Vondlepark; try them with this.'

She pushed a small dish of strawberries towards him. They looked to be slightly stewed, as if a jam-making session had been interrupted. He spread some on one of the poffertjes and popped it into his mouth. It was exquisite.

'It's compote, made from wild strawberries,' Rani explained.

The three of them continued eating. Rani and Ashri continually trying to persuade him to taste new dishes or combinations he would normally have considered absurd, frequently nudging each other at some unseen joke, perhaps an expression on his face, or spilled food, and occasionally giggling like schoolgirls. It was obvious to Arthur that Rani took great interest in her cooking or perhaps food in general. She seemed to need to explain where she had obtained a recipe for this, or how she had learned to make that. It wasn't as if she were showing off, he thought, just unable to hide her passion. Ashri's obvious enthusiasm appeared to be of no less intensity. Eventually Rani pushed herself away from the table.

'Well, some of us have work to do. I'm going to let Ashri show you around today. If there is anything you want to see in particular, just ask her. I'm sorry, I so wanted to do this myself, but I have to process all these orders that I've worked so hard at getting.

'And,' she continued with a knowing look at Ashri, 'I'm going to be a little shorthanded, now that I'm losing my best helper.'

She rose gracefully to her feet and as she walked towards the door it struck Arthur that to have such elegance, she must have studied ballet, or at least dance of some kind , in her youth.

As she reached the door, she paused, gave a backwards glance directly at Arthur and wrinkled her nose with a little grimace. Arthur felt himself turning to jelly.

'Rani said you might like to see the rest of the house,' Ashri said, rising to her feet. 'You were an architect, is that right?'

Arthur followed her example, very carefully. He expected his knees to complain after kneeling for so long, but found he could stand easily without the slightest hint of pain.

'Uh, yes, until I retired,' he paused, 'a few years ago now. And yes, I'd love to see the rest of the house.' He glanced at the table, 'Shouldn't we do something with these, though? I don't mind helping out.'

'Don't be silly, they'll be taken care of.'

Ashri grasped him by the hand, pulling him along behind her. She reminded Arthur of an impatient child, wanting to show something wondrous to a parent.

The first room, entered through the hallway, was a less formal sitting room, containing two couches facing each other across a low table on which were strewn well-thumbed glossy magazines in several languages. A rattan chair stood next to a table near the window and bookshelves covered one wall. A single large modern painting, with swirls of bright complementary colours, hung on the one otherwise empty wall. The couches and chair were of dark leather with squidgy, comfortable-looking cushions and the two tables were of light oak, as were the bookshelves.

Arthur examined the books briefly. Most were in English, some in Italian, a few in French and the remainder had titles in a mixture of different characters he assumed were of Indian languages. On closer examination, several appeared to be Japanese. From the titles that he could understand, he could see they were arranged by subject; economics, business studies, home design, a large section of cookbooks, nearly as many classics and a mixture of fiction and biographies. He noticed some were by authors he had read, but more he had only heard of, never quite finding the time to try. They had the well-worn look of books from second-hand shops, bought to read, not to impress, and possibly explained in part, Rani's conversational ability.

He looked at the large window and realized that on this side of the house, the sun would only light the room for the last few hours of the day. It was an inviting room, he thought, not one he could ever be bored in.

'Come on,' Ashri said, impatiently tugging at his hand, 'we haven't got all day'.

He had momentarily forgotten she was still holding his hand. He looked at her and seeing the twinkle in her eyes, realized she was teasing him. She took his other hand and pulled him closer to her. Although the twinkle remained, he was stunned by the directness of her gaze. She seemed to be looking directly into his soul.

'Actually, we do have all day, but if you'd rather stay here and read instead of spending it with me out in the countryside, you can. It's up to you.'

She affected a hurt look, tilted her head down with an exaggerated pout, and looked at him from under her brows.

'Oh please,' he said, trying to join in her mood. 'I do want to spend it with you. I do, I do, I do. The countryside sounds wonderful. Or, anywhere else you choose to take me.'

She released both his hands and gave him an exuberant hug, turning her head to rest briefly with one cheek against his chest. Then, grabbing one of his hands again, she started tugging at him, leading him into the hallway.

'Rani said I had to show you the rest of the house, first,' she said over her shoulder, then nodding at a doorway they were passing, 'kitchen,' and continued walking.

'Wait, please, 'Arthur said, unable to hide a chuckle. 'Could we at least peek in? Rani may have asked you to show me around because she knows that I'm interested in houses. I used to be an architect, you know.'

'I know, you just told me that.' she laughed, turning and leading him back through the doorway. Spreading her arms in a grand gesture like an impresario announcing some wonderful illusion, she repeated, 'Kitchen!'

Arthur looked about quickly. The kitchen was much larger than he expected, with white painted walls and matching white painted wooden cabinets lining two of them. Work surfaces of stainless steel ran all along one side with a large sink in the centre.

The ceiling was almost of double height, sloping upwards towards the outer wall, with shallow windows set just below it and running the full length. Low, translucent flames licked slowly behind a glass door set in the adjacent wall. Above the glass door was a larger stainless steel door that Arthur assumed was an oven. He could immediately see the economy of the design. The double height would act very like a chimney, to remove heat from the work area. The kitchen was large enough and fitted to a standard that could have been used for a restaurant or some similar commercial enterprise. No concession had been made to style, only to function. This was not a *lifestyle* kitchen-diner from the glossy magazines. Only a small table and two chairs indicated that it was used at any time for eating.

A very pretty young woman in a short, white tee shirt and denim shorts stood at the sink, washing dishes.

Ashri strode across the room to her and they exchanged affectionate kisses on both cheeks. The young woman had to twist, somewhat awkwardly and extend both wet hands so as not to drip.

'This is Aszli,' announced Ashri.

Arthur replied to her smiling 'Hello' and joined them, then felt his ribs being prodded by Ashri's elbow.

'Go on, then,' she said, nodding her head in Aszli's direction.

Arthur leaned over and was warmly kissed on both cheeks in a similar manner as he had been the previous evening, except that Aszli held her sudsy hands away from him.

'Sorry we can't stay,' said Ashri, grasping Arthur's hand once again and tugging him towards the door. 'I'm giving him the grand tour. We'll see you later.'

Aszli laughed and said something to Ashri that Arthur was unable to understand. Ashri laughed in turn as they re-entered the hallway and Arthur gave her a questioning look as they started up the stairs.

'She only wished me good luck.'

'Yeah, that's what it sounded like to me.'

'Don't get any ideas, she's only sixteen.'

Arthur was appalled at the implication. 'I didn't mean anything like that,' he protested, before the flash of her eyes told him he was again being teased.

As they walked along the top landing, Ashri allowed him a quick peek in the rooms, indicating each in turn, 'Your room... Rani's room... my room... guest room... bathroom, you've seen... Rani's office.'

The first four were decorated in a simple, yet elegant style with vases of fresh flowers in each of the occupied rooms. He had thought the whole house to be painted a creamy white, but noticed the bedrooms were in several different pale colours. Small differences in the furniture and bedding kept them from looking too similar.

Arthur liked the near-minimalist look. He thought the rooms warm and welcoming like the rest of house and was impressed by the lack of clutter.

They entered the last, fitted out as an office with desk, filing cabinets and a worktable covered with stacks of papers. Rani looked up from the computer she was using and gestured for them to sit.

'What do you think?' Rani asked and before Arthur could reply, 'I'm so sorry I couldn't show you around myself, I really need to get these into our system as quickly as possible.'

Arthur followed her glance at the stacks of papers on the table. They appeared to be order paperwork for various items.

'That's okay,' he said. 'Ashri has done a wonderful job. It's a beautiful house. I'm really impressed.'

'I'm so glad you like it, some people think it's a bit stark.'

'No, no, I love the simplicity. I hate cluttered rooms.'

His assertion made Arthur suddenly think of his own home and he wondered how Ester was coping. He knew when he returned she would complain for weeks at having to fix her own breakfasts. He knew also there would be a fortnight's newspapers and magazines strewn about the various rooms to tidy. In the kitchen there would be a sink full of unwashed dishes, as she would be using directly from the dishwasher instead of putting the clean dishes away so that it could be reloaded. He reassured himself that she wasn't lazy; she just had a total lack of logistics. He thought of the complaints she would make about her hours spent dusting and tidying. She hated dust and the slightest evidence of it, as sunlight reflected off shiny surfaces, would result in endless grumbles about his housekeeping skills, but she continued, despite his protests, to cover every horizontal surface with little objects she had found on holidays or the shops she liked to browse in. Her own efforts at dusting were quick swipes around the vases, tea light holders and figurines, without ever picking one up to actually clean the surface on which they rested.

Something Rani said brought Arthur back to the present.

'Sorry, you said you lived in Japan?'

'For nearly three years, I was trying to establish new markets for mother. She ran the business then. I was really impressed by many of their design ideas. I tried to incorporate some of them when I decorated this house; at least the principle, or concept behind the design, if not the actual design or product itself. The bathroom you've seen is straight from Japan.'

'That must have taken some organising,' Arthur said, remembering her telling him the only alternative route to their climb yesterday, was a rough, narrow track, necessitating a two-day journey by jeep.

'Yes,' she laughed, 'but I think it was worth it'.

Arthur noticed Ashri impatiently shifting from one foot to the other.

'I think someone's trying to tell us something.'

'Is that all you can talk about?' Ashri asked, 'This house will still be here tomorrow.'

'And I have tons of work.'

Rani reached for Arthur's hand, at the same time presenting a cheek. Arthur kissed her softly on both cheeks, in what was becoming a very pleasant routine. Rani squeezed his hand.

'Later, then.'

'Later.' He returned the squeeze before releasing her hand.

'Come on,' Ashri pleaded, insistently.

Without his noticing, she had added a matching scarf to her ensemble, draping it around her shoulders and over the back of her head. She was carrying a light canvas shoulder bag; similar to the one Rani had worn on their climb.

They had descended the stairs and were approaching the door when Arthur remembered his bare feet. His shoes were no longer by the door.

'I've forgotten my shoes,' he said, slightly embarrassed. He looked down and saw that the soft pink adhesive pads he used to avoid his toes rubbing against his shoes were gone. Rani must have removed them last night when she was bathing him. He tried desperately to hide, even from Ester, the awful accoutrements that accompanied old age. What must Rani think of him? He felt he was really a dreadfully sad old man.

'Ah, Rani's taken care of that,' Ashri replied, producing a pair of slippers from a cupboard near the front door. 'Try these on.'

They looked like bedroom slippers with cut-away sides, but they had firm soles and fitted perfectly. They were also very comfortable when he tried a few tentative steps and far more supportive than they looked.

'They go very well with the pyjamas,' he laughed, 'but I've never dressed like this to go out before'.

'Oh, stop worrying, everyone will love you.' Ashri said, as she pulled him firmly across the veranda and down the steps.

Their route initially retraced the one he and Rani had taken the night before. Arthur noticed that many of the houses they passed were similar in appearance to Rani's with the broad-leaved trees that lined their path giving welcome shade from the rapidly warming sun. Although there were no pavements and the street was covered with fine sandy gravel, it was quite smooth and easy to walk on.

Ashri chattered away, making comments about the owners of these houses, their businesses and the various amusing incidents that had happened to them. Arthur, following half a pace behind, knew he would remember little of her conversation, occupied as he was despite himself, with the swell of her hips below the deliciously coloured, soft, smooth skin of her exposed waist. Feeling as if he was some aging pervert, he tried to tear his eyes away and concentrate on her chatter.

After a short time Ashri took a side turning into a narrower street with more modest houses and fewer trees. Where there were long gaps between the trees, Ashri showed him how to avoid the direct sun by walking in the shadows of the houses. Arthur thought he recognized the street as the one taken by the women of the previous evening. Before long they came to a wide square bordered by a river on the far side.

Small shops with open fronts and colourful displays of goods were scattered about the other three sides and more of the broad-leaved trees in the central square gave plentiful shade. The village was only moderately busy with a few young women, mostly accompanied by toddlers, using the shops. A few women, engaged in animated conversation, were seated at tables under the trees, apparently served from a café in the middle of the square.

They had encountered several women on their passage so far, all of whom had greeted Ashri with good natured banter or in some cases shy giggling, and had looked at Arthur in a curious manner until they were introduced. Arthur wondered if they somehow knew of his arrangement with Rani and if perhaps this was frowned upon, but their friendly attitude put him at ease. On at least two occasions the women had touched, or actually stroked his arm when introduced. They all seemed to have some knowledge of English and after the usual, 'Hello, Arthur, it's very nice to meet you,' had made fairly suggestive comments to him, such as, 'Ah, that Ashri, she's a lucky girl, eh?' and 'You will make her a happy girl tonight, no?' The conversation would then continue in their own language, inevitably ending in much laughter as they made their farewells. They seemed to be under the impression that he and Ashri were together and made no reference to Rani. Ashri did little to correct the mistake, taking his arm possessively as they continued.

Ashri stopped in one of the little shops where a similar exchange was made with the shopkeeper, a young woman of similar age to Ashri. As they chatted Arthur admired the neat display of fruits and vegetables that were laid out in flat baskets and supported at waist height by wooden benches. Inside, the walls were lined with shelves filled with smaller baskets and boxes of dried items. Although the shop had an open front, he could see that the hinged canopy doubled as a door, swinging down to make it secure when not in use. The general air of purposeful efficiency was enhanced by the almost total lack of advertising and packaging. It reminded him more of a European market than the fairly chaotic appearing shops he had seen from the bus when they had passed through villages en route.

Looking around, he saw that the adjoining shops, although offering a variety of different goods, had a similar orderly appearance. The next shop was a flower seller run by an older woman, with beautiful displays arranged by their colour. Arthur idly wondered if the whole village decorated their homes as Rani did and if so, he was certain she would be kept very busy. The shop on the opposite side appeared to sell nothing except dried fish. They were graduated in size from tiny minnows to fish large enough to make a meal for a family, all heaped in similar flat baskets to those in the greengrocer's.

In his fascination with the shops, Arthur didn't see the items that Ashri purchased, but turned back in time to see the shopkeeper making a note in a small book and passing it to Ashri. She took the book, made a notation in it and passed it back. He watched the page carefully torn from the book and placed in a box on the shelf behind as they left. Arthur remembered hearing of mining villages in England once having company stores that ran a "tick" and assumed this to be similar accounting system.

They made their way to the tables beneath the trees and ordered coffees from the young waitress who had greeted Ashri as if she were an old friend. To find an empty table they'd had to contend with considerable banter and friendly jibes from the other women seated nearby. The café had more of a southern European feel to it than anything he had expected to find in India and despite knowing that much coffee was grown in India, Arthur was surprised to be drinking cappuccino in such a remote area.

Arthur had noted that most of these women were little older than Ashri and each was accompanied by an infant of the age where they were just starting to try and walk; pulling themselves up to a standing position on their mother's lap or standing on wobbly legs as their arms were supported above them. Could they have attended the same antenatal classes, Arthur asked himself and then wondered if that was feasible in a village as small as this. Still, it seemed odd to see so many of so similar age at one time. Perhaps it was just a coincidence or maybe their husbands were all sailors on the same ship and given leave together. He must remember to ask Ashri later.

Their coffees arrived and he asked Ashri about the "payment" he had seen made.

'Oh, we don't use money here,' Ashri explained, 'or not for everyday things. We settle up each week at the gathering. Most of the time it's just a matter of trading tickets and we have to use money when we go outside of course, so the tickets do have a monetary value.'

'It seems such a simple system, but I suppose it would only work somewhere so small.'

'The whole valley uses the same type of tickets so we can go to any of the villages, although we can tell which village any ticket comes from by their colour.'

'I would think it would be easy to cheat, you know, to fake someone's signature or something.'

'I can't think anyone in the valley would do that,' Ashri looked shocked. 'That's appalling to even consider. It would only ever happen once.'

It must be wonderful, thought Arthur, to be so young and so naïve. He looked at her in admiration; she was so similar in appearance to Rani it was disturbing. Yet, where he was continually in awe of Rani's air of sophistication and serenity, Ashri's youthful enthusiasm only made him feel protective. If he and Ester had had a daughter, is this how he would have felt about her? The thought momentarily saddened him until Ashri reached across the table and grasped his hand.

'Arthur, what's the matter? Has a ghost passed by?

'Something like that. I'm sorry, I'm just being a silly old man, you know; thinking of things that might have been.'

'Come on then, let's get you out into the sunshine. I'll be right back.'

Ashri made her way to the front of the café, where he watched her make a similar notation as she had made in the greengrocers. Again, there was the banter with the waitress and with the other women still seated at the tables as they made their exit. Arthur was beginning to relax and enjoy the attention, smiling at the women when they made comments to Ashri. He had noticed that their comments to each other in their own language invariably caused only slightly suppressed hilarity. If he was to be the object of a joke, he was determined he was going to enjoy it. It was such a welcome change from being invisible.

Ashri led him to the open area of the square, pointing to a stone circle blackened by countless bonfires. Surrounding the circle was a larger circle of worn wooden benches. The nearest buildings on either side had a greater concentration of the sconces he had noticed the night before, and the stonework above them was also blackened.

With all of the torches and a bonfire as well, the square should be quite well lit at night, he reasoned to himself.

'This is where the gathering takes place.'

'You've mentioned the "gathering" a couple of times. What is it?'

'It's the *gathering*,' she said, bemused at his lack of comprehension. 'It's where we meet most evenings. To talk about things and make plans. As I said a few minutes ago, we regularly make the weighing up of our debts then. Sometimes the storytellers tell stories, sometimes we sing and dance, and sometimes we drink too much aqui and make fools of ourselves. It's always fun, and it's always interesting, unless there's a correction to be made. That can be very sad, of course, but it doesn't happen very often.'

'A correction, what's that?'

Ashri looked suddenly very serious, almost sad, 'It's like you said, you know, when someone does something wrong. Like, someone cheating at something.'

'And? What happens then? Is there a trial, or something?

'Something, let's not talk about it.' The look of sadness left her as suddenly as it had arrived. 'Come, let's walk by the river.'

She turned and started walking towards a low stone jetty where two long boats, filled with an assortment of boxes and baskets, were being unloaded. Women in the boats were heaving the goods to others on the jetty. They in turn, were carrying them to various shops in the square.

Arthur found the design of the boats quite interesting and tried to get a closer look without getting in the way of the women working. They were quite narrow, but long and, even loaded as they were, sat lightly in the water. He could make out pointed paddles with 'tee' shaped handles stowed at the stern. Except for their sharply pointed and raised prows they reminded him of Canadian canoes.

Sudden memories of the years he had spent in America flooded into his head. He'd had a girlfriend whose parents owned a lakeside summer home in the Ozarks and they had spent several weekends there together. The lake was deserted by October and she had taught him to paddle a canoe on their first visit. Afternoons were spent with him slowly navigating the canoe about the lake while she lay facing him on a folded blanket, reading aloud from Wordsworth, Byron or one of her other favourite poets. The evenings were cool enough to require a fire in the huge stone fireplace and its flickering glow reflected off the vaulted pine ceiling as they sat together on a fur rug sipping her father's wine. She had been so beautiful and he had never been in love before. Remembering now, it all seemed a bit clichéd, but at the time he had thought it was just like a Cary Grant movie.

So very long ago, he reflected; he hadn't thought of her in years, perhaps decades, and suddenly wondered what she was like now. Had she grown fat and wrinkly, surrounded by hordes of grandchildren or was she still a virgin?

He smiled as he remembered that she had never once let him kiss her open-mouthed, *French kissing* as the Americans had called it, let alone feel her breasts or caress the silkiness of her inner thighs. Still, it was before the sexual revolution of the sixties had taken hold and at a time when every young man was expected to gain experience with women of loose morals, but still marry a virgin. And, she had been the type one wanted to marry.

'You can stay there and look at the boats all day if you want to,' Ashri called, interrupting his reminiscences, 'but I'm going for a walk. And, I've got our lunch.'

Arthur turned and found that she was walking backwards along the riverbank, dangling her shoulder bag behind her as if to entice him.

31

'I'm sorry,' he apologised, hurrying to catch up, 'I guess I was daydreaming. I didn't mean to hold you up.'

As he grew closer he could see from the little laughter lines around her eyes that she was teasing him once again. He resolved to try and avoid being distracted for any length of time; for some reason, she seemed to constantly want his full attention.

They had left the square behind them and walked along the lane with the river on one side and a mixture of houses and other buildings on their other side. As the noise of the square faded, Arthur could hear the sound of children chanting. It was coming from a low building set back from their path. It seemed to be in the strange language the locals used, but there was something familiar about the "*duh te duh te duhhh, de, duh te duh te duhh*" sound. He had just about identified it as the multiplication table, when they abruptly changed to English and confirmed his guess. It was surprising, he thought, that he had not identified the building as a school immediately. Of course they would need a school in a village of this size, but there were so many things so unexpected about the day; perhaps it wasn't that astonishing after all, to find that the ordinary did come as a surprise.

He could hear Ashri tittering about something that had happened to her while attending that very school and tried to both listen to her and at the same time observe the unrolling surroundings.

Presently she pulled him into a side street and into another low building, not unlike the school they had passed.

'This is where I work,' she pointed out. 'Come; they're all dying to meet you.'

A few days earlier and the prospect of meeting a friend's workmates would have been intimidating for Arthur, but already he was beginning to enjoy the attentiveness of everyone he met. Even though he could understand little of the actual conversations, the implications were very obvious. The friendliness he was faced with did much to put him at ease and that they thought he was in a relationship with this young woman was completely flattering.

The inside of the building appeared to be a larger version of Rani's office. There were several modern desks, complete with computers and comfortable looking office chairs. The artwork decorating the walls even appeared to be by the same artists as graced her house. The physical layout too, was similar in concept with overhanging trees and awnings shading the windows, so that the interior was still a comfortable temperature, while outside, they had been starting to feel the heat of the day.

There was the usual fuss that Arthur had already come to expect. The half dozen women of varying ages made comments similar to those he had heard in the square and he could feel them touching him, sometimes gingerly, sometimes with no attempt to hide their interest, as Ashri introduced him. There were the usual kisses on both cheeks, but also lingering caresses on his back and firm squeezes of both his arms. He felt a completely overt, and not unpleasant, grasp of one buttock as Ashri showed him her desk and explained her role in the business. By the time she had made their farewells, he was more than a little reluctant to leave the attention behind.

Within minutes they had resumed their walk by the river and as they neared the outskirts of the village Arthur could see new houses being built. Two appeared nearly finished, but the third was still in a state of construction. A woman was manually mixing mortar with a shovel near the front opening and from within came the sound of banging. Outside, there were stacks of the lightweight bricks that seemed to be commonplace and various other materials that would eventually disappear into the interior. Scaffolding of bamboo and wooden planks tied together with fine rope surrounded the building. Arthur knew from experience that the rickety appearance was misleading. He could see that every section was well triangulated and would support much more than the casual observer would imagine.

At the top a young woman was fitting roofing tiles. As she caught sight of them, she gave a loud whistle, waved, and shouted.

'Hey Ashri, is that your man?'

Ashri, apparently pleased to see her, responded 'Yes Zanli, he is completely mine.'

'Don't you use him all up.'

'I am going to drain him dry. There will be nothing left of him when I am through.'

'Oh, that's not fair,' the young woman gave an exaggerated pout. 'Think of the rest of us, I want him too, you know.'

Arthur was slightly shocked by this light-hearted exchange, but flattered at the same time; he had never imagined conversations about him could be of this character. Although he had been unable to understand Ashri's earlier conversations, he had inferred from the nudges and winks that they were possibly of a similar nature.

Their conversation switched to the local language they all seemed to use and there was an amount of giggling. Arthur couldn't decide whether they regularly wanted to talk about something that he was not to be included in or if it was simply that the women they encountered did not have the extent of English that Rani and Ashri had.

Ashri caught his eye and shook her head as if disgusted, while snorting under her breath, 'Builders, they're all the same!'

The gleam in her eyes however, betrayed the affection she so obviously felt for Zanli.

They continued to trade remarks that caused both to laugh as he and Ashri walked on, but as they were nearly out of earshot Zanli directed a final remark to him.

'Arthur, don't let her wear you out. I can't wait to be with you!

He had been fascinated by the woman's appearance. She was tall, wearing a baseball cap with her long dark hair pulled through the adjustment hole at the back and her hands were protected from the tiles by heavy leather gloves. Only a pair of American-style bib overalls completed her outfit, nothing more. As she had turned from her work, he had tried to avert his eyes, but couldn't resist a glimpse at her exposure. She was, he supposed, handsome rather than beautiful, almost statuesque, but the thought that this creature could be attracted to him was somehow just a little bit scary.

They had walked little more than a few paces when they became aware of faint laughter and the sound of splashing, coming from the river. The river was bending away from them and the trees that bordered it were no longer so closely spaced. As they grew closer, an area where the riverbank had eroded into a natural slipway was revealed. Flat layers of stone graduated downwards like steps to the water's edge, bordering a small beach alongside. A collection of baskets filled with wet laundry and empty white plastic buckets was randomly scattered over the stones. One or two young women were still working on the lower steps, scrubbing at the items in their buckets.

Beyond were several others; some up to their waists in the water, splashing each other with their hands or in one case, one of the buckets, amidst great laughter. Another smaller, but older group on the far side of the opening were resting or eating in the shade of overhanging trees, joining in the laughter at the results of the communal drenching. Several turned and waved at them, called Ashri and Arthur by their names, and invited them both to join them in the water, but preoccupied with their own fun, failed to tease Ashri to the extent that earlier groups had. Amongst them Arthur recognized Aszli who continued to wave at them long after the other women had resumed their play. Most of the women were only wearing simple white cotton sarongs, which in the water had turned quite translucent. The tops that had not been discarded, but soaked from their owner's activities, gave even less efforts towards modesty.

Arthur stood momentarily transfixed by this uninhibited display, until Ashri roughly pulling on his arm, made him realize he was staring.

'Come on,' she said in mock fury, 'Aszli's far too young for you.'

'I wasn't just looking at her,' he protested, then embarrassed at what he had said, 'I mean, I couldn't help looking. They were…'

'I think you fancy her,' she taunted, walking more quickly as she added in a singsong, 'Arthur fancies Aszli.'

'Please,' he said, trying to catch up with her, 'I wouldn't lust after someone's maid.'

Ashri stopped abruptly turning to face him. Her anger was evident and obviously not feigned.

'I cannot believe you just said that. I would never have thought of you as a snob. In fact, she's far too good for you.'

Arthur was stunned. Her outburst was so unexpected; he couldn't think of a reply for a few moments and she had resumed walking away from him, hurriedly, before he had collected his thoughts. He ran after her and caught at her shoulder, but she pulled away and continued her pace.

'Please,' he cried, 'please stop. Let me explain.'

Ashri slowed, then stopped without turning, but let him catch up. Arthur had to overtake, then turn about and found her glaring at him.

'That came out completely wrong,' he pleaded. 'I didn't mean to imply that I was better than her; that I'm too good to be attracted to her. It's just that she works in a house where I'm a guest. For a man to make advances to someone in that position would be an... an abuse of... of their own position. And, as you said, she is very young, far too young for me. She is very pretty, but I don't fancy her. Not because she's a maid, but because to do so would be completely wrong.'

Her expression softened slightly. 'That's all right then, I suppose. But, anyway she's not a maid.'

'Okay.'

'She's a learner,' she said emphatically, 'do you know what that means?'

'No,' he smiled, looking her directly in the eyes, hoping to appear sincere; this was a side of Ashri he couldn't have known existed. He far preferred the laughing, teasing, confident Ashri. 'Would you like to tell me?'

His ploy appeared to have worked and the slightest hint of a smile crept back across her face. It was as if the sun had come out from behind a cloud. He swore he could even hear faint music playing in the background.

'As a learner Aszli will work alongside Rani for at least three years. The purpose is not to have someone merely to do her housework. The purpose is to avoid her vast knowledge going to waste.' The smile had nearly returned completely.

'So she's like an apprentice?'

'Much more than that. Rani has spent almost half her life outside the valley, most of it in foreign countries. She's built a small empire that conducts business all over the world. Aszli, with any luck, will learn not only to help the business continue, but also how to conduct herself in an appropriate manner and eventually how to run a well-ordered home of her own.'

'I see. It sounds like quite an undertaking and I would imagine not particularly easy. I'm sorry if I underestimated her, I just didn't know.'

Ashri calmly took his hand and started walking again, pulling him into a matching pace alongside her.

'I forgive you; as you said, you didn't know. Maybe it will teach you not to jump to conclusions. Everything here is not necessarily as you may expect.'

Chapter Three

The trees alongside the riverbank were more widely spaced and they were approaching fields bordering the river, when Arthur first noticed the windmills. Or wind pumps, he supposed was the correct terminology. As they came abreast of the first one, his curiosity about things mechanical prompted him to examine them more closely and he persuaded Ashri to pause as he took a closer look.

At first glance they looked to be quite crude, almost Heath Robinson in appearance, with a triangular tower made of bamboo, held together in the same manner, as the scaffolding on the building site had been. Atop the tower was a shaft with five sails on one end, much like the individual sails on a boat. On the other end of the shaft was a chain sprocket. The sails were made of canvas, wrapped around the mast sections, with a boom for each that restricted its angle. It looked like the strength of the wind could be adjusted for by unwrapping more or less of the canvas.

The shaft was connected to the pumping mechanism below with a chain, which seemed to be just another chain running through a pipe whose lower end was submerged in the water. Small diaphragms were placed around the lower chain at regular intervals and were pulled through the pipe by the turning of the sails. As each diaphragm was exposed, a flood of water erupted from the top of the pipe, spilling into a trough that led to a small irrigation ditch running alongside the field.

Arthur stood open-mouthed at the simplicity of the design. With the flexibility of the sails, there was no need to have the complication, as on more conventional designs, of a swivelling cap that could be turned into the wind. He imagined that these would perform adequately over a large variation of wind directions and even though there was only a gentle breeze, the sails were turning at a moderate rate.

Each mechanism was relatively small; the towers were little more than two or three metres high and the flow from one pump would be of little use for irrigating a whole field, but there were many wind-pumps, regularly spaced as far as he could see. Between them, he imagined, they were probably quite effective, as the adjacent fields were lush and green.

Ashri pulled at him once again. 'You can ask Zanli all about these old pumps when you see her again. It's getting hot and we've some way to go before we can stop for lunch.'

'Zanli? The girl on the building site?' Being reminded that there were plans for him to see her again gave him a pleasant, but slightly uneasy feeling.

'Yes, she knows about everything mechanical.'

They walked on in silence in the heat of the sun. Arthur stopped thinking about the wind pumps and contentedly remembered the fleeting sidelong glimpse he'd had of Zanli's breasts and imagined what it might be like to bury his face in them.

They had walked for some time, leaving the open fields behind, and were surrounded by forest when another gap in the riverbank appeared, similar to the one where the women had been doing their laundry. Ashri led him to a spot that was in partial shade at the very edge of the river. By now, the river had widened and the opposite rocky bank rose gently towards the mountains beyond. A small stream tumbled down the hillside, gurgling into stair-stepped pools before ending with a gentle splashing in the river.

He watched, fascinated, as Ashri produced their lunch from the bag she had been carrying. She had carried it all morning without the slightest hint of effort, yet it contained a folded picnic rug, quantities of fruit, bottles of beer, little covered dishes and plates of various pastry things. There were also what appeared to be several different sorts of pakoras. Arthur was suddenly ashamed that he had not once offered to carry it for her.

When she had unfolded the rug onto the long grass and carefully placed all of the items, she sat down, removed her shoes and dangled her feet in the water. He rolled up his pyjama legs and followed her example. The refreshing coolness of the water and the tranquillity of the setting invoked a wonderful sense of peace. Ashri repeatedly thrust bits of the food at him to try with pauses only to say, 'try these,' or 'Rani made these herself,' or 'aren't these wonderful? Aszli makes them almost as good as Rani'. He couldn't empty his mouth long enough to reply; he could only watch her in complete awe.

The broken shade gave a dappled effect on her face, reminding him of a Renoir painting. She had the same prominent cheekbones as Rani, the same intense turquoise eyes and the same long, dark brown hair with reddish highlights. They both had the same perfectly shaped noses, the same full lips and the same finely chiselled chins, yet Ashri was so different. As she joked with him or teased him or questioned him about something she hadn't understood, her eyes revealed her every mood. She would never be a successful poker player, he thought, she makes no effort to hide any emotion. Rani in contrast, was so, so measured he supposed was the right description. Her eyes, though just as captivating, seldom revealed what she was thinking. Her movements were more graceful and her overall manner was one of style. In contrast Ashri at times reminded him of a kitten he and Ester once had.

Perhaps it was just a matter of experience, he thought. Rani was older, had obviously travelled extensively and had lived abroad. Ashri, he imagined, might never have been out of the valley.

When they had finished their lunch, Ashri after refusing Arthur's offer of help, repacked the empty containers into her bag. She pulled the rug further from the water's edge into deeper shade, folded her bag under one corner to affect a pillow and indicated for him to lie down. When she was satisfied he was comfortable, she snuggled up alongside him, pulled his arm around her shoulder and rested her head on his chest. The warmth of her body next to his was welcome in the coolness of the shade. The smell of her hair was of young animal, orange blossom and cakes baking.

'We should have a little nap, a siesta? To let our food settle, don't you think?' she asked.

'Mmm, yes,' was all he could think of in reply.

They lay together quietly for a few minutes, until Ashri rolled over and raised herself on one elbow, to face him.

41

'English is a funny language, isn't it?'

'Perhaps,' the question took Arthur completely by surprise, 'why do you ask?'

'You have letters that have the same pronunciation as others. And there doesn't seem to be any rules as to how to use them.' Her expression was completely sincere

'I wouldn't have thought you had any trouble; your English is absolutely perfect. Give me an example.'

'Well, the letter "gee". Sometimes you pronounce it "jhee" and sometimes you pronounce it "guh". For instance, how would you pronounce "g", "i", "b"?'

'Gib, I guess,' He pronounced it softly, as if starting with a "j". 'Sometimes it depends on the letter following.'

'But, if it had a "b", "o", "n", after it?'

He thought for a moment, 'Okay, "gibbon", with a hard "gee".'

'And there's *give* and *gibe*, it gets very confusing.'

'I, uh, guess you just learn from experience.'

'Then there's "k" and "c". I can give you similar examples. Why don't you give just one sound to each letter? Or make some sensible rules, or something?'

'Actually, I didn't invent the language. Please don't blame me.' He couldn't resist smiling at her sober, wide eyes.

'Oh, I am going to blame you.' She dug a knuckle into his ribs, hard enough to make him wince, and laughed back at him. 'I think it's all your fault. You should be ashamed of such a system.'

'I'll try to change it to your satisfaction,' he gasped, when he had recovered from laughing, 'first thing in the morning'.

'Try to sort out some of your words, while you're at it. Fancy, for instance.'

'Why is that confusing?'

'Well, it means intricate or excessively adorned and it means to imagine, doesn't it? So why does it also mean sexual desire?'

'I think that's a legitimate usage. If I remember correctly, it used to confuse Americans when I lived there, but I suppose that it meant at one time,' he stopped, worrying where his explanation was heading, 'that one *imagined* oneself making love to someone. You see, I might say that I *fancied* making love to someone. Then it just got shortened to where *fancy* meant wanting to make love to them.'

'So, when you said you didn't fancy Aszli, you really meant you wouldn't want to make love to her?'

'I think I probably meant that I knew I shouldn't want to. Does that sound confusing? In the back of my mind, if I'm honest, I probably do.' His explanation was sounding decidedly woolly and evasive, even to his own ears. 'If I was seventeen again, I would find her captivating, but I'm an old man and I mustn't let myself even think about someone so young.'

'So, does that mean you don't fancy me?' Her earnestness was endearing; she was looking directly into his soul.

He would not, could not, lie or be evasive to anyone so trusting.

'Yes, rightly or wrongly, if I'm honest. Of course, I fancy you.'

Ashri seemed pleased by his answer, laid her head back on his chest and hugged him. They lay together like that until her slow rhythmic breathing told him she had fallen asleep. He was not far behind.

Chapter Four

Arthur was dreaming. Ester needed his help to open a tin, despite the new electric tin opener sitting prominently on the worktop. He had just sat down to watch the six o'clock news and she had volunteered to prepare the tea for a change, but the news didn't make any sense. This was the fourth interruption he'd had in approximately the same number of minutes.

'Arthur, wake up!'

He opened his eyes, unable to think where he was for a few moments. Ashri was kneeling over him, shaking him by the shoulder.

'I didn't mean to sleep so long. It's time we started back. I'm really sorry.'

Arthur stretched, feeling wonderfully refreshed as he slowly recalled their morning together. The sun was lower in the sky and the heat had gone from the day, leaving a still warm, but pleasant temperature.

'Ummh, that's okay,' he yawned, stretching again. 'I've had a really nice sleep.'

'So did I, Rani told me to let you have a nap, as you were probably still tired from yesterday,' she was folding up the rug and shoving it determinedly into her bag, 'but I wanted to show you the crocus fields.'

'I'm going to be here for a couple of weeks. I don't have to do everything the first day,' he said, patiently, 'there'll be time to see them later'.

'You don't understand, it's not that simple. We'll have to go straight back now or it will be too dark by the time we get to the village.'

'I don't mind. I think I can make it in one go. Let me carry your bag.'

'Oh, now that it's empty, you're offering to carry it for me. You're such a gentleman.'

He didn't have to look at her; from the tone of her voice he knew that she was teasing him once again. It was reassuring that she was so consistent.

'I am so sorry. I had no idea that you had so much stuff in it. It must have weighed a ton.' He took the bag from her, 'actually, it's still pretty heavy. Can I change my mind?'

He half expected another knuckle in the ribs, but Ashri only laughed, grabbed his hand and started walking quickly in the direction they had come from earlier. They walked silently hand-in-hand until the pathway became too narrow. Ashri relinquished her hold on his hand and took up the lead in front of him. She had folded her shawl and draped it over the bag he was carrying, leaving the smooth, golden brown expanse of her waist exposed.

He could only think of what Ester would give to have skin like that and of the hundreds of hours she must have lain in the sun trying to achieve a "healthy" tan. When they did get some actual sun at home, he would often arrive home from work to find her still dozing in the sun lounger on their airless patio. She had always insisted on sunny holidays, even though his pale complexion resisted any attempt at tanning and burned painfully if not completely covered with high factor sun cream.

He had never objected. He could relax under a sunshade, read a book, listen to the sound of the crashing waves and after the sun was lower, go for a walk along the beach. He had made excuses of needing to get some exercise after their lunch, but Ester would always tease him on his return with, 'seen any pretty girls, dear?' It never seemed to bother her how much he looked at other women; he couldn't decide whether she trusted him completely or just didn't think him capable of getting involved with anyone. Now, after all that sun and despite the endless drenching in sun cream, the skin on her face was beginning to resemble that of a much older woman's.

'I just realized, I've been out in the sun most of the day. I didn't think to ask for any sun cream and I must be as red as a lobster,' he said. 'God, I'll pay for this tomorrow. Probably won't get any sleep tonight, either.'

Ashri stopped and examined his face. 'No, you're not burnt at all. Didn't Rani bathe you last night? That should have given you enough protection. You may not get any sleep tonight, but it won't be because of sunburn.' She looked at him as though they had just shared the most enormous joke. Rani must have told her of their assignation; she seemed to know about everything else.

It was nearly dark as they entered the village and Ashri led him on a circuitous route back to Rani's house. At one point they could hear the sound of music and riotous laughter coming from the square. Arthur was inquisitive from what he had heard so far, and would have welcomed a glimpse of the gathering that Ashri had described.

'We have avoided it,' she explained, 'so those women don't catch a glimpse of you. A couple glasses of aqui and some of them would eat you up.'

The prospect didn't sound so very terrifying to Arthur.

When they ascended the steps to Rani's veranda it was nearly a repeat of the previous evening, except he was with Ashri instead of Rani and he assumed it must be Rani waiting for them in the shadows. Except, as they grew closer, he could see that it wasn't Rani, but Aszli.

'Rani's already gone to the gathering,' she explained to Ashri, 'come in the kitchen with me and I'll show you what we've made for your supper'.

As the two of them disappeared, Arthur couldn't help but feeling disappointed. No, actually hurt. Rani had been so specific only a few hours earlier. True, he'd had a wonderful day; Ashri was delightful company. He couldn't think of anyone he would rather have spent the time with, except Rani herself, of course. And perhaps he shouldn't jump to conclusions; perhaps Rani had only gone to the gathering for a short time. Perhaps she had something so important to discuss it couldn't be postponed. Perhaps she would only stay for a short time and be home in time to spend the rest of the evening with him. Another couple of hours with Ashri wouldn't be an unpleasant way to spend the evening.

As the two of them returned from the kitchen, Aszli asked, 'You're sure you can find everything you need? I don't mind helping.'

'No, I'm quite capable of taking a few minutes to serve what you've obviously laboured hours over,' Ashri replied, 'get on and enjoy the gathering.'

Aszli leaned forward to kiss Ashri on both cheeks and then repeated the manoeuvre with Arthur, taking both his hands in hers, holding them and his gaze rather longer than necessary.

'Don't forget what I said,' she said with a meaningful look at Ashri, 'Rani said specifically to tell you, we'll be very late back.'

Despite the excitement of Aszli's kiss, Arthur felt the bottom fall out of his stomach. So much for the hope that Rani would be returning early, Arthur thought, it would serve her right if he worked on seducing Ashri. He was positive that only this morning she had repeated her promise. Sure, last night he really had been far too exhausted to be of any use in bed and any attempt would have only been embarrassing. But tonight, he was very well rested and being in the company of a beautiful, flirtatious young woman all day hadn't made him anticipate the evening with Rani any less.

As they stood together waving goodbye to Aszli, Ashri slipped her arm around Arthur's waist and pulled him closer to her.

Yes, thought Arthur, looking down at her. The whole village seemed to think they were meant to be together and she was so warm and friendly, as though they had known each other for years. Why not just take one's time and see what develops over the evening?

Oh, you stupid old man, his conscience screamed back, she's a wonderful, but rather naïve young woman who is being friendly and well-mannered for her mother's sake. There is absolutely no possibility that someone so young and beautiful would be attracted to a sad old man, not even if you plied her with booze all night. Don't do something you'll regret and be despised by both daughter and mother.

They had made their way into the dining room where Ashri gestured for him to sit down, and then disappeared once more into the kitchen. She reappeared only moments later carrying an enormous tray completely covered with little dishes and a bottle of wine.

'Rani told me you mentioned liking a complete meal of antipasti' she said, 'so we've tried to accommodate. I hope you like it'.

She proceeded to place dishes of roasted yellow and red peppers, sun-dried tomatoes, olives, shredded green beans fried in lardons and garlic, an aubergine paste, artichokes in oil and a platter of several different types of salami and thinly cut, dried ham on the table followed by a small basket of foccacio. Arthur was fascinated with her speed and the artistic arrangement she achieved with such little sign of effort, humming a familiar sounding tune as she worked.

'That's "Your Little Hand Is Frozen", isn't it?' he asked.

'Tiny,' she corrected, pausing to fill his glass, "Your Tiny Hand is Frozen". "*Che gelida manina.*" Try the wine.'

'Rossini?' he held the glass to one of the candles to observe the colour, swirled the wine, breathed deeply of the fumes, then sipped thoughtfully, 'that's really very good; it's like a... Cabernet Franc?'

'It's one we make here. It's a mix of Cabernet Sauvignon and a native Indian grape. And no, it's not Rossini, it's Puccini.'

'My mistake. You're an opera fan?'

'Oh yes, I adore opera,' her eyes looked dreamily at the very mention, 'I've only been to one live, but Rani has lots of recordings. She became a fan when she lived in Italy. Now, she finds DVDs that we can play on the computer. Do you like it, too?'

'I, I like the music, but for performances, I prefer ballet.'

Ashri smiled at him as if he had revealed some deep secret. 'Of course, you like the pretty girls, don't you?' then in a sing-song voice, 'Arthur likes the pretty girls, Arthur likes the pretty dancers. Opera singers are too fat for Arthur.'

'No, no,' he protested, 'it's not that. Well, perhaps a little. Sometimes the sight of overweight, middle-aged woman playing the part of a young princess requires more imagination than I can muster.

'If her musical skill is enough, it shouldn't take that much imagination and you're meant to be listening to the music.'

'True, I think it's more a case of, I like the music, I like the splendour of the settings, the costumes and everything, but the plots are always so, so tragic.'

'You mean "boy meets girl, boy falls in love with girl, girl dies? You can't cope with that?'

'Yes, something like that. Don't they ever have a happy ending? This is nice, what is it?'

'Pickled aubergine, try the artichokes,' she said offering the dish, 'Have you never experienced tragedy? Had a lover leave you? A close friend or one of your family die?'

'All of that, I suppose.'

'So?'

'What do mean, so?'

"I mean, tell me about your family. Which one died?'

'All of them, I guess. My parents were both killed in a car accident.

'How old were you?'

'Oh, I was grown and had left home years earlier. Twenty-six, I think. We weren't very close. I only visited them a few times after I left university. They only seemed to have time for each other. I think I was a big disappointment for them.'

'Why do you think that?' she looked at him solemnly, 'did you have brothers or sisters?'

'I had a brother. Much older than me, I never met him. He died a year or two before I was born' he sighed, the thought seemed to depress him. 'Our whole house was like a shrine to him. There were pictures of him in every room.'

'I don't think that's so terrible, under the circumstances, that is.'

'He was about eleven when he died, but I always heard how wonderful he was at everything. If I got a good report at school, I was told how Charles, that was his name, Charles always got *wonderful* grades. If I did well at a sport, I was never given a pat on the back, only told what a wonderful sportsman Charles had been.'

'That's so sad. It sounds like your parents must have loved him very much and never overcame their grief. And it's not unusual to deify someone when they die too young. They must have expected you to stop the hurting when you came along and maybe they were disappointed when it didn't. I'm sure that they must have loved you very much; maybe they just didn't want to let themselves feel too deeply, in case they lost you as well. Try not to think unkindly of them.'

Arthur had never thought of the situation from that viewpoint before. Perhaps it was the effects of the wine; perhaps it was this unexpected wisdom from someone so young, but he had the distinct impression of an ancient accumulated bitterness flowing away from him, leaving him light-headed and smiling.

'What about you? Any tragedy in your life?' He noticed the momentary, uncharacteristic change in her expression and quickly reached across to take her hand. 'Sorry, perhaps it's something you'd rather not talk about. I didn't mean to pry.'

'No, no, it's okay. My life's not very exciting, I suppose.' Her smile re-established itself in its rightful place. 'I've travelled some with Rani, but I'm usually too busy to see much or get involved like she did. I've never been in love. Not much chance of having any tragic events here in this valley, it's so peaceful. The worst thing that ever happened to me was when mother left me.'

Arthur was puzzled. 'You mean when Rani went to Italy or Japan?'

'No silly, that was long ago, when I was very little. When Rani lived abroad, my mother ran the business here. When Rani came home, they couldn't get along so she went to live in Boston, in Rani's house there. She's been there ever since.'

'I guess I had the wrong end of the stick, I had assumed Rani was your mother, the two of you are so much alike.'

'Well, we would be alike,' Ashri laughed, 'Rani's my greatmama, grandmother to you, of course we're alike.'

'Why didn't your mother take you with her?' Arthur immediately regretted his question; he didn't want to see her face cloud over again. When would he learn to be more thoughtful? 'Or, is that private?'

His lack of diplomacy appeared not to have bothered Ashri.

'We didn't get along very well, either. Everything I said or did, seemed to upset her. I *was* thirteen!' She laughed, 'And Rani said I could learn so much more with her. So, I lived here and when I finished my schooling, I became a learner with her.'

'Ah, I see why you were so defensive of Aszli. You've been through the process yourself.'

'Yes perhaps, Rani's a strict taskmaster, but it's very rewarding in the end. I know I'm good at what I do with the business and I can't wait to run a home of my own. Having a daughter is a little more daunting, but I want to prove I can do a better job of it than Zetla. I'm so excited, I can hardly wait to get started.'

They had long finished the meal and the wine, and had been sipping at small glasses of the intoxicating juice mixture Rani had given him the night before; glasses that were refilled several times by Ashri. Ashri drained the last of hers and suddenly stood up, as if having made a decision.

'Come on, you,' her eyes were large and round and almost completely dark. 'There's no time like the present.'

As she pulled him to his feet, Arthur staggered slightly. His head was really very light, but he was unable to tell whether it was from the wine, the digestive or what seemed to be about to happen.

They ascended the stairs hand-in-hand, or rather finger-in-finger. Ashri had linked her index finger around his, and once again was leading him as if he had no idea of where to go. Arthur wondered how much of the day they had spent connected in this manner. Some of it had been to show him the way, an appreciable amount had been he believed, to indicate possession (This is my man! Don't go near him), and thankfully, much of the time had been to show affection. There had been frequent little squeezes when she had wanted to bring something to his attention without attracting attention to herself. There had been the times in the village square when one or other of the toddlers had performed a particularly endearing action and she had squeezed his hand hard enough to cause pain. He should have recognized it immediately; it was so similar to times with Ester when they had still entertained hopes of having children of their own. Today, he had been so engrossed in the physical activities of the village, he had hardly been aware of the emotional needs of his companion. Would he ever live long enough, he thought, to be sensitive to the unspoken language of others? Perhaps there was still time to make amends. Whatever was to happen tonight, he was to be a willing and wholehearted participant.

Chapter Five

Ashri led him into the bathroom and finally released his finger while she pulled a chrome, free standing towel rack laden with white fluffy towels closer to the curious, saucer-shaped bathtub. Oddly, he noticed a laundry bin next to where the towel rack had stood that appeared to match. Perhaps laundry sack was a better description, as it consisted of a large white cotton bag, suspended by its handles within a chrome tubular frame. Both rack and bin could obviously be folded away if not needed and were of the same economy of design that Arthur found impressive.

The minimum of work for the maximum of reward was how he had always described his own design philosophy. He was absolutely sure he had seen both items in a large Scandinavian chain store of home furnishings. How telling of Rani that she would have chosen items so simple, yet so functional to accompany her expensive Japanese suite.

While Arthur had allowed his attention to be diverted, Ashri had adjusted the temperature of the water silently flowing into the tub. She selected a lidded soapstone container from several of varying sizes on a glass shelf, considered her choice and then replaced it with another. She measured a generous amount of white crystals into her hand, and then sprinkled it into the bath water where it foamed and effervesced. A thin cloud hung for a few moments over the bath water and when it had cleared, the water had turned a creamy, opaque white. A delightful smell of vanilla and cinnamon and orange blossom wafted from the tub as the cloud dispersed.

'That's quite a trick.' Arthur said in amazement. 'I've never seen bath salts quite like that before.'

'They're something that's exclusive to the valley for now, but we're trying to develop a market abroad,' Ashri said as she took a handful of dried petals from a carved dish on the same shelf and scattered them into the bath.

'But let's not talk about business now. Come over here and get your… is it kit you say? Get your kit off?' Ashri laughed, 'That sounds so funny. Did I say it right?'

Arthur started to unbutton his jacket, suddenly self-conscious again, but Ashri pushed his hands away with an impatient, 'here, let me do that'. Grasping the shoulders, she pushed it so that the jacket fell away behind him. As he turned to retrieve the jacket from the floor, Ashri grabbed the elasticized waist of his pyjamas together with his boxer shorts and in one motion pulled them to the floor. He found the bunched material around his ankles momentarily confining and would have fallen over had she not caught and supported him. They were both laughing so hard it took them some minutes of pulling, hopping and balancing on one leg to extricate him from the unhelpful articles.

As soon as his feet were free, Ashri scooped up his clothes and sent them into the laundry bin in one well-aimed toss.

'Goal,' she cried enthusiastically, 'now get in that tub and get scrubbing'.

They were both still laughing as she left the room and Arthur tentatively tried climbing into the bath. The elegant shape sacrificed some of its suitableness, he thought. The wide rim and shallow bowl-like shape meant stepping over the raised edge onto an inclined surface covered with, what he found to be, a very slippery material.

'Ooooh, Health and Safety wouldn't like *that* back home,' he laughed aloud. 'Old folks could have a very nasty fall.'

He tried to sit in the middle of the tub where the water was deepest, but his extended feet were raised by the inclined sides and he ended by kneeling, his legs tucked under him, with the water just covering his upper thighs. The water was not only the colour of cream, but also a similar consistency with an incredible silky feeling when he rubbed it between his fingers. He couldn't think what the feeling reminded him of, as he tried rubbing his hand against his legs; there was almost no resistance at all.

'Make room for me,' he heard Ashri shout behind him. He hadn't heard her re-enter over his splashing and before he could turn around, she had climbed into the bath with him. Putting one hand on either of his shoulders and stepping astride him, she lowered herself to sit astraddle his thighs.

'Let's get you really clean. You're probably *very* dirty after your long day,' she said, handing Arthur a washcloth and dipping another into the water. She squeezed the dripping cloth above his head, sending a small torrent of the silky, aromatic water cascading down his face and neck before starting to work scrubbing him.

The close proximity of this young woman and the uninhibited manner in which she had joined him, had an immediate and not unexpected effect on Arthur. The silky water added a delicious dimension to Ashri's movements as she squirmed about, causing Arthur to panic, a sudden fear of peaking too early plaguing him. He also remembered that the calendar, rather than a clock, measured his recovery time these days.

An embarrassing memory suddenly returned to haunt him. He had almost never been unfaithful to Ester, more from lack of opportunity than good character, he imagined, but on one occasion shortly before retiring, he had attended an exhibition for the company with a female colleague. A tiring day, a pleasant dinner, a shared bottle of wine and they had ended up together in her room on their last night. They had worked together for years; she was nearly his age, and was hardly anyone's idea of a raving beauty, but she was vulnerable from a husband's abandonment and he was wearing glasses tinted with too many glasses of Shiraz.

They had scarcely climbed into bed together, he was sure it was their first long kiss, when his years of neglect erupted all too soon. Despite her sincere protestations of 'It really doesn't matter,' her frantic efforts at trying to revive him, and even showering together with their soapy bodies rubbing against each other, he was unable to recover adequately. He had made a half-hearted attempt at gratifying her in another way that seemed to go on forever with little result until she had eventually cried out unconvincingly. Probably, he thought, just to finish the whole sordid episode.

But it hadn't ended there; she had repeated her admonitions of it not mattering, that she really just wanted to be cuddled, and they had fallen into a wine-fuelled sleep together, her head on his arm. He had awakened, pinned to the edge of the bed, his arm aching with pins and needles and her snoring, loudly enough to wake the entire hotel, directly into his face. He had managed to slip from under her and into his trousers and shirt. Gathering the rest of his belongings by the curtain-filtered light of streetlamps below, he returned barefooted to his own room for a comfortable few hours' sleep.

The next morning she wouldn't look at him and refused to sit at his table for breakfast. He had tried to make an excuse of needing to phone Ester and having locked himself out of her room, but it sounded lame, even to him. He knew she had never forgiven him. It remained one of those things that if his life could be lived over, he would do a little differently.

He placed his hand on Ashri's shoulder to stop her oscillation, saying, 'Slow down, we don't want this to be over too quickly.'

She reluctantly did as he asked and taking his face between both of her hands, looked directly into his eyes. 'Rani said to tell you, you are not to worry about anything. The aqui will slow you down and give lots of staying power.' Her look was earnest, but bemused. 'She said you would know what that means.'

Arthur couldn't quite suppress a slight giggle. 'If that's what Granny Rani says, then I'll totally believe it. I'd believe anything Granny Rani says. If she says you're gonna get laid tonight, you're gonna get laid.'

Ashri's look was of even greater bemusement. 'Does that mean fuck? It is fuck you say, isn't it? It's a funny word to say. Did I say it right?' She laughed as he nodded while trying to suppress another giggle. She had drawn the word into a drawl, pronouncing it, 'fffuckuh'. 'I am going to fffuckuh you. You are going to fffuckuh me. It sounds like doing something *to* someone. We say *oolontha*.'

The word sounded quite distinctive to Arthur, starting as a guttural sound, almost a cough, in the back of the throat and ending in a very nasal sound. He was quite sure he had heard it several times earlier in the day, particularly in Ashri's conversation with Zanli, the overall clad girl on the rooftop.

'It means the gift, or giving to someone,' she explained. 'It's almost sacred here.'

It struck Arthur that this was a far better interpretation. Suddenly, remembering young male friends expressing their admiration of a passing female with, 'Cor, I'd like to give her one,' the words didn't sound quite so crude after all.

'I like to think of it as *sharing*,' he said, 'You know, sharing an experience together. Not doing something to someone, but sharing something mutually enjoyable.'

Ashri thought for a moment. 'Yes, part of it is sharing, but most of it is your giving me something, something that I can't actually share with you.'

Ashri added hot water to the tub, dipped her washcloth into the water again and pushed it directly into his face, rubbing briskly.

'We've got to get you really clean, you dirty boy,' she said, retrieving the washcloth he had dropped, and thrusting it into his hand, 'but you're not helping out. You're a very lazy boy. You can start anywhere.' She arched her back and spread her arms wide, 'I'm sure I'm very dirty too!'

Arthur dutifully took the washcloth and began to slowly, carefully and meticulously remove the last imagined speck of dirt from her face, before working his way down her neck, shoulders and arms. Deciding that the washcloth wasn't quite up to the job, he repeated the entire operation, beginning-to-end with his bare hands. Ashri, meanwhile, had worked her way up to the top of his head and with a comb she repeatedly dipped into the water, was combing through his hair. With his thinning hair, the operation took very little time and handing it to him, she indicated he should reciprocate.

He was afraid her hair might knot and protest against the passage of the comb, but instead with the slipperiness of the water, it separated easily, allowing itself to be combed into very artistic styles. He experimented first with piling it on top of her head, then all to one side, *a la* Veronica Lake, back-to-front, so that it completely covered her face and finally parted in the middle, to fall gracefully either side of her head in her original style.

Ashri raised one hand above her head letting water cascade down on to them. The water flowed down the underside of her arm and Arthur was suddenly aware of the beauty of her armpit. Ester had always shaved hers on a regular basis, but they were more often than not textured with a slight bristle and fairly unpleasant to touch. Ashri's were decorated with a growth of soft downy hair, now plastered to her skin from the water, and so inviting to touch that he was unable to resist kissing it gently. She laughed, protectively dropping her arm, but he persuaded her to raise it above her head again and with a fingertip, traced the flow of water from her elbow, down the equally wonderfully shaped upper arm and across her armpit, before diverting it to flow over her adjacent breast. With some repositioning of her arm and body he was able to find an angle where the water ran down her arm in one continuous flow before falling off the curve of her breast.

'When I go back home, I'm going to become a sculptor,' he said with complete conviction, 'just so that I can recreate this. It would make a fantastic water feature for my garden. No, that would be selfish; I would have to put it in a public park somewhere, to share the beauty of this with the whole world.'

'That's very noble of you, but don't you think you should concentrate on the matter at hand?'

Ashri had been exploring every nook and cranny of his body that was reachable and now, pushed him over to lie on his back so that she could unfold his legs, then changed her own position so that they lay side by side, but head to toe. She began washing the soles of his feet and then each individual toe, before inserting her fingers between his toes and squeezing them lightly. Arthur found this excruciatingly enjoyable; he tried to do the same to her, but found his fingers too large to all go between her toes at once and had to content himself with one toe at a time. He lay admiring her feet; they were so perfectly formed with no sign of corns or calluses, or having worn ill-fitting shoes. Her toenails were carefully trimmed and coated with a clear varnish.

He nearly burst into tears comparing them in his mind to Ester's poor feet. Hers had been for half-a-lifetime too often crammed into "stylish" shoes that had caused corns, bunions and misshapen toes. He remembered that they had once been as young and unsullied as these in front of him. Perhaps a pair of beautiful feet would be added to his list of things to sculpt.

Without warning Ashri said, 'It's time we were thinking of bed. We've used up most of the hot water for the morning and I've got better things in mind than building the fire up now.'

She sat up to fiddle with the water controls. A gentle spring rain started falling from the immense showerhead as the fragrant water they had wallowed in slowly drained away. Together, they helped each other to their feet and started chasing the bath water from each other's body. When they were satisfied there was nothing hiding anywhere, Ashri stopped the water flowing, they clambered from the tub and rubbed each other dry with the luxuriant towels.

Arthur stood next to her as she ran a comb through her long hair and wondered just what the next step should be; should he take her in his arms again and lead her to his room? Before he could make a decision, she opened another jar from the shelf and sprinkled some of its contents into her hand, which she proceeded to rub all over his body. Talcum powder, he guessed, with a similar smell to the bath salts, and held out his hand, assuming she would want the same treatment. Even if she didn't, he thought it would be tremendous fun to apply. Ashri held up her hand to stop him and when she had finished her current task, opened a different jar.

'Here, use this one, she said huskily, 'they go together better than one on its own'.

Arthur did as he was told, sprinkling a small amount of the powder into his palm as he had watched Ashri do, and proceeded to lightly rub it all over her bare skin. The powder gave her skin the same silky feel that it had had in the bathwater and was just as enjoyable as he had expected. He applied the same concentration that he had in washing her body and could easily follow his progress, as in the candlelight the powder left a very faint greenish tinge on her skin. Even so, some areas took repeated applications before he was satisfied he had completely covered them. He had just about reached the part where he was satisfied with his coverage when Ashri pulled away and blew out the few remaining candles. Once again, as she had spent so much of the day, she linked her index finger around his and started leading him towards his room.

Chapter Six

Most of the candles, that earlier had illuminated the landing, had burned out. The few more enduring gave just enough light for Ashri and Arthur to find their way into his room and to the side of his bed. They stood together in the darkness; the linked fingers became an embrace and their bodies seemed to be trying to join together as one. Arthur saw his hand leave a little trail of sparks or phosphorescence as it slid across Ashri's shoulders and down her back.

Maybe those powders were something other than mere talcum, he thought. Again a long-forgotten memory surfaced, of the first time he and Ester had holidayed together in Ibiza. On their way home from an evening of drinking and dancing, they had gone swimming together late at night. Heads emptied of inhibitions, they had divested themselves of their clothes and plunged eagerly into the warm sea. The first flashes of light they supposed were reflections of the stars in the ripples they had caused, but as the water deepened around them and their splashes grew stronger, so too did the intensity of the flashes. Eventually, they realized it was phosphorescence in the water, something both had read about, but never seen before. They played together like children; swimming underwater, splashing each other, competing with each other to see who could make the more intense flashes until nearly, but not quite, exhausted, they emerged from the water and made love in the wet sand, uncaring of any discomfort, the sky already turning a faint lilac.

Ashri unexpectedly gave Arthur a strong push. His back was to the bed and he fell over backward, somewhat clumsily, onto it. Before he could position himself better, she had landed directly on top of him and was raining little kitten kisses down his eyelids, his neck and across his chest. He responded similarly, wherever he could reach and once tried to kiss her on the lips. She interceded with a finger placed over her lips as Rani had, how long ago? The drying powders allowed their bodies to move together almost as easily as they had in the bath and they spent rather a long time exploring each other as they had earlier, just in case they had forgotten or overlooked something, exclaiming occasionally at the light show they were creating.

Arthur had managed to get his full length on to the bed and Ashri was lying facing him, her legs slightly spread to help balance herself. She raised herself to her elbows and put both her hands behind his neck. He could just make out her huge dark eyes, only inches from his. Her mouth was open and he could feel her breath on his face. He could barely hear her voice; it was so low and husky with emotion.

'We mustn't put this off any longer, let's do it!'

Arthur was sure he was ready as her soft wet mouth clamped on to his. He thought later that he should have had some inkling from the pyrotechnics that had occurred the times he had nearly kissed Rani, but the bolt of lightning that went through him was completely unexpected. He had a vision of having tinkered with a car, when he was young and it had been the thing to do to be knowledgeable about those things. He had touched the sparkplug lead on a running engine and had received several painful shocks before he could get his hand away.

They were nothing compared to what he was experiencing. His back arched involuntarily in spasm; he would have thrown Ashri from on top of him if she had not clung so tightly. A brilliant flash of light burst through his head and every part of his body was in pain. The blood pounded in his ears like the sound of a machine gun. He would have screamed if his mouth had not been filled by Ashri's tongue. He tried frantically to pull his head away, or shake it from side to side, anything to dislodge the source of that unbearable pain.

She continued to grip his neck with a strength she couldn't have imagined she possessed and to probe his mouth with her burning tongue, sending ever-greater explosions of agony into his body. It seemed a lifetime since he'd had a breath, or had been without pain, when she suddenly removed her mouth from his. He gasped for air and at the same time tried desperately to push her away, but she hadn't relaxed her grip on his neck and before he could recover, her tongue had found its way on to his again.

A fresh shower of white-hot lava burned its way through his body; a body so rigid in spasm he was unable to offer any sign of resistance. Ashri had locked her legs completely around him and was effectively riding him as a rodeo rider rides a bucking bronco. He could only wonder what he could have done to her, to make her so want to kill him.

Again she released him for a few moments, all too briefly, before her searing tongue sought his once more. It seemed there was a different dimension to the pain this time. Perhaps his body had been numbed with the previous exposure or perhaps he had just lost all strength to resist, but even though it was no less intense, he seemed almost able to tolerate the onslaught. Hell, he thought, he was an old man; his life hadn't been perfect, he hadn't accomplished any of the things he had set out to do with the optimism of youth, but it had been good fun most of the time. He was sure that someone, somewhere would be heard to offer their attempt at condolences to Ester with a clichéd, 'Well, Arthur certainly had a good innings.' Not that it could be taken literally, of course, he had never had the slightest interest in cricket.

If it was to be his death, he resolved, let it come quickly. When the next wave arrived, he made no attempt to struggle and let his body embrace the fresh pain. The spasms had subsided and strangely, he found, now that he was not struggling so, that he could breathe normally. The pain permeated as before, but somehow, didn't seem so debilitating. It seemed somehow, he didn't believe he could be thinking this, almost enjoyable. Was he becoming, he searched for the word; immune? Hardened? Or, simply so out of his mind that he couldn't tell which way was up?

It was a much longer interval before Ashri had to give him another rest and with her resumption of his torture, came the realization. This was not pain; this was happiness, joy, bliss, ecstasy, all rolled into one. This was pure, raw, unrefined pleasure in such potency that his body, never having been exposed to such a concentration before, had resisted as foreign. The more he welcomed it into him, the more enjoyable it was and he began eagerly returning Ashri's kisses.

With his lack of resistance, Ashri no longer had to hold him so tightly. Arthur found that her kisses were not the only source of the sensation; it resulted from everywhere their bodies touched. And everywhere they touched, the phosphorescent glow appeared, bathing them in its soft eerie light.

Arthur was watching the trail of light from his hand illuminate one of Ashri's breasts when he became aware that he could actually feel what it was like to have breasts. No, that wasn't quite right, he was feeling... he squeezed her breast more firmly, it's smooth rounded shape fitting so perfectly into his hand; the hard, little nipple gripped between his forefinger and thumb, he was feeling Ashri's reaction to his touch.

The more he searched, the more he became aware of. He could feel what she was feeling, and he could feel that she was feeling what he was feeling.

It was like one of those infinity mirrors he had seen in a novelty shop somewhere, where two mirrors faced each other within a frame, with a row of tiny lights sandwiched between and attached to the inner surface of the frame. One of the mirrors was of the one-way type, allowing the lights to be seen, and their reflection, and the reflection of the reflection and so on and so on, creating a tunnel of the lights that eventually faded out, apparently in the far distance.

Each of their touches was like that, he could feel her, and he could feel her feeling him feeling her. He realized how she had been able to hold him for just the right length of time when he had been struggling; she had been feeling his pain, or his reaction to the overwhelming sensation. He no longer thought of it as pain. He realized also that she must have been feeling the same sensation, but perhaps had, with her youth, a greater tolerance or had been warned what to expect.

They continued to explore every aspect of the sensation and every possibility of creating it. They no longer had to be kissing to create the feeling, but if it waned, they only had to touch their mouths together, their lips and tongues joining in their own embrace, to send instant deluges of the mind distorting sensation flooding through them.

When they finally joined together, Arthur wasn't sure whether he had entered her, she had enveloped him, or they had simply melted and run together, but the sensation rose to another order of magnitude altogether. With their newfound ability to feel what the other was feeling, they were able to discover infinite ways to mutually tease, to excite, to prolong the level of intensity they were experiencing until, after what seemed hours, their passion could no longer be contained. It was unthinkable that the sensation could increase to even greater heights, but they were no longer in control and could only scream, again and again, as paroxysms of pleasure racked their bodies over and over.

Chapter Seven

Arthur awoke to find he was alone. The last thing he remembered was their going off to sleep together. He had been lying on his back with Ashri curled on her side next to him; one of her legs over his, one of her arms over his chest and her head nestled on his arm. He had not moved in the night; he was still lying just as he was when he had fallen asleep. He had probably been too exhausted to move. More of the events of the previous evening returned and he could feel a smile creep across his face. More like a self-satisfied grin, he admitted to himself, and resolved to try and avoid going around all day looking quite so smug.

As he thought about their lovemaking he wondered if there had been something hallucinogenic in their drinks, perhaps in the aqui. He knew he was a little drunk, but could they have really felt the intensity of sensation he remembered and what about the ability to feel what the other was feeling? Could that have really been possible? He would have to find Ashri and compare notes. He could just imagine the conversation, *How was it for you, baby?* No, surely he could come up with something a little more subtle.

He suddenly remembered the weird sensation after their lovemaking. It had been like gently floating down from a great height as his muscles relaxed and his body returned to normal. He had not been able to tell if Ashri experienced the same; the ability to feel what she was feeling had subsided. In a strange way though, the floating sensation had been almost as enjoyable as the events that had gone on before. Perhaps it was just that, as the sexual experience had been so much more intense, the resulting afterglow would also be appropriately heightened.

Arthur swung his legs out of the bed, sat up and stretched luxuriantly. Everything still seemed to be in working order and as he glanced around the room, he saw fresh clothes had been left for him, along with a light cotton bathrobe. He slipped into the robe and found his way to the bathroom. It was immaculate. Fresh towels had been put on the towel rack, shaving accessories had been placed near the basin and there was no indication at all of anything that had taken place there the night before.

A dark cloud of guilt wafted over Arthur as he thought of the previous evening. What could he have been thinking about? And after that pretentious twaddle he had given Ashri yesterday about how a man should behave when a guest in someone's home. Sure, he had been a little drunk, perhaps a lot drunk, but he should have resisted his natural impulses.

He didn't know what he could say to Rani; would she ask him to leave? He had, after all, followed her halfway around the world, to be with her, not her granddaughter. Admittedly, she had reneged on a promise, but wasn't that a woman's prerogative?

Trying to postpone the inevitable confrontation, Arthur had a leisurely shave, brushed his hair into an approximation of order and returned to his room where he investigated the clothes that had been left. The white cotton shirt appeared to have been made for him, with just the right amount of looseness and the khaki, knee length shorts were an equally good fit. If Rani's estimate was correct, he thought, his bag should be arriving sometime soon; would it arrive in time to be simply repacked for his exit? In the meantime though, he was being looked after rather well.

The house seemed unusually quiet and he was unable to tell the time, but he suspected he had slept much later than he had the day before. Mottled sunlight came through the window as before, but the room was warmer and he could hear the occasional passing of pedestrians outside. He decided it was time to look for Ashri; he would really like to feel her in his arms again and wondered what she would have planned for him today.

He quietly passed the bathroom and looked first in the room she had said was hers, and then in the guest room. There was no sign of her in either one and the rooms didn't look as though they had been used. With some apprehension, he hazarded a peek in Rani's office, but the whirring of her computer was the only sign of activity.

Downstairs, the dining table was set for two places, but no one was to be seen in any of the rooms. In the kitchen, he heard voices and following the sound, found another short corridor and a doorway beyond, leading onto a shady courtyard with vine covered walls. Rani and Aszli, were seated at a patio table and looked up at his entrance.

'We thought you were going to sleep all day,' Rani said with a faint smile, 'you must have been thoroughly worn out. Ashri should have been more careful so as not to tire you too much. Are you ready for some breakfast?'

Feeling dreadfully awkward Arthur was grateful for the change of subject. 'Yes, please. Shall I go back to the dining room?'

'Come say "good morning" first,' she said, beckoning with one hand, 'we're not in any hurry'.

Arthur hesitantly walked to her side. He felt like a schoolboy about to be chastised, but took her hand and remembering their routine, kissed her on both cheeks.

'Good morning,' he said, looking directly into her eyes, unable to see any sign that would help him read her mood.

'Aren't you forgetting someone?' She nodded her head in Aszli's direction.

Arthur turned, found both his hands immediately taken and was kissed on both cheeks, just as before. And like before, she held his hands firmly, gazing deeply into his eyes as they exchanged greetings. Perhaps Ashri was right; perhaps he did *fancy* her. He couldn't believe he could be feeling such an attraction to someone so young. It was like cradle-snatching; whatever was happening to him?

The sound of Rani's chair being pushed back, brought Arthur back to his senses.

'I think we're ready for our breakfast now, Aszli,' Rani said, with the faintest hint of mischief in her voice. 'That is, if you can put him down for a few minutes.'

Arthur reluctantly followed Rani into the dining room with a sense of foreboding. Perhaps he shouldn't have taken Ashri at her word. It was after all, only her word. Rani's expression had been so enigmatic. Did she despise him? Yes, there was a hint of laughter in her eyes, but was she hiding her anger or disappointment to find he would succumb to temptation so easily?

He realized he hadn't put up much resistance and any excuse he could think of just sounded feeble. Sure, Rani had gone out for the evening when she had effectively promised him a night of intimacy, but what woman isn't prone to changes of mind. And, he certainly wasn't going to fall back on the old clichéd excuse of too much to drink.

How would that make him look? 'I'm sorry I made love to your granddaughter, but she got me drunk.' No, all he could do was apologize profusely and sincerely; try and show he was serious and hope she didn't throw him out.

More importantly though, he couldn't bear to be the cause of a rift between Ashri and Rani. It was obvious how close the two were and how Ashri had thought of Rani as more of a mother than her own. To cause a breakup between them for a few hours' pleasure was unforgivably weak of him. He had to do something to rectify this, even if it meant leaving.

Rani was already seated as he reached the dining room. The table laid for two reminded him of Ashri's absence. He could only hope he wasn't too late and she hadn't done something drastic, like throwing Ashri out.

Arthur pulled the cushion on the opposite side of the table around so that it was alongside Rani, then knelt on it and reached for her hand. She looked at him bemused; it was fairly unusual for someone to sit with their back to the table just as their breakfast was about to be served. He was on the verge of blurting out his apologies when Aszli came in carrying a tray laden with their breakfast.

She seemed equally puzzled by his curious seating position, but said nothing as she proceeded to unload her tray.

'Did you want your things moved around where you can reach them?' she asked when she had finished.

'No, no thanks, I'll move back in a minute,' Arthur replied, 'I just wanted a private word with Rani.'

'Enjoy your breakfast, then.' She said as she turned to leave the room.

'Thank you, Aszli,' Rani said cheerily.

'Yes, thanks,' mumbled Arthur, still disconcerted by the interruption.

Aszli's expression had been quite poker-faced as she left, but Arthur was sure he had heard a not totally successful attempt to suppress a giggle from the hallway.

'So, how was it for you?' Rani asked brightly, still holding his hand.

'Sorry?' Arthur asked, not sure he had heard correctly. Could she read his mind or had she overheard him voicing his earlier conversation with himself aloud?

'I simply asked how your evening with Ashri went. Did you enjoy yourself?'

'It was fine,' Arthur replied. Could she possibly not know what had taken place?

'Fine? Is that all you can say? I did, after all, promise you the best sex you would have ever experienced. I'm sorry if it was a disappointment.'

'No, not at all. It was wonderful, it's just, uh, I thought you would be angry. I thought you brought me here to, uh, you know—'

'You thought I wanted your body?' she said, trying to suppress a laugh with similar success as Aszli's. 'Well, yes, I do. Absolutely. It's just not my turn.'

'You could have told me it was all right. I've been worrying how to apologize ever since I woke up.'

'Would you have been comfortable if I had explained beforehand? No, I don't think so. You would have been the perfect English gentleman and found a dozen excuses not to go to bed with Ashri. You would have left her feeling unwanted and dreadful. I thought this was the best way and I'm sorry if I've made you worry unnecessarily.' She took his other hand in hers and met his gaze on an equal level. 'Can you forgive me? Can we still be friends?'

'I feel as though I should think I've been tricked, or taken advantage of, somehow, but in light of what I've been given, I mean, you didn't exaggerate—that really was the most wonderful night! Everything I've experienced before just pales into insignificance.'

'Can I change the subject for just a minute? Did you ever get a chance to read that article I gave you at the airport?'

'The one on Molly fish? No, not really. I glanced at it, but I'm afraid I just shoved it in my bag and forgot about it. I'm not very interested in tropical fish. I had a friend that kept them, though. Why? Was it important?'

'Not really. I thought it might help you to understand something about the way we live here. Try and find time to read it when your bag arrives.'

'Sure'

'Then if you're not angry with me for tricking you—and I'm not angry with you for bedding Ashri, perhaps you could let go of my hands and get seated at the table so we can have our breakfast.'

Arthur resumed what he had begun to think of as his customary place at the table with an immeasurable sense of relief. It seemed as if a great burden had been removed from him. His appetite, which was completely missing only a few minutes earlier, had suddenly returned. He started to spoon a mixture of fruit into a dish and load one of the little fried cakes on top when he remembered they were only the two.

'Is Ashri not joining us for breakfast?' he asked. 'I've not seen her this morning.'

'I'm afraid that Ashri has left.' Rani replied solemnly. 'She wanted to see you this morning, but I thought we should let you sleep.'

'But she'll be around later, won't she? There is so much I wanted to say to her.'

'I don't think that would be wise at the moment. She became a little bit possessive and I've sent her to her other home for a few days. You can see her again when she cools down.'

'How can you do that?' Arthur was suddenly angry. 'You can't just throw her at me one minute and then take her away the next. Are you jealous after all?

'Stop! Let me explain,' Rani interrupted him in mid-flow. 'She needs to rest; I mean complete rest, for a day or two. She mustn't get herself excited. It's very important. And yes, I'm very jealous of you. Do you think I want to see you go off with all these young things?

But, it's my duty and they come first.'

Arthur pondered for a moment. *All these young things,* she had said. Who else did she have in mind?

As if in answer, Rani continued, 'And, if I can change the subject, you shouldn't eat too much breakfast. Zanli has your day all planned out. It's quite late, she wants to take you out to lunch and she will be here soon.'

'Zanli? The girl roofer?' Arthur asked. His anger was completely forgotten, but the excitement remained. What had she said to him as he and Ashri had left yesterday? *I can't wait to be with you, Arthur.* So, she wasn't just teasing him?

'I thought that might change your attitude. Ashri said you seemed quite impressed by her. Am I forgiven?'

'Yes. I'll just have to learn that Granny Rani knows best,' he replied, ducking her mock blow, 'but I'm starving. I really need to eat a bite of something'.

'Go on, then, but don't you *ever* call me that again. Or, I won't be responsible for the consequences.'

Chapter Eight

Arthur found it difficult to believe that his holiday could get much better. He was seated opposite Zanli in a small open-air restaurant, overlooking the river, in village Number Three. Attractively laid tables, covered with starched white tablecloths, were placed under the broad-leaved trees in such a fashion as to afford a view from each. Overhead, Chinese lanterns were strung between the trees and even though they were not lit, gave the setting a festive look. Arthur could imagine that at dusk or with the moon rising, the place would look very romantic.

'It would be nice if we could come here one evening, don't you think?' he asked.

'I don't think that would be a good idea,' she replied with a frown, 'it can get pretty wild when everyone comes in after the gathering'.

Arthur couldn't quite imagine this being the setting of anything "wild", but said nothing further on the subject.

The only other customers were a group of four colourfully, but elegantly, dressed middle-aged women, seated at a distant table. They had made a great fuss over Zanli and Arthur when they entered, but after his day out with Ashri, he had come to expect this treatment.

Arthur thought that the table arrangement must cause considerable extra steps for the waiting staff, but appreciated that the spacing gave a considerable amount of privacy. He was still in considerable awe of Zanli and was grateful no one was close enough to hear him if he made a fool of himself.

They had not had an opportunity to converse much on their journey across country and both were still feeling their way about the other. Zanli was explaining that all the villages in the valley were located on the river and were numbered in order of their position.

Number One, the village in which she and Rani lived, was the highest and closest to the point where the small streams coming out of the nearby mountains formed the river. Number Two was the next along the flow, but because of the river's winding course, Number Three was actually closer to them. That was why, she had continued to explain, they had ridden their bicycles along the lane through the barley fields instead of following the lane along the river.

'I like the idea of having a number for a name,' Arthur said, trying nervously not to stare at Zanli. 'It's such a simple system and it tells one where as well as who.'

'It seems to work very well here and it has been used for so long, most of us have forgotten they had a... another name,' Zanli said earnestly, concentrating on her English. 'They were long and complicated. For instance, our village was called something like, *Village on The River Near Where The Streams Fall From The Mountain With The Crooked Peak.*'

'Can you imagine writing that as an address on all your letters?' Arthur asked.

They both laughed.

'And if the street was called, *Street That Starts at The River And Goes Past The Baker's Shop Towards The Field With The Red Cows?*' she laughed again.

'You don't actually have streets named like that, do you?' Arthur asked incredulously.

'No, I was only teasing you,' she laughed once more 'It is called Red Cow Lane, only.'

Arthur could feel himself starting to feel more at ease. He loved the sound of her laughter. It sounded so incredibly feminine when he thought of how he had first seen her in builder's overalls.

He had been almost tongue-tied earlier, when she had walked into Rani's dining room. She was dressed in a similar fashion to him, in a white short-sleeved shirt and loose knee-length khaki shorts, but the effect on her was stunning. Arthur had made a comment about 'Bobbsey Twins' which neither she nor Rani had understood. He had quickly abandoned his fumbling effort to explain and simply let his eyes drink in her appearance instead.

She was even taller than he had realized; he was above average height, but she towered over him. He had also realized his assessment the previous day was mistaken; she was not merely handsome, but incredibly beautiful. Her long shining hair was loosely tied with a ribbon at the nape of her neck and looked as though it had been brushed for hours. Her nose was strong and straight above full lips tinted with just a hint of additional colour. Emerald green eyes, the lids lined with a generous application of kohl, smiled all the way into his soul as they went through the routine of greeting. And, like Aszli, she had continued to hold both his hands in a firm grip for far longer than seemed to be required. Her demeanour was not the loud, brash builder of the day before, but quiet and somewhat subdued, almost shy.

Arthur had gathered from the conversation, that Zanli was borrowing a pair of bicycles from Rani for their expedition. He couldn't remember when he had last used one; some long ago holiday when Ester was more energetic, perhaps. Would he still be able to ride one adequately and not be an embarrassment?

He needn't have worried. It had taken several adjustments of the seat on one of the bicycles to accommodate Zanli's incredibly long legs and it became obvious that she was even less experienced than he was. The cycles, though shiny and new looking, were of an old-fashioned design with very large wheels, which necessitated a sit up and beg style. Their passage through the countryside was leisurely; Arthur let Zanli lead where the way was narrow, which limited their conversation, but gave him a wonderful view. By the time they had reached the restaurant they had had to stop to get their breath back several times and were both ready for food and drink.

Arthur glanced out at the river to see three of the long narrow boats passing by line astern. Two women, one in the bow and one in the stern, were paddling each. He nodded in the direction of the boats.

'I really would love to try one of those. They look great fun.' he said, more to fill a sudden chasm in their exchange, than a serious wish, then added as an afterthought, 'Although it must be hard work to paddle one all day, plus loading and unloading at either end. They must be very fit.'

'We will have to ask Rani if she can arrange for you to ride along on one.' Zanli said without any great enthusiasm.

There was another pause while Arthur wondered if he was just being entertained for the day or if he was expected to make love to this magnificent woman. Surely, Ashri was just a fluke; some twisted joke between grandmother and granddaughter. But he remembered hearing student friends of his in America, telling of how fathers or uncles had taken them to brothels for their first sexual experiences. Was there something similar going on here? Was he being used as a, how could he describe it? A stud? The idea was ridiculous; who in their right mind would choose someone as old as him? Still, perhaps Rani had recognized him as someone caring, considerate, and experienced.

As he had let his mind wander, his eyes had lost the 'trying not to stare' battle. After the warmth of their noonday ride, Zanli had unbuttoned an extra button or two of her blouse and her generous cleavage was like some eye-magnet, snapping his eyes back in its direction whenever he forgot to apply conscious effort to look elsewhere.

'We just wanted to say goodbye to you, Zanli and to wish you a happy day.'

Arthur turned in the direction of the voice. One of the four women they had encountered on arriving stood directly behind him. The other three were a pace behind her, tittering like schoolgirls awaiting a treat. Arthur stood up, pushing his chair back as he arose and went through what he had come to believe was the normal double kiss and prolonged holding of hands with each of them. He could feel them crowding closer and suddenly their hands were all over him, exploring far too intimately as they made laughing comments in their own language to Zanli and to each other.

The women left the restaurant and he sat back down, wishing for the proverbial swallowing from the earth, anything to make him disappear. He felt so small, perhaps no one could see him after all.

Zanli had kept a straight face throughout the episode, but when they were out of earshot, she burst into laughter. Arthur thought that was definitely the way to make him feel better.

'Those *dirty* old women,' she said, nearly choking, 'they did that deliberately. Did you see the way they pressed themselves against you? Of course, you would have felt it, wouldn't you? One of them said to me, she could not stop herself from giving you a little squeeze. I am so sorry if they offended you.' She thought for a moment, 'Please do not be embarrassed. It really was very funny. And they did not mean any harm. It is just that they do not see someone like you very often, but it does not stop them wanting that feeling again.'

She reached across the table and took one of his hands. 'I could have done the same yesterday. When I first saw you, I wanted to eat you up; just devour you. I was so envious of Ashri. I did not think I could possibly wait another day.' She pulled him closer to her, lowering her voice. 'I am going to be so good to you tonight. I am going to be the best you have ever had.'

So there it was. Arthur no longer felt any humiliation. There was no longer any confusion or doubt about it; it had been made as plain as it could be, he was going to get laid again tonight.

Chapter Nine

They were both on their second glass of the cold white wine before their starters were finally served. Oversized plain white china plates covered with melon and air-dried ham were placed in front of them, along with a basket of, what appeared to be, Irish soda bread. He had let Zanli order for both of them and fare of this type was not quite what he had expected in the middle of India.

Zanli watched him as he buttered the bread and tried the melon and ham.

'Do you approve of my choice?' she asked.

'It's lovely,' he said, his mouth still full, 'but isn't it terribly expensive to import things like this?'

'Oh, none of this is imported. I would think that everything you have eaten since arriving here has been grown or made in the valley: mostly by one of Rani's companies. We do not import very much into the valley.'

'But is there any demand here for this type of food? I'd been expecting to be eating curries for my entire stay and I've not had one yet.'

'I will have to have a word with Rani and tell her you are disappointed with the catering,' she said, mock seriously. 'It is something that Ashri is gambling on. Rani is always looking for new ventures to bring money into the valley and Ashri believes there is enough demand in the large cities like Delhi and Mumbai for European food to warrant a trial. We are all, what is it you say? Crossing our fingers? It does not seem the best time to be having a baby perhaps, but maybe she will have it all sorted out by the time her daughter is born.'

Arthur sat silently chewing his food for a few moments. Ashri hadn't said in so many words that she was totally inexperienced and from her performance, she might have been studying how to make love for a thousand years. Somehow though, she had made him think he was the first. Not that it made the slightest difference. Even though he was only to be here for a couple of weeks and even if he was to make love to someone as beautiful as Zanli every night, he could never forget her. He knew he must find a way to see her again soon.

'Ashri told me you wanted to know all about the wind pumps,' Zanli said, between mouthfuls.

'Yes, I was curious, that's all. I've never seen anything like them before and they seem such a simple solution,' he replied and then realizing the importance of her statement. 'When did you see Ashri?'

'This morning, before I came to Rani's, why?'

'It doesn't matter I suppose, it's just that I wanted so badly to talk to her, to see her again.' Not wanting to offend Zanli by talking about her friend, he tried to change the subject back. 'Tell me how you know about the wind pumps.'

Zanli had finished the last of her food and sat looking down into her lap, a resigned expression on her face and her voice so quiet he could barely hear her, 'I am sure that she will find a way to see you again. You are all that she could talk about this morning. She did not want me to see you today or to, to... you know... with you tonight. I only hope that you will feel this way about me by tomorrow.'

To Arthur she looked as if he had actually struck her; how, with so little effort on his part could he have caused so much hurt? He pushed their plates to one side and took both her hands in his. He seemed to have spent an unbelievable amount of time in the last two days holding hands with one woman or another.

'Please Zanli,'

'I do not think you are really interested in the wind pumps.'

'I am, really, but they are not important.' Arthur consciously tried to make his voice as sincere as he could. 'You are important to me. Everything about you is important to me, what you have done, where you have been, what you want from the future.

'But you are still thinking about Ashri. I can tell.' At least she was looking at him now, but her voice was still barely audible.

'I can't deny that I have thought of Ashri today. She is a lovely person and we had a great time yesterday. And last night was just incredible. It has been years since I made love to anyone, so of course it is natural I will continue to think about her. But I can't think of how to tell you just how happy I am that we are together like this. I can hardly breath, I am so excited that we will be together tonight and I can't wait to hold you in my arms. I love the look of your smile and the sound of your laughter; please give me a smile and let me hear you laugh.'

Zanli looked at him and the faintest flicker of a smile crossed her face.

'I used to work keeping the wind pumps repaired.'

'How did you get involved in that?'

'When I left engineering college, I worked for the electricity company. They have many small hydroelectric generators in the mountains where the streams have a sharp fall and you can get a lot of pressure with only a few hundred meters of pipe. But they are remote and need a lot of maintenance.

'So you do have electricity here?'

'Yes, of course, why?'

'Rani seems to only light her house with candles. And I've seen the streets lit with torches. But then, I've seen several computers too, haven't I? Perhaps it was a silly question.'

'Not so silly. Many with older homes, like Rani, like to keep the traditional look and feel. It is the same reason that we use torches for streetlights. It is probably more expensive to use the candles and torches, and lots more effort, but we like it that way.'

'I'm sorry I interrupted; go on, please.'

'That's all right. I am glad you are interested. Anyway, my job was to check the generators regularly and I was camping out on my own most nights. Mother was worried and the job came up repairing the wind pumps. They are scattered all along the river and even if I had to be away overnight, it was always near one of the villages. Was there a reason you were so curious about the pumps?'

'Not really, it's just that they seem such a simple and economical solution to pumping the water out of the river for irrigation.'

'The rotating sails are a timeless design; probably almost as old as boats themselves. They are not as efficient as ones that can turn into the wind, but so much easier to make. And the pumping mechanisms are similar to what were used for a hundred years by American farmers. They collected rainwater in underground cisterns and only needed a simple pumping mechanism that could be easily repaired.'

'Why did you change from that to being a roofer?'

'Mother's business was growing and she needed more help. And I'm not just a roofer. I can do nearly all of the jobs in building a house. The wiring, the plumbing, most masonry work. I am not so good at carpentry yet, but I will learn.'

Arthur looked at the hands he was still holding. He could feel the strength in them, but they were soft, with no sign of calluses and though the nails were cut fairly short, they were carefully shaped and polished.

'Your hands don't look like those of a builder, or of an engineer for that matter.'

'I wear gloves all the time at work. I have lots of different gloves for the different jobs I do. My mother teases me about the amount of time I spend looking after my hands, but I do not want them to look like hers. Would you like to meet her? And my auntie?'

'Of course,' Arthur replied automatically, thinking that he would never understand any woman. One minute she had been upset because he had only mentioned Ashri, and the next she was inviting him home to meet her family. Perhaps he had to obtain their permission before he could be with her or maybe, with any luck, they just wanted a look at him. Whatever he was to face, he was sure it would be worth it, but he wasn't sure he would ever understand why they had chosen him.

Near the outskirts of the village they could hear the rhythmic sound of a drum, accompanied by the haunting sound of flutes and the jangling of small cymbals. At the first crossroads, Zanli slowed to a stop to let a procession pass. It consisted of several dozen women, dressed similarly to the four they had seen in the restaurant. Although the music was sombre, the women appeared to be in a festive mood. It seemed as though they were taking it in turn to tell a story or joke at which the others would laugh appreciatively. Occasionally one would burst into song and the others would join in on a chorus.

They were walking slowly and Arthur realized it would take several minutes before their way was clear. He turned to Zanli, to find her with hands crossed on her chest, almost touching her throat and her head bowed reverentially. When in Rome, he thought and adopted her stance, turning back to see several women carrying a litter on their shoulders. On the litter was, what at first appeared to be, a mound of bright red cloth, but as it drew closer, he could see the face of a woman exposed.

When the procession had passed, Zanli waited until they were nearly out of sight before uncrossing her hands and raising her head.

'That was a funeral, I presume?' asked Arthur.

'They were taking her to the mountains, to set her free,' Zanli said.

'Was it someone you knew? You seemed upset. The others didn't appear to be in mourning exactly.'

'I knew her of course, everyone here did, but we were not close, if you know what I mean. I was only being respectful of her position. I was not asked to celebrate. That is what we do when someone has lived a long, useful life and it is her time to go to dreamland. If we mourn them, we do it privately.'

Chapter Ten

They rode on for some time until Arthur suspected they had taken a wrong turning. He was sure their route was not the one they had used that morning.

'Are you sure we are on the right road?' he asked, 'I don't think this is the road back to Village One.'

'You have been here two days and you think you know the roads better than me?' she laughed. 'You probably believe the myth about it not being possible to have a womb and a sense of direction at the same time.'

'I'm sorry; I didn't mean to imply that you didn't know your way around.'

'You are right though, this is not the road we used earlier. Be patient and I will show you why we have come this way.'

Another ten minutes of riding and they had joined the lane which ran alongside the river. A few minutes more and as they rounded a bend, field after field of purple crocuses came into view. Groups of women, their heads protected from the sun with turban-like scarves were kneeling in the fields, picking the tiny stamens. Another group was spreading them on the ground to dry. Zanli braked to a stop.

'This is why we have come this way,' she explained, 'this is what Ashri wanted to show you yesterday, but you slept too long. She made me promise I would show you today. She didn't want you to go home without seeing this.'

'Thank you. It's really beautiful. What are they doing?'

'It is the *kashmirajanman*, saffron. It used to be our main source of income from the outside world, but there are too many others now, that can grow it as cheaply or cheaper than we can. This is all that is left. Rani has found a few specialist buyers that she exports directly to, but one day, it will all be gone.'

'That sounds very sad. I hate to think that this would all disappear.'

'Very few want to do the work, now. It is very hard, very tiring. If we brought in workers from outside the valley, from the surrounding villages, it might be possible to keep going, and there have been suggestions for that, but we all know that it would not work.'

'Could you mechanize, or something?' Arthur asked, his mind already filled with visions of buzzing machinery.

'I think it has been tried in other parts of the world, but without any great success. Anyway, we must carry on.' Zanli said, carefully treading on one of the bicycle's pedals as she swung her other leg over the seat.

'Hey, you're getting pretty good with that,' Arthur said, with admiration. 'I'll have to work to catch up.'

They rode along the lane by the river and had gone only a short distance before Arthur recognized the place where he and Ashri had spent the previous afternoon. He smiled as he remembered their falling asleep with her in his arms. He could only hope that the coming evening went as well as the previous; so far the day had been a little disappointing.

A few more minutes and they were alongside the first of the wind pumps. Zanli slowed to a stop again.

'Did you want to have a closer look?' she asked as Arthur braked to a stop beside her.

'I don't think so. You can see the mechanisms from here. I was just amazed by their simplicity.'

'Yes, there is that. They work very well until they go wrong. Then they can be very dangerous.'

'I hadn't thought of that'

'There aren't any brakes on them and the only way to stop the sails turning is to jam them with a long pole. If one of the chains break, the sails spin much faster and you can't get close enough to put the pole in, because the chain flails around so. You have to dive in with the pole and time it just right so that the chain doesn't hit you. I have heard of serious injuries. I think that is why mother didn't like me working with them.'

'At home we tend to think we've gone overboard about health and safety. We make lots of jokes about it, but I'm sure that we wouldn't be allowed to use a mechanism like that if it could cause injuries. Maybe it's not such a bad thing after all.'

Arthur looked at Zanli wistfully. She was so beautiful. Why, he wondered, were they stood here talking boring twaddle about machines or saffron production when they both knew they wanted to be making love? Couldn't he just take her in his arms right now and find a hidden place along the riverside?

'I am sure I know what you are thinking,' she said, 'but we must be patient. I want you so much I can taste it, but we have to do the ritual. You know, the day together, the dinner, the bathing, and then the lovemaking. It has to be in the right order. You understand? Come, let us go see my family.'

With that she was astride her bicycle and pedalling along the lane at such a pace that Arthur was panting by the time he had caught up with her. She slowed to let him ride abreast as the lane was wider here, but they continued wordlessly. Soon they passed the opening in the riverbank where he had seen the learners doing laundry the day before. Arthur glanced towards the river and noticing the bank was deserted turned back to hear a stifled snort from Zanli. He looked in her direction. She was looking at the ground with an amused look on her face and her lips pressed together as if trying not to laugh.

It took only minutes before they were at the house where he had first seen Zanli on the roof. She indicated they were to stop; they dismounted and parked the bicycles in front of the house. He had heard someone shout as they came to a halt and as they reached the top step of the porch they were greeted by the three women waiting there.

Two of the women were, he guessed, approximately Rani's age. Both had their hair protected with loose turban-like affairs, much like he had seen being worn in the crocus fields, and were wearing long voluminous skirts and loose, long sleeved blouses. These were so spattered with paint that it was impossible to determine the original colour. The third was closer to Zanli's age, but two or three years younger. She was wearing a tee shirt and jeans, similarly spattered with paint. Her long dark hair was pulled through the adjustment hole of a speckled baseball cap, just as Zanli's had been on the previous day.

Almost before he had stopped he was being gazed at, kissed and his hands held by first one and then the next. He was aware that Zanli was telling him their names, but knew he wouldn't remember any of them. He had found the close resemblance between Rani and Ashri a little disturbing, but these four women were absolutely uncanny. It was like looking at the same woman at three different ages and in slightly different situations.

'I'm sorry,' he said, addressing the woman he could at least remember was Zanli's mother, 'I'm not very good at remembering one name, let alone three at once.'

'I suspect that our names sound quite foreign to you as well,' she replied in a strong, but easily understandable accent. 'I am Alethi, Zanli's mother.'

'And I am Nalethi, her sister and Zanli's aunt.' the other older woman said, with an identical accent.

'And I am her daughter, Zanli's cousin, Xanthli,' the young woman wearing the baseball cap said. Her accent and tone of voice was identical to that of Zanli.

'Zan-thli?' he asked. 'Isn't that confusing?'

'No, Xanthli,' she corrected, emphasizing the 'x' sound at the beginning of her name.

'Ah, sorry,' he apologized.

Arthur looked first at Xanthli and then at Zanli. Despite the modest amount of make-up Zanli was wearing, the very different clothes and the small age difference, they were unnervingly similar. Having only seen them together for a few minutes, he could already see similar mannerisms. He was sure he would not be able to tell them apart if they were dressed alike.

They had been moving into the interior of the house as they conversed; into the smell of fresh paint and plaster.

'Did you enjoy your meal?' one of the older women asked.

As they had moved, Arthur couldn't remember which was which. He would have to look for a prominent paint spot on each when he got them sorted out again, he told himself.

'Oh, yes,' replied Zanli, before he could answer, 'it was everything I expected. Although I think Arthur got a little more than he expected.'

At that, Zanli proceeded to relate in great detail, the incident with the four women at the restaurant. Arthur could only look away with embarrassment.

One of the older women, he was almost positive it was Alethi, took his hand and pulled him towards her, putting her other arm around his shoulders and hugging him comfortingly.

'Oooh, I hope you will not think too badly of us if some behave in a manner that they should not,' she said, sympathetically. 'Our own daughters can get up to mischief if we do not watch them closely.'

'Mother!' Zanli protested innocently, 'I do not know what you could possibly mean.'

'Perhaps you can explain to me why this roof that was completed months ago suddenly needed some attention yesterday.'

'I... I thought that there may have been some slippage of the tiles. We do not want it to leak, do we?'

'Bah! And although the weather was just the same as it has been for weeks, why it suddenly seemed so hot to you that you had to remove your shirt.'

'Okay, I admit it. Atti said she would bring Arthur by for me to see what he was like and I wanted him to like me.' She turned to Arthur, 'Is that so wrong of me?'

'But you have probably given this nice man the wrong impression of us,' replied Alethi before Arthur could answer, 'and our customs'.

'From what I've seen so far,' Arthur searched for a diplomatic answer, 'I really like your customs. Everyone I've met seems really nice.'

'And there is no reason for you to stand there looking innocent,' Alethi mock scolded Xanthli. 'Do you think I did not see you plotting with the learners the other night?'

Zanli covered her mouth with her hand, trying unsuccessfully to contain her laughter.

'I am sure that was a hit,' she said to Xanthli, taking Arthur's arm. 'You should have seen Arthur looking at the washing place as we rode past it on the way here.'

She looked back at Arthur, still unable to contain her laughter, 'I think you were disappointed that there was no one there today. Were you not?'

'I don't know what you mean,' he protested, 'I only looked that way because, uh, because…'

'Because you wanted to see,' she interrupted, 'if there were any young girls showing off their titties'.

'Zani!' scolded Alethi.

The humour of the situation struck Arthur and he found himself joining in the laughter.

'You mean that was a set up too? I'd be very disappointed if I found out that doesn't occur on a regular basis. It was so enchanting.'

'Oh no,' said Xanthli, 'the washing takes place a couple times a week. We just thought it would be nice if Ashri would take you past at the right time so they could get a look at you.'

'And you at them,' Zanli elbowed him in the ribs. 'Come on, we should let these women get back to their work.'

'You are just afraid we will tell Arthur more of your secrets.' This was, Arthur was almost positive, from Nalethi, unless they had changed positions without his noticing.

They made their farewells and were soon approaching the crossroads, near the school Arthur had seen the day before, when they had to stop for dozens of little girls. They were all in neat blue uniforms with white blouses and socks, pouring out of the front door and flooding into the street. Laughing groups of varying sizes, different classes Arthur presumed, were going their various ways at the crossroads, some calling excitedly over their shoulders in a mixture of English and the strange tongue he was unable to understand, to friends on different routes.

How beautiful he thought, and then wondered if perhaps this was also staged for his benefit. No, he thought guiltily; don't question everything you see just because you've had a couple of pranks pulled on you. Learn to accept and enjoy what you see.

'Ashri was telling me yesterday about some of the things she used to get up to, when she went to school there,' Arthur said, more to fill in the quiet spaces than to start an actual conversation. 'Did you go there as well?'

'Oh, yes, we were best friends,' she laughed, 'and always in trouble. We were friends with Yetti back then too, but she was never in trouble, even though she was the instigator half the time. She always knew the answer to every question and always had her homework in on time, so our teachers would never believe she could be part of our gang. You haven't met her yet, have you?'

'Who?'

'Yetti, Yeathili, that is. She is tomorrow.'

'I'm sorry, I don't know what you mean.'

'Yeathili,' Zanli spoke patiently. 'You will be spending tomorrow with her, but you have not yet met her, have you?'

'No,' Arthur replied, completely puzzled, 'no one has said anything to me about another woman'.

'Then it is time that you meet her.'

And with that, Zanli set off once again at a hurried pace. The roadway had almost cleared of the children and she rang her bell furiously at the stragglers slowly walking along the sides of the road. Her sudden departure caught Arthur completely off guard. They had passed several cross streets and he was starting to think he would never catch her when she came to a halt in front of a large house.

The area looked familiar; Arthur thought they must be close to Rani's house. The house was of a similar design, but even larger, with its veranda running the full width. More of the tall, large-leaved trees in front gave shade to the garden, from the still warm, late afternoon sun. Individual awnings shaded the upper windows and a gracefully curving path ran from the front steps to a gate where it met the road.

Zanli dropped her bicycle and ran up the path. Arthur could hear her shouting 'Noni, Noni' as she went through the front door.

He assumed he was meant to follow and carefully leaned his bicycle against the gatepost. At the entrance he stopped, unsure for a moment if he should enter without an invitation, then tentatively stepped through the open doorway.

The interior was dim in contrast to the afternoon sunshine and it took several seconds for his eyes to adjust.

'Come on,' Zanli called impatiently, from further along the entrance hall. 'Come and meet my Noni.'

In the dim light, Arthur could just make out another woman that she was talking to. As he drew closer, he could see that it was an older version of Zanli's mother. The woman's hair was pulled back into a bun and was almost completely grey, but the face, aside from the hint of a few lines, was nearly identical. She stood very erect; her height and demeanour giving her an air of serenity, reinforced by the pale coloured sari and matching scarf she was wearing.

'This is my Noni,' said Zanli excitedly as he joined them. 'My great mother, I mean grandmother. She does not speak much English I'm afraid, but I can translate for you.'

'You do not have to apologize for me, Zanethili,' she said quietly, 'I can speak enough to tell this beautiful man how honoured and how grateful we are to have him here.'

She extended a hand to Arthur. It was the first time since arriving in this place he had not had the two-handed, doubly kissed greeting and a tiny worry wormed its way into his awareness that this was somehow, a sign of disapproval.

'I'm very honoured to meet you,' he replied, 'I've just met Zani's – I mean Zanli's – mother, aunt and cousin. Now it's almost the whole family.'

'You are making me a happy woman,' she continued as though she had not heard him. 'It will be–'

She paused, then said something to Zanli that Arthur didn't understand.

'Wonderful,' Zanli whispered.

'Wonderful, yes, *wunderbar*,' she continued, 'to have this house filled with baby daughters again. It has been far too quiet for far too long.'

Arthur looked questioningly at Zanli.

'Yes, we are all going to live here together,' she laughed. 'Atti, Yetti and I. Noni will look after us when we have our babies. It will be almost like being at school again.'

'You're all having babies?'

'Of course, the babies you are giving us. That is why Noni is so grateful. She told me she is so envious of us. She said she is not too old to make you sing, if there is anything left when we are done with you. She has been rehearsing her little speech all afternoon, but she did not expect us quite this early.'

Arthur stood quietly for a moment as the impact of what she had just said sank in, but before he could ask further questions, Zanli began conversing with Noni in their own language. After a short exchange, she turned once again to Arthur.

'I am sorry, but Yeathili is not here. She has gone out with Ashri. It is of no importance, you will meet her tomorrow. Now I must take you back to Rani's so that I can get ready for tonight.'

As they approached Rani's house, Arthur could see a battered jeep parked in front. Somehow this looked out of place on the narrow lanes in this neighbourhood until the realization stuck him that, aside from a tuk tuk he had spotted in village Number Three, this was the first motorized vehicle he had seen since arriving.

'Ah, the delivery is just too late,' Zanli said with a hint of disappointment. They were cycling slowly for once, at little more than a walking pace. 'I wanted to borrow Rani's car to take you to the lake today, but she was nearly out of fuel.'

As if on cue, Arthur could see that the woman who had been unloading boxes and bags from the jeep, was now straining from the weight of two jerry cans she was carrying around to the back of the house.

'Perhaps,' Zanli continued, 'Yetti will take you there, tomorrow. Let us hope so; it is so beautiful there, I don't want you to miss it. It seems that each of us is destined to complete the wishes of the other. The one before. I showed you the crocus fields that Atti wanted to show you. I hope that Yetti will show you the lake. I wonder what Yetti will want to do for you that Simili will get to do instead?'

Arthur was no longer surprised to hear yet another name. He was beginning to believe that nothing in this place could surprise him when the woman from the jeep emerged from the back of the house and with a rattle from a not completely suppressed exhaust, drove off. Her hands, arms and face, in fact, all of the skin he could see that was not covered by the tee shirt and jeans she was wearing, was approximately the colour of a green olive.

Arthur thought he was beginning to recognize a wind-up when he saw one and made no comment. He followed Zanli's lead and together they walked their bikes around to the back of the house.

Zanli showed him the entrance to, what he now realized was, a small garage bordering the courtyard at the back. She showed him where to hang the bikes on the wall and when he had finished, pointed to the small 4x4, an open topped Japanese model that Arthur recognized as being nearly twenty years old. Despite its age, it appeared to be in excellent condition.

'That's what I wanted to borrow today. It's not exactly a Maserati, but it's good enough to take us anywhere in the valley.'

'And Rani would have let you borrow it if she'd had enough petrol?'

'Oh yes, I have used it many times. I keep it in good running order for her. She trusts me with her Maserati when we are in Italy. She is very generous. With everything. She may be very rich, but she would give you anything she has if you needed it.'

As they left the garage Zanli turned towards the front of the house, but stopped as Arthur started to follow.

'I must go back to Noni's and get ready for you tonight. You can get in through there,' she said, indicating the narrow passageway between the garage and the house.

She put an arm around him, pulled him towards her and wrapped him in a firm embrace. One hand stroked the back of his head and pulled it onto her chest and she began running her fingers through his hair as she lightly kissed the top of his head. Their relative heights seemed exaggerated to him; he had never been held by anyone so tall and he could not tell whether it was his own or her heart he could hear beating.

'Until tonight,' she whispered and disappeared in a run.

Chapter Eleven

He wandered through the courtyard into the kitchen, where Aszli seemed suddenly very busy with something in the large sink. As he entered, he thought he saw a flash of something brightly coloured going out the far door, but it had been so brief that it might have been just a trick of the light, he told himself.

'Rani is in the study, if you want to see her,' Aszli said. 'Can I bring you a pot of tea?'

'Oh yes, please.' The thought of tea seemed suddenly very welcome, 'I can't think of anything I'd rather have right now.'

'We have Earl Grey or English Breakfast or Darjeeling? And would you like anything with it? Cake? Or perhaps some biscuits?'

'Earl Grey sounds very nice. Umm, cake or biscuits? Why don't you surprise me?

'If you wait with Rani, I will bring it in a few minutes' she said, with a bemused expression.

In the study, Arthur found Rani sitting on one of the couches, her legs folded underneath her and a magazine on her lap. She was dressed in what Arthur had begun to think of as her "office clothes" and he could see a pair of shoes where she had left them by the end of the couch. He started to take the couch opposite, but she sat upright, unfolded her legs and patted the cushion next to hers. He was completely unable to resist such an invitation. As he made himself comfortable she slipped one hand around his upper arm and pulled him closer to her, then laid her cheek against his shoulder for a few moments.

'I think we may be getting some tea before long, which one did you choose?' she asked.

'Earl Grey, I think,' he replied.

'And cake or biscuits?'

'I left it to Aszli's discretion.'

'She'll probably bring us enough to feed a small army. I have a real problem with my weight if I leave it to Aszli's discretion.'

'That is if I remember correctly. I usually feel quite distracted when Aszli looks at me and I don't always remember what I've said.'

'I wonder why that is,' Rani laughed and squeezed his arm, 'Ashri thinks you have a crush on her.'

'On Aszli? Not really, but I do feel a little strange when I'm around her.'

'Lust, perhaps?' she laughed again, putting a finger to her lips as Aszli entered carrying a large silver tray. It was loaded with a white china teapot, cups, plates and a large salver heaped with an assortment of biscuits and slices of several different types of cake.

'Do you see what I mean?' Rani asked, 'we shall have to eat all this now, it's all far too good to let any of it go to waste.'

Arthur barely heard her; Aszli's eyes seemed to have never left his as she deposited the tray on the table, poured tea into the two cups, added milk and arranged the plates in front of them. He was aware that Rani thanked her, but it seemed to him that time had stood still until she had left the room. He tried his tea.

'That's very good,' he said appreciatively.

'You would say, at the end of a long day, nothing hits the spot as well as a good cup of tea?'

From the sound of her voice, Arthur was unable to tell if she was teasing him, or was completely serious. He had heard the cliché so many times, but as he took another sip of tea, her quiet giggle and expression explained where Ashri's talent for wind-ups came from.

'Perhaps, I'm partial to a cold beer in hot weather, too. I'm a little surprised to find you drink tea like this. Don't you prepare it a little differently?

'I learned to drink it like this in Italy.' She held the salver out for Arthur to make a choice. 'I used to stay occasionally in a little hotel on Ischia. It was quite modest, but it had a nice pool and was in a lovely position up on the cliff tops, overlooking the town and the port. Although you couldn't quite see Naples for one of the other islands, you could just see Vesuvius in the distance. Every day at five o'clock, they would offer their English guests tea and cake, or biscuits round the pool. They served me one day by mistake and after that I had to pretend to be English.'

Arthur took a piece of cake and carefully placed it on his plate.

'Couldn't they tell from your passport?'

'I'm sure they knew that I was neither English nor even Italian, but they make such wonderful hosts. They would never let on, or say anything to embarrass a guest.'

Arthur let the conversation come to a lull as he filled his mouth with cake.

'So, have you had a good day?' Rani asked.

'It's been interesting.' He thought for a moment, 'Yes, it's been fun. I'm not sure I quite understand Zanli, though.'

'But you like her?' There was a note of concern in Rani's voice.

'Oh yes, I like her,' he thought for another moment. 'Maybe I'm just apprehensive. Ashri was so easy, so natural. I wasn't expecting anything from her and I was thinking about you most of the time. You know, looking forward to the evening with you. After what you had said yesterday morning.'

Rani looked at him over the rim of her cup as she took a sip. 'And now you are looking forward to an evening with Zanli?'

'Mmm, yes,' Arthur mumbled through the mouthful of cake he had just taken. It had looked like fruitcake, but was surprisingly sweet and tasted of honey; almost like Greek pastries he had had on holiday. He quickly took another sip of tea.

'But you don't know what to expect of tonight? Or, perhaps more important, what is expected of you?'

'Maybe that's it.' He decided after the initial surprise that the cake was really very good. He took another mouthful.

'You only have to be yourself. Can you dance?'

His timing never was very good, he thought, he waited until his mouth was empty before answering.

'Sure, a little.'

'I mean dance properly,' she laughed, 'not just wiggling your hips and waving your arms around in an embarrassing fashion, you know, after you've had too much to drink at a wedding or an office party?'

'Have you been watching me?' Her laughter was infectious, 'Ester and I took evening classes in ballroom dancing for two or three years. It was some time ago and we were never very good, but we enjoyed it at the time; well, most of the time.'

'But you can do the foxtrot, or perhaps a waltz?'

'I think I might just remember how. I won't make any promises about how good I am and you might think about getting some workman's steel toe-capped shoes. Why?'

'It isn't for me that I'm asking; it's for Zanli. I'm sure that she has some of the shoes you described, but I think she has something a little more elegant in mind. She loves old Hollywood films from the thirties and forties and wants to have an evening styled along those lines tonight. And, she loves to dance.'

'Well, I can certainly try. I think we saw my bag being delivered a while ago, but I don't think I've brought anything suitable to wear.'

Rani smiled at him. 'Oh, leave that to me. Have I let you down, yet?'

'No, I can't think of any way that you've let me down,' he paused, then touched her arm and as she met his eyes, continued, 'except to keep fobbing me off with these beautiful young women, when I really want to be with you'.

Rani put her other hand over his and smiled at him again. 'You can be quite charming when you want to, can't you? I can't imagine why you would want to be with an old woman like me when you can be with these "beautiful young women".'

'I... I didn't mean it like that,' Arthur stammered. 'Compared to me, you're still a young woman too, and you're very beautiful.'

'Thank you,' she said.

Arthur could see she was trying to be sincere, but her eyes still revealed a spirit of mischief. He was reminded of Ashri's continual teasing and decided to change the subject.

'If Zanli is a very good dancer, she may find me a little disappointing. Ester always complained that I couldn't lead properly. She often went off on a tangent on reversals, instead of following me and if I tried turning her, she would complain that I was pulling her about too much.'

He thought for a moment.

'Of course, if she forgot a step on the sequence dances, that was my fault, too,' he laughed. 'I just remembered why we stopped going to the classes.'

'Did you not suggest that for one to lead, the other must be prepared to follow?'

'No-o,' he looked skywards. 'I think that might have just started another argument.'

'Well, you will find Zanli a very good dancer. And, a good dancer can make even a mediocre partner look good, not that I'm suggesting for a moment that you are mediocre. I think the two of you will get on very well.'

Arthur lifted his cup to his lips and took a sip, but the tea had gone cold. He put the cup back down.

'Have you finished?' Rani asked, 'I can have Aszli make another pot. We haven't even made a dent in the cakes.'

'I think I've had enough.'

'Then let me see if we can find you something to wear tonight.' Rani rose to her feet. 'Come with me.'

Rani led him to her bedroom, where the door he had noticed on the opposite wall, opened to a walk-in wardrobe running the full length of the room. Dozens of outfits, ranging from expensive suits, cocktail dresses and casual arrangements, through to traditional Indian styles, lined most of the rail along one wall, but at the far end, a row of men's suits took up an appreciable amount of the space.

She pulled out a grey, double-breasted suit that looked expensive, but its excessive lapels made it look out of date. Arthur thought that if Zanli wanted a 'forties' evening, this would be perfect. Rani held it to his chest and observed the result.

'No,' she said, shaking her head. 'It doesn't do anything for you. Your grey hair is lovely; it makes you look very mature, but you need some contrast or it can look wishy-washy.'

'Oh, thanks. Wishy-washy, eh? I'll try and remember that.'

'You know I didn't mean it as a criticism, but tonight, you must be perfect. Here try this one on.'

101

She handed him a dinner suit. He slipped the jacket on. It fitted perfectly.

'And the trousers,' she said emphatically. 'It's no good if they don't both fit.'

He hesitated for a moment.

'Don't be coy,' she continued, laughing once more. 'Don't forget, I've seen more than your legs before now.'

Arthur unbuttoned the knee-length shorts and stepped out of them. The trousers at first seemed a little long and a little loose, until he remembered he wasn't wearing shoes and the trousers were probably meant for braces and a cummerbund. Rani rummaged in drawers below the hanging suits and produced a pair of highly polished black pumps, and as if reading his mind, braces. She followed these with a dark blue cummerbund and a matching bow tie.

'If you'd like to take this stuff back to your room,' she said, handing him the shoes and accessories, 'I'll see if I can find a shirt for you.'

Arthur bent to pick up the shorts he had discarded, but Rani interrupted him. 'Don't bother with those; I'll take care of them.'

He made his way back to his room; put the tie and the cummerbund on the table next to his bed and the shoes of the floor. He removed the jacket and laid it carefully across the bed as Rani came in, holding out a white shirt to him. It was folded as if it had just come from the laundry.

'Do you keep spares of everything?' he said, completely puzzled, 'or has all this been planned for a very long time?'

'There's no mystery,' she laughed; 'All the clothes you've borrowed were my husband's. You just happen to be the same size.'

'I don't think you've ever mentioned that you were married, before. I had assumed that you were, because Ashri told me you had two daughters, but I'm aware that in today's world, you can't always make assumptions.'

'I've actually had two husbands.'

'What happened to them? No, don't answer that. I'm sorry; I'm being nosy and blurting out the first thing that comes into my mind again.'

'It's all right; I haven't been what you would call lucky, with husbands. Neither of them lasted very long. They're both dead now.'

'I'm sorry. I shouldn't have asked. I didn't mean to stir up unpleasant memories.'

'No, I said it was all right. It was a very long time ago. That's why the styles of these clothes may look a little dated. When I said I wasn't lucky, I didn't mean it because they were dead. I was very young and didn't make very good choices. I didn't grieve much for either of them.'

She moved closer to him and put both arms around him. 'Now, I just take lovers.'

Despite her laughter and joking manner, Arthur was unsure whether she was joking or not; after all, she did seem quite practiced at this.

'I think we'd better get you into the shower,' she said and sniffed in an exaggerated manner, 'or you'll be making an impression tonight, but not the sort you want'.

'Well, I have been riding a bicycle in the heat all afternoon, whose idea was that?'

'I'm afraid I suggested the bicycles,' she replied, leading him towards the bathroom, 'Zanli wanted to borrow my jeep so that she could show you the lake. I told her a little white lie; that I didn't have enough petrol until another shipment came. I know it was selfish of me, but I wanted to show you the lake myself. Is that too awful of me?' She turned her head and looked at him over her shoulder as they crossed the landing.

Arthur couldn't remember another woman ever having told a lie so that she could be with him. It gave him a very strange feeling.

'You remember how to use this?' Rani asked indicating the control wand of the bath, as they arrived in the bathroom.

Arthur nodded; the thought of Rani lying, so that she could be entertaining him later, still perplexed him. And yet, she was leaving him in the arms of Zanli tonight.

Rani turned to leave, but hesitated at the doorway, 'just shout if you get in a muddle. Of course, you'll be having the ritual bath with Zanli later, but she knows how the controls work. She should, as it's her own design and she fitted it for me.'

Chapter Twelve

Arthur was putting the finishing touches to his bow tie when Rani re-entered his room. He found it hard to believe that she had showered, applied make-up and was already dressed in the length of time it had taken him just to put on his trousers, shirt and shoes. Admittedly, he'd had to adjust the braces and work out how the cummerbund fastened. Finding the shirt had French cuffs he had wasted time looking for cuff links. Eventually he had spotted a pair prominently displayed on his bedside table where Rani had thoughtfully left them. And the shoes were of a quality Arthur had never hoped to afford so he had probably wasted considerable time admiring them. Although they were buffed to such a shine that he could almost see his reflection, they were fully lined and in such soft leather, that on his feet, they felt more like gloves than shoes.

Rani was dressed in royal blue, in much the same style as the women Arthur had noticed on his first night, but with a look of elegance that had escaped them.

'I thought perhaps you could use some help with your tie,' she said.

***

He had only just turned off the shower when she had appeared behind him with an oversized towel and started rubbing him dry.

'There isn't a lot of privacy in this house, is there?' he had asked, jokingly.

'Would you really want there to be?' She had said, giving him a firm squeeze on the buttock through the towel, 'I should have told you, I needed to get in the shower right behind you or I'll be late for the gathering.'

105

He had turned around and put both hands around her waist. 'If you'd said, we could have showered together; just think how much water we could have saved.'

Laughing, she had pushed him away from her. Her white cotton bathrobe was only loosely tied and it had soon opened revealingly from her movements. 'I don't think it would have saved any time at all, and in fact, I probably would have never got to the gathering. Now, *you* get out of here and let *me* get in the shower.'

Arthur had pulled the towel around him and started to leave the room, making a heroic attempt to resist turning back, as he heard the shower start again and the splashing as Rani stepped in. At the last moment, he was unable to resist the temptation and had looked back, only to find Rani watching him, giving a shake of her head and a little waggle of her finger, like a mother to a naughty child.

'You should be thinking of Zanli,' she had said, disapprovingly, 'just think how crushed she would be to arrive here and find us together.'

He had thought the sight of her standing there, drenched with the fine, soft rain from the oversized shower was completely worth any reduction in her regard for him. He had found himself almost skipping back to his room, a wide grin on his face that would simply not go away.

***

Arthur fought the temptation to embrace this wonderful creature standing in front of him, but contented himself instead, with the memory of her standing naked in the shower.

'No,' he said, 'I'm quite able to tie my own tie.'

'I wouldn't have thought you were the type to wear a bow tie,' she replied, 'I always associated them with more pretentious men.'

'I may not have spent that much time in dinner jackets, but most of my working life, I was hunched over a drawing board. Long ties get soiled far too easily. In later years when we used computers for drawing, they could still get caught in the machinery if we had to go into the factory.' He moved closer to her and lowered his voice. 'But if you think it needs improving, I can untie it and you can help me to tie it again.'

She saw the gleam in his eyes and gave him a little push. 'No, I think it's absolutely fine. It's not very wise for me to get that close.'

Turning to the bed, she picked up his jacket and handed it to him. 'Let's see how you look in the complete outfit.'

When the jacket was in place, had been tugged here and there, then smoothed down in the appropriate places, she gave an appreciative 'Mmm, very nice. Zanli's a very lucky girl.'

They went down the stairs together. Arthur was surprised to find the lower hallway had been transformed. Chinese lanterns, like those he had seen at the restaurant, had been strung from the ceiling and the console table had been removed, giving the room a more spacious look. He followed Rani into the dining room to find the theme continued there. The usual low table and cushions were gone and instead, a small table of what he considered "normal" height and two dark lacquered bentwood chairs were in their place. The table was set for two places with Rani's simple white china, graceful cutlery and an array of stylish glassware. Only a few candles were lit, but the subdued lighting from the colourful lanterns resulted in an intimate, yet festive atmosphere. Music, he thought he recognized it as Gershwin, was coming from somewhere, although he couldn't see any speakers.

'Do you approve?' Rani asked, 'Zanli insisted on the lanterns at the last minute.'

'Wow, it's stunning!' Arthur circled round, taking in the decorations, 'how did you manage all this? It's less than an hour since we went up to shower.'

'I think Aszli has had some help,' she replied as if that explained everything, 'would you like to wait for Zanli in the study?'

The study had been decorated with a few of the same lanterns, but otherwise seemed unchanged from earlier. Rani disappeared in the direction of the kitchen, only to re-appear a minute later carrying an ice bucket with a bottle of sparkling wine. Aszli, dressed the same as Rani, but in burgundy, followed her, carrying a tray with two glasses. They set them down on the table between the two couches.

'We really have to leave you now,' Rani said, 'Zanli should be along any minute.' She slipped her arms inside his jacket and gave him a prolonged hug. Her musky scent and the feel of her warm body against his, made him fervently wish she were staying. She gave him a lingering kiss on the cheek and released him. Aszli gave him her usual protracted, two handed, double kiss, complete with her deep disquieting gaze and when his senses had recovered, they were gone.

Chapter Thirteen

Arthur wandered around the colourfully decorated rooms, noting the effect with admiration and looking, without result, for the source of the music. He at last settled on one of the couches in the study and was toying with opening the wine, torn between good manners and the desire for something alcoholic to quiet his uneasiness. He was on the verge of reaching for the bottle when a sound to one side made him turn. Zanli stood in the doorway watching him.

Any questions of how she had entered so silently were banished by the impact her appearance had on him. She stood for a few seconds like a model at the end of the catwalk, before twirling gracefully on the ball of one foot to show off the complete effect. Her long hair was parted on one side and fell to her shoulders as before, but had tiny ribbons, woven into it on both sides, that held it away from her face. The long neckline of the navy-blue dress extended almost to her waist, but the hemline had given up long before it reached her knees. Over the dress she was wearing a cream-coloured jacket in a style Arthur thought had once been called *bolero*. It was just long enough to match her neckline and failed to meet at the front by quite a few inches, offering he thought, very little protection from the elements. The matching navy shoes had tiny cream bows and four-inch heels, making her already impressive height, even more intimidating. As a finishing touch, she wore gloves that matched the jacket, and accentuated the graceful movements of her hands.

Zanli finished her twirl and stood with her back to Arthur, swaying for a few minutes in time to the music. She raised her hands to her shoulders and very slowly let the top slide off. To Arthur the implication was obvious and as he leapt to his feet to assist with the task, he realized his lightheaded feeling was only partly because he had not been breathing since she entered the room.

As she tried to slip out of the jacket, Zanli's gloves kept snagging on the snugly fitting sleeves and they both laughed as the jacket bunched up at her back, effectively trapping her arms behind her. It became obvious they were attempting things in the wrong order. She tried removing the offending gloves behind her back, but there were small buttons at the wrist of each, which she found difficult to unfasten.

'Oh, I did want this to look seductive,' she laughed, 'and I've made such a mess of things.'

'No you haven't,' he replied. 'You look wonderful.'

Arthur patiently held her jacket so that she could move her hands in front of her and remove the gloves where she could see what she was doing. When she had finally rid herself of them, he let the top slip down her arms and again caught his breath. The dress was halter style, revealing bare shoulders and a flawless back nearly to her waist.

He made no attempt to resist the temptation and leaning forward, slipped his arms around her waist and lightly kissed the back of her neck. She leaned back into him and together they began swaying in time to the music again.

'Do you approve?' she whispered, turning her head enough so that he could just hear.

'Oh yes, I approve,' he replied huskily. There was something definitely wrong with his breathing; maybe he needed to sit down. 'Would you like some wine?'

'Mmm, that would be nice,' she said.

As one, they stopped their swaying; she turned to face him and took one of his hands, allowing him to lead her to the couch where he had been sitting. He carefully opened the wine, covering the cork with the corner of the tea towel that had been wrapped around the ice bucket, and cautiously filled two glasses, trying not to let the foaming liquid overflow.

As they sipped the wine, another silence crept in, but there was nothing awkward about it this time. Arthur was fully aware he was staring and just as aware that Zanli was returning his stare over the rim of her glass. Finally, she broke the silence.

'I think we are too much alike, you and I.'

Arthur could see very little similarity between them. She was young and beautiful. He was, well older, and certainly not beautiful: although he did try, of course. She was single, he was married, by law if not completely in spirit. She had her complete future in front of her; he was clinging to perhaps, his last chance to enjoy himself before he was too old for adventure.

'How do you mean?'

'I am always being told I am too interested in things, in machines, in systems, in how *things* work, and how they function. That I am not interested enough in people. Watching you today, I think you probably suffer from the same complaint.'

'Oh?' was all Arthur could say; it sounded very familiar.

'I do not necessarily agree that they are right. Yes, mechanical or electrical things interest me. I love being able to fathom out a system or make something work that did not before, but I think I like my friends and my family and I am interested in what affects them. I just find it difficult to talk about personal things or how I *feel* about people. I do not think I can change that much, or even want to. Perhaps having a daughter will change me and I will be able to show my feelings in a better way. That is why I am sometimes a little brash or loud. I hope you will forgive me if I was like that yesterday.'

Arthur felt tears welling up in his eyes and could not think what to say. He put his arm around her and pulled her close. When he could speak, his voice was husky.

'You don't have anything to be forgiven for. I thought you were wonderful yesterday. I couldn't stop thinking about you. And you are right, we are quite alike in some ways.'

They sat like that for several minutes until he remembered Rani telling him of Zanli's love of dancing.

'Rani tells me you like to dance.'

'Oh yes,' she looked at him with bright eyes. 'I absolutely love to. Are you asking me to dance with you?'

'Only on the understanding, that I make no great claims about my ability. And, that you agree to say "stop" if I'm not good enough for you. I don't want to damage your toes.'

'I am sure you will be fine; I think perhaps you are overly modest. First though, I am going to change the music.'

She rose and walked to the bookcase, opening one of the doors to the lower closed section. Within, was a fairly comprehensive, if older, hi-fi unit, with a turntable for records and twin cassette and CD players. To one side were stacks of CDs and below, stacked on end from one side of the cabinet to the other, were dozens of LPs, still in their original brightly coloured sleeves. From these she selected a few, then shuffled them about before choosing one, with a, 'Yes, I think, perhaps; no, it must be this one to start.'

When the record was in place and the turntable started, she adjusted the volume until the music swelled about the room. It was a big orchestra with a vaguely familiar sound playing a slow waltz., but not one Arthur could identify His chest tightened; he loved waltzes, but they had always caused an argument when he had danced with Ester. She could never remember which foot to start on and often tried to steer him in the direction she wanted to go, instead of letting him lead.

Zanli seemed to fall into his arms and without counting, or even nodding to the music, they both started as one. Within seconds they had adjusted to each other's stride and went swirling out of the room and into the hallway. Rani was right, he thought, he had never danced so well. Zanli had a firm grasp on his shoulder, a light touch to his extended arm and was incredibly light on her feet for someone so tall. They were so close, with their legs interwoven and their bodies pressed together; he could feel every movement of her body.

His hand on her back could feel the strength of firm muscles under the bare skin, but fearing that it might soon feel clammy to her, he slid it down to the small of her back where the dark blue material of her dress insulated it. He was undecided which was the more sensual.

Together they whirled up and down the length of the hallway. Any variations Arthur tried were followed effortlessly by Zanli as though they had danced together for years. When he made actual mistakes, she immediately responded to them and avoided being kicked or stepped upon, except for one occasion. The record ended and they parted. Zanli slid her arm around his waist and they walked back to the table where their glasses waited. Arthur felt as if he had just experienced dancing as a pleasure, instead of as an effort, for the very first time.

'Perhaps we should sit for a few minutes,' Zanli said, topping up their glasses. 'I don't want to wear you out.'

'Good idea,' Arthur responded, 'but only for a few minutes. I could dance with you all night.'

Zanli looked at him with exaggeratedly wide eyes, blinking slowly, her head tilted slightly downwards so her eyelashes seemed be touching her brows.

'Not all night, I hope,' she said. 'I think we may have more important things to do.'

'Oh yes, I hadn't forgotten,' Arthur exclaimed, raising the bubbling glass to his lips, 'but you're such a terrific dancer. Wherever did you learn to dance like that?'

'Rani taught me most of what I know,' she replied, mirroring his action with her own glass.

'I didn't even know she danced. I think Ashri said that you often danced at the gathering, but I had supposed it was traditional Indian dancing.'

'Yes, that is more like what we do there, although it is *our* traditional dances,' Zanli said. 'Not Indian, but they are similar.'

She leaned back luxuriantly into the couch; the halter top suddenly almost as revealing as had been the bib overalls when Arthur had first seen her. He tried desperately to keep his eyes trained on hers, thinking there would be time enough for that later.

'I'm not sure I understand the difference.'

'Let us just say there are many different "traditional" styles. Anyway, Rani was a professional dancer when she was a young woman. Shall we have another go?'

Arthur watched as Zanli put another record on the turntable and carefully lowered the stylus. The music started and suddenly Zanli was in his arms again. The wine had stifled some of his inhibitions, but he still found himself trying not to think too much about what lay ahead with this beautiful woman he was holding. Better to concentrate on the dancing instead, he told himself.

Zanli at first made a few cautious little suggestions to improve his style and posture. Then, when she found him agreeable, was soon teaching him new steps and routines. Arthur had often watched a popular program on the television, where professional dancers paired with celebrities and taught them to dance to competition level. Originally, he had only watched because Ester wanted to watch, but he had quickly become fascinated with the colour, the music, the overall gaiety of the show and not to mention, the beauty of the female dancers. He had often felt envious of the amount of instruction and practice time the celebrities received.

Tonight, he thought, is the closest he would ever come to that and it was wonderful. Zanli had the ability to show a step so simply and to explain the timing in such a manner, that when they tried the step together, in time to the music, it all came together easily. Sometimes, of course, he still made dreadful mistakes and they fell into each other's arms laughing, but he would insist on trying again straight away and after another attempt or two could usually master it.

He had long discarded his jacket and they had stopped several times to sip at the wine, or for Zanli to change records, when she suddenly held up her hand to get his attention.

'I think it's time for us to eat,' she said, glancing in the direction of the dining room.

Arthur followed her look and in the dim light caught sight of movement between the dining room and the kitchen, but he couldn't see who it was.

'Oh, I was just getting started,' he said, pretending to be a reluctant school boy, 'do we have to stop?'

'Yes we do,' she replied sternly, 'Ashri will be very angry with us if we let her dinner get cold.'

Arthur was grateful he had his back turned as he reached to retrieve his jacket. He felt as if the breath had suddenly been sucked from him again.

'Ashri?' he inquired, slowly putting the jacket on, 'Ashri has made dinner for us? I thought Rani had sent her away.'

'Yes, she did, but Ashri has promised not to cause a problem. And she knows that I cannot cook anything. I am completely hopeless in

114

a kitchen. And she wanted to do something to make amends for the little spat we had this morning.'

'But didn't she have to rest or something?'

'Yes, but she has insisted. Anyway, she is so good at choosing menus and she promised she would not exert too much effort. She would prepare something light,' Zanli gave a giggle, 'something that would not sit heavily for later.'

The thought that Ashri had been right there, so near to them, perhaps watching them dancing, laughing and enjoying themselves, tore at Arthur's heart. What had Rani said? That she had become too possessive. Did that mean she felt as deeply as he did about their brief relationship? He wanted to run and find her, to hold her in his arms again, explain that his day with Zanli, though enjoyable, was not of his own making.

He looked down at Zanli's bare shoulders as he held her chair. Could he bear to hurt her? Was she not looking expectantly to an evening of pleasure? Of passion, even? Did she not also deserve to be treated with consideration? Were her feelings not equally important? How had he reached this situation? Why were these young women so like busses, suddenly showing up in threes after so long a wait for one?

'Are you going to stand there all night?' Zanli asked, looking around at him.

Arthur put his hands lightly on Zanli's shoulders and kissed the top of her head. She tilted her head to one side, letting him push her hair out of the way. He lightly kissed the side of her throat that was revealed, then lifting her hair a bit more, the nape of her neck, and finally, let it drop back into place before moving to his own chair.

'I was just soaking up how very beautiful you are,' he said softly, having made his decision, 'and how lucky I am.'

Zanli smiled up at him warmly. He knew he had made the right decision.

Chapter Fourteen

Arthur looked at the dinner that was already laid out before them. It did indeed look to be a very light meal. Two large white dinner plates were heaped with some kind of a salad. Their matching side plates each had only a small stack of tiny pancakes, or crepes, and a bottle of wine stood in a bucket filled with ice. He noticed the glasses had been chilled; a slight mist was beginning to form on both of them.

'Well, this looks very...' he said, reaching for the wine bottle, '... um, nice'.

'I think you will like it, once you have tried it.' Zanli responded quickly, 'it is one of my favourites, of all of the things Ashri has made for me over the years.'

Arthur cautiously sniffed the wine. He had thought it would be too cold and would have lost much of its flavour, but the bouquet was intense. The wine was surprisingly dry after the sweetness of the smell and Arthur took another sip appreciatively.

'Um, that's really very good,' he said, taking another small sip, 'I wasn't going to have any more wine after the amount of champagne we've had, but we can't let this go to waste.'

'Go on and try your salad,' Zanli urged, putting down her fork, 'it is at just the right temperature. If you let it get cold, it will not be nearly as good.'

Arthur cut through one of the asparagus spears that lay on top, dipped it into a pool of the dressing, and raised it to his lips. The texture of the asparagus was perfect and the sharp vinaigrette dressing tasted of anchovies. He poked at the salad and could see tiny new potatoes and chunks of what appeared to be smoked fish amongst the mixture of spinach and coriander leaves. The whole assembly was dusted with a mixture of seeds. He carefully selected a forkful and took another bite.

'God, that's fabulous,' he cried, when his mouth was empty, 'I hadn't expected it to be anything like this.'

'Did I not tell you,' Zanli said, 'that Ashri is a wonderful cook. Wherever we have travelled with Rani, I always look at her cars or at the machinery in her factories, Yetti spends all her time in the local museums and libraries, but Ashri would always end up in the restaurants we liked best: pestering the chefs to tell her their secrets. And they were always flattered to be asked and would let her spend as much time in their kitchens as she wanted. If we could not find her, we always knew where to look.'

Arthur tried one of the little crepes. It was thin and light, tasting of black pepper and parmigiano; it seemed a perfect accompaniment to the salad.

'All three of you travel with Rani?' Arthur asked between bites, 'I hadn't realized that. Where did you go?'

'Oh, we have been to Italy and Germany and Holland and Switzerland, oh and of course, to England once or twice. And in India, we have been to Delhi, Mumbai, Kolkata and several other places. Yetti has not travelled with us so much for the last few years, since she started at the university, but sometimes we go to Germany to see her.'

'This is just for holidays? I know Rani has lived in Italy and Japan, and didn't she say, in Amsterdam?'

'No, no, we go to work. Well, I suppose they were holidays for us, when we were little, but Rani is going to see how her businesses are doing. And Ashri is going to learn the businesses, and I go to look at the systems they use and learn about them if they are new and advise if they are old and need replacing, or updating.'

'Rani has businesses in all these countries? I thought she was mainly an exporter. What kind of businesses?'

'You know, cosmetics, um, fashion, food production. That kind of thing. Her biggest cosmetic company is in America, but Ashri's mother runs that. I think Rani leaves her to run it by herself, so they don't argue.'

They both sipped at their wine before filling their mouths with the salad. The only sound to be heard were appreciative 'Ummms' and quiet chewing.

'You said that Rani taught you *most* of what you know about dancing. Where else did you learn?

'In Italy. We were in a little town in the very north. Rani has a factory there, making leather goods. Not in the little town, itself, but in a more industrial town nearby. It was just Rani and me; she wanted me to look at some of the cutting machinery they were using and whether we could introduce computerized equipment.'

'That sounds interesting.' Arthur was suddenly alert. 'Did you?'

'Uh no, it would have taken far too long to, to, how do you say, recue? To pay for itself? I would spend my mornings in the factory, go back to our hotel in the afternoon to do some calculations and in the late afternoons, Rani would take me to a tea dance.'

'That sounds a lovely way to spend the day,' Arthur was using his fork to push the remainder of his crepes around his plate, mopping up the last of the dressing. 'I didn't know anyone still had tea dances.'

Zanli raised her glass and slowly waved it in front of him to indicate that it was empty. Arthur was surprised to find the bottle had scarcely enough to top up their glasses. He hadn't wanted to drink too much.

The events of the previous evening had kept returning to him through the day and he had found it difficult to believe it had taken place quite as he remembered. He knew he had drunk more than he had intended, but he didn't think that it was enough to distort his memory quite so much. But then, he couldn't possibly have experienced such a feeling as he remembered. Tonight, he was determined to remember everything accurately.

'I can open another bottle,' Zanli offered. 'I'm sure Ashri will have put more in to chill.'

Arthur shook his head. 'Not for me, please, but go ahead if you want more.'

'No, I think my legs may be a little wobbly as it is.'

The thought of her legs being wobbly, stirred something within Arthur. He realized that much of her height was because of those long legs. Sitting opposite him, she didn't seem particularly tall. Would she wrap them around him as Ashri had last night?

'Anyway,' Zanli continued, 'the hotel we were staying in had once been the royal palace of the Australian royal family and the gardens at the front–'

'I don't think you mean the Australian royal family,' Arthur interrupted, laughing. 'They don't have one.'

Zanli giggled, 'did I say Australian? I meant Austrian. Uhh... where was I?'

'The gardens,' Arthur prompted.

'The gardens at the front,' Zanli repeated, 'had been turned into a park that was open to the public. There was a large open area with kiosks serving drinks or coffee and lots of tables and chairs, and they would play music, and everyone would dance.'

She suddenly appeared to have remembered something very important. 'Would you like some dessert? Or pudding, is that what you call it? I know Ashri has made us something. It will be in the refrigerator.'

'I don't think I could eat another bite. That didn't look much to begin with,' he indicated the empty plates, 'but it was very satisfying'.

'Some coffee, perhaps?'

Arthur remembered her earlier description of her skills in the kitchen. He didn't think Ashri would have made the coffee in advance.

'It might keep me awake.'

Zanli smacked the back of his hand that was resting on the table and looked at him fiercely. '*I* will keep you awake. You will not have a chance to sleep until we hear the birds singing.'

Arthur was not entirely sure if she was just teasing him or completely sincere. Perhaps it would be better to appease her.

'Okay then, just the coffee.'

Zanli picked up their empty plates and disappeared into the kitchen. She returned in only a few minutes with a cafetiere, cups and saucers, two glasses and a decanter, all balanced on a serving tray. So, Arthur thought, Ashri must have had it all ready, after all. He should have trusted her.

Silently, as if concentrating, Zanli depressed the plunger on the cafetiere and poured coffee into their cups, then reached for the decanter.

'No more to drink for me, thanks.' Arthur said, remembering his resolution to try and remember things.

'You must,' Zanli appeared shocked, 'it is just aqui, for later. It will help you, you know, with the pain.'

She poured her own glass to the brim, then looked at him questioningly once more. He shook his head.

'And you and Rani danced there, in this park, or garden?' Arthur asked, trying to return to their conversation.

'Not with each other, or at least not very much; we didn't have much chance.'

'Why was that?' Arthur asked. He could imagine that two beautiful women would not be left to dance together in Italy, but he had to ask.

'All the old men wanted to dance with us. They were absolutely lovely,' Zanli shut her eyes for a moment as if remembering the scene. 'It was so beautiful there. The sun would be low and shining on all the flowers surrounding us, and the whole garden smelled of blossom. The sun would have set before we left, with only the candles on the tables lighting the dance area. That made it even more romantic.'

'Wasn't it difficult to dance in a garden?'

'On no, the dance area was paved with marble, or was it, uh, that Italian limestone?'

'Travertine?'

'Yes, I think so,' she paused for a moment, 'I think they swept it down each day, just before the dancing started. Couples would start drifting in; they were mostly elderly and so sweet to watch. They have such style there. Then the singles would start to appear; there were always more men than women, and they dressed so, so smart? You know, they were in, perhaps their best suits, but the styles would not be quite up to date. As if they were trying to impress. What is the word I am looking for?'

'Dapper?' Arthur suggested.

'Yes, I think that is what I am looking for,' she nodded, 'yes, dapper. The men would be dapper. They were just beautiful, and so charming, and they would flatter us endlessly. I wanted to bring them all home with me. Some of them were very good dancers and wanted to show off their skills, so I had lots and lots of practice. They were forever telling us how beautiful we were, and I think to them, we may have appeared to be beautiful.'

'I think that goes without saying,' Arthur laughed.

Zanli appeared puzzled. 'What do you mean?'

'I mean it should be obvious to anyone that you are beautiful. You are indeed very beautiful.'

Zanli's expression softened; she sank into her chair in a more relaxed manner and seemed to beam at him. She reached across the table and touched his hand.

'You are very nice. I had hoped so much that you would like me.'

'How could I not like you?' Arthur asked softly, 'you are just incredible. Not just beautiful, but obviously very clever as well. I can't quite understand why you want to be with an old man like me, but I'm not complaining. I must be the luckiest guy in the world.'

Chapter Fifteen

Arthur had never been enamoured with oral sex. He had grown up in a world where homosexuality was unacceptable and myths flourished. As a result he was, as a young man and much embarrassed by in later life, truly homophobic. It was not until he was nearly middle-aged that a greater coverage on television and in films, plus discovering that some of his close friends were of this formerly despised persuasion that he slowly came to accept that it was not quite as despicable as he had imagined. He was surprised to admit that he could accept two people finding each other attractive or falling in love, even though they were of the same sex. He no longer felt uncomfortable to see two men holding hands in public; only self-conscious that he had once been so narrow-minded.

He had however, at an early age confused the acts committed by those he so feared, with the supposed evil of the participants themselves. In other words, if *queers*, for that was the usual description when he was young, were bad because they performed oral sex, then oral sex must be wrong. Full stop.

This was further reinforced when he went to a mid-western university in America. There he had first encountered the widely-used term of abuse, of *cocksucker*. It was used to indicate such a level of loathsomeness, evident in the tone of voice invariably used, that even after changing his views completely, he still shuddered at hearing it. Looking back, he knew he had been very naïve, but probably little more than other, apparently confident, young men around him. He could still remember comments about some young women that his roommates had found less than attractive; comments that he had found disgusting, offering alternatives to normal sexual relations.

Added to that, he knew that there were young women at his university, from what were called *good families,* in other words relatively wealthy, who were subject to such pressure to remain virgins until marriage, that they had learned to perform fellatio fairly readily to reduce the pressure to submit to full intercourse.

Arthur painfully remembered a young woman he had been strongly attracted to shortly after starting at his university; one that he had felt at the time was completely out of his league. Her general appearance, the style and quality of her clothing, her diction and overall demeanour, all indicated a background of considerably greater affluence than Arthur's modest upbringing. He had made several fairly feeble excuses to speak to her and her welcoming smile eventually gave him the courage to ask her for a date. Expecting immediate rejection, perhaps scornfully administered, he was dumbfounded when she agreed. Her manner made him think she was actually pleased to have been asked. They had decided upon the cinema for the following Saturday night, which gave him four days to worry if she would have changed her mind in the meantime. Every possible scenario had flashed before his eyes, from her receiving a better offer from another of less modest means or greater sporting skills, to a car crash in which she was seriously, perhaps fatally, injured. He tried to console himself that he suffered from a ridiculously overactive imagination.

She had offered to collect him from his hall of residence, or dorm, as the Americans called their relatively well-appointed student accommodation. As he waited for her to arrive at the agreed location in front of the building, he was all too aware that his humble selection of apparel was drab and outdated in comparison to the flashy clothes worn by his fellow students. The arranged time passed without her appearing, and although he was convinced it was a waste of time, but having nothing better to do, he continued to wait. Nearly twenty minutes had passed and he was on the verge of returning to his room when he heard his name called.

The sudden relief at her actually appearing was almost immediately negated by the appearance of the car she was driving. He knew it to be an expensive and desirable model. Although from one of the popular brands, it was the very top of their range; a low-to-the-ground sports coupe that had only just been released to the public. It also looked as if it had only just that moment been driven from the dealer's showroom. Very much in awe, he stammered some words of admiration as he slid into the passenger seat, even more intimidated by their relative positions on the scale of wealth. She had explained the car had been a recent birthday present, her twenty-first he distinctly remembered her saying, as she competently threaded through the early evening traffic, a barely muted roar from the many cylindered engine, trailing in their wake.

The film had been *North by Northwest*. He hadn't remembered telling her, but she seemed to know he was an architectural student and she told him she had chosen that particular film to gauge his reaction to the modern cantilevered cliff-top house of James Mason's character. He was greatly impressed by the fact she seemed to know more about him than he knew about her. Later in a popular bar filled with students, most of whom could not drink alcoholic drinks legally, but where the financial interests of the proprietors were gratefully put before their legal responsibilities, he had expressed admiration for the design. Of course, he had seen pictures of similar designs in various magazines, but he was thoughtful enough not to mention this, even going so far as to slightly exaggerate his surprise at the design. She had responded by telling him of her love of the architecture she had seen on a visit to England and of her sadness at seeing so many grand buildings devastated by the war, but still not restored. He realized she was the first person he had met in America who knew anything about England, let alone having visited it.

When they left the bar, she had asked him to drive and seemed to be amused at his reluctance. He had made excuses of his inexperience with left-hand drive, the automatic gearbox and the contrast in power to the Morris Minor in which he had taken lessons, but she had insisted. He had found the car, despite its power, almost ridiculously easy to drive, once he had suppressed his tendency to stamp upon a non-existent clutch and wave his left hand at a gear lever that wasn't there. She had almost completely stifled a giggle at each of these actions, as she directed him to a local park. The road wound picturesquely through a wood, past the last of the streetlights, and into an unlit area where the occasional car was already discretely parked.

Long before he had found a suitable place to park, she had nestled against him; stroking his inner thigh with one hand while she lightly ran her tongue around the rim of his ear. The car had hardly stopped before she was unfastening his trousers and lowering her wetted lips over his manhood. Torn between his repugnance at the act and the guilty pleasure he was receiving from it, he had silently allowed her to continue, but when she had later tried to kiss him, he had avoided her lips. She had slowly, almost methodically, sat erect, pushed his hand away from where it had meandered, straightened her skirt and asked him to let her regain her position behind the wheel. Quickly, but wordlessly, she drove back to the campus, the sporty exhaust roaring and the tyres protesting as she accelerated away from traffic lights or tight bends. Within minutes she had squealed to a halt in front of his dormitory, raising a cloud of the recently fallen leaves. He had tried to offer an apology, but the look of hurt on her face told him it was an action destined for failure and his words came out as an undecipherable mumble.

'You drive like a girl!' had been her only angry words as she sped away amidst a flurry of fallen leaves and more squeals from the overworked tyres. So quickly had she accelerated that the still open passenger door slammed shut, barely missing him.

***

Before meeting Ester, his longest relationship had been with a girl named Amy, a girl he had lived with for several years. It had been a loving, but almost at times, too intense partnership. Arthur knew that Amy had a promiscuous past and her experience far exceeded his own, numbering by her own admission, many scores. Her promiscuity was perhaps not altogether in the past, he sometimes thought. Her explanations of where she had been at times did not always sound completely valid, but he decided what he didn't know wouldn't hurt him.

Amy had loved the excitement of outdoor sex; the more public the place, and the greater risk of being caught the better, and she was more often than not, the initiating one. Sometimes the locations were far too public for Arthur's liking. There had been very few of their country walks that did not result in her pulling him into a barely secluded, or only slightly hidden place, sometimes only a few feet from footpaths where others might be walking. Rare were the evenings spent in a pub or restaurant that on their way home, did not result in a sexual encounter in his car, even though they would be later sharing a comfortable bed. Arthur always kept a blanket folded up in his boot and on summer evenings they would occasionally walk along the banks of the Thames to a quiet place and make love under the stars.

One evening, on holiday together, they had been in a pub, when she had suddenly told him to put down his drink and follow her. He thought her to be headed for the car, but instead she had turned the opposite way and persuaded him to follow her up a densely wooded and precipitously steep slope. The ground underfoot was slippery from mud and wet leaves; several times only the trees stopped them from sliding back down, but with one of them pushing the other, while bracing themselves against an adjacent tree, and the other then pulling with an arm wrapped around the next nearest tree, they somehow arrived at the top to find a grassy cliff-top, overlooking the surf that crashed against the rocky shore below. A nearly full moon lit the scene with a soft light that seemed almost as bright as daylight. Amy's button-fronted denim dress had been quickly removed and stretched out on the soft grass and after long and intense love-making, they had fallen asleep in each other's arms. Hours later they had awakened to a sky turning pink, rubbed the chill from each other's limbs, dressed hurriedly and made a cautious descent to his car.

But even with Amy, fellatio had seemed awkward. He had long overcome his disgust, but it still seemed somehow wrong. He knew that to some men it was a way of demonstrating power over their partners, but to him it was more often than not, just uncomfortable. Over the years, in the magazines that girlfriends brought home, he had read so many complaints about men's ignorance of women's "parts" and of their inability to even find a clitoris, let alone a "G spot".

It seemed ironic to him that none of their articles had ever explained to women the working of a penis; of the various sensitive areas; the places that could be manipulated for instant arousal or the places that were so sensitive that careless handling could cause intense pain.

Of course, with Ester it had never been a problem. She had never offered and he had never asked. For the first few years their couplings had been fairly frequent, but uninspiring. Ester was a willing, but submissive and patriotic partner, rarely initiating sexual activity and always reluctant to vary from her usual "missionary" position, even insisting on her usual left-hand side of the bed which required him awkwardly using his left hand for caressing. Any attempt towards oral sex on his part was invariably met with a, 'No, please don't' and after twenty-four years, he still had no idea of how she tasted. On the rare occasions she had made the opening play in bed, it had always consisted of a grope at his genitals with a teasing remark along the lines of 'What's this funny little thing, then?', or 'Is this all you've got? That's not going to excite anyone, is it?' Words guaranteed to have the exact opposite effect to that desired.

It had been almost a relief when, after nearly twenty years together, Ester had quietly and without explanation, announced that she was no longer interested in any form of sexual activity. Arthur, who had worked hard to maintain, what he felt was merely a normal relationship and had never for a moment thought that he might be imposing anything out of the ordinary upon her, had readily, but carefully, trying not to appear too eager to escape from an unpleasant task, agreed.

None of these thoughts, or memories, was going through Arthur's mind at the time though; he was almost out of his mind from the sensations he was experiencing, being the recipient of the most intimately teasing and yet, seemingly endless foreplay he had ever experienced.

Chapter Sixteen

When Arthur and Zanli had finished their dinner they had resumed their dancing. Zanli had put on successively slower pieces of music and they had simply swayed back and forth in time to the music, holding each other tighter and tighter until they seemed to have melded into one being. It didn't even seem unusual for Arthur to rest his head on her shoulder instead of the other way round. Finally, she looked down at him with dilated eyes and said, 'It's time, come.'

He had followed her up the stairs and into the bathroom, where they slowly and silently disrobed each other, even taking time to carefully fold their clothes before stepping into the rapidly filling bath. In contrast to the playfulness that had been so much a part of the previous night with Ashri, they had set about washing each other with a dedication to thoroughness. Then, with the same slow silent determination, they had towelled each other dry, their eyes never leaving the other's. With a final dusting of the various, talcum-like powders, they had almost carried each other to Arthur's bed.

Almost immediately, Zanli had locked him in her arms and her open mouth had clamped on his. The pain he had experienced seemed much greater than the night before. Perhaps he had not really remembered the full extent of it, or remembering the wonderful exhilaration when it had subsided had led him to think it was not as bad as it had really been. It also seemed to continue for much longer, but he steeled himself against it, stifling the screams that welled up and tried to escape. He had tried to relax and embrace the pain, but he was beginning to think he could endure it no longer when finally the wave of delirious pleasure engulfed him and the *"infinity mirror"* effect let him feel the same pleasure washing over Zanli.

He had kissed every square centimetre of her body, feeling her pleasure with every kiss and was in turn being kissed as frequently in return. The colourful trails of phosphorescence as they stroked and caressed each other seemed brighter and more long-lasting than they had before and at times illuminated the room with the glow from their bodies. His kisses had started with the fingertips of one hand, across her palm, up her inner wrist, continuing up the full length of her arm and lingering on each breast, before proceeding on a symmetrical path down the other arm. Her pleasure was a delight to him as she slowly stroked his back and neck, kissing his ears in turn, as he made his exploration.

Turning his attention to her toes, he left a trail of kisses on the sole of her foot, up her calf, on the back of her knee and up her inner thigh. He had barely completed his circuit when she had pushed him onto his back, straddling him and forcing him into her. Then, pulling him into a seated position, she pulled his face into her welcoming cleavage. Her fingers found pressure points in unrelated parts of his body that gave great surges of delight as with rising and falling hips, she had brought them both to a pinnacle, like some great display of fireworks.

Chapter Seventeen

They had lain in each other's arms for only a short time when the contrasting wave of relaxation and gratification softly flooded over him. He was floating. The room and Zanli, disappeared, followed quickly by the earth, the solar system and perhaps the entire universe. The shrinking effect reminded him of his childhood and of an old black and white television as it was turned off; the picture rapidly shrinking to a dot before finally being extinguished completely.

The feeling of floating turned to one of falling; falling at an incredible speed. Only the faint glow he seemed to generate lit the way ahead, but there was nothing to see, only total blackness. Faster and faster he went; he could feel himself accelerating at such a rate and for so long that he was sure he must by now be travelling at many times the speed of light. Was that possible? But then, he was only a tiny burst of pure energy; no weightiness of flesh and blood, no eyes to see, no ears to hear with, nor even any lungs or need for breathing. Yet, he had an awareness of the way ahead. If there was something to see in the blackness, he was sure he would see it. If there was anything to hear, he knew with complete confidence that it would not go undetected. If by any chance some smell was to fill the void, he knew without even thinking, that it would seem to him as some wonderful perfume.

After what seemed hours the darkness ahead was less dark, he could see the beginnings of a faint glow in the distance. As he continued at this impossible pace, the glow slowly grew in size and brightness until it filled his entire awareness of the way ahead.

A long forgotten memory scrambled to the surface of his mind. Very late on a dark, cold, crisp nigh Hhe had been in an airliner on his way to Chicago. Only the occasional farm or faint lights from a car, as some late-night reveller made their way home, relieved the blackness of this dark Midwestern flatness. The city had, like this, first appeared only as a faint glow on the horizon, but as he watched, it slowly grew to cover the entire earth below them from horizon to horizon, yet with no distinguishable features. Their descent had at first revealed only the curving, brightly lit paths of motorways, then major roads and finally the individual streets as they flew over a whole world of streetlights. The memory dimmed and disappeared, as a dream upon awakening, leaving him momentarily wondering what he had been thinking about.

Arthur gradually overtook another glow of energy like himself. Their encounter as they briefly melded together told him everything essential about the other being, though whether it had been male or female, man or beast, he was unable to determine. Only the nature of the spirit was there, no history of its actual life, but an instant love, more intense than any he had ever known, was formed between them. It caused him to think about himself. He could remember nothing. He knew he had once had memories, both good and bad; had he not just remembered something about; about what? He'd had worries about things he should have done; things he could have said to help alleviate someone's pain, concerns about his future, his health; all gone and replaced with a wonderful lightness, a feeling that it no longer mattered, and a commitment to understanding the meaning of his present existence.

As they grew closer to the main body of light, he could see it was simply made up of millions upon millions, more likely billions upon billions, of tiny bursts of energy, like themselves. They overtook more and more, sometimes wisping through each other in microseconds. The same bond of love was formed each time and as the bursts became more closely spaced, the magnitude of love he could feel was almost unbearably intense. The brilliant whiteness surrounding them was made up of every colour of the rainbow and many that were impossible to describe, possibly from another spectrum altogether. He was also now aware of an unbelievably beautiful music around them, faint at first, but louder as they progressed into the denser, main body of the glow. This seemed to be an emission from each individual glow in sheer delight at the bond of love formed, as one passed through another. Combined, the infinite number of transitions created a chorus of unbounded exquisiteness.

In the distance, no louder than a faint whisper at first, Arthur heard his name called. The voice seemed to be from the direction he had just come, if there was such a thing as direction in this place, and unable to comprehend how anyone could know his name here, he slowed his pace. Without thinking or knowing why, he was drawn to the sound. It was Rani. Who was Rani and why would she be calling him?

Torn between the incredible love, joy and bliss he had found in this immense, impossibly beautiful, glowing world and the sound of her voice, he was soon travelling back at a similar speed to the one with which he had arrived. As her voice became louder the black and white television effect was reversed and his old world rapidly grew to fill his awareness.

Arthur awoke to find he was in Rani's arms. She was rocking him gently from side-to-side, tears streaming down her face. Sitting at the foot of his bed were Ashri and Aszli, concerned looks on their tearful faces. Zanli, a light robe thrown around her shoulders, was half collapsed across the bed, half kneeling at the side of it. Although her face was hidden by her folded arms, he could hear her sobbing loudly. His body felt icy cold and the warmth from Rani's arms was very welcome. Pins and needles were torturing him everywhere as though his whole body had gone to sleep.

As he struggled to sit upright, Rani realized he had awakened. 'Oh, Arthur, Arthur,' she cried, 'you've come back to me!' She held him even more tightly and rocked him all the harder, pressing her face against his. He could feel the wetness of her tears and taste their saltiness. Inexplicably, she suddenly released him from one arm and aimed a flat-handed blow at Zanli.

'You stupid girl,' she hissed as her hand made a cracking sound against Zanli's shoulder. Zanli shrunk away towards Ashri and Aszli, but sobbed even harder. It was a side to Rani, Arthur would never have expected.

'Why?' he managed to ask, with a mouth that felt as if some mad dentist had gone berserk with novocaine, 'What has Zanli done?'

'She's a very stupid girl,' Rani replied, her voice tinged with bitterness, 'and a very selfish girl'.

'But, what has she done?' Arthur asked again, thoroughly puzzled by this sudden change in their relationship.

Rani ignored the question and pulled him even tighter into her arms.

'Oh, Arthur, Arthur,' she repeated, 'I can't believe you came back when I called.' She used the back of her wrist to wipe unsuccessfully at the tears running down her face.

'But, but...' he tried to protest that he had only fallen asleep, as Rani interrupted him.

'Quick, you two,' she directed at Ashri and Aszli, 'rub his arms. He's freezing cold.'

She raised one leg to the level of the bed and prodded Zanli with her foot. 'You, girl! Rub his feet and legs. That's all you're good for.'

With the four of them rubbing him at once, the warmth slowly returned to his body and the feeling of pins and needles dissipated. He was unaware that Aszli was no longer there, until she thrust a cup of hot tea towards him and told him to drink it. That seemed a very distant possibility to Arthur as Rani was still pressing his face into her bosom while stroking his head and the back of his neck. She relaxed her hold and let him sit up; the tea tasted more of aqui than tea, but was never-the-less extremely welcome. The birds had started their early morning chorus and the sky was turning a faint pink as Rani pulled a light coverlet over him, kissed him on the forehead and told him to get some sleep. He felt her weight as she sat back down on the opposite side of his bed, but by the time she had reached over to take one of his hands in hers, he had drifted into a peaceful sleep.

Chapter Eighteen

Arthur awoke from a troubled sleep. The earlier dream had returned to haunt him with its intense feelings of love, the wonder and brilliance of the colours and the musical sounds, but mostly of the freedom from all his earthly worries and responsibilities. He now found himself worrying about any possible meaning. He couldn't believe for a moment that it was anything other than a dream, and yet, at the time it had seemed so natural and so terribly real. Not being of a religious nature, he had never thought for any length of time, of life, or even any awareness, after death. He had always assumed that when the end came, it was indeed the end, and it was better to try and get everything in while one had the chance. If, he thought, by some preposterous chance it was real, or even some long-hidden memory from somewhere deep in his psyche, then death, as they say, could hold no fear for him.

The contempt Rani had shown to Zanli, however, was very disturbing and the more he thought about it, the more it puzzled him. Even if they thought he had actually died, why would Rani hold Zanli responsible? Their evening together had been wonderful; their lovemaking rapturous. She had not prepared the food they had eaten, so even if he had been accidentally poisoned, it could not have been her fault.

Last night he had deliberately refused the aqui and the exaggerated effects he had felt during lovemaking had been just the same as with Ashri. If they were a hallucination, then the aqui was not to blame. He could think of nothing else he had eaten that had been the same as the previous night. All of the food had been completely different.

Probably he had led himself down a blind alley; perhaps the aqui had no hallucinatory effects, the dream was just a dream, and the exaggerated intensity of the lovemaking was completely real. Possibly it could be explained by his long abstinence or some hormonal change due to his increasing years, but the effect seemed to have been as much larger-than-life for both Ashri and Zanli. There was obviously something here he could not understand without some explanation.

But the trouble between Rani and Zanli worried him far more. He realized that he loved them both and could not bear to think of them so at odds with each other. He must find the cause of the dispute and attempt to be a peacemaker.

He sat up in bed, swung his legs out and his feet had only just touched the floor when Ashri's smiling, but obviously concerned face appeared around the door.

'Are you okay?' she inquired, quietly, 'Can I get you anything?'

Arthur thought for a moment. He felt suddenly wonderful. The numbness had disappeared and despite his fretful sleep, he felt completely rested.

'You can give me a hug,' he replied.

Ashri literally threw herself into his outstretched arms, pulling him firmly against her and at the same time kissing him repeatedly on his forehead and both cheeks.

'You are alright, then?' She asked, pausing in her kissing long enough to look directly into his eyes, 'Please say you are alright.'

'I'm okay, honest,' he reassured her, 'I've never felt better. But I don't understand what's going on. Why did you disappear yesterday? And why is Rani so angry with Zanli? That seems so unlike Rani. And, I can't think of anything Zanli has done.'

He paused for a moment, but although Ashri appeared to be searching for an answer, she said nothing.

'If it had been yesterday,' he continued, 'you know, after our making love, I would have understood. I was expecting Rani to be angry yesterday morning, but she said it was intended all along that I was to make love to you and she made it quite clear that I was to sleep with Zanli last night. And, I think there is someone else lined up for me today.'

'Yetti, I mean Yeathili,' prompted Ashri.

'Yes, Yeathili,' he said, a note of frustration creeping into his voice. 'I wish someone would just explain things to me. I'm not complaining; I just want to know what is expected of me.'

'I think Rani will explain everything soon,' Ashri said softly, 'but first, can I ask you one thing?'

'Sure,' said Arthur, 'anything.'

'Did you refuse to drink the aqui last night?'

'I told Zanli that I didn't want any, yes.'

'But, she tried to get you to drink it?'

'Yes, she was even a little insistent. I was a little worried that I might have committed a faux pas by refusing her hospitality.' Arthur fretted that he might have caused his hostess some loss of face, or in his ignorance of their customs, overstepped some unstated rule.

'Why would you not drink it, then? Don't you like it?'

'It was a little strange to begin with, but it's very good. Yes, I quite like it.'

He remembered Rani saying she had become *a little possessive*, but her eyes were so sincere and concerned he felt desire again welling up within him. He looked at the colourful sari she was wearing; at the expanse of smooth golden skin that was revealed around her waist; skin that he had touched and kissed; skin that had pressed against his own and regretfully told himself that this was not the time.

'It's silly, really,' Arthur took one of her hands in his, trying to explain made him feel even more embarrassed, 'I thought what we had experienced might have been a hallucination. I didn't think it could be real, somehow. The only thing that I could think might have had hallucinatory effects was the aqui. It was the slightly unusual taste, I suppose.'

'And you didn't want the same thing to happen with Zanli?' Ashri appeared bemused.

'I wanted to remember only what was real. I didn't want to have a false memory.'

'And you think ours was, somehow... false?'

The hurt look in her eyes felt to Arthur as if he had stabbed her. He couldn't bear to think he had caused her pain and felt for her other hand.

'It was so many times better than anything I had ever known, I didn't think it possible to feel the way I felt. I remember every second of our being together, and now I'm convinced everything was real, it seems even better.'

'Okay,' Ashri said as if that explained everything; the hurt look faded as quickly as it had appeared. She pulled one of her hands free and raised it to lightly stroke his cheek. 'I think you could do with a shave. Would you like for me to give you a shave?'

Arthur's thoughts went back to his first evening and Rani's administrations. Would Ashri be as accomplished, he wondered. He knew there was only one way to find out.

'Yes, please.'

Chapter Nineteen

Rani pulled the little open jeep to a halt, only yards from the jetty. A couple of women unloading boats feigned diving for cover, even though it was obvious they were in no danger. Most of their progress through the small town had been of a similar nature, with some women calling out to her and some shouting mock abuse. It appeared to Arthur that everyone knew her and, in his estimation, were actually treating her with great affection. She must have stopped at least a dozen times to converse with someone, usually in an animated manner, which had also required introductions to him with much handholding and cheek kissing.

He'd had little chance to converse at any length with Rani. As he had been getting dressed, she had entered his room to announce that she would be spending the day with him. He didn't ask what had happened to the elusive Yetti (an unfortunate choice of name in his estimation; in his mind he had formed a little prayer that she wouldn't be covered in hair and have big feet), but hoped that if he was to spend the day with Rani, that he would finally spend the night as well.

Rani had hurried him to the little jeep Zanli had pointed out the previous day. It was parked in front of the house and already loaded with an interesting looking picnic basket, surrounded with folded rugs. She drove quickly out of the village, leaving a cloud of dust behind, and shortly turned off the road he and Zanli had cycled along the day before.

'This is a shorter route,' she said, 'but you may find it a little rougher'.

Arthur found it a lot rougher. All of the roads they had used before, though unpaved, were well maintained and quite smooth. They had gone only a few yards on this side road when the surface deteriorated to a series of potholes. It reminded him of one of the roads the coach had used on his earlier holiday, when taking them to a remote tiger reserve. Their guide had joked that in some places the roads had a few potholes and in some places, the potholes had an occasional bit of road. He decided to start looking for any sign of a road.

Rani drove as if she was in some kind of a race and appeared to enjoy the challenge of seeing how many of the potholes she could hit, although, Arthur had to admit, there was little chance of missing many. Neither had fastened seatbelts; there seemed little point when there appeared to be no other vehicles on the road and Arthur looked around for handholds to help keep him in his seat. Rani, of course, had the steering wheel to help her, but he was flung around uncomfortably until he found that he could brace himself with his feet, pushing his back firmly into the seat. He realized the wisdom of the manner in which the picnic basket had been packed amongst the rugs.

The road rose from the valley floor, twisting and turning through a dense forest of very tall trees. Large ferns, and shrubby plants covered with small blue flowers, lined the roadside. As they continued to climb, the air grew cooler. Arthur could see only occasional glimpses of the valley they had left, usually as they were skidding around a hairpin bend, but enough to show him that already they were high above it. In a less dense area where a few rays of sunshine penetrated the canopy above, Rani coasted to a stop and, holding a forefinger to her lips, turned off the engine. At first he could hear nothing above the tinkling of the engine and exhaust as hot metal cooled, but after a few seconds, he was aware of the surrounding birdsong. It was as if they were in the middle of an entire orchestra of birds and it gradually increased in intensity as the noise of their intrusion was forgotten.

'Isn't it wonderful?' Rani whispered to him.

'It is, indeed,' was Arthur's whispered reply, 'I could listen to this all day.'

'Well, not today, I'm afraid. Perhaps I can suggest to Yeathili that she brings you up this way tomorrow.

Ah, thought Arthur, the promise of Yeathili once again. Was it a promise or, he thought again of the image the name Yetti had inspired, a threat?

'That would be nice,' was all he could manage, weakly.

'We could have spent more time here, if someone wasn't such a sleepyhead,' Rani reached over and rustled his hair with one hand as she restarted the engine with the other, 'and had to lie in half the day.'

Her affectionate, almost motherly, touch, it seemed a little possessive as well, prompted a stir within him. Please God, he prayed to himself silently, please, let me spend the night with this woman.

As they proceeded up the rough and winding road, Arthur found himself concentrating on Rani, rather than on the adjacent countryside, as he had been earlier. She was dressed in a similar manner as she had been on their first days in India, in a long, loose skirt and matching blouse. Before climbing into the jeep, she had reached between her legs and pulled the front and back together into a loose knot, instead of tucking the hem into her waistband, as she had for their climb up the mountain.

The arrangement effectively kept her skirt from falling on the dusty floor of the jeep, but had amused him. The many old men he had seen on his earlier visit to India, standing at the roadside, working in the fields, or wobbling about on their rickety old bicycles, did the same with the skirt-like things they wore. The invariably skinny legs of the old men, though, were no match at all for the long and beautifully shaped legs now exposed.

He remembered the sensuous feel of those legs around him as she had shaved him the first night. It had been too much to hope that Ashri would adopt a similar stance when she had given him a shave; she had cradled his head in her lap, admittedly, but had covered her pressed-together knees with a towel. The shave had been just as professional as Rani's though, he must remember to ask them where they had learned such a skill.

The trees around them suddenly thinned out and the road levelled off. They emerged from the forest into bright sunshine and a clear blue sky overhead, broken only by the occasional puffy white cloud. Ahead of them lay a range of gently rounded, green-clad hills that appeared to be covered entirely in grass except for the occasional small grove of trees. Arthur felt he could almost be in the Lake District. Except for the clear blue sky, he thought, his entire experience with the Lake District had been with grey skies and drizzling rain. The road was less rough now, though not enough to engage in any prolonged conversation, and they made better time. Soon, they were descending again, not through forest, but terraced fields covered with pale green vegetation. They passed the occasional thatched roof cottage of brown stone, usually with a thin column of smoke nearby. As they continued to descend, the terraced fields gave way to smaller fields with rows of shiny leaved bushes covered in red berries. These were in turn replaced by larger fields of tall palm trees, again planted in neat rows, but almost as quickly as these had appeared they were back in open country again, looking down on a small town.

The road was smoother as they entered the town, but they still found it impossible to converse as Rani was kept busy, both avoiding the women walking along the roadside and maintaining a running stream of good-natured banter with them as they passed by. It seemed that everyone knew Rani and she knew everyone. Arthur watched her and the animated expression on her face. It was obvious how much she was enjoying herself and hoped some of the enjoyment was the result of being with him. After the previous two days, he was no longer surprised by the attention directed at him, but was still flattered by the number of hands that reached into the slowly moving jeep to pat his shoulder or grasp his knee. On more than one occasion when Rani brought the jeep to a momentary halt, lips brushed his cheek.

They were passing a row of surprisingly neat little shops, threading their way through the crowds of women who seemed to be busily going from one to the next, when it occurred to Arthur they were lucky not to be also harassed by the ubiquitous small motorcycles he had seen on his earlier holiday. He remembered the coach journey; at each small town they encountered they would be surrounded by hordes of buzzing mopeds and small bikes, usually with at least two men on each one.

Their guide had explained it was the custom for anyone riding solo to pick up the first pedestrian he met going the same way. The coach would laboriously overtake throngs of them, often missing them by only centimetres when the way cleared, only to be again overtaken by even more of them as they slowed for the next tuk tuk, wandering cow or other obstacle. It was obvious this town was much larger than any of the villages he had seen in the last two days, but he had only seen one or two mopeds and a few tuk tuks and he was sure they were all driven or ridden by women.

He glanced over at Rani. She still had her skirt loosely tied between her legs and at the sight, it suddenly struck him what else was missing. The old men. They had been everywhere on his holiday; standing by the roadside, idly watching their coach go by, lounging in front of the chai shacks, or without warning, obliviously turning their bicycles directly into the path of the coach. He had been nearly flung from his seat countless times, as their driver had had to brake sharply to avoid another, intent on self-destruction. This was his third day and he could not remember having seen a single old man in the villages, by the roadside or working in the fields. In fact, now that he thought of it, no men at all.

He remembered, on his first day with Ashri, thinking the men might be working away somewhere, but he couldn't even remember seeing any little boys. There was a girl's school in Rani's village. Zanli and he had had to wait for the noisily chattering clutch in their brightly coloured uniforms to clear the road before they could continue their journey. He had just assumed there was a counterpart somewhere of equally exuberant little boys. Perhaps he was wrong. He glanced once again at the women they were passing. Many were accompanied by young girls, it must be Saturday he reasoned, of varying ages from toddlers to teenagers, but he couldn't spot a single small boy.

And there didn't seem to be any of the picturesque chai shacks for the men to loiter about. Their guide had suggested to the passengers that trying one would be quite an experience, as their coach had stopped at one on their first day. The front had been a chaotic display of bottled water, soft drinks, coconuts, sweets and assorted spices and nuts. A young man attended a small wood fire, burning on a stone platform at waist level, only about a metre or less below the smoke blackened, thatched roof. Several of the other tourists had made laughing comments about health and safety, or fire marshals, as they queued to be served.

Arthur had watched as the young man heated milk to near boiling in a pan over the fire, then poured it through a sieve filled with loose tea, into another pan. He had made an elaborate show of pouring from one pan, held high above his head and almost touching the blackened roof, to the other, to aerate and cool the mixture, before pouring it into tiny metal cups. Ester had refused to even taste the tea, pointing out the rudimentary washing facilities for the used cups, but Arthur had found the hot sweet tea surprisingly refreshing and had gratefully drunk her cup as well.

Many old men had clustered around watching them, enthusing over having photographs taken, and inquisitively looking at the small displays on the tourists' digital cameras. It was as if they were flattered that these Westerners would want to take photos of them. Their sombre faces would light up with wide grins, and the little sideways nodding of their heads. The movement had caused one severely spoken English woman to compare them with nodding dogs for car parcel shelves. Arthur had been careful to avoid the woman for the rest of their holiday, not wanting to be associated with such narrow views.

For the rest of the journey through the town, Arthur watched carefully for any sign of men, but saw only women. Women shopping. Women conversing in the streets. Women sitting in western-styled coffee bars or outdoor cafes, along bustling yet peaceful, shady avenues. There was even a row of the little grey jeeps, like the one the green woman had driven, with yet another green woman loading parcels into one, but not one man. This was indeed a puzzle.

Equally puzzling was the order of everything. Neat little shops with carefully written signs overhead stood next to other shops that appeared just as painstakingly designed. With hoardings in a different language, the shops could have fitted into any European high street. The colourful chaos he had seen everywhere on his earlier holiday was, now that he had taken notice, completely absent. This was equally beautiful, but was a pastiche of India, as if a colony of Swiss or Austrians had decided to settle in the region, then left it to be populated by local women. It was like a film with the actors correctly dressed in the appropriate costumes, but the set produced by someone who had never been to the area or even bothered to research what it should look like. He must see if Rani could explain the conundrum for him, if only he could ever get her to himself.

Chapter Twenty

After a few more minutes of joking and raucous laughter with Rani, the two women that had been unloading the boats had helped both of them out of the jeep. Despite Arthur's reassurance that he could manage a picnic basket and a couple of rugs, they had insisted on carrying those items to the little boat moored at the far end of the jetty. They had made a great show of stowing the basket out of the sun, in front of the stubby mast, and under the furled sail that ran the full length of the hull. The two rugs were draped over the polished wooden seats near the stern and as one held the boat steady, the other extended a hand, first to Rani then to Arthur, to help them into the boat. Arthur was aware of being helped a little more than was necessary as the woman put her other arm around his waist and, letting his body brush against hers, held him momentarily, before reluctantly lowering him onto the deck.

There had been a few more minutes of behaviour that Arthur thought would have been entirely appropriate for teenage boys, while he noted their appearance. Both had scarves casually wound around their heads into impromptu turbans, apparently to protect them from the sun, but wore only the tight-fitting tee shirts and loose denim shorts that he had seen on many of the workers in the fields. Their exposed faces, waists, muscular arms and legs were all unprotected and the effects of the sun had darkened them to a rich chocolate. He couldn't begin to guess their ages, but after very careful consideration, had managed to narrow it down to somewhere between twenty and fifty. Although they were doing the work one would normally think of as more suitable for a man, their movements were entirely feminine, and he found them sensuously attractive.

Finally, Rani went through the motions of introducing Arthur to them. Even though he could not understand their language, it seemed suddenly obvious that was what they had been pestering her for all along. As Rani repeated their names and first one, then the other pulled him into a firm embrace, their bodies held tightly against his while they held their cheeks equally tightly pressed against his on, for a moment or two. Not for them the double hand hold, the deep gaze and the kisses on both cheeks; this was completely unsubtle and utterly passionate. Arthur had half expected them to be unpleasant perhaps, in view of the strenuous type of work they were doing; for them to smell of stale sweat, but they both exuded an aroma of coconut, cinnamon and other spices which with the warmth of their bodies, was overpoweringly sensual. It was only after they had climbed out of the boat and untied the ropes holding it to the jetty, that Arthur noticed the deep look of longing in their eyes.

Arthur found a seat on the rug next to Rani, but continued to watch the two women, returning their smiles and exuberant waves, as she started the engine and reversed the boat away from the jetty and into the lake. There was only the slightest breeze creating small ripples on the surface of the crystal-clear water and the boat, once Rani's practiced hand on the tiller had turned it so that it faced away from the town, left little wake. Despite the feeble putt-putting sound of its engine the boat moved surprisingly quickly. The two figures on the jetty were almost reduced to invisibility by the distance, before their waving stopped.

Arthur had noticed many of the canoe-like boats he had seen on his first day with Ashri, drawn up onto the beach near the jetty. Fishing nets were spread around and over them to dry and as they had begun their journey into the lake, he had seen one or two more, headed in the direction they had come from, but as the town faded from view, Rani's boat seemed to be the only one on the entire lake. At first, the opposite shore had been hidden by the moisture rising from the midday sun, only a very faint, pale blue trace of the mountains beyond revealing that there even was an opposite shore. Before long, both shores merged into the almost white sky. Although the air seemed clear and they were able to see a great distance, the horizon in all directions disappeared and they could have been floating on the surface of an unknown and otherwise unoccupied planet. Rani cut the engine and as the boat slowed to a stop, even the sound of the water splashing against the bow diminished. There was complete silence. The ripples they had seen on the surface near the jetty had ceased and the water was like a mirror, reflecting only the white sky.

Arthur looked at Rani, to find she was smiling at him expectantly.

'It's like another world,' he whispered softly, not wanting to disturb the quiet.

'And we're the only ones in it,' Rani whispered back, her smile widening, 'we can have complete privacy here. Do you see why I didn't want you to experience this with anyone else? Why I was a little selfish?'

Arthur reached to touch her arm. 'I'm so glad you were. As much as I've loved being with Ashri and Zanli, it's you I want to share things with. And this is really special.' he put his arm around her, drawing her closer to him. 'Thank you.'

They sat like that for several minutes, their heads touching, until Rani abruptly stood up, narrowly avoiding the furled sail and boom above her.

'It's time for a swim,' she said, starting to unfasten her top. 'You do swim, don't you?'

Arthur watched fascinated as she untied the little bow at the front, then pulled at the two tapered overlapping halves. The blouse parted, revealing her breasts, as she pulled her arms out of the short, tight-fitting sleeves.

'I'm sorry,' he apologised, suddenly realizing he was openly gazing at her, 'I didn't mean to stare.'

Rani pushed her shoulders back, lifting her breasts even more prominently, her arms out to her sides and her palms turned up.

'Why? They are meant to attract you,' she said matter-of-factly. 'I would be offended if you pretended to ignore them, or turned away in mock modesty.'

She slowly untied another bow at her waist and her skirt fell away, disclosing a similar lack of under-things. Arthur felt his breath catch in his throat as she turned, stepped onto the gunwale and, with the smallest of splashes, dived gracefully into the water.

Her exit left the boat rocking gently and Arthur had to balance carefully as he removed his own clothes and plunged into the water after her. The water, in contrast to the heat of the day, was at first cooler than he had expected. After a few strokes he looked up to see Rani, some distance away, doing a competitive looking crawl, face down, breathing on the fourth stroke and going at twice his pace. Arthur knew that he was a fairly strong swimmer, usually adopting a side or breaststroke, but he had never been fast. It was several minutes before he caught up to where Rani was treading water while she waited for him.

'Showoff!' he accused, between breaths. 'I suppose you think you're pretty good, don't you?' Rani just laughed.

'Isn't this wonderful?' she asked after a short pause. 'There ought to be a law against swimming in a costume, don't you think?'

Arthur was suddenly aware of the freedom he felt in the water around him; his body had become accustomed to the temperature and was now comfortable. He was also aware of the nearness of Rani and the thought that she was feeling the same unrestrained lack of restrictions.

'Yeah,' he sighed, 'it's pretty good. I don't think I'll ever wear a pair of swimming trunks again; it might cause a sensation at my local pool when I go home, though'.

'Perhaps you shouldn't go home, then,' Rani laughed, 'or, perhaps we should head back to the boat.'

Arthur looked over his shoulder. The boat seemed a long way away. 'I'm not going to race you back, I'm going to take my time and enjoy this.' He rolled onto his back and started a slow backstroke, little more than a sculling movement that was completely silent. Rani watched him for a moment, then moved alongside him, matching his pace.

When they reached the boat, Rani put one hand on the transom, braced a foot against the rudder and launched herself into the boat, almost as gracefully as she had left it. Arthur managed to restrain himself from comparing her verbally to Aphrodite, but when he tried the same manoeuvre, the rudder swung to one side and he fell back into the water with a resounding splash.

'Here,' Rani said, 'let me give you a hand'. She extended one hand to his while she braced one knee against the tiller to hold it in place. Between them, he was soon pulled into the boat.

'I'm not sure that we packed any towels,' Rani said, stretching out on one of the rugs that covered the seats. 'Anyway, I just want to lie here in the sun to dry off.'

Arthur looked at her reclining figure. Her arms were behind her head, supporting it in her interlocked palms. One leg was fully extended, the other bent at the knee, resting against the gunwale. His eyes traced a path from her slightly flattened breasts, down the unblemished, golden tan skin, to the mound at the base of her belly. As he felt the desire rising within him, he tried to think of other things, but was unable to take his eyes off her. He stood there, trying to decide what to do next; to take a seat at the stern behind her, or to lie down on the opposite side. He would have sat on the deck next to her, had there been room, but there was barely enough width to walk between her and the engine cover.

As if aware of his dilemma, Rani opened her eyes and looked up at him. She moved forward to take up less room, then patted the seat behind her and said, 'Sit here with me.'

Arthur struggled past her, banging his knee on the tiller, and slid into the indicated seat. As soon as he was seated, Rani lifted herself into a half-sitting position and leaned back against his chest.

'You must think I'm an awful tease,' Rani said, wriggling against him and turning her head to kiss his chest 'but we can't actually make love today; it isn't right for me and you are supposed to be resting. We can't have another episode like last night.'

The disappointment welled up within Arthur. He was unable to answer, only pulling her more firmly against him.

'When we make love,' Rani continued in a whisper, 'and I promise it will be soon, I want to be the best you've ever had. I want to be perfect for you. But for now, could you just hold me?'

Her arms were folded against her chest; Arthur put both his arms over hers and pulled her even tighter into his own chest. He lightly kissed the side of her neck, just behind her ears, over and over. Her still damp hair, smelling of the fresh lake water, rubbed against his face as she turned her head to give him better access.

'I could hold you forever,' he said huskily, 'if you let me'.

Chapter Twenty-One

'Tell me about Ester'

Arthur nearly choked on the small savoury pastry he was eating. They had awakened after a short nap; his back was numb where he had been resting against the gunwale and his neck ached where his head had tipped forward against Rani's. Their bodies seemed totally dry until Rani had attempted to stand up. The moisture trapped between them had had the effect of a suction cup and the two of them made an audible slurping sound as they parted.

'Arthur!' Rani had laughed.

'It wasn't me!' he had protested. 'At least, not like that.'

They had both laughed as they rubbed the remaining dampness from each other's bodies and had then quickly donned their clothing. The sun was lower in the sky and the air, though still comfortably warm, had cooled slightly. With the cooler air, the visibility had improved and the mountains surrounding them seemed close enough to touch. Only the distance to the barely visible shorelines gave an indication of how far away they were from the little town.

Rani had retrieved their picnic bag from its hiding place and rapidly laid out its contents on the engine cover, handing a bottle of wine, corkscrew and glasses to Arthur, saying, 'I don't know about you, but I'm famished.'

'Yes, me too,' Arthur had replied, struggling with the cork. 'It seems like a very long time since breakfast.'

'A little longer for some than others,' she'd said, giving him a motherly pat on the head.

'I don't know what you mean. And after all, we have had a bit of exercise,' He'd handed her a glass of the dark red wine.

'What? Two hundred meters of *very* leisurely swimming?'

Arthur had ignored the playful gibe, turning his attention to the food instead. The assortment of dishes looked fairly similar to those he had enjoyed with Ashri and he eagerly accepted the dish of small cakes, nuts and olives she offered.

'What do you want to know about her?' he said when he had emptied his mouth. He felt a twinge of guilt; he had barely thought of Ester in, how many days? This was his third day here, but it had taken another two, or was it three, days of travelling to get to this valley. He couldn't remember with the time difference. And Ester had been so helpful in driving him to Heathrow, in asking if he had everything he needed for his trip, in writing lists of what he should take. From the time he had apprehensively told her of his planned trip, she had been surprisingly enthusiastic, rushing out to buy him new clothes for his journey, assuring him repeatedly, that she would be okay, and that she could manage in his absence.

'Well, anything, everything, what she's like, how you met, how you feel about her.'

Arthur had so many questions he wanted to ask Rani, questions about the reason for her anger with Zanli, why there were no men in the valley and why-the-hell the women who drove the jeeps, painted themselves green. He was slightly annoyed at the distraction, but the sincere look in her eyes told him she was not just making conversation. He took a sip of his wine.

'Uhh... she's very beautiful, she's a lot younger than me, nearly eighteen years, and she has a... a great sense of humour.' Arthur thought of her frequent and inexplicable flashes of completely unreasonable anger in the last few years. Perhaps it was better not to tell Rani everything.

'How did you meet?'

'I worked for her father.'

Arthur had a vision of the first time he had seen her as an adult. He remembered the way she had held her head, the sway of her hips, the way her breasts had strained against the confinement of her starched white shirt and her confident walk as she went through his drawing office into Max's domain. He remembered the way she had looked directly at him when she emerged with her father a few

154

minutes later. Max had simply said, 'My daughter, Ester,' to everyone in general.

He had not been able to concentrate on his work for devising complicated ways to meet her. He had seen her when she was younger, of course. Max had several pictures of both his children in his office and Arthur had regularly asked after them, often to be told in detail of their latest exploits. He had been to Max's house at various times in the years he had worked for him. There had been Christmas parties for the entire staff and he had been invited to join Max and his wife on a number of social occasions. He had remembered Ester as a gangling, self-conscious and not very pretty teenager. She had always been quiet, apparently in awe of her older brother who was very self-assured, a little cocky and always hogging the limelight.

He needn't have wasted any time thinking of far-fetched schemes; Max had stopped at Arthur's desk on his return and looked over the blueprints on his drawing board before saying in an off-hand manner, 'Artie, we're having a few friends over this evening, nothing special, completely casual, but if you'd like to take pot-luck with us? Oh, and bring your young lady if she's free. What's her name? Amy?'

Arthur had explained that he and Amy had parted a few weeks earlier. That evening he had been seated next to Ester; they had spent the evening almost completely ignoring the others around them, talking animatedly about her travels and two months later they were engaged.

'It couldn't have been that simple,' Rani said 'Come on, tell me the whole story. I want to hear every detail.' She prodded Arthur's chest forcefully, almost making him choke on the mouthful of food he was chewing.

Between bites of the welcome pastries, Arthur related the story to Rani, leaving out as much of the detail as he dared. He had his own questions to ask, but before he had a chance, Rani was probing for more.

'What was her father like? Did you get on with him?'

'I guess he was like the father I wished I'd had. He was a strong character, uh… you know, strong-willed, knew what he wanted out of life, but could take the time to make you feel appreciated. Charismatic is probably an overused term, but it would certainly apply to him. He had made his name out of trying to create workable social housing. He'd seen some of the failures of "the projects" in America, slum clearance, that is, and had worked out a lot of the reasons they failed. The government accepted his proposals, but when the time came for implementation, they tried to do the job as cheaply as possible and cut back on the very items that would stop the same thing happening here, I mean in England.'

'I understand.'

'He had already begun to see that the pretty curving paths developers always wanted and the little groves of decorative trees or shrubs, would always be ignored and the shortest routes would be used, even if it meant trashing the lawns and beating down the pretty little groves of trees. He had seen that it was important to use good quality materials, to keep buildings regularly maintained, and to keep entrances secure; to provide centres where tenants could meet and develop a sense of community. Sure, all of these things cost extra, but if it gave quality living for lots of people, it would have been worth it in the long run. In many places in America, high-rise apartments were very desirable places to live. Instead, our government provided cheapjack housing that no one wanted and because the developments were never maintained properly, they were an enormous waste of money. I'm sorry, I must be boring you. It was Max's pet subject and he made a believer out of me.'

'It sounds like you had a lot of respect for him.'

'I did. He... did have, perhaps I'm being petty, one thing that used to annoy most of us.'

'Go on.'

'I said he could make us feel appreciated, and he did when we were in the office. There wasn't a draughtsman, or an engineer, or a secretary that he didn't take the time to find out about their family and any problems they might have and he had generous ways of showing his appreciation when we won a contract, or completed a project.'

'Yes, I see...I think.'

'But he always took personal credit for everything! He hadn't sat at a drawing board in all the time I knew him. Sure, it was his business, he managed it skilfully, he chose talented people to work for him, but we went out and got the business, usually by choosing the latest techniques and coming up with design innovations, most of which were our own. When it came time to deliver a proposal to a board of directors or to stand in front of television cameras, it was always "I", everything. "I decided to solve your problem by, such and such..." "I created a new approach to people traffic management here..." "I've given you a ..." as if he did everything single-handed. You see how that could cause a problem after a while?'

'Sure, but you said he made you feel appreciated in other ways. Maybe it was just his way of trying to give a personal touch to potential customers. To make them feel as if *he* really was concerned about the building they wanted.'

'I know, I know, I told myself that many times.'

Rani shared the last of the bottle between their glasses and pushed more of the dip onto Arthur's plate.

'Did you ever speak to him about it? Or, to Ester?'

'No! Max had enough good qualities that he could be allowed the occasional fault here and there. If it was a fault. I mean, you've just justified his behaviour. And we were probably being petty, as I've said.'

'You said had; had good qualities.'

'He died less than a year after Ester and I were married. I couldn't have asked for a better father-in-law and I guess I still miss him.'

'How did he die? He couldn't have been all that old. I presume it wasn't old age.'

'It was a plane crash. He was coming back from looking at a prospective project in Germany. The developers offered him a lift in their private jet, but none of them made it home.'

'So, now I know a lot about your father-in-law, but you still haven't told me much about Ester.'

Chapter Twenty-Two

'Look, I'll tell you more about Ester,' Arthur paused, the late afternoon sky had turned to a reddish colour, even though the sun was still well above the horizon; he wondered where the time had gone, 'but will you answer something for me first?'

'If I can.'

'Where are all the men? I don't think I've seen another man since I've been here.'

'You never did get around to reading that article I gave you, did you? And I suppose you really haven't had time since your bag arrived.'

'Are you trying to change the subject?' he laughed, 'Why is it so important that I read about tropical fish?'

'No, I promise I'll answer your question,' Rani sat her glass down and took one of his hands in hers. 'I'll explain as much as I can, but it may take some time and it's getting late. Can we head back, first?'

Between them they quickly gathered the remains from their meal into the picnic bag and stowed it beneath the sail, where it had been before. Rani resumed her place at the tiller, patted the seat beside her and as Arthur sat down, turned the key to fire the little engine into life.

'I did glance at that article,' Arthur had to raise his voice a little. His head was very near Rani's, 'but I'm just not that interested in tropical fish. A few years ago, it seemed all my friends were keeping fish. I thought they were great in a dentist's waiting room, you know, very relaxing and all, but not for me. A neighbour kept Molly fish. I didn't think they were very exciting. There were more colourful fish about.'

'The article was about Amazon Mollies.' Rani turned her head to smile at him. Arthur wondered if there was just the slightest hint of condescension to it.

'His were from Texas and Mexico,' Arthur said, a little puzzled, 'I didn't think these would be that different.'

'Believe me, they are very different,' Rani gave a little laugh, 'they're not named after the river, but because there are no male Amazon Mollies.'

'But...' Arthur stopped as the significance of what she had said set in, 'but how do they reproduce?'

'They borrow a male from another species,' Rani's pupils were beginning to dilate. She was smiling at him in a positively intriguing manner, 'they don't actually use any of his genetic material; he only acts as a... a catalyst, I guess. Essentially, the females just clone themselves, but they need a male to... to set them off.'

'And this is important,' Arthur struggled to make a connection, 'in what way?'

Rani made a corrective movement to the tiller. A small breeze was picking up and the waves made soft slapping noises as they splashed against the bow.

'We could have raised the sail and saved some fuel,' she observed, 'but we're more than halfway back. I don't suppose it's worth the effort, now.'

She turned back to Arthur who was still pondering her last remark. He noticed again her odd smile; perhaps she was only teasing him. After all, there was a great resemblance between Rani and Ashri.

'Don't you think it's a little ironic that those who first noted the fishes' behaviour named them after a supposedly mythical race, when in fact, they were mimicking, almost exactly, the actions of that actual race?'

'This is another little joke, isn't it?' Arthur laughed nervously after a pause. 'You've all been setting me up, ever since I got here.' He sat for a few moments looking questioningly at Rani. Her curious expression hadn't changed and she said nothing. There was only the sound from the engine and the splashing of waves against the bow.

'You're not telling me you are Amazons,' he groped for any memories of his Greek history. 'I think you're in the wrong place. Didn't they live to the north of Greece, Turkey or Anatolia, or some such place?'

The expression still hadn't changed on Rani's face. It wasn't smugness, he told himself, and he didn't think it was satisfaction at having successfully perpetrated another joke at his expense. He suddenly remembered something he had read, somewhere. 'Didn't Amazons cut off their right breast? 'He reached across and gently caressed the article mentioned. 'Nope, this appears to be all there.'

'Trust you,' Rani said, shaking her head and laughing 'and we wore rather sexy looking armour, too. So I couldn't possibly be an Amazon; I'm not wearing armour.'

'It's just so unbelievable,' Arthur still struggled whether to accept what Rani was telling him, or to search for some evidence of another joke. 'Does that mean you've killed all the men? Isn't that what Herodotus called the Amazons? Killers of men?'

'*Androktones*, yes, killers of men,' Rani said, 'but that was a long time ago. Herodotus wrote, two thousand years ago? Two and a half thousand? We have been misunderstood all that time by anyone who came in contact with us. Yes, we lived further west at one time, so it could have been in what is now Romania or the Ukraine, but we were nomadic and were feared wherever we went, until we found this valley. We have been isolated here for most of the time since. And we are still feared by the people in the surrounding villages, the few who know about us, that is. Fortunately, these hill people are very backward and not believed by the more, shall we say, enlightened?'

'It just doesn't seem possible,' Arthur was slowly beginning to believe Rani, 'how could you have kept this a secret?'

'It is true, we were once killers of men,' she said softly, ignoring his question, 'not intentionally, at least not in most cases, and we were never the "warrior maidens" we were portrayed to be. We have always tried to be peaceful.'

'You were just the victims of adverse publicity?'

'I think the ancient Greeks gave the label of Amazon to any tribe of people, whose women fought alongside their men. Even Artemisia was called an Amazon by some historians.'

'Artemisia?'

'Of Halicarnassus,' she smiled at his bemusement, 'one of Xerxes' generals, at the battle of Salamis. It was she who advised him not to engage the Greeks at sea, but still, fought so valiantly when he ignored her advice.'

'Xerxes was…Persian? Son of Darius? Sorry, but my knowledge of ancient history isn't all that good.'

'Yes, you've heard of Thermopylae, Marathon and all that? Anyway, that was all roughly of the same time, but she was clearly not one of us. According to our history, we never fought against others.'

'So.' Arthur paused to think; he would have to phrase his next question carefully. 'If you didn't go into battle, how did you get the reputation of being killers'

'It is a long story,' Rani said, turning off the engine and holding up one hand. 'Later.'

The boat came to a controlled stop as she brought it effortlessly alongside the jetty. Before Arthur could even stand up, she had jumped out with one of the mooring ropes and secured the bow. She pointed to the rope at the stern, indicated he was to throw it to her and had made that fast by the time he had folded the rugs and retrieved the picnic basket.

The flat stones of the jetty seemed to be moving under Arthur's feet as he climbed out of the boat and joined Rani. She grabbed his buttocks playfully as they started making their way to her jeep. 'Mister wobbly legs, are you?' she teased.

'I think I've sat on those hard seats too long.'

'And you did get a lot of exercise with all that swimming.' Her mood seemed suddenly buoyant. She almost danced along next to Arthur.

Within minutes they had reached the jeep; the women helping them onto the boat must have parked it out of the way, Arthur reasoned as he loaded the items he was carrying. In front of them, the buildings of the town were bathed in a pale rosy light. He turned and looked behind. A thin crescent of the sun, still just visible above the distant mountains, turned the sky to red and was reflected back by the water of the lake. All the shops looked closed, but upper storey windows were lit from within, creating contrasting orangey coloured squares. Otherwise, there was little evidence of life.

'There doesn't seem to be many people about,' he said, as they climbed into the jeep. 'Does everyone have early nights here?'

'They will all be having their evening meal,' Rani said, putting the jeep into gear and letting the clutch out with a lurch, 'and getting ready for the gathering. Almost everyone goes to the Saturday gatherings.'

'This is the big night out, is it?'

'Oh yes, all the serious stuff, the politics, the problems are all left behind. This is the night we sing and dance and forget about any disagreements. There will be a lot of aqui drunk tonight. And, there will be a lot of thick heads tomorrow.'

With no one on the road, Rani sped along at an alarming pace. The wind blowing around them felt refreshing to Arthur, but he held on tightly to the grab handle set into the dash. He had had enough experience of Rani's driving from the morning to give him warning.

'I'm going to take the river road back,' Rani shouted above the noise of the tyres and engine, 'it's a little bit further, but the road is much smoother. '

Although the road was, admittedly smoother, Arthur thought, the bumps were just as severe because of the speed at which they were hitting them. He noticed that the light was fading quickly, dusk never seemed to last long in the tropics, and the headlights penetration was feeble compared to their pace. He wondered if Rani was just addicted to adrenalin or if she had an actual death wish.

He would have liked to continue the conversation they'd had on the boat, but the effort of shouting over the noise of the engine and tyres made it impossible. Several times they slowed slightly at the outskirts of the villages they passed though, but all too quickly they were left behind as she resumed her frantic speed. Soon they passed through a village that Arthur recognized as the one he and Zanli had had lunch in and only minutes later they were pulling into the drive at the back of Rani's house.

Chapter Twenty-Three

'Are you hungry?' Rani asked, as they entered the kitchen, 'I could put some things on a tray and bring them up.'

Arthur thought for a moment, it didn't seem that long ago that they'd eaten, but the suggestion seemed, somehow, very attractive.

'You're sure you don't want to go to your gathering? Isn't it the big night of the week?'

'I shall not be attending the gathering tonight. We can sit and talk all night if you want to.'

'I guess it's all the fresh air,' he laughed as he added, 'and all that exercise. Yes, I could probably eat a little something. Especially, if there is a bit more of that wine to go with it.'

'If you let me have first shower, I'll organize something while you're getting cleaned up. We can eat sitting on your bed and be very, very decadent.'

'If we showered together,' there was a note of hopefulness in his voice; he put his hands around her waist, 'we could save a lot of water.'

'No, no, no. It sounds an attractive proposition,' her eyes flashed, as she pushed him away, 'but we must let you rest, so you mustn't excite yourself'.

Rani ceased her pushing and as quickly hugged him to her. Her eyes were sincere as she looked up at him. 'Are you forgetting you died only last night?'

***

Arthur had been standing under the soft, warm, relaxing water of the shower for a long time, thinking of the afternoon's conversation with Rani. Her explanation, if indeed it was an explanation and not another joke, had only raised more questions in his mind. By the time he had dried and donned the soft, towelling robe that had been left for him, he could see Rani, dressed in a matching white robe, entering his room with a tray of assorted small dishes and glasses. He followed her as she sat the tray in the middle of his bed and piled pillows against the headboard. Together they carefully sat on his bed and reclined against the improvised backrest. Without speaking, they each reached for a glass of wine; their eyes met and they burst into laughter, then raised the glasses and clinked them lightly together, before taking a sip.

'Arthur, did you not notice anything different about Ashri or Zanli, in the time you were with them? I mean, when you were making love to them?'

'Well, they both had their right breasts,' he laughed nervously, savouring the memory of his time with them, at the same time, suddenly painfully aware that he was speaking to Ashri's grandmother. 'But no, nothing physically different.'

'I didn't mean appearance. I meant the lovemaking itself. Anything about the... the intensity?'

She was so sincere, he knew this was not a joking matter, but Arthur had never before discussed one woman's lovemaking with another, especially when one was the grandmother of the other.

'Well,' he murmured apprehensively, 'it was... very... intense.'

'Yes?' She was watching him with a questioning look, willing him to give her the answer she wanted. It reminded him of a school teacher, patiently trying to extract the correct answer from an unsure student.

'It was... fantastic,' he almost blurted the words out, in relief at the approving look on her face, 'it was unlike anything I've ever experienced. They were just... indescribable!'

'Didn't I promise you the best sex you'd ever had?' a broad smile appeared on Rani's face; the warmth of it went straight to Arthur's heart, 'but is that all? Nothing else?'

'Like...?'

'Did you not feel any pain?'

'Oh,' the memory made Arthur catch his breath. 'Yes. That was pretty... uh... intense, as well. I really thought Ashri was trying to kill me. I tried desperately to push her away, but when I gave into it, it turned into the most indescribable pleasure. I was half-expecting it with Zanli and thought if I just relaxed, it would be okay, but it was even worse with her, at least, to begin with.'

'If you had been Ashri's age,' Rani sat her glass down and put her hand on Arthur's arm, 'it would have killed you, Arthur'.

'Why? I don't understand. I would have thought a younger man would have been stronger.'

'It is something to do, so I have been told, with testosterone levels. We apparently secrete; you will forgive me if I get this wrong and I may not be using the correct medical terms. I can ask Neanthi if you want an exact explanation; we secrete an enzyme that reacts unfavourably with testosterone. If the testosterone level is too high, as it would be for most young men, it almost always results in death.'

'And with an older man?'

'Their testosterone level is usually just enough lower that they can survive the experience in most cases, and if they, or their partner, don't get too greedy.'

'Greedy?'

'You know, to try and have too many orgasms. Or, too close together.'

'Is that what you thought Zanli had done? Been greedy?'

'I didn't know at the time you had refused the aqui. I should have known Zanli better. I should have trusted her. I feel terrible and I will try to make it up to her. I hope she can forgive me.' Rani brushed at a tear in either eye, 'It's just that, all of a sudden, you mean so very much to me. I couldn't bear to think of being without you. Can you forgive me for being selfish?'

'I don't think you have anything to be forgiven for.' Arthur leaned over protectively, to kiss her on the cheek; remembering only at the last moment to avoid her lips. Her robe had gaped partially open, inviting his gaze. She followed his eyes, then pulled her robe together.

'Not tonight,' Rani scolded, 'I keep telling you. You need your rest.'

Arthur sat his empty wine glass on the tray in front of them and picked up one of the smaller glasses filled with the golden liquid. There was still a faint warmth to the glass.

'And the aqui?' he asked, 'what does it do? I had suspected it might be hallucinogenic, but Ashri told me that wasn't the case.'

'You were not all that far off, I suppose. It's great for pain relief, amongst other things. If you drank enough of this,' Rani raised the glass to her lips, 'you could probably walk through fire'.

'What's it made of? It is really very pleasant, but it has an unusual taste.'

Rani burst into such laughter that Arthur momentarily feared he would have to do something to calm her hysterics. He had never seen her so volatile and was perplexed by the sudden outburst.

'Oh Arthur,' she said, trying desperately to recover her composure, 'you are priceless! I am telling you the greatest secret known to mankind, something only a very few outside this valley know and all all want to know is, how the aqui is made.'

'I'm sorry, I do understand the significance of what you're telling me, but it's just too fantastic. I guess it's more than my mind can take in. I've just had the most unbelievable two nights and now I'm here with you. You've already told me I'm supposed to spend tomorrow with another young woman, which I assume will end with our making love. Rani, that's more sex than I've had in the last five years. I'd begun to believe I'd had my life's quota, but I'm not so old that I don't still have a healthy libido. I wouldn't have cared if you'd told me you were aliens from Mars, I'm just so grateful that I'm here with you; I can hardly think of anything else.'

Rani looked at him sympathetically, 'You don't have marital relations ... sex... with Ester?'

'No. Not for a long time. Please, would you put those things away? If we're to have a serious conversation, that is.'

'I didn't realize,' Rani began, pulling her robe closed again. Arthur didn't know if she meant she didn't know her breasts were exposed or if she didn't know he wasn't sexually active.

'So, aqui,' she continued, speaking quickly, 'it's something you would call a fruit brandy. It's made by collecting the juices from rotting fruit. You know, the fruit hangs in a porous bag and the juice collects in a bowl underneath. It's only mildly alcoholic, but it gets distilled once or twice which seriously raises its alcohol level. Like schnapps, there are a lot of different varieties. Some have things added, bark of certain trees, mushrooms, or herbs to give it different qualities. In fact, some *are* mildly hallucinogenic, but oddly enough, not this. I can assure you that everything you experienced was completely real.'

'Okay,' Arthur said, 'I feel suitably chastened. Go on with your story. I am interested, I promise you. And I'm beginning to believe you aren't pulling my leg.'

'You're sure I'm not boring you? I could get Zanli back to explain about windpumps.'

'Don't remind me.' He almost whimpered, 'I'm sorry I'm such an anorak.'

'You did ask why we were called killers of men.'

'I know, please go on.'

'Think about what happens in an invasion,' Rani said, with a seriously look, 'the defending army has retreated, or fled, leaving all the women behind. So what is the first thing the invading army does?'

'I see,' Arthur answered, beginning to understand, 'they rape all the women?'

'Exactly. Except in our history, there would not have been a retreating army. We never had to depend upon an army. The tales of our being great warriors were entirely fabricated to explain something that no foreigner understood, the death of all their virile, young soldiers.'

'That must have been pretty hard for someone like the Greeks, with their reputation as such accomplished fighters, to accept.'

'Greeks, Persians, Scythians. Throughout history, every country was always trying to gain more territory. And according to our history, it was very profitable to sell their armour back to them, or to the highest bidder. We may have even dressed up in the captured armour to explain the defeat of the vanquished army, rather than have anyone discover the real reason.'

'That's almost funny.' Arthur could feel his eyelids drooping, despite the excitement of Rani's tale.

'I can see you're about ready for sleep,' Rani said softly. 'You can ask Yetti all about this tomorrow. She is our historian, after all.'

She rose from the bed, taking the tray with her.

'Oh, don't leave,' Arthur said, 'it's not that late. Stay with me a little longer.'

'I'm just getting rid of the tray,' she replied, 'I'm not going anywhere tonight. Let me have your robe.'

He let her help him out of his robe and gratefully let her pull the light covering over him, then leaned forward as she plumped up their pillows. She walked around to the other side of the bed and let her own robe fall to the floor before climbing in beside him. Arthur turned on his side as she nestled against him, resting her head on his outstretched arm. The warmth and smell of her body was intoxicating as he lightly kissed the back of her neck. Putting his other arm around her, he tenderly cupped one of the breasts that had spent the day pleading for his attention.

'Don't get too excited,' she whispered softly, as his body relaxed against hers, 'some types of aqui can also give you a very good night's sleep.'

Chapter Twenty-Four

Arthur awoke to find Rani still next to him. She was lying on her back, her head turned towards him, with an amused look on her face.

'Good morning, sleepyhead,' she said quietly, as her eyelids slowly half-closed over those startling turquoise eyes, then opened wide again, 'did you have a good night's sleep?'

His arm that been supporting her head was completely numb and he tried flexing it to restore circulation, then rubbed it vigorously as the feeling of pins and needles set in. It reminded him momentarily of awakening from his dream a night earlier.

'Ooh,' he protested. 'Umm, yes. I had a wonderful sleep. But I dreamed that I was in bed with the most beautiful, adorable woman, an Amazon actually, and she wouldn't let me make love to her.'

Rani lightly stroked his face with one hand. 'We never use that term here, but it's okay. You're unlikely to be able to pronounce the word we use for ourselves. I've heard of your attempt at *the gift*.'

Arthur was sure he had only tried pronouncing *oolontha* with Ashri. Admittedly, Ashri had been amused at the time, but he wondered if it was so funny that she had to relate it to Rani, or did they discuss everything about him.

'And what do you call this place?' Arthur tried changing the subject, 'Zanli told me about the names of the villages, but what do you call the area we are in? This valley?'

'Just that. In English, anyway. It's too complicated to try and translate it from the old language. I suppose you could come up with "safe haven" or something of similar meaning, but it wouldn't be a literal translation. In Sanskrit, it is the same as "valley", so in English, we just use that.'

'I suppose we should make an attempt at getting up,' Arthur said, yawning and stretching his arms above his head.

'I can see you're eager to meet the gorgeous Yeathili,' Rani teased. 'So quick to discard the old woman you've tired of.'

Arthur turned and taking her in his arms, pulled her on top of him. 'I could never tire of you,' he murmured, as she lightly kissed his neck and face. 'And if you're an "old woman," then I must be prehistoric.'

At the light sound of footsteps, Arthur turned towards the doorway to see Ashri entering the room carrying a tray covered with cups and a teapot. She was followed cautiously, by Zanli. They were dressed in identical white bathrobes, similar to those he and Rani had used the previous night. Arthur wondered if Rani bought them in bulk.

'Leave them alone together,' Ashri said to Zanli in mock scorn, 'and what do they get up to? It's disgusting; you can't trust them to behave like adults for a minute.'

Zanli said nothing.

'And look at this,' she continued in the same vein, trying to find room on the side table to sit the tray down, 'they really are like teenagers that can't be bothered to pick up after themselves'.

Zanli removed the previous night's tray, still covered with the remains of their evening meal, and sat it on the floor, making room for Ashri to sit her tray down. Ashri picked up two cups and walked to Arthur's side of the bed.

'Scootch over,' she said, handing Arthur one of the cups, as she rested one cheek on the edge of the bed. Arthur sat up, accepted the cup and dutifully moved closer to Rani. He put his free arm around Ashri's waist and pulled her closer to him. She put her free arm around his shoulders, kissed him on the forehead, then froze. Arthur turned to see where she was looking.

Zanli stood holding two cups, looking bewildered at Rani's outstretched arms. 'Please, Zanli,' he heard Rani say quietly, 'just set the cups down and come to me'. Zanli did as she was asked and stood just out of reach as Rani continued, 'I was so very, very wrong. Can you ever forgive me?'

Zanli didn't respond, but looked uncomfortable as she shifted her weight from one foot to the other.

'It was evil of me to think so unkindly of you,' Rani went on, 'you who have been my faithful friend and helper for so long. This man means so much to me and I was out of my head with grief, but that does not excuse my unkind words. Please say that you can find it in your heart to forgive me.'

Tears were streaming down her face as she slid out of the bed and knelt low in front of Zanli. Arthur could not see her face, but from the bobbing motion of her back, he assumed that she was kissing Zanli's feet. Zanli bent forward and struggled to lift Rani up to a kneeling position.

'There is nothing to forgive,' she said, her eyes filling, 'I should have acted sooner, but I panicked and didn't know what to do. I wanted to get Noni, but I was afraid to leave him.'

Rani, still crying, put her arms around Zanli's legs and clung to her. Zanli bent once again and pulled at Rani, trying to lift her to her feet.

'Don't do this Rani, you have nothing to be forgiven for, but if it helps, then I forgive you.'

Rani allowed herself to be helped back into the bed, before accepted the cup of tea that Zanli had retrieved. Zanli picked up her own cup and took up a position mirroring Ashri's, one arm around the shoulders of Rani. Her height let her easily lean over to kiss the top of Arthur's head.

'Good morning, my darling Arthur.'

Arthur replied in kind as he lifted his head and kissed Zanli on the cheek. He had felt an awkward outsider during this display of emotion and was grateful that it appeared to have been resolved. Neither his upbringing, nor his years with Ester had prepared him for anything like this and the fact that he had been the object of the dispute had doubled his embarrassment. He felt relieved when Rani wiped at her tears with the back of her hand and addressed Ashri in an almost normal tone of voice.

'So, why are you here?' she said with only a slight sniffle. 'I thought all three of you were staying at Neanthi's.'

'We were, but Yetti wanted to be all refreshed for today and left with the learners. We stayed on at the gathering. It was quite late when we came back'

173

'And what?' Rani asked, 'you had forgotten where you were staying. It's only a couple of hundred metres to Neanthi's.'

'No,' Zanli interrupted, 'but last night, that could have been a couple hundred kays'.

'And,' added Ashri, laughing, 'we knew the food would be better here, this morning.'

'But Neanthi is an excellent cook,' Rani protested.

'Yes,' Zanli said, 'but she will prepare what she thinks we need; it will have all the right nutrients in it, but it may not be what we want. And she will scold us for drinking too much.'

Rani allowed herself a little laugh, 'and you think I am not going to scold you for drinking too much in your delicate condition? And for coming in singing and falling down in the early hours?'

Ashri reached over Arthur's head and ruffled Rani's hair. 'You couldn't have heard us; you were both snoring and tucked up so close together, it was impossible to tell just how many there were of you in the bed.'

'Okay,' Rani accepted, 'but you will have to make breakfast for all of us. It is Sunday and Aszli has gone to her mother's.'

'We know,' Zanli said, getting out of the bed and heading for the door. 'We were with her last night. She left with the other learners at the same time as Yetti. There were a few others that couldn't stay the course; they had really good excuses, but we knew they just couldn't keep up with us. Aszli really wanted to stay.'

'Yes,' added Ashri, following her, 'and she told us she'd made a large bowl of batter for waffles. We only have to fold in some beaten egg whites this morning.'

'Umm,' they heard Zanli say from the hallway, 'waffles! With chocolate sauce!'

'With chocolate sauce!'

'And whipped cream!'

'And whipped cream!'

'And mango compote,' the food-related conversation continued until they were out of earshot.

Arthur felt as if he had been on a roller coaster. He dreaded any kind of argument or discord, especially in public and even more if was between people he cared for, but the happy scene that had just happened made him aware of the love he felt for these three people. His love for Ashri and Zanli had transformed from a sexual passion to an intense protective, almost paternal, love that made him feel quite guilty when he thought of the intimate pleasure he had received with both.

He had to keep telling himself that despite his feelings, they were not related to him, and they were easily old enough to have made up their own minds, so it wasn't as if he had actually committed incest or seduced anyone underage, but the feelings of guilt persisted. He still felt overwhelming desire for Rani, but also a love of an intensity he realized he had never known before. He also knew there was something he must confess to Rani.

'Rani.'

She was holding her face in her hands, her body shaking slightly. At her name she looked up, her eyes streaming. She was laughing and crying at the same time.

'I am so lucky, Arthur, I don't know what I would do without them.'

She turned to him, laid her cheek against his shoulder and put her arms around him.

'Rani,' he repeated, stroking the top of her head.

'We should get up soon,' she replied, 'or those two will have eaten everything, but I want to hold on to you for just a little longer'.

'Rani,' he said once again, 'I've never had children. I mean, I've never fathered any children.'

Rani looked up at him. 'This will be a new experience for you, then. If you decided to stay here, that is.'

This was the second time she had hinted at the possibility of his staying and it confused his thinking process, but he was determined to persevere with what he had to tell her. 'No, you don't understand. I don't think I can. Have children, that is.'

Rani ran a finger lightly across his lips to stop him speaking. 'Shhh, it isn't important.'

'But it is,' he protested. 'Those two seem to assume that I am going to get them pregnant after one night and from what they have said, I assume you are pushing this Yetti at me for the same reason.

It just doesn't work like that and I really feel like a fraud. I couldn't get my first girlfriend, well my first long-time partner, pregnant. We really worked at it, but it never happened. That was before IVF and all that, and I've never been tested, but she got pregnant right away with her next boyfriend. She left me because she wanted children so badly and it worked out for her. Ester and I've never had to... you know, use anything. It's never bothered her; she's never complained, I don't think she ever actually liked children, she always said how they would ruin her figure and take up all her time. She didn't want the responsi...'

The finger Rani had run across his lips was now firmly pressed against them, interrupting him in mid-flow. 'I said it wasn't important. The role you play in getting them to conceive is not the same as with your kind. It is called gynogenesis; at least I think that's what Neanthi calls it; we do not need your sperm. We only need the act of making love to trigger us, if we are in the right state. Like a...' she paused to find the right word, '... catalyst? The article on the Molly fish explained all the technicalities of the process; that is why I wanted you to read it. We are slightly different, of course. I think it said that with the fish, it is the sperm that triggers the process; with us, it is just the act itself. We don't need or use any of the DNA of the father. We are essentially just clones of our own mothers.'

The similarities between Ashri and Rani, between Zanli, her mother, her aunt and her cousin suddenly made sense to Arthur. He had noticed many such similarities as they drove through the town yesterday and had been beginning to think perhaps he was falling into the trap of thinking, that to his eyes, all Indian women looked the same. It came as a relief to him, that no matter how absurd the explanation sounded, it was better than he had imagined.

'I think it's time we were up,' Rani said, starting to get out of the bed. Arthur reached to delay her and caught her by the inside of her thigh. Her skin felt invitingly silky to his touch and he was unable to resist stroking the smooth surface.

'No, ooh, Arthur,' she protested, pushing ineffectively at his hand. 'Those girls will have eaten all the waffles, if we don't get up soon.'

Arthur looked up at Rani; at the wonderful muscle tone of her upper arms. Then let his eyes drift down her stomach, hips and thighs. He couldn't help but compare this firm smooth body to Ester's. Even though they must be of a similar age, and Ester had admittedly worked hard at keeping off any excess weight, her inner thighs had already started to sag in much the same way as her upper arms. She had described the sagging flesh as "bingo wings" and now shunned short sleeved or sleeveless tops and the shorts she had once lived in.

His hand continued to stroke her inner thigh, slowly moving upwards.

'No, Arthur,' Rani repeated, firmly this time and pushed his hand away, 'it would not be right to keep Yeathili waiting. We must both get up now.'

Chapter Twenty-Five

Arthur watched expectantly as Yetti unloaded the picnic basket and placed its contents in an orderly fashion on the rug he had just spread out. Their lunch had at first appeared to be very similar to the one he and Ashri had shared on his first day, but as he looked closer he could see numerous differences. He was also suddenly aware of considerable hunger, despite his generous breakfast.

'I think there are some cushions in the back of the jeep,' Yetti said. 'If you wouldn't mind getting them while I finish this. It would be a little more comfortable.'

'Sure,' Arthur agreed, as he headed back the few metres to the jeep, parked at the side of the lane.

The spot she had chosen for their picnic was in the shade of a small grove of trees. The location gave a panoramic view of the rolling green hills and distant mountains that Arthur had seen on the previous day. They had retraced much of yesterday's route, stopping in almost the same spot to listen to the birdlife in the forest before turning on to a different road that led higher into the hills.

After climbing for some time with the air gradually cooling, they had driven around a blind bend and seen before them, hill after hill covered in convoluted patterns of intense green growth. Arthur had seen similar on his previous holiday and recognized them as tea plantings. The green hedge-like growth was punctuated with the occasional full-grown tree covered in large brilliant orange blossoms and as they continued to drive, the roadside was decorated at regular intervals with plants growing two to three metres high and topped with bright red leaves. Arthur was sure that despite their unusual height they were poinsettias. Several times he could see groups of far away workers lining the twisting pathways between the hedges and he assumed they were harvesting the leaves, but the distance was too great for him to be sure.

Further along, Yetti had had to brake suddenly as they exited a tight bend and wait as a herd of goats crossed the road. Several of the animals, apparently curious about the jeep or its occupants, kept breaking away from the herd and returning to sniff at the tyres and other parts of the vehicle. One brave goat even leapt onto the bonnet before being chased off by the two patient women attending them. When the way was finally clear, Yetti had released the clutch and they continued as before.

Eventually she had stopped in front of some industrial looking buildings on one of the higher hills. There was a continual hum from within and a pleasant aroma coming from them that seemed familiar, but one that Arthur couldn't quite identify. A faint breeze, smelling of fresh growing things, wafted around them and mixed with the aroma coming from the complex. He'd wondered why she had stopped here, but she had simply motioned for him to follow her. After a few moments of walking on a rough paved path that skirted the larger of the buildings, they turned a corner and he could see a small, open-air, but shady café, overlooking the vast plantation. Without consulting Arthur for his preference, Yetti spoke to the young waitress who had appeared almost immediately and ordered tea for the two of them.

'Rani suggested that you might like to see where her tea is grown,' Yetti said, settling into one of the comfortable-looking, Lloyd loom-styled, chairs, 'and I always love coming here. Haven't been for a couple of years, but still, it doesn't change and it's just as I remembered.'

Arthur looked about him as he sat down. Their table was near the edge of the paved area, giving an excellent view of the verdant green hillside below.

'All this belongs to Rani?' he asked, incredulously. He was beginning to think he could not be surprised by anything, but the extent of her endeavours just seemed to keep increasing. 'It's quite impressive.'

'Most of it,' Yetti replied. 'It was owned by a large group once, but was very run-down and not producing enough to make it worthwhile.

Rani's mother was part of the group and when Rani took over her mother's business a number of years ago, she found a way to export the tea directly to customers abroad, instead of selling it to larger producers in India. She bought out most of the other owners and put a lot of investment in new equipment; the fields were not producing enough, so Rani travelled around to other tea growing areas and studied the way they did things there. She even went to China to see their tea plantations. I would have loved to have gone with her, but she took only Zanli. Did you know that they have plantations there that have existed for three or four thousand years?'

'I had no idea. How do they keep the soil from wearing out? I thought crop rotation was essential for most agricultural things. And how do they keep the fields here, so neat and clean? There isn't a weed in sight; it's just bare earth between the rows of tea plants.'

Yetti burst into laughter. 'Ashri warned me that you might ask a lot of technical questions.' When she had regained control, she continued, 'I am sorry that I do not have an answer about the crop rotation or the soil wearing out. You will have to ask Rani about that; I can tell you that they keep the fields here free of weeds with goats.'

'With goats? Like the ones we saw? How do they stop them from eating the tea plants, or do you call them bushes? They are a sort of shrub, aren't they? I thought goats would eat just about anything.'

'The goats do not like the taste of tea. They find it very bitter. They only drink cappuccinos.'

Arthur did not need to see the sparkle in Yetti's eyes to tell him she was teasing him. She momentarily covered her mouth to suppress her giggles. 'The last bit was a joke,' she added unnecessarily, when she had recovered her composure. 'Cappuccinos are very out of fashion now, the latest thing is lattes.'

They both paused for a few moments, smiling at each other and enjoying the lack of tension between them, or the need to impress each other. It was obvious to both that what was to be, would be. Quickly, Yetti resumed her guide duties.

'Most of the labour in the fields is still manual and fairly intensive. The replanting and restoration of the fields has provided work for many more people, though.'

She paused as the waitress delivered their tea, but was interrupted by the girl's whispered comment as she started to pour milk into their cups. Arthur couldn't understand what Yetti said to her in reply, but from her questioning tone, he assumed she was simply asking the girl to repeat her comment. The girl giggled shyly and cupped her hand around Yetti's ear before speaking even more softly.

Yetti suppressed a laugh and smiled at Arthur. 'She wants to touch you and asked me if it was okay. Is that all right with you? She has never seen a man before.'

Arthur was growing accustomed to the attention directed towards him and remembered the warm reception he had received at the jetty with Rani. He had hardly nodded his acquiescence when the young woman started running her fingers lightly over his face. Within seconds she had grasped both his hands and was gazing into his eyes before kissing him on both cheeks in much the same manner and intensity he had received from Aszli. She eventually released him and skipped back towards the enclosed café, but the sound of further giggling prevented any further conversation with Yetti.

Two smiling faces were peering questioningly from around the corner of the building and he nodded to them. Within minutes he was surrounded by a small crowd of women, he assumed them to be the entire workforce of the buildings behind them, touching him, kissing his cheeks, gazing into his eyes, even taking his hand and surreptitiously pressing it to a breast or inner thigh.

***

'You can put the cushions there, and there,' Yetti said, pointing to one side of the picnic rug, when he returned from the jeep.

'And if you sit here,' she continued, almost pushing him on to one of the newly placed seats and sitting down opposite him, 'then we can talk comfortably, but still be able to reach everything'.

Arthur watched, fascinated, as Yetti pushed one of the plates covered with the little pastries towards him. He had felt comfortable in her presence since she had first walked into the slight chaos of Rani's breakfast room. The simple white blouse and dark skirt she wore had contrasted sharply to the bathrobes Ashri and Zanli were still wearing and her neat bobbed hair and small dark framed glasses gave her a slightly scholarly look. Her clothes did look somewhat out of place for the upcoming picnic and the drive through the mountains that Rani had promised for the day, but she had explained that most of her older clothes were still packed away and this would have to do. Zanli had protested because Yetti was being allowed to use Rani's jeep when she had not, but Rani assured her that her turn would come soon.

'After all,' she had said, 'it's not as if Arthur is going to leave tomorrow. I'm sure he is going to be here for some time, yet'.

Yetti looked up to see him watching her as she chose a pastry for herself. 'I'm sorry that I laughed back there,' she said, not sounding the slightest bit sorry, 'you looked so funny. Most men I know would be delighted to have all those women making a fuss over them.'

'It seems to happen all the time, but I'm getting used to it. Was that true what you said about the waitress? That she'd never seem a man before.'

'Of course. Hasn't Rami explained to you who we are?'

'Yes, but it sounds so incredible. There must be some men about though, otherwise how do you...'

'Replicate?'

'I was thinking, *reproduce*, but yes; Rani said you still needed men to... to...'

'Get us started? To be a catalyst? Yes, we still need men. But it's more complicated than that. We really do *need* men! There was a man living in Village Ten for most of my life, a friend of Rani's, but he died a couple of years ago.'

'One man? Surely one man isn't enough to satisfy all these women?' Arthur laughed and helped himself to a slice of something that looked a bit like quiche, but had a strong nutty flavour, 'Not when they act as they do.'

'No, you're right. One man isn't enough to satisfy all these women. On paper it almost works out. The valley needs somewhere around two hundred births a year, just to keep the population from shrinking. That's theoretically possible if the man is shared out and given sufficient rest.'

'Like a... a stud animal?'

'Exactly. But women need much more than that. We've lived like this for a long time, but I believe that each village should have at least one man. Perhaps, several.'

'And that's why the women here act as they do? Because there are not enough men?'

'They are *obsessed* by men. In the gatherings, that's all they talk about. Especially after the business is over and the aqui starts to flow. The women who have had a daughter can only talk about how wonderful it was to have been with a man and those that haven't can only dream about what it will be like for them.'

'So, it's like forbidden fruit?'

'Not so much forbidden, more like non-existent.'

'Couldn't you persuade more men to come here and live? Wouldn't that solve the problem? Or, at least help?'

Yetti paused as she took a mouthful of food and seemed for a few moments to be lost in thought before replying. 'I think it would help, but it's more complicated than that. We have a history, sometimes a rather unpleasant history.'

Arthur was about to ask for an explanation, but Yetti smiled and put a finger to his lips as she said, 'Let's change the subject; are you looking forward to making love to me tonight?'

He didn't have to think about it; he had felt completely at ease with her from the moment they met. Perhaps, he thought, it was just that he was comfortable with the situation. He had not known what was expected of him with Ashri. He had been a little annoyed with Rani and a little drunk or he wouldn't have allowed himself to make love to her. He hadn't been completely at ease with Zanli, even though he knew by then what was expected of him, but he had still found her intimidating.

Of course, he was learning more about this valley and its people all the time, but the more he found out, the stranger it all seemed. From first seeing Yetti, and possibly the relief at finding she didn't fit the image her name had conjured in his mind, he had felt a strong attraction however, and even though they had spoken only a few words on their travels; the noise of the jeep tended to make conversation almost impossible and the pandemonium at the tea plantation precluded any serious discussion, he felt as if he knew her already. Still, he knew little *about* her.

'Definitely,' he smiled at her, 'but tell me more about yourself. I only know that you've been living abroad. I have no idea what you do.'

'I have been living in Germany for the last few years.'

'Oh, I love Germany. Whereabouts? What do you do there?'

'Give me a chance,' Yetti laughed as she poured wine into their glasses. 'I live in Fribourg. I lecture at the university there.'

'Sorry,' Arthur apologized, somewhat chastened. 'It's just that I always welcomed a chance to work in Germany even though our clients, we had several there, were usually a little demanding, but I've never been to Fribourg. I've heard it's nice; do you like it?'

'It's a beautiful and I know I will miss it.'

'Will you go back?'

'I have to. I have so much work to do there and I have so many friends that I will miss. I probably won't go back until my daughter is old enough to travel, though. Perhaps not until she can start school.'

'That means you will be here for some time, then. I'm sure that should make Ashri and Zanli happy. They keep talking about you. I think it's because they have missed you.'

'It seems like a dream come true, that we should all three have our babies together. It's something we used to talk about when we were little, but as we grew older, we came to realize that it was unlikely to happen.'

'What do you lecture in?' Arthur asked, trying to change the subject.

'History. Greek and Middle Eastern. But my real job is research. I'm trying to tie up, to coordinate, if you like, the history of our people, which has been an oral tradition, with more accepted, recorded history.'

'Sounds fascinating. How did you get interested in such a subject?'

'I was a learner to our village storyteller,' Yetti paused and to Arthur, appeared to stare into the distance for a moment before meeting his eyes again. 'It has always been one of the traditions of our gatherings, and in our schools, that a storyteller recites tales of our past. These have been learned word for word and passed down from generation to generation. Until recently though, we have not had a written history. The woman to whom I was a learner, had started to record as much as she could; then I became interested and continued to add to her work as she trained me.'

'I've always accepted that the stories about Amazons were just myths. Like Atlantis or... dragons, or... the Cyclops that Odysseus encountered on his journey home. You don't lecture about your history at the university though, do you?'

'No,' Yetti laughed, 'I don't think that would be a very good idea. It's better for us that everyone thinks we are just mythical creatures.'

'I understand, but I always associated Amazons with the Greeks. I didn't expect to find them in India.'

'That's because the earliest writers of history, or at least Western history, were Greek. It is said that Herodotus invented the very idea of written history. Nearly two hundred years before the time of Alexander the Great, he travelled around much of the world that was known to the Greeks, recording folk tales, religious habits, stories of battles, stories of population migrations and especially stories of their sexual habits. If you read the stories about them though, the Amazons were always just beyond the lands that the Greeks were familiar with. A bit like the dragons you mentioned inhabiting any area that you couldn't get to. Did you realize that less than two hundred years ago, it was still generally accepted in Europe that the Alps were full of dragons?'

Arthur noticed the amused look in Yetti's eyes and assumed she was joking, again. 'What?' he said in feigned astonishment, 'are you trying to tell me they aren't?'

Yetti reached across to him and put a hand on his wrist. 'No, I wasn't joking. When aristocratic young men from England were travelling to Italy, to make what was called the Grand Tour, to admire the great architecture, to see the wonderful Renaissance paintings and sculpture and to sample the delights of the sophisticated brothels, most were fully convinced that dragons actually existed in the mountains they had to pass through to get there.'

'I didn't know that. You mean actual **winged, fire-breathing,** dragons? Not something like komodo dragons?' Arthur paused as Yetti nodded affirmatively. 'God, it sounds ridiculous, but I guess it just shows how attitudes, well, not attitudes exactly, perhaps accepted uh… common knowledge,' Arthur held up both hands and waggled his index fingers to indicate quotation marks as he said the last two words, 'can change as we become better informed'.

'I'm of the opinion our people would be better off if we made our existence known and stopped hiding away,' Yetti's expression had changed to one of seriousness. 'Yes, there would be a period when the world's scientists would want to study us; would be poking into our lives and trying to see what makes us tick. We are after all, at least according to Neanthi, an entirely different species, not just slightly different humans.'

'I didn't realize that, either,' Arthur paused. 'So where did you come from? I said to Rani that I thought Amazons, if they ever existed at all, had been from much further west and she told me that you had migrated here from somewhere to the west.'

'That's something I'm trying to determine. Our oral history would indicate that we have seldom been able to settle in one place for long. Whether *long* means a decade, a century or a thousand years I have no way of telling except when one of our stories coincides with accepted written history.'

'And are you able to do that?'

'Occasionally, but far too seldom. For instance, Neanthi believes we are a separate species, not a mutation, as Neanderthals were completely separate from Homo sapiens. They probably had a common ancestor but had divided at an earlier stage.'

'But you look just like us,' Arthur protested. 'I don't think I would agree with her.'

'I was about to say the same thing. According to one of our folk tales, at one time a very long time ago, we were normal, but then for some unknown reason, we started producing more daughters than sons. As in many cultures today, sons were valued more. They would grow to help in their fathers' work. When the fathers grew too old to work, the sons were there to support and provided for them in their old age. Daughters were not valued. One had to provide for them until they were grown, but then they married and went to live with someone else's family, no longer helping out the parents that had raised them. Our husbands were very angry and beat us a lot for producing daughters.'

Arthur smiled; Yetti's words poured out effortlessly and she seemed to be settling into a comfortable routine. She must have repeated this tale many times, he thought.

'The more their husbands beat them,' she continued, 'the more daughters our great, great mothers produced. The mothers were always blamed if they produced a daughter, but the fathers always took the credit if a son was produced.'

'So,' Arthur laughed, 'nothing has changed in all that time'.

'No,' Yetti agreed, 'not very much. Anyway, the beatings became so frequent and so severe that our great, great mothers grew fearful for their very lives. Finally, all the women met in secret when the men were out hunting, or fighting a war somewhere, and agreed to rid themselves of their burden at the next full moon. The husbands returned and at the next full moon, all the wives contrived to organize a great gathering with much music, dancing, and drinking of wine, ostensibly to celebrate their husbands return. But, when the men had staggered to their beds and fallen into a drunken stupor, their hearts were all pierced with their own knives that they each carried at their waists.'

'Wow, that's what I like,' Arthur laughed appreciatively, 'a good moral tale. That should teach men not to beat their wives.'

'Thank you, I'm glad you appreciated it,' Yetti declared triumphantly. 'I know hundreds more like that, if you had the time to listen to them.'

'Umh,' Arthur nodded, picking at the remaining morsels on his plate. Their eyes met as he continued, 'I could find the time.'

'But I don't suppose that you believe any of it for a moment,' Yetti poured more of the wine into their glasses, 'I don't suppose I do either, but most of them link together in some way and all of them taken together can be quite convincing. For instance, part of the story I've just told you is about how our gatherings originated and how we came to govern ourselves in such a simple and straightforward way.'

'It doesn't really agree with what Rani told me about your... your secretions? You know, the hazard you pose to normal younger men.'

'Oh, believe me,' Yetti smiled, 'we have stories about how that came about, too. As I said, one story taken on its own sounds naive and simplistic, but when you see how they interweave and reinforce each other, it is easy to understand that there may be some truth behind them. Just like most religions, don't you think?'

'Do your stories explain how you have been able to roam over such a large part of the globe without anyone actually believing in your existence?'

'Oh, yes,' her smile changed to laughter, 'but surely you only have to think about the situation to work that out for yourself. Powerful women have been tolerated as queens, but individually and usually in societies that still suppressed the common woman. There have been some matriarchal cultures such as Greece in very ancient times, but in general, they are the exceptions.'

'I still don't see how you could have managed to keep your existence secret all this time.'

'Think about it, cultures that have been aware of us invariably resented us. We've never been warlike, as we've been portrayed, but because they were afraid of us and because they didn't understand us, we have been harassed, invaded, and driven from place to place. There have been many attempts to take advantage of us or completely annihilate us. We never sought acquisition of great amounts of territory, but we may have been guilty of defending ourselves, rather... *enthusiastically*, at times.'

'Rani said that you may have wiped out whole armies. When they saw you didn't try to defend yourselves, when they, uh...'

'Resorted to rape?'

'Yes. It wouldn't have all happened simultaneously. I would have thought that when the first few saw what was happening to their companions, they would have simply slaughtered the rest of you.'

'You're talking as if I was there,' Yetti said, her eyes sparkling with amusement.'I only know the stories. Anyway, it mostly comes down to one thing; no one ever wants to talk about their defeats.'

She paused, for a moment, 'You do realize that we have considerably greater physical strength than ordinary humans?'

189

Arthur suddenly remembered the effortless manner in which Rani had climbed the mountain on their approach to the valley and how her swimming had left him so far behind; how powerless he had been to resist Ashri's embrace when they had first kissed and the amazing speed Zanli had shown when riding a bicycle.

'Sometimes, I can be pretty dense,' he said, 'and it often leaves me feeling a little foolish'.

Yetti looked concerned. Her dark eyes grew larger as she stroked his arm. 'You mustn't be embarrassed; this is all very new to you. I wouldn't expect you to understand everything about us immediately.'

'I've been here a few days, now. I could have asked about some of the things that puzzled me, instead of just waiting for an explanation.'

'Perhaps we should have had more explanations ready, instead of waiting for you to ask questions,' she pulled him to her and gently kissed his cheek, leaving her arm resting around his neck. 'There is another thing you probably wouldn't have noticed. Many of us, not me I might add, but an appreciable percentage of us, have a hypnotic power. Just by looking at you, they can make you do things.'

'Aszli?' Arthur asked slowly, with a sudden clarity of thought.

'Um huh,' Yetti nodded, pulling him even closer.

Chapter Twenty-Six

'How did it go, yesterday?' Rani asked, matter-of-factly.

She was dressed in, what Arthur thought of as, her office clothes, as if she had been up for hours. He had only just descended to the dining room for his breakfast, at Aszli's insistence, and was still in one of the thick towelling bathrobes. Aszli had poured a cup of coffee for him before disappearing up the stairs, presumably to tell Rani he was up. He had not seen her come back down the stairs, but she had reappeared from the direction of the kitchen bearing a plate of hot croissants, just as Rani had entered. The pace, with which things were happening, was almost too much for Arthur's head.

'Umm...'Arthur hesitated, lingering over a sip of coffee.

'I only meant, did you enjoy your time with Yetti?' Rani laughed. 'No, that's not quite right either, I meant, was she interesting company? I wasn't enquiring about the more intimate details.'

'I really enjoyed myself,' Arthur said, after a pause while he selected his words, 'yes, Yetti is great company; she's very fascinating, I mean, with all her stories and everything. I felt... I think we both felt, comfortable with each other. The day just flew by.'

'Yetti was probably more comfortable with you than the other girls have been,' Rani said, 'because she has had more experience with men. Ashri and Zanli have travelled with me and have both seen men; we have dined with men that I was doing business with and they have danced with men, in Zanli's case rather enthusiastically, but neither had ever had, what you would call, a boyfriend.'

'And Yetti has?'

'Yes. I know this because she has sought my advice on the subject on more than one occasion.'

'About men?'

'I don't think she would mind if I tell you. Yes, she asked my advice about a boyfriend. She wanted to marry him and of course, she knew that I had been married twice. She asked how I had avoided kissing my husbands and she asked what the difference was between sex without kissing and sex with kissing.'

'What did you tell her?'

Rani felt the weight of the coffee pot, then let it hover over Arthur's cup as she looked questioningly at him. He nodded and she filled his cup, before topping up her own.

'About the difference in sex? Probably the same thing you could tell her. When we have sex with a man without kissing, it is much the same as you must have experienced before coming here. It is very nice. It can be great fun. It can vary according to how one feels about the other person, but it is not like what you have found here, is it?'

'No, not quite,' Arthur smiled at the memory. '*Normal* sex would seem a little tame now.'

'Exactly. Would you say our way is a hundred times better? A thousand times better? It is almost impossible to describe the difference.'

'True,' Arthur took a sip from his cup and found that its contents had cooled. His expression must have shown and Rani quickly tried her own.

'Oh, I'll get Aszli to make a fresh pot,' she said, setting her cup down, but before she could call out, Aszli had already appeared and started clearing the table.

'I'm sorry,' she apologized, nervously. 'I should have...'

'No, no,' Rani interrupted, affectionately placing an arm around Aszli's waist, 'it's okay. We are not in any hurry.'

'Poor girl,' Rani said to Arthur when she had left the room. 'She thinks she has to anticipate my every whim.'

'And the kissing?' Arthur noticed how Aszli had unexpectedly avoided his eyes, remembered what Yetti had said about her and thought it prudent to change the subject, 'What did you tell her about that?'

'Oh, that she would have to use her imagination,' she laughed, 'there any number of ways. And if the worst came to the worst, she could always give in.'

'I don't understand. Wouldn't that, wouldn't it be, fatal? For the young man, I mean.'

'I only meant it as a little joke, but I think it upset her. I think she really loved him,' she paused; her expression turned to sadness. 'It is very hard, if you really love someone. There are far too many that indulge in what we call *heiress tourism*. They go abroad and find a rich husband, then after a couple of years, just *give in*. They come back much richer and with a daughter to boot. There isn't any way that they are going to get caught. Their husbands die of completely natural causes. And, if there is an inquest, they have everyone's support because they are pregnant.'

'Wow,' Arthur said, shaking his head, 'doesn't anyone get suspicious?'

'I have, perhaps, uuh, oversimplified things. They go to different parts of the world, where others have not been. They wait for a respectful time before returning to the valley, or perhaps even stay in their new homes,' she shrugged, then reached across the table, taking hold of Arthur's wrist and looking into his eyes sincerely. 'We can be very devious, Arthur. Please don't judge us too harshly, though. It is how we have survived.'

'Huhh,' Arthur shook his head, incredulously, 'is that what happened to you? Were you an *heiress tourist*? Didn't you go abroad and have a couple of husbands die on you?'

Rani gripped his wrist so hard that it hurt. Her eyes glistened. 'Arthur, if you believe anything I have said, please believe this. I did not intentionally kill either of my husbands. I did not even go abroad with the intention of finding a husband. I went abroad to pursue my dancing career and I fell in love.'

She fell silent as Aszli came back into the dining room, carrying a tray with fresh cups and another pot of coffee. Arthur watched as Aszli placed the cups in front of them and filled them from the silver pot. She ventured a sideways glance at him, but averted her eyes when she saw he was watching her, then quickly left the room.

'I do believe you,' he said to Rani, suddenly ashamed that he had doubted her. 'It wasn't my intention to judge you. I remembered that you'd said something about marrying; how did you describe it, unwisely?'

'I was very young when I met my first husband,' Rani looked away as if lost in thought for a moment, before turning back and looking directly at Arthur with large dark eyes, the turquoise of her irises almost completely hidden. 'I thought he was the most wonderful thing I had ever seen. He had seen me dance and followed me on tour for several weeks, not telling me he would be there, and then suddenly I would spot him in the audience. The first couple of times, I almost forgot my routine, but then I began to expect him; looking for him at each new performance and would have been very disappointed if he hadn't been there.'

'He sounds like, what I think used to be called, a stage door Johnny,' Arthur laughed, 'I've only ever heard of them in films. No one I knew ever had the time or money to indulge in something like that.'

'It was very romantic,' Rani went on, 'and yes, he didn't work in the family business at that time; he had only just left university. And he didn't have to worry about money. Our tour had started in Milan and gone on to several large cities in Europe, before crossing the Atlantic. I really hadn't expected him to follow me that far, but on our first night in San Francisco, there he was in the front row.'

'Now that is romantic,' Arthur agreed. 'Please, go on.'

'It wasn't as if he was just watching me dance. Right from the beginning we were having dinner together and, you know, just spending time together when I could get away from rehearsals. We were in beautiful cities, Rome, Geneva, Madrid, and London with wonderful places to go, and things to see. And he was wonderful company, and we were just so happy together.'

'So, where did it all go wrong?'

'Fairy tales don't really live happily ever after. We got married; that's where it went wrong. The tour ended in New York and I finally had some free time. We flew back to Las Vegas and were married there. When we returned to Milan, his parents were horrified. They thought that I was a gold-digger; that I had talked him into marriage. They tried to get the marriage annulled. They insisted that I give up dancing; that he join the family firm. They were, I suppose you would call them social climbers and were involved in all sorts of charities.

194

They eventually discovered that I was actually an asset to their social aspirations and insisted that we attend all their functions. They were very nice to me in public; you would have thought that I was their first choice for a daughter-in-law, but as soon as we were out of sight of their friends, the carping, the little digs, the petty complaints would resume.'

'Doesn't sound as if it was very nice for you. Didn't you ever consider leaving?'

Rani pointed at the two untouched cups. 'These will get cold and Aszli will be annoyed,' she said, 'and it's better *not* to annoy Aszli'.

They each raised a cup to their lips, as if an object reflected in a mirror, drank deeply of the cooling liquid and sat them down. Rani topped up both cups from the pot.

'Why,' Arthur asked, slightly puzzled, both from the remark and the unaccustomed aloofness of Aszli, 'does she get upset easily?'

'No, not at all. I don't know why I said that. Aszli has a very even temper.'

The remark seemed to Arthur as a straight man's set-up, waiting for the punch line; he laughed, 'You mean, she's angry all the time?'

'No,' Rani laughed. 'I didn't mean to imply that. She's lovely to have around, she's a very hard worker, she learns easily,' she paused, 'and she *adores* you'.

Rani's sudden laughter seemed to lighten the mood. Arthur noticed the little lines that had appeared around her eyes and resolved to try and make them appear more frequently. Still, he wanted to hear the end of the story, but before he could prompt her, Rani continued.

'No, I never thought of leaving. I was very much in love with Roberto and I just wanted to make things better for us. He had started working with his father in their perfume business; at first just to appease him, but when he found he was actually good at the business, he became very enthused with it. He worked long hours and then started to travel quite a bit. Their perfume was well known and sought after, but this was long before globalization and there were many countries where they had no representation. He wanted to expand, and produce other products, skin care, moisturizers and the like, but his father was very conservative and thought it would cheapen their image.

'I ended up having to spend far too much time with my mother-in-law and in desperation, I convinced him to let me work in the business, as well. After all, I had learned about business from my mother, but instead of wanting to help her, I had only ever wanted to dance. I had never thought that I would actually put to good use all the things I had resented having to learn.'

'It sounds as if things did improve for you.'

'Well, yes. For a while, but I saw less and less of Roberto and it was worse when his father died. It meant that Roberto could follow some of his ambitions with the business and we expanded, but at the same time he became demanding about having a child. His mother had moaned about my not getting pregnant by the time we had been married six weeks, but once his father died, he was almost as insistent as his mother. Of course, I would have loved to have given him a child, but there is no way that I could get pregnant with *normal* sex and if I gave him our kind of sex it would have been fatal for him.'

'I think that's called, being between a rock and a hard place,' Arthur ventured, 'so what did you do?'

'Nothing. Well, not right away, that is. We carried on working together, living together, at least when he was around; I tried desperately to make him happy and at times we almost captured that old feeling, but I saw less and less of him. We carried on like that for a few years, but we made love less frequently and he almost stopped complaining about me not giving him children.'

'Couldn't you try to explain your situation to him?'

'Do you think he would have listened for a minute? No, I think they would have tried to lock me up for being an imbecile. By that time, he would probably have wanted to divorce me, but I was an important part of the business. I suppose that he had affairs; he often smelled of perfume if he had been out late, but it was always one of our products.'

Rani stopped and the sad expression that had returned, disappeared as she smiled once again at Arthur. 'Funny isn't? Most women begin to suspect another woman, if their husband comes home smelling of perfume. All Roberto had to do was give his girlfriends one of our products. If I had ever accused him of smelling of perfume, he could have said something to the effect that, that was our business.'

'So you don't actually know if he had affairs?'

'Oh, he confessed to me of having affairs. Or, rather he bragged about having affairs. He came home very late one night, quite drunk, which was very unusual for him; he never drank very much. Yes, a glass or two of wine with dinner, sometimes at lunch, but I had only seen him tipsy a few times, usually after something to celebrate. But this night he came into my room, we hadn't been sleeping together for a year or two, and tried to get me to have sex with him. There was something very unpleasant about him and I didn't feel like making love to him under the circumstances. I told him to go to one of his whores, if he wanted sex. He became very angry and forced himself upon me.'

'And that killed him?' Arthur asked in astonishment. 'Just like that?'

Rani moved their cups to one side and took both his hands in hers. 'Well, perhaps not quite *just like that*. I was in hospital for several days from the beating he gave me first, and it took weeks for the bruises to go away. I told the police he had had some kind of a seizure while we were making love and the bruises were a result of that. I don't think they believed me, but when the coroner's report came back, it simply stated that he had died of a heart attack. He had often complained about my excuses for not kissing him and when he raped me, for that's what it was, even if it was in the days when a husband couldn't be convicted of forcing himself on his wife, I simply *gave in*. You have experienced the *hug* we give when we first kiss. It's not something we can control. It's a reflex action for us and it's not something many men have ever escaped from.'

She released his hands and sat back in her chair. 'So, there it is; an unfortunate story. I never set out to kill him, it wasn't intentional and I wouldn't have chosen for it to happen as it did. His mother died shortly afterwards; I think she just couldn't bear to be in a world without her son, and I inherited the business.'

As Rani pushed her chair back, Arthur noticed again how the darkness of her eyes had obscured their normal deep turquoise colouring; she stood up and leaned over to kiss him on the forehead.

'I must get back to work now, but Zanli and Ashri are expecting you at Neanthi's house this afternoon, if you would like to join them, that is. You remember how to get there, don't you?' she asked and when he had nodded, added, 'I do hope you believe what I've told you; I'd really hate to think that you were suspicious of me.'

Chapter Twenty-Seven

Still thinking about the story she had told him, Arthur waited for Rani to negotiate the stairs before he arose from the dining table and followed after her. He found no difficulty in his mind of absolving her for any wrongdoing and felt a little guilty about encouraging her to relate, what must have been for her, a very distressing time. By the time he had reached the top, she was out of sight; resuming work in her office, he presumed.

He took his time washing and getting dressed before descending the stairs again. There was no one in sight on the ground floor, but the breakfast things had been cleared away. He had a sudden impulse to see if Aszli was in the kitchen or the courtyard, but the thought of how Ashri would tease him, if he mentioned that he had talked to her, convinced him to resist the urge.

He emerged into warm sunshine, pleasantly surprised at how the thick walls of the old house and the trees which shaded the windows kept the interior so much cooler than the air outside. Pausing for a moment to get his bearings, he started walking in the direction of the house where Zanli had introduced him to her grandmother. The change in temperature was soon forgotten as he quickly acclimatized; there was a faint breeze that smelled of blossom and the pathway was partially shaded. He had remembered the bicycle ride as having been no more than a couple of hundred yards, but distracted by the pleasant atmosphere and his admiration of the grand old houses lining the street, he became aware that he had walked much further than he realized. He was starting to worry that he had passed the right house without recognizing it and was starting to consider turning back when he spotted Ashri standing in the veranda of a house to his right.

She must have seen him at the same time and came running to meet him with outstretched arms. As they met she enveloped him within an embrace that nearly stopped his breathing as she plastered his cheeks and neck with a series of little kisses.

'Oh, Arthur, Arthur, we had begun to think Rani was going to keep you there all day,' she said, releasing him and, as she had so often on their day together, linked a finger with one of his to direct him towards the house from which she had emerged. 'Come and see what we've been doing.'

As they reached the top of the stairs Zanli appeared at the door and the performance he had just experienced with Ashri was repeated in an only slightly less air of abandonment.

Finally, after the display of affection had subsided they each took an arm and pulled him into the house. He had only seen the interior of the hallway at his earlier visit, but had not realized the impressive size of the building. At the end of the hall was a rather grand stairway, wide enough for the three of them, that swept around in a semi-circle as it led to the upper floor. Arthur half expected to encounter Rhett Butler and Scarlet O'Hara as the two girls chattered away either side of him, excitedly urging him to hurry. At the top of the stairs they led him past a series of doors, along a balconied corridor that overlooked the hallway below.

'Look,' said Zanli, when they had at last reached their destination and entered the door centred on the end of the corridor. 'It's our new nursery.'

'It was Neanthi's bedroom,' echoed Ashri, 'wasn't it kind of her to give it up for us?'

Arthur looked about him. The room must have occupied the entire front of the house and seemed far too large to have been a bedroom for just one person, but as a nursery, it had ample room for three sets of little beds, matching chests, and chairs. Alongside each of the chairs were standard lamps with gaily decorated shades. The space between meant that one baby could probably cry without waking the others and would allow lots of room for rocking horses and doll's buggies when they were a little older.

He was towed around the room, first in one direction and then another, and looked on admiringly as the two showed him the new baby beds:

'Look, the bottoms can be positioned at different levels to adjust for their growing!'

'Yes, and the railings stop them falling out when they get more adventurous,'

The chests alongside; 'See, we've already filled them with all the new clothes they will need, until they are two or three!'

The matching rocking chairs; 'Noni told us that babies nurse much better and are much happier, if they are rocked at the same time!'

And the new curtains; 'We can shut out the light for their afternoon naps with the Venetian blinds behind!'

The smell of fresh paint, new fabrics and carpeting filled the room despite the open windows. The colours of the walls and new furniture were in soft pastels and the whole room could have been a display for an expensive furniture showroom. This, thought Arthur, was not the result of one or two afternoon's work.

When the tour of the nursery was completed and he had made the appropriate comments of approval, he was shown the newly redecorated bedrooms that they were using. Two beds occupied the first room, but the second contained only one.

'This is Yetti's room,' explained Zanli, 'we've doubled up while the last bedroom is being decorated. Mama and Auntie are working in there now. They should be finished in a day or two.'

Once it had been pointed out, the sound of scraping was just discernible to Arthur through the thick walls.

'So, where is Yetti?' he asked, 'I haven't seen her since last night.'

'She is resting,' replied Ashri, 'in my old room at Rani's. It is very important for us to get a full day of rest, after the event, in order to conceive, you see.'

Arthur took one of her hands in his and said softly, 'I think perhaps you didn't rest as much as you should have, after our... event, did you? I thought I kept getting a glance of you when Zanli and I were having dinner. Shouldn't you have been resting?'

'I did for most of the day,' Ashri lowered her eyes, 'but there were things that I wanted to be just right for the two of you. It's all right, you needn't worry, Aszli did most of the work. All I did was a little supervising.'

***

'Every time I ask you to tell me about Ester,' Rani looked at him in a very serious fashion, 'you find a way to avoid the conversation. If you don't want to talk about her, you know, if it is too private, you needn't tell me. I'm only curious.'

Arthur gave a sigh worthy of an Australian soap opera, 'Its okay, I suppose I thought I might feel guilty if I talked about her. I think I fell in love with her the first time I saw her, after she was grown, that is. I think I said that I'd seen her lots of times when she was a teenager, skinny and wearing braces; a bit awkward. Then there was a gap, must have been four or five years, maybe six, when I just didn't see her at all. Either I was away when they were having family gatherings, or perhaps she was. I know that I was at their house several times over that period, but I just never saw her.'

'So, she was a beauty. What else? Does she like to cook, for instance?'

'Yes, she's a great cook. She's good at entertaining, full stop.'

'Does that mean she has become fat and jolly?' Rani's eyes twinkled. Arthur began to wonder if he was being teased again.

'No, she is definitely not *fat and jolly*. She may have put on a little weight at one time or another, but she works to control it and is almost as slim and elegant as when we were first together. If anything, she is even more elegant now. Perhaps elegant isn't quite the right word. She has great dress sense, true. Perhaps *composure* is the word I'm looking for. *Elegant* to me, implies people being intimidated by her and she is the exact opposite of that. She knows how to put people at ease, almost immediately, whether it's when meeting people with one of her charities or at a dinner party for one of my clients.'

'She sounds far too good to be true,' Rani said, smiling again, 'and too much competition for me. I think I hate her already.'

Arthur laughed, 'She's really very like you, when I stop to think about it.'

'See, I said I would hate her; I couldn't bear to be around anyone like me. Why do you think my daughters do not live here? Does she not have *any* faults?'

'I shouldn't talk about her faults.'

'Go on, maybe if you tell me about her faults, I can begin to like her,' she laughed again. 'Its only people that are perfect that I dislike.'

'I'm sure you'll start to love her soon,' Arthur could not resist joining in with her infectious laughter.

He looked at the assortment of teacups and plates in front of them, empty except for the last few dregs and some crumbs; he had arrived back from his visit with Ashri and Zanli just in time for afternoon tea.

'Is it too early in the day for some of your aqui?' he asked. He wasn't accustomed to drinking at this time in the day, but rarely thought about waiting for any particular time and the way this conversation was going, it seemed somehow appropriate.

'Probably,' Rani replied, 'but I often have a small sherry about this time of day, or I'm sure there is a bottle of white wine cooling somewhere'.

'That sounds even better.'

Aszli was immediately in front of them clearing away their tea things; did she stand around the corner and listen in to their conversation, he wondered, or was it just coincidence. As if in answer, she returned within minutes with two glasses and an ice bucket, an opened bottle visible, poking out of the ice. He had not heard Rani utter a word, other than to thank her.

'You're doing it again,' Rani said as she half-filled their glasses and pushed the bottle back into the ice.

'I'm sorry, doing what?'

'You found a way of avoiding the conversation, again,' she said, and took a cautious sip. 'Umm, still, that was a good suggestion. Now, go on with your story.

Arthur thought for a moment. 'I once heard, or perhaps read somewhere, it's too long ago for me to remember, that the key to a happy marriage was to remember your wife's virtues and forget any faults she might have,' he paused for effect, 'and to do the exact opposite for your mistress'.

Rani burst into almost uncontrolled laughter, nearly spilling her wine. 'And did that work for you?' she asked when she had recovered.

'I don't know.' It was so much fun making her laugh, perhaps he could keep this up, 'I've never had a mistress,' he paused again, looking at her very seriously, 'but I'm working on it'.

The resulting laughter was so rewarding, he continued; for some reason, he adopted a ridiculous Irish accent, 'when I got married, I knew she was Mrs. Right,' the timing was crucial, 'I just didn't know her first name was Always.'

'Stop it,' Rani said when she had finished laughing. 'You're still trying to distract me. Tell me one thing you would change about Ester, if it was possible.'

Arthur's smile vacated his face as he looked into the distance, 'I suppose there is one thing. She thinks there is only one way to do things. Her way. I've had some modest success in my life, a reasonable education, a good career and I've seen a bit of the world, Hell, I've even won an award or two for my work, but she still treats me as if I'm a halfwit.'

'How do you mean?' Rani was suddenly all ears.

'Well, we share the cooking and the cleaning. I end up doing most of the cleaning, really, but she does more of the cooking. We could afford a cleaner or a housekeeper, but Ester has this need for privacy or something, and won't let me hire anyone. She doesn't want anyone else in the house, not even for an hour or two a week. When I'm working about the house, she tends to stand over me and tell me I'm doing it wrong. Or tell me that her way is better.'

'There are different ways of doing things. Don't we all think our way is best?' Rani asked.

'Sure, but there are limits. And speaking of cleaning, she just cannot see her own mess. She receives a couple of magazines a week and is a compulsive newspaper reader. She can never tidy up a paper and throw it away; there are stacks of magazines all over the house dating back years, but if I try to get rid of any of them, she complains that there was a recipe in one of them that she wanted to save or an article that she wanted to read. At the same time, if *I* leave a book on the coffee table...' he left the sentence unfinished.

'This sounds wonderful,' Rani said, actually rubbing her hands together. 'I'm beginning to love her already.'

'I wish you hadn't got me started; I feel terrible talking behind her back. Especially when she can't defend herself. Sometimes I even have to admit that her ideas might be better, and thank her for her suggestion,' Arthur tried to think of an example, 'driving! She drives me crazy when we're going anywhere. I think I'm probably about average behind the wheel. I try to concentrate on what I'm doing; I can look at a map and work out how to get there and I've only had a couple of minor prangs when I was younger. I've learned to drive carefully, and considerately, not accelerate like a hot-rodder or brake too sharply, you know, think about the comfort of my passengers. I've driven hundreds of thousands of miles in half a dozen different countries, yet whenever we go out I get this constant barrage of, "There's a red light ahead! Watch out for that car! It's a thirty mile an hour speed limit here!"'

'Maybe there's something about your driving that makes her feel unsafe or perhaps she's just trying to be helpful.'

'I'm sure she is, but it's the inequality I dislike. She's actually a pretty good driver too, if… if she concentrates on what she's doing. But if she's talking, we zigzag down motorways, because she can't talk and keep her steering wheel straight at the same time. She forgets where she's supposed to turn. She's always getting lost if she's on her own and she has written off several cars. Of course, it was never her fault.'

'Of course.'

'But if I try and be helpful, and believe me, I've learned to keep my voice calm and not shout; I may have been a bit sarcastic when I was younger, but that's long behind me, I've had to manage enough people and I know sarcasm doesn't work, it just inflames anyone.'

'I think I would agree with you.'

'So, if I see that she's in the wrong lane and mention that we need to turn left shortly, she might shout, "I know!" or "Why didn't you tell me earlier?" or "Who's driving this car?"'

'How old is Ester?' Rani asked, as if trying to change the subject.

'I think I know what you are getting at,' Arthur felt ashamed of his outburst, it was thoroughly disloyal. 'She's not really old enough to be going through the change, and shouldn't be anyway, she had a hysterectomy several years ago, but this has only been in the last few. It is as if she's constantly suffering PMT, though.'

'Do you know if she has health problems? Or, if there's something worrying her? Have you asked her?' Rani looked concerned. The mood had completely changed.

'I've tried to talk to her; she doesn't think there is anything wrong. Not with her, that is,' Arthur couldn't help laughing. 'She did suggest that *I* might be paranoid.'

Rani lifted the bottle from its cooler and looked at it. It was empty. 'Shall we go in to dinner?' she asked.

Arthur had not noticed that it had grown dark as they talked and that candles had been lit everywhere. The atmosphere was once again cosy and inviting as they went in to the dining room where the table was laid for two. On the plates in front of them was, what Arthur assumed was to be, their starter. He couldn't identify the steaming dish in front of him; it resembled a small meat pie that had been crushed completely until the gravy spilled out, then covered with melted cheese. Even so, it still looked appetizing and smelled wonderful. Rani lifted a bottle from another ice bucket by the side of the table and filled their glasses as they sat down.

'I don't think you've told me anything about Ester,' Rani said, carefully putting a fork into her starter, 'that is any more than the little niggles that occur between people that have been married for a long time'.

'Trust you to take her side,' Arthur laughed, 'and you're right, of course. All I've been doing is airing little grievances like we blokes do when we get together on our own at the pub. Of course, it's the same thing our wives do when they're having lunch together, you know,' Arthur affected a falsetto voice, 'My husband never thinks to take the rubbish out,' changed it slightly in pitch, 'well, mine seems to think toilet paper just replaces itself, all on its own and simply doesn't know how to put the seat back down,' before resuming his normal voice, 'She does a lot that makes me very proud of her. She spends a lot of time with a couple of charities, fundraising and helping in a charity shop one day a week, you know that sort of thing.'

'I think I'm beginning to dislike her again,' Rani almost giggled, and then gently blew on a forkful of the hot concoction. 'Can't you think of anything else that annoys you.'

'Sure, there are other things, but I've probably said too much already. She's really generous about most things, yet she can be surprisingly mean about the silliest of little things.' He took a tentative stab at his own starter and followed Rani's lead of carefully blowing on the still steaming forkful. 'Probably the thing that annoys me the most is comparing me to her brother.'

'Mmm,' Rani closed her eyes in obvious appreciation. 'Why should that annoy you? She probably cares very much for her brother.'

'That's the problem,' Arthur said through a mouthful, 'God, that's good! It doesn't taste anything like I expected it to. What is it?'

'I'll explain later, 'Rani took another mouthful, 'but it's my absolute favourite. Tell me about Ester's brother.'

'Ester seems to think I dress too conservatively. If we're going out, she often criticizes my clothes and says that I should take a lesson from Charles.'

'And does Charles, I assume that is her brother's name, dress fashionably?'

'Maybe in her eyes, 'Arthur replied, between mouthfuls, 'I would say *flamboyantly*. He certainly spends enough money on clothes. That was one of the complaints his wife had. He has to have all his suits made at Saville Row. And, I have to admit he wears them well; he is tall and used to be athletic, although he has put on quite a bit of weight now, but they are far too *show-offey*, too *look at me,* if you know what I mean.'

'I'm not sure, try and explain what you mean,' Rani said, mopping up the last of her starter.

'Ester's parents used to live in a little village on the Thames. We would often have Sunday lunch with them and later, go for a walk by the river. We had to pass a pub that had been turned into a restaurant; a restaurant that catered, for some reason, the food really wasn't all that good, to *show-busi* types. But, even worse, to people that wanted to be seen *with* show-busi types.'

'I think I can see where you're going,' Rani paused to let Aszli clear away their plates.

'You could see the car park from the road and the customers going into the restaurant,' Arthur chuckled, thinking about it, 'the cars were mostly very expensive, but finished in ridiculous colours that were totally unsuitable for the models involved. Too bright, too loud, too garish. And the clothes the customers wore were very much the same. Most of the men looked as if they were about to present some dreadful panel show on the television.'

'If I haven't been there,' Rani smiled, 'I've certainly been to a couple of places like that'.

'Anyway, I think that is what must have influenced Charles.'

He stopped as Aszli sat their main course in front of them. It appeared to be a slight variation on the warm salad he had shared with Zanli. Rani watched him as he examined it.

'You expressed how much you liked this, a couple of nights ago,' Rani said, 'and Aszli has tried to copy Ashri's recipe. I hope it lives up to her standard and you enjoy it.'

'I'm sure I will,' he replied, tasting his first bite, 'that's every bit as good; a little different perhaps, but wonderful, all the same.'

'Back to Ester,' Rani said, 'if she is fond of her brother, then her appreciation of his dress sense is probably a little distorted. It is just a matter of taste, after all.'

'I know, I know,' Arthur agreed, 'and I'm being a little petty. There are other reasons for my dislike of any comparisons, though.'

'Go on,' Rani urged, conspiratorially, 'we have all evening. And it's not as if I'm going to tell anyone else. But, I do love a bit of gossip.'

Arthur thought for a minute that she was going to rub her hands together in anticipation. 'I told you that Max, Ester's father, died just short of a year after we married. Well, I had been, more or less, a general manager of the business for several years. Max was more than a figurehead, he had been a great architect in his own right, and his success had made him a public figure, but I did the day-to-day running of the business and just kept him informed, consulting him if I had doubts about a decision, but he nearly always agreed with my choices. It was a privately owned, limited company and had written into its constitution that only family members could be on the board of directors. Even though I was in charge of what we undertook or the conditions we agreed to on any contracts, I was never a director.'

'Did you feel as if you were undervalued?' Rani looked sympathetic.

'Not really,' Arthur paused again as he refilled their glasses. 'It wasn't like that. I was very well looked after financially and after we married, as Ester was on the board, we had her share of any profits, as well.'

'I see.'

'No, I didn't mean to imply that I felt sorry for myself, or anything like that. The problem arose when Max died. Charles convinced his mother and sister to let him take over the business. He had no experience, he wasn't an architect, and he had only dabbled in a few wild ventures that had invariably failed, but he can be very persuasive. He might have made a fortune selling double-glazing if he had applied himself, but he didn't know how to run a business. He took on ridiculous contracts with disproportionate penalty clauses, spent our reserves on foolish projects so that we couldn't pay suppliers in time to get discounts and generally upset all of our staff when their pay checks bounced.'

'Couldn't you appeal to Ester and her mother before it was too late?'

'I tried, believe me. But he was, and is, very convincing. I was making a mountain out of a molehill, he had everything in hand, it would only take one good contract and we would be back on our feet. I couldn't make Ester or her mother understand how useless, no… not just useless, how disastrous he was, until it was too late. It had taken just three years for him to turn a very profitable company with an admirable reputation, into a bankrupt laughing stock with an enormous amount of debts.

'Fortunately, my reputation meant that I had no problem finding something else, in fact something better; most of the better staff had seen the writing on the wall and had already done the same, but there were several of the administrative staff that had a bad time of it.'

'At least you must have felt vindicated with Ester and her mother.'

'No, not really. As I said Charles can be very persuasive; he convinced them it was entirely my fault. That I hadn't pulled my weight; that I had sabotaged all his best propositions and had ruined his influence over our best architects and the staff.'

'And Ester believed him?'

'Still does, as far as I know. There were other problems as well, a little later, more personal, but almost as bad.' Arthur sat back in his chair; they had both finished their main course and Aszli was clearing away their plates.

'Shall I serve the desert, now?' she asked of Rani.

'Give us a few minutes while we finish our wine, if you don't mind,' Rani replied, affectionately putting a hand on Aszli's wrist. 'Is that all right with you, Arthur?'

'Sure, if we aren't keeping Aszli from her gathering. Or, if she wants to get away, she could serve our dessert now, and we could help ourselves when we're ready.'

'You can speak to her directly,' Rani laughed, 'you don't need me to translate.'

He looked at Aszli, he hadn't thought about it, but perhaps he had been avoiding her eyes. They drilled into his consciousness, big, dark, round, soft, smiling eyes that could see into his soul. He couldn't take his eyes away from hers.

'It is okay,' she was slowly saying to him as if he were a child. 'I will not be going to the gathering tonight. I would prefer to stay and serve you. But thank you so much for your consideration.'

'Tell me about the other problems,' Rani said when Aszli had left the room and Arthur's breathing had returned to normal.

'Sorry, what?'

'You said there were other problems later, more personal.'

'Oh, yes. Charles had married a couple of years before we did, his wife was Italian, and they had an infant son; I guess he was about six months old when Ester and I married. He was a lovely little boy, happy, laughed at everything, seldom cried. His mother obviously adored him and was, as far as I could see, a very good mother; you could see just by looking at her how proud she was of him and how happy he made her.'

'It sounds an ideal relationship.'

'Yes, it was; at least between mother and son. Between father and son, it was different. It was as if Charles was jealous of his son. At family gatherings, if anyone made too much fuss of little Tony, his name was Antonio, he had to change the subject, start telling a story about what *he* had been doing, or take all the credit for his son's behaviour. I found out later that Charles never paid any attention at all to his son when they were at home. But it was seldom that he was at home with his family. He seemed to need to carouse, to be out drinking with his cronies.'

'This is beginning to sound so familiar.' Rani couldn't resist a little laugh, 'except for the baby, that is.'

'I thought it might,' Arthur agreed. 'Anyway, as the boy grew a little older, he was such a little bundle of joy, always giggling and doing funny things, I found myself volunteering to entertain him. First at our family gatherings where, by this time, his father would be in another room entertaining his mother and sister with his latest wonderful achievements, and before long, at any opportunity I could find.'

'Are you sure it was just the little boy you were fond of?' Rani was looking at him knowingly. 'You haven't even mentioned the mother's name. Don't you think that's a bit strange?'

'Yes, I have to admit I was drawn to Pia. At first, I probably just felt sorry for her, but the more time we spent together, the more I found myself wanting to be with her. And not to just share her son. It was the closest I ever went to really cheating on Ester.'

'So, what happened?'

'After the business went bust, Charles became even more difficult to live with. Pia decided to leave him and asked me to join her. She had family in Australia and wanted to make a new start there. I was really torn; I knew I still loved Ester and couldn't bear to think of leaving her, even though things had cooled between us with the collapse of the business. But I knew that I loved Pia and her son as well. I often consider that I may have made the wrong choice.'

'Do you know what happened to her?' Rani emptied the last of the wine into their glasses. It seemed to be a recurring feature of their relationship.

'Yes, we still keep in touch,' Arthur took a very large sip of his wine. 'We exchange letters three of four times a year. She regularly sent me pictures of Tony growing up; he has graduated and, funnily enough, became an architect as well. I had set up a trust fund to finance his education. She remarried a few years after the divorce, I think happily, and had two more children. I don't know if her husband knows that we were as close as we were; I visited them once when I was in Australia on business, but I've never told Ester that I'm in touch with her. Pia always sent her letters to my office until I retired and now we communicate by email. Ester, of course, believed Charles's side of the story and thinks it was all her fault. As far as I know, Charles doesn't even know where they live and has never been in touch since having divorce papers served.'

'You really are the most surprising man,' Rani said, 'I'm beginning to see why you don't like being compared to Ester's brother, though.'

'I guess I told Ashri, but you wouldn't know. I never knew my older brother. I don't mean to imply that there was anything about him that was like Charles, as far as I know he was a good scholar, a great sportsman and very well behaved, but I was always compared to him unfavourably too, and his name was also Charles.'

Chapter Twenty-Eight

They lay in each other's arms unable to sleep. At first Rani had turned on her side, one leg over his and her head on his chest, but after a while had turned so that her back was to him and they had curled together like nesting spoons. Neither position was conducive to Arthur suppressing his desire for her. He had to admit though, it was very pleasant simply lying next to her and holding her in his arms; something he missed with Ester. Her desire to watch television in bed, programs that Arthur felt prevented him from concentrating on the book he was reading, had led them to sleep in separate bedrooms. Even then, he could hear the sounds of her television set through the bedroom walls.

Why, he had once asked her, did the programs they put on late at night have to contain so much shouting, so much violence and aggression, so much clamorous music? Wouldn't it make more sense to show the quietly narrated nature programs with their soft, almost soporific, backing tracks late at night, to help lull people to sleep?

Eventually Rani volunteered to go downstairs to make them another cup of tea.

'We could just sit and talk some more,' she suggested, 'if you can't get to sleep'.

Arthur agreed that it was a very good idea; he was wide-awake and certainly didn't want Rani to go back to her own room. She returned ten minutes later, laden with a tray that would make Aszli proud, complete with teapot, milk jug, cups and an assortment of biscuits. When she resumed her place in bed and passed him a cup of tea and a biscuit, he asked her about her reluctance to make love to him. Was it because of fear, he asked, that she would become pregnant as easily as Ashri, Zanli and Yetti. He was taken aback by her sudden outburst of laughter.

'Oh Arthur,' she had said, 'do you know nothing? Can't you see that I'm far too old to bear children?'

Arthur didn't think she looked too old; he was quite sure he had known women older than Rani who had given birth and couldn't resist telling her so.

'Any way,' Rani continued, 'you must save up all your strength for Simili, tomorrow.'

She had asked him when he returned from his afternoon with Ashri and Zanli if he minded spending the day with another young woman. He had remembered Ashri mentioning the girl's name so matter-of-factly earlier; it seemed already to be accepted and he could only agree. Strange, he thought, that no one had told him anything about the girl, but he thought he had noticed a slight curl of the lip when Ashri had said her name. Perhaps it was just his imagination, or perhaps she was again showing a little jealousy.

'What would Ester think,' Rani asked, interrupting his thoughts, 'if she knew what you were doing here?'

'What...?' Arthur replied, 'Do you mean...? Yes, of course you do. She would probably be very angry, disappointed in me, you know, hurt is probably the best description.'

'Does it make you feel guilty?'

Arthur sipped his tea while he thought about his feelings, 'No, I'm not depriving her of anything. It's not as if by making love to these young women that I'm not making love to her.'

'Would you be angry with her if you found out she was having an affair?'

'Perhaps.'

'Why?'

'Umm... it's a different matter,' Arthur said hesitantly, he wasn't sure he was on very solid ground.

'Isn't that a bit of a double-standard?' Rani's large eyes were smiling ambiguously over her cup.

'No,' Arthur protested, 'I would have made love to Ester at any time in the last few years, but she doesn't want to, so if I'm making love to someone else, I'm not depriving her of anything. I'm not making love to someone else instead of her, if I had my way, it would be making love to someone else in addition to her. I'm not leaving her to run off with someone else. I may be spending some time here, but I will be going back to her. We have taken separate holidays before; she goes off with her girlfriends to sunny beaches, I go skiing with my friends.'

'But, don't you have rules against committing adultery?'

Was Rani just playing the devil's advocate? Wasn't she the one that had invited him here in the first place?

'I think the condemnation of adultery is often an overreaction. If you have some standards, adultery doesn't have to be such a bad thing. It's not as if sexual intercourse, or even love, is a material thing, something you can see or hold. And it's not as if we are allotted a given amount that can be used up if we spread it around too much. Sure, in most western cultures we pretend to disapprove of it, yet a very large percentage of us seem to indulge in it at some time or other. Most of us could be accused of simply worrying about our image, but isn't that just hypocrisy?'

'Probably,' Rani said. She turned to put their empty cups back on the tray on the bedside table, and then settled back comfortably, leaning against Arthur again. 'You know, in some countries, if a woman commits adultery, she is stoned to death. If a man commits adultery, he may get a slap on the wrist and told not to do again, or not to get caught. The woman he commits it with still gets stoned to death. And his wife probably gets stoned to death as well, because it was all her fault in the first place that he was tempted to go astray.'

'Now that's the kind of double-standard I've hated all my life,' Arthur felt himself stiffen with rage at the very thought of such a situation, 'but I'm ashamed to say I've never taken any active part in trying to prevent such things happening. Maybe back in the years when women were trying to gain equal rights; I may have given a couple of friends some encouragement.'

'Of course, there is a valid argument against adultery,' Rani said. 'There was a time in the distant past when a man needed to know his sons were his own and he needed to know that in his old age he could depend upon those sons to support him. Not something that we have to worry about, of course, but the argument went that if his sons learned they were not really his, they might end up supporting their real father instead.'

'But you could say that there is just as valid an argument to support polygamy, for instance.' Arthur argued, 'if you lived in deeply rural America in the nineteenth century, like the Mormons, death during childbirth was very high. If a farmer, herdsman, or rancher already had a few children and his wife died with the birth of the latest one, remember back then you only had two methods of birth control, abstention or abstention, then he needed another wife quickly. He needed to spend all his time working to support his family, working in the fields or tending his herds; it wasn't as if those jobs were part time. If he had to stay at home cooking and cleaning and looking after young children, he wasn't going to have any income if his animals died or his crops weren't harvested. So, having another wife or two around the house meant that they could look after each other during childbirth or if they just got sick, and the children would still be looked after, the kitchen garden would be tended and the farmer had supper on the table when he came in from the fields.'

Rani didn't seem convinced. 'Wouldn't it have been better to let one woman share two husbands? When there was heavy work to do, both could work in the fields, or whatever, and when there was only enough outside work for one, the other could look after the children, clean the house and fix a few meals for a change,' she looked inquisitively at Arthur, a pronounced twinkle in her eyes. 'Why is it that the men, and I'm asking this as someone who loves them dearly, always seem to make things work to their own advantage?'

'I don't know,' Arthur replied, resignedly, 'it just seems to be the way things are, but going back to our argument about adultery. In this day and age, at least in the western world, none of what we've said applies any longer. I just believe you shouldn't hurt people. Don't commit adultery if you're stupid enough to get caught, because it's going to hurts someone you care for.'

'And if you don't get caught? Does that make it okay?' Rani laughed again; the tinkling sound of tiny bells washed over Arthur. 'It appears as if you've given this a lot of thought.'

'Yeah, I suppose. I even made up my own rules once, when I was much younger,' Arthur said, 'I had a friend, years ago before I was married, that I would take out for a meal, or for a drink, or to the occasional party, when I was free. We were never involved romantically, just friends, but we liked doing the same things. She always seemed to be free even though she was popular, had a lot of friends and was very attractive. I found out after several years that she had been seeing a married man. He had strung her along with continual excuses why he couldn't tell his wife just then, you know? And when his wife did find out about her and divorced him, do you think he married her? Did he hell. She had wasted all those years on a selfish bastard.'

'And because of this, you made up your own rules,' Rani seemed suddenly interested instead of just making conversation. 'So what were the rules?'

'I thought if you were married – or later on when cohabiting became acceptable, if you had a partner – you should never get involved with someone that didn't already have someone. So they weren't forever waiting around for you to find a few brief minutes to spend with them.'

'Didn't that just mean that you were always going to hurt two people?'

'No, rule number two was, never get involved with someone you were capable of falling in love with.'

'Now that sounds really very shallow.'

'Absolutely. If you're going to commit adultery, be aware it's a crime for the selfish and the shallow. Admit it at the beginning; don't try to make excuses why you're doing it. You know you're doing it because you're selfish. You want something extra, something you're not really entitled to. But you shouldn't try to justify it by saying you're in love, or that you just couldn't help falling in love. If you wanted to look for someone else, someone to fall in love with, then it must mean your marriage wasn't worth saving,' Arthur stopped to take a deep breath, 'I thought if I was ever tempted, I should have the decency to get out of one relationship before I got involved with someone else.'

'That doesn't justify it though, and it doesn't make it right, does it? You can't just say, "I do it because I'm selfish, but that's okay, because I'm not going to let myself fall in love," and think that makes it acceptable.'

'I didn't say that anything justified it; the rules were just to try to make me think about what I might do. The last rule was if you found you were falling in love to get out of the situation straight away.'

Rani shook her head in bemusement, 'So with all these great rules, were you ever guilty of adultery? I mean, did you cheat on Ester before you came here?'

'I guess I've broken all my rules haven't I?' Arthur tried to laugh, but felt shamed. 'Technically, I suppose the answer is yes. I did stray once – it isn't an excuse, but I was quite drunk. It wasn't very good and I was, I think we were both, very embarrassed later. I've often strayed in my mind; I fall in love with every woman I meet, but you can't be tried for just thinking. There was, of course, the one time that I told you about, when it almost happened, but it would have meant making a complete commitment and I couldn't have left Ester.'

'With your sister-in-law?' Rani looked at him curiously. 'And you've broken *all* your rules coming here?'

'Well, I've been unfaithful to Ester, I've uhh... *been involved* with three young women that don't have anyone else, I've fallen in love with you and I didn't have the decency to let Ester know what I was up to before I left. Let's see, have I left anything out?'

'But you didn't really know what was going to happen when you agreed to come here, did you?'

'Maybe that lets me off the hook a little,' Arthur smiled. 'I thought it was just a lark; I didn't really expect anything like it has turned out to be.'

Rani stroked his bare arm with one hand, 'do you think Ester has been unfaithful to you?'

Arthur gave a small chuckle. 'I don't think so.'

'You seem to think that's funny.' Her hand felt warm against his skin. The cooling night air gently wafting through the open window had felt refreshing, but it would soon be time to pull the coverlet up around them. 'Don't you think she would ever cheat on you?'

'Ester has never really enjoyed sex; it was more like she endured it because she loved me. She was a once a week at the most type of person, you know lights out, covers up around your chin, don't make a move until it's over and maybe it'll never happen again. I tried to get her to talk about her problems when we were younger. She just wouldn't talk. She'd clam up completely. I even tried to get her to discuss it with someone professional, a marriage counsellor, a psychologist or anyone that could help and she simply got angry at the suggestion.'

'And you think because of that she wouldn't find anyone else attractive?'

'I think the desire for sex is the usual motivation for straying. Perhaps if you stop caring for the one you're with, or if they treat you badly, you start looking for someone else, but if everything else is okay, then maybe sex isn't all that important.'

'So, you have a good relationship with Ester, otherwise?'

Arthur pulled the light covering around them, carefully tucking it over Rani's shoulders, then leaned over to blow out the last candle, leaving the room lit only by the pale moonlight coming through the open window. He stared at the pattern of shadows from the tree outside, before snuggling comfortably back against Rani's warm body. 'We sit and talk for lengthy periods almost every day, we enjoy each other's company, God, she even laughs at my jokes. I don't know many other couples that can say that. Most of our friends are usually so busy with their children, with their social commitments, with their hobbies or their individual interests, that they seldom have time for each other. We have our individual interests and we go our separate ways for part of the time, nearly every day, but in the evening we're both interested in hearing what the other has been doing. And we don't always bury ourselves in a book or the television and ignore the other. I know a lot of couples that you just wonder why they're still living together. It seems obvious they don't even like each other. We're not like that. Maybe it's a blessing in disguise that we never had children. We depend so much on each other.'

'It sounds like a much better relationship than I had imagined,' Rani said sleepily, once again stroking his encircling arm. 'Somehow I had imagined you were a little like the last couple you described.'

Chapter Twenty-Nine

'Do you know how to use one of these?' Zanli asked, producing a small radio handset from the pocket of her slacks. It was only slightly larger than the palm of her hand. 'You simply turn it on here...' she punched one of the buttons on the brightly coloured panel and it crackled as it came to life, then pointed at the thumbwheel barely projecting from one side, '... and adjust the volume here. I have already set the channel to mine'.

'I've used something similar on a few building sites,' Arthur replied, examining the object as she thrust it into his hand. 'Why?'

'We don't have any cell phones here,' she explained, 'and satellite phones are too expensive for most of us, but these work almost as well over a short range. They come in very handy at times.'

'Yes?' Arthur was puzzled why she was giving the two-way radio to him, 'but as I understand it, you're dropping me off at Simili's and presumably, you'll be picking me up in the morning. Why should I need this?'

'I have a bad feeling about this,' Zanli replied, a concerned look on her face, 'I tried to talk Rani out of letting you go.'

'It's okay,' Arthur put his hand lightly on her shoulder and gave it a friendly little pat. 'I promise I won't fall in love with her or anything. You'll still be my special one.'

'Do not joke about this.' The tightness in Zanli's voice revealed her concern, 'Simili was the only girl in our class that we did not like. She was the greediest person I have ever known and according to Zetla, her mother was the very same.'

'It's okay,' Arthur repeated, trying to make light of the situation. 'I'll let her eat all the cakes.'

Zanli took both of his hands in hers and looked him directly in the eyes, 'Arthur, I am serious; her mother was a *tourist* and she is a fat, greedy cow. I am afraid she will try and use you all up.'

Arthur tried to think where he had heard the expression before; wasn't it a joking remark between Ashri and Zanli herself, on his first day. It didn't sound particularly threatening to Arthur. 'I'm sure you're worrying about nothing. Shouldn't we be going? Simili is probably wondering what has happened to us.'

He leaned over the small console separating the two seats and kissed Zanli on the cheek. She leaned towards him in turn, pulling him firmly into her arms and, pushing aside the collar of his *kurti*, left a trail of open-mouthed kisses on the side of his neck from just below his ear to the top of his shoulder. The effect of her warm breath and soft lips was unexpectedly provocative. She smiled at him warmly for a few seconds, her eyes only inches from his, before releasing him and turning back to the steering wheel of Rani's jeep.

***

He and Rani had been lazily taking their time over the last of the coffee as they finished their breakfast and Arthur was just about to ask Rani for the plan of the day, how was he to find this Simili they had discussed, when Zanli had arrived. Arthur soon found that Zanli was at last going to have the chance to chauffer him to his destination.

They left Rani sitting in the dining room and after exchanging greetings with Aszli, exited via the courtyard at the back of the kitchen. Rani's jeep stood waiting for them just outside the vine covered garage, its paintwork gleaming in the bright morning sunshine. As they both climbed in, Arthur was amazed to see the interior was as spotless as the outside; as though it had just been valeted for resale. Every trace of the dust and mud accumulated from Rani's mad drive and Yetti's cross-country venture had been completely eradicated. Arthur wondered if this was the work of Zanli, but her carefully manicured hands, loose, beige slacks and long-sleeved white blouse did not appear to be commensurate with such fastidious car cleaning.

'We are going to Village Two, today,' she said, as she pushed the gear lever into first and released the clutch. 'I do not think you have been there yet?'

'No, I don't think so,' replied Arthur, 'although Rani may have driven through on our way back from Ten'.

'I hardly think so,' Zanli said with a laugh. 'She said she had left it too late and had to take the quickest possible way back. She was terrified that you might get stopped going through one of the villages, if the gatherings were in full swing. Even her clout would not have mattered if those women had gotten too excited.'

'I don't understand.'

'I think you would, if you saw one of the gatherings once they get going.' She turned to glance at him again; a slightly mischievous look on her face. Arthur wished she would keep her eyes on the road; although she was driving at a pace slightly less than Rani's, the narrow, gravelled lane was rutted in places and tended to throw the little jeep about.

'You've seen how mad they are to get their hands on you, even in the middle of the day? Well, consider two or three hundred like that, but with their inhibitions dulled from too much aqui. You wouldn't last five minutes.'

She turned towards him and smiled again, but he could tell she was not joking. Perhaps this wasn't such a paradise as he had imagined.

'Anyway,' she continued, 'although Village Two is the next one downriver, it is much further away than Village Three, where we had lunch together'. Zanli turned towards him once more and wrinkled her nose. It was wonderfully intimate gesture that spoke to Arthur of a shared confidence.

'That is because of the way the river meanders,' she went on. 'Did you know the word meander comes from the original river of that name in Caria and Phrygia that flowed into the Aegean near Miletus? Or, that the river was named after the river God with the same name? I have not been there, but it must have really wandered about, don't you think?'

Arthur could not resist laughing out loud. 'Oh Zanli,' he exclaimed, affectionately stroking her knee. 'We were meant to be together. Anyone else would be constantly bored with the useless little bits of information that fascinate us.'

'I learned that from Yetti,' she smiled at him yet again, 'I thought it would impress you. But I have to admit it, she is the one filled with such ancient knowledge.'

Within minutes she had pulled to a stop at the side of the road and implored him to accept the two-way radio. When he had finally convinced her that it was unnecessary and promised to heed her warning, she had pulled slowly back onto the narrow road.

The road wandered through fields of grain and long grasses, periodically broken with small groups of workers in an odd mixture of clothing. All had their heads bound up with scarves or lengths of fabric and were cutting the hay, binding it and carrying the shocks on their heads to where others were piling it into conveniently sized stacks. A mixture of brown and white, and grey and white cows grazed in the clearings and the workers invariably waved enthusiastically at the passing jeep. The smell of the newly cut grass, mixed with the smell of blossom and hot sun on growing vegetation, wafted around and assaulted their senses. Before long, the fields gave way to plantations of tall, curving, coconut palms, laid out in chequerboard fashion, their bare trunks allowing glimpses of the elusive river. Soon, they were entering, what Arthur assumed to be Village Two, which at first appeared very like Village One. On the outskirts they passed simple thatched-roofed, workers' cottages made of roughly cut, brown stone. In the centre was a similar looking, leafy square with shops on three sides and the river bordering the fourth, but the throng of women in colourful saris that had caused Rani to slow to a walking pace in Village Ten was thankfully absent. A small handful of women were idly browsing about the shops and a few more were sitting at tables under the trees, but Zanli hardly slowed as they passed through.

They had gone only a short distance from the centre before the houses grew larger and larger. Each seemed to vie with its neighbour for an appearance of grandeur; large carefully tended lawns, many with sprinklers throwing up little rainbows in the bright sun, separated the houses from the road. Several had long drives leading through wrought-iron gates that were set between high brick or stone pillars. The walls lining the road however, were no more than waist high, so as not to obstruct the passersby's view of the magnificent houses. An absence of the large trees and shady avenues that contributed to the peaceful atmosphere of Rani's village, hinted to Arthur that these were all very recently built.

'This is where Mama and Auntie make most of their money,' Zanli said to him conspiratorially. 'They are full of, what I think you call, bling.'

Arthur nodded in agreement. They looked perfect for an estate of footballers or successful used car dealers and their wives.

'We have to bring in much marble,' she continued, turning into the driveway of one that had its gates already opened, 'not to mention gold-plated taps, expensive furniture and luxurious brocades, to furnish these to the wishes of their new owners. It is really difficult with the state of the roads through the mountains, but as I said, it is much more profitable than the lovely little houses you saw us working on your first day.'

***

Arthur felt the slightest twinge of disappointment as the young woman Zanli introduced as Simili, held out her hand in greeting. It wasn't because of the coolness of her manner or the fact that she had not indulged in the usual two-handed embrace, complete with the passionate look of longing that he had so quickly become accustomed to. Nor was he disappointed that she had averted her dark eyes demurely when he looked directly at her. It was only that she looked so normal. Because he remembered Zanli describing her as a 'fat cow' and the way Ashri had screwed up her face in distaste at the mere mention of her name, he was expecting someone much larger or of far less pleasing appearance.

Most of his adult life Arthur had, if not actually fantasized about, at least been occasionally curious, what it would be like to make love to a very large woman. Or, a woman who was just exceedingly ugly. There had been a woman approaching middle age he had often been tempted by, who had for several years, worked in their administrative offices. She could not by any stretch of the imagination be described as ugly; she had a warm, outgoing personality and a very pretty face with large round eyes that looked at him soulfully each time he entered her office, but she was very overweight. He had heard her described by a colleague as fat; he felt this was unkind and had tried to find a more delicate description, but phrases such as pleasingly plump, roly-poly or Rubensesque struck him as euphemistically twee. She had large melon-shaped breasts over a well-rounded belly and from behind her hips and buttocks were large, but pleasantly rounded. She often wore blouses straining against the pressures from within and held together by one or two buttons too few, revealing a cavernous cleavage.

At their annual Christmas party she had always made a point of kissing him under the mistletoe, prolonged open-mouthed kisses, her ample body pressed against his and her arms firmly holding him until he responded in kind. He had often wondered what it would feel like to simply immerse himself in her softness and was sure that he had only had to say the word. Knowing it would offend Ester if she ever found out, perhaps just knowing that it was wrong, but mostly being afraid that it would entangle him in a relationship that he would quickly want out of, prevented him from ever "saying the word", but he was unable to eradicate the images in his head of what it might be like to make love to her.

Equally, he was unable to walk down the street and see a woman with a pleasing, or at least an acceptable shape, but an ugly face, without again wondering the same thing. Would he find an ugly face repugnant up close? Would he be able to overcome any inhibitions against kissing someone ugly if he knew the rewards were, in the end, well worth it? He had never had the courage to find out and the images remained simply in his imagination.

When he had first been told of his impending encounter with Simili and noticed the remarks, reinforced by Zanli's warning, he had imagined that she would be something unusual, but the only evidence he could detect was of her size. She seemed to be almost perfectly proportioned for her height, perhaps a kilo or two overweight at most, but was only a few centimetres shorter than Zanli. Her apparent shyness contrasted strongly to her appearance. She was wearing a matching ensemble comprising a tightly fitting short-sleeved blouse, the fronts of which crossed over just below her breasts, then wound around her waist and tied at the front. It was similar in style to the one Rani had worn on their day out together, but was in a rich gold-coloured silk with small burgundy coloured embroidered figures in a regular pattern. The skirt, in the same fabric, started at her hips and fell straight to her ankles. It appeared to have been wound around her, ending in a scarf that continued loosely around her back, before being casually thrown over one shoulder. The gap between the two exposed an attractively shaped waist and part of a softly rounded belly with smooth golden brown skin. Arthur had seen a similar style worn by air hostesses on one of the Malaysian or Sri Lankan airlines, but not as elegantly as this. Her dark hair was cut to curve inwards, just brushing the tops of her shoulders. He could only wonder how anyone this beautiful and shy could be so obviously disliked by those he cared for. It was, he decided, probably just a schoolgirl thing that they had clung onto.

Distracted as he was, he realized Zanli had been explaining to him that Simili spoke only a little English, but probably, she added with just a touch of sarcasm, enough for their purposes. The conversation between the two women had, until now, been in their own language, but after a show of affectionately, almost possessively, kissing him goodbye, she had said to Simili, her eyes glaring aggressively, 'Take *very* good care of him. I'll be back tomorrow.'

Zanli had only shut the door behind her when Simili smiled down at Arthur, she was at least half a head taller than he, and held out her hand to him.

'Come,' she said softly. 'I show you my house.'

He was reminded of Ashri as he put his hand in hers. She turned and led him towards one of the doors leading off the hallway they were standing in.

'My kitchen,' she said proudly, gesturing about the room. Arthur was unreservedly impressed by both the size and the design. The walls were lined with units he recognized as being from an expensive German firm; a mixture of stainless steel and gleaming lacquered black fronts with gold-flecked grey granite work surfaces and double inset sinks. As she walked about, Simili stroked the surfaces with one hand, opening a couple of the cabinet doors to reveal interior lighting illuminating the ornate chinaware within. She stopped at one corner to open the doors of the lower unit. As the door opened a clever arrangement of sliding shelves emerged, revealing rows of shining enamelled pots before lifting them to be within reach.

Everything could have come straight from a showroom; he saw nothing that appeared to have ever been used. Simili shyly took his hand again and led him into the dining room. An enormous table with at least four chairs down either side, plus two larger chairs at both ends, took centre stage. A sideboard stood to one side of the table and a matching, but smaller, chest of drawers stood the other. The design was very ornate, very fussy, but in highly polished, interestingly grained wood with many layers of clear lacquer giving a deep rich look to the surface. Arthur was sure he had seen similar from an Italian manufacturer at one of the home shows he still attended from time to time. Above the table were two elaborate chandeliers, large enough to light a small ballroom. The shelves of the sideboard were laden with an odd mixture of objects in silver, gold and brass.

'It's, ummh... very nice,' he commented as she led him through the door at the opposite end.

The living room was furnished with an L-shaped sofa and matching footstool in white leather with a large glass-topped coffee table nestling in the centre of the L. The depth of the seats on the sofa looked to be far too great to sit on comfortably, without the overabundance of red silk cushions dotted about to support one's back. Arthur smiled and wondered if it was ever used for backup sleeping accommodation; it could probably sleep at least three people comfortably, he thought, without one knowing the other two were even there. Opposite this stood one of the largest flat-screen televisions he had ever seen. He wondered if it was only used for playing DVDs, he had not seen another television since arriving and wondered if there could be any reception in this remote area. There were two white console tables with oversized red vases of flowers and one other matching leather chair, but the room was so large that it still looked under furnished. One end of the room was almost completely glass, with sliding doors pulled open that overlooked a patio. The patio was shaded with an enormous green and white striped awning that extended over most of it. Beyond, he could see a garden with putting green quality lawns and carefully manicured shrubs.

A marble staircase with a polished brass handrail and glass panels dominated the opposite end and appeared to be the next objective on Simili's tour. 'I show you... beds... room?'

'Bedrooms.' Arthur corrected.

'Yes,' she smiled, 'bed... rooms.'

Arthur lost count of the number of bedrooms. Each was expensively furnished with oversized beds and matching chests of drawers and bedside tables. Some of the beds had ornate gilt bedsteads; others were adorned with elaborate headboards of biscuited upholstery in plush fabrics; all were littered with brightly coloured pillows and duvets that appeared to be of silk.

There were several bathrooms, some en suite, in various colours of granite. One that appeared to be the largest held a bath easily big enough for four people to bathe in at the same time. Arthur wondered if he and Simili would be sharing it later. Off the main bedroom was a bathroom with walls, floors, twin basins and the shower, all in reddish-brown granite. Above the bath were two small louvered doors, not unlike a serving hatch between a kitchen and dining room that would enable one bathing to carry on a conversation with someone on the nearby bed.

The walls of nearly all the rooms were decorated with large paintings of tigers; close up paintings of tigers' heads, paintings of complete animals, tigers engaged in devouring their kill, and tigers gazing purposefully into the far distance. The rendition of the animals was by a skilful artist, but the support of every painting was of burnished copper; copper which had been scored with hundreds of tiny grooves radiating from the centre and catching the light in such a manner as to simulate a halo around the animal, regardless of the angle from which it was viewed. Despite the accurate rendition of the animals, the overall effect to Arthur was of something cheap and tawdry, as if it had been won at some carnival sideshow. He could not help but compare this garish display with the quiet good taste of Rani's beautiful home.

When Simili had completed her tour and Arthur had made the correct complimentary noises, she led him back to the living room and indicated he was to sit next to her on the amazing sofa. As he sat down, he could not resist clowning about and pretending to fall over, provoking unrestrained laughter from Simili. She hastily piled cushions behind him for support. They sat in an awkward silence for a few minutes until Simili stood up and disappeared in the direction of the dining room, after shaking her head and indicating with a finger for Arthur to remain seated when he had also started to rise.

She returned within minutes, carrying a silver tray with two tumbler-sized gold-rimmed glasses. They were filled with a slightly amber-coloured, familiar looking liquid. Arthur accepted the offered glass as she took the remaining and sat the tray on the low table in front of them. This time she sat so close that one of her knees was rubbing against his.

'Cheers,' Arthur said, raising the glass to his lips. It was some form of aqui, but with an unusual taste, a little like melon, but spicier. After the fieriness of the first sip receded, the aftertaste reminded him of something from his past. It took a few seconds to identify it, but it suddenly reminded him of his earlier years in America where he had developed a fondness for pumpkin pie. This had a similar bland sweetness that had been made more interesting with the addition of cinnamon and nutmeg.

'Che...ers,' Simili echoed, raising her glass and taking a large gulp. Arthur was amazed; such a mouthful would have completely taken his breath away, but she seemed unfazed and looked at him over the top of her glass with large provocative eyes.

'Your house is nice,' Arthur said, trying to initiate a conversation. He tried in his mind to justify the little lie with the excuse of wanting to avoid offending, but knowing it was a deliberate compromise.

'Yes,' she replied, and took another large sip.

'Do you live here all on your own?'

'Ye...es?'

'Have you lived here very long?'

'Ummh, yes?'

'Still, everything looks very new.'

'Ye...es...'

'Your kitchen,' Arthur said, thinking of the unused look, 'it's very grand, do you like to cook?' When she didn't reply, but merely looked at him in an unnerving manner, he continued, 'I mean, you have room to entertain many guests, do you like to have friends stay?'

Again, she didn't reply but merely sat her empty glass on the coffee table. As she leapt to her feet and disappeared in the direction of the dining room once again, Arthur noticed that the glass had left a wet ring around its bottom. Simili reappeared within moments carrying a jug that matched the gold-rimmed glasses in one hand and a small towel in the other. She sat the half-filled jug carefully on the tray in front of them and wiped the bottom of her glass with the towel before placing it alongside the jug. After a feverish wipe at the wet ring, she painstakingly folded the towel and placed it beside the tray. Arthur was undecided whether this display was one of obsessiveness or merely nervousness because of the situation.

He suddenly realized Simili was asking him a question even though he was unable to understand her. She pointed at the glass in his hand, raised the jug, and looked at him in a questioning manner. 'Oh yes, please,' he nodded, extending his hand. She took the glass from him and holding it over the tray, carefully topped up its hardly dented contents. Handing it back to him she repeated the procedure with her own glass.

'Che...ers,' she repeated, taking an unladylike gulp that half-emptied the glass.

Her action encouraged Arthur to at least try and show his appreciation of the spicy, sweet liquid. He took a much larger sip than before and swallowed quickly, but it still scalded his throat and mouth. Determined not to look a wimp, he took another as soon as the burning subsided and he found it less fiery. By the time he had drained his glass, his mouth was either numb or he had become accustomed to its effect. Simili had already sat her empty glass on the tray and placed his beside it.

She stroked his knee a few times and stood up, pulling Arthur to his feet as well. 'I show you... garden.'

They walked hand in hand across the patio and onto the lush grass lawn, past the tinkling fountain in the centre of a large round pool and into a smaller shrub enclosed space. He noticed in a far corner of the garden the top of a large satellite dish protruding above a row of shrubs. The answer to the question he had had in his mind about the television set was so simple.

Simili had released his hand and lagged behind him as he admired the display of blossom in the circular beds adjacent to the shrubs. When he turned back to her, he saw she had untied the overlapping belts of her top and had exposed her breasts to his view. The implication was made more obvious by her slight swaying from side to side and he reached out to touch her. She suddenly grasped his head in both hands and pulled him roughly towards her, nearly causing him to stumble. With one quick motion, she forced his head down and pulled it firmly into her bosom, wiping it from one side to the other. He could feel her affectionately rubbing his ears as he flicked his tongue at a moving target, before pulling his head to the other side, making little whimpering noises as she did.

His first thought on seeing her unclad was that her breasts didn't look quite real; too large, too much like those on the covers of magazines on the top shelves of his local newsagent. He had often wondered what surgically enhanced breasts felt like; would there be an unnatural firmness where the implants were located, or would they even taste differently. He had never had the chance to find out. But these were of a wonderful texture, the perfect mixture of firmness and softness. There was no difference in the feel anywhere his face made contact. And every part of his face was making contact. She kept moving his head around so that one moment his chin was pushed into their yielding pliability and the next, his forehead. His eye sockets would be alternately filled with firm and fully erect nipples, causing him to suddenly close his eyes in defence, before he would again have his mouth centred over one or the other.

The rubbing of his ears became more and more animated, almost furious, and then ceased as she put one hand around the back of his neck, but continued to pull his head forcefully into her breasts. He felt the other hand feeling at his collar and then move further down as she tried to unbutton his *kurti*. After more impatient struggles with the unyielding fastenings a growl-like snarl came from her throat and he felt the jacket being savagely ripped apart and pushed off his shoulders. A moment later he was lifted bodily off his feet leaving his legs dangling in mid-air. Simili had released the hold on his neck and he was able to take a couple of deep breaths as she removed the loose pyjamas, pushing them clear of his legs and feet. For a moment when his feet touched the ground again, he was able to stand and admire this passionate creature in front of him, until she put a hand on each of his shoulders, forcing him to his knees. Before he could regain his balance, she had pushed him over backwards and he could feel the soft warm grass welcoming him. She stepped forward, straddling him and in one motion, unwrapped the sash and long skirt she was wearing. He had a glimpse of long shapely legs as his eyes were drawn up to the dark triangle where they joined together. She lowered herself to her knees, then reaching between her thighs, guided him into her.

This isn't too bad, Arthur thought as he watched her above him, her breasts brushing his face with each thrust of her hips. After his unbelievable experiences with Ashri, Zanli, and Yetti, he had worried that normal sexual relationships might be disappointing when he returned to England. If he were to ever resume normal marital relations with Ester that is, but even without the prolonged foreplay he had come to expect or the explosive kissing of his recent encounters, he was finding this wonderfully enjoyable.

Suddenly Simili grasped his head with both hands again as she had earlier, but instead of pulling his face into her breasts, held him immovable as she locked her mouth onto his. The same fireworks he had felt with the other young women exploded inside his head and the intense, unbearable pain surged through his entire body. Almost immediately, he was turned into a volcano as white-hot lava erupted from within him. The epicentre of his pain was centred on the searing torrent of burning liquid and his own hips thrust upwards in a series of involuntary spasms. Somewhere on the periphery of his awareness, he felt Simili must have been feeling the same as her body stiffened and clung to his. She removed her mouth from his just long enough to give one long piercing scream of agony, before clamping her lips over his again.

They lay on their backs together in the grass, panting. Arthur was ashamed of his early delivery, a problem that had plagued him from his youth. Over the years he had learned to think of other things or to work on puzzles in his head in order to slow his mad rush towards completion, instead of concentrating too much on the very thing he wanted. Simili spoke so little English, he thought, would she be able to understand his apology? Could she comprehend that at his age, recovery to make a second attempt might take all evening?

His thoughts were interrupted as she suddenly leapt to her feet, bent over him and grabbed one of his hands. 'Come,' she grunted, and pulled him to his feet. He was unable to stop himself laughing as a ridiculous thought occurred to him. She looked at him questioningly, but he knew he would be unable to explain and just shook his head. She sat off at a run, firmly holding on to his hand, with him stumbling along behind. Water splashed under their feet as she took a shortcut through the shallow pool and seconds later passed through the opened sliding glass doors. Simili paused momentarily in front of the enormous couch before turning and lowering herself onto the white leather. Without releasing the hold on Arthur's hand she pulled him to his knees, then with her other hand savagely pulled his head between her parted legs.

The blinding euphoria he had expected to feel a few minutes earlier flooded over him, as his tongue tasted the wetness there. She continued to rub his face around in the same manner as she had around her breasts and he could feel the heightened awareness of each other that had developed with his previous couplings. He could share the mounting pleasure that Simili was feeling and at the same time could feel himself responding. He could also feel her pleasure in knowing he was responding. The intensity of the shared ecstasy rose, ascended and soared until she threw her head back and again screamed with delight.

Before their mutual pleasure could plunge into the peaceful calmness Arthur expected, Simili lifted him bodily, thrusting his fully recovered state fully into her and pulling his mouth down to meet her own. Once again, the elation they shared rose even further as she guided him rhythmically in and out, until after only a few more minutes their unbearably stimulating experience was repeated. Unable to stop himself, Arthur joined in Simili's screams as the culmination of their efforts went on and on; seemingly for far longer than the preceding contributory labours.

As the floating sensation arrived, Arthur rolled over onto the expanse of leather and relaxed, feeling Simili's warm form next to him, still gently caressing his skin. He could not help but smile with contentment. His fears of a disappointing encounter withdrew and he smiled inwardly, secretly pleased that he had recovered so quickly.

Before he could relish the sensation for very long, Simili had risen and pulled him to his feet once again. Wordlessly, she again took one of his hands and guided him towards the dining room. As they entered, Arthur looked around, but could see no reason for their being there. Perhaps, he thought, she was going to offer him something more to drink, but she turned to him and again locked him into a firm embrace. Her lips engaged his and he felt the surge of pleasure engulfing him again. He was almost unaware of the cool marble beneath him as she pushed him to the floor before lowering herself on top of him. She continued to hold him in her arms for several minutes, her kissing becoming more and more passionate as the shared pyrotechnics of pleasure wafted over them both. As she released her hold around his shoulders and waist, moving her hands to either side of his face, he felt her envelope him once again.

God, he thought, this must be paradise. To be able to respond and perform twice so quickly was unheard of, at least for anyone of his age, but to still be enlarged and ready for a third attempt was unbelievable. When she had rocked back and forth to bring them to another peak of mutual sensation, savagely slapping the sides of his face all the while, he was finally beginning to feel exhausted.

A sudden weariness overcame him and he was almost unable to rise. Simili impatiently pulled him to his feet. He could feel her nibbling at the back of his neck and shoulders as she pushed him towards the kitchen. Thoughts that were so out of place in this situation filled his head and he couldn't help chuckling to himself. He vividly remembered friends of his, many years ago, laughing as they related how, when they were first married, they had wanted to make love in every room of their new home. I'll bet, he thought to himself, they hadn't been able to do it all in one evening.

By the time they had finished in the kitchen, Arthur's legs were so weak, he was incapable of standing. Everything about him was limp and floppy except for the one part which seemed to have grown enormously. As Simili tried to get him to a standing position, he caught sight of himself and he couldn't help laughing aloud. He remembered seeing a nature film about whales; narwhales in particular. At the time they had seemed a little awkward, despite having an entire ocean to swim in they seemed to flock together and always looked as if they were in danger of spearing each other with their long protruding tusks. Arthur laughed again as he reminded himself not to get too close to walls or furniture, as he might do irreparable damage to something.

Simili appeared to give up trying to get Arthur to stand and grasping his head in a wrestler's arm lock, simply started dragging him along behind her. The backs of Arthur's ankles and calves bounced from step to step as she ascended the stairs and he was unable to breath with her wrist across his throat, but he felt no pain. He laughed again as another image from so long ago filled his head. His dear Phyllis was kneeling in front of a little girl, showing her how to hold a kitten.

Of course, it was the same friends he had thought of only a little earlier; he and Ski had found a litter of kittens at an old house they had been renovating. They had seen the body of the mother cat at the side of the driveway, presumably killed by a passing car and a day or two later, three mewling kittens, their eyes barely open, had emerged from their hiding place. Two of the kittens had gone to one of the other the workers and Ski had taken the remaining one home to his two daughters. When Arthur and Phyllis had visited a few days later, Jennifer, the elder of the two was dragging the protesting kitten around wherever she went, one arm around its neck. Phyllis had patiently shown her how to support the kitten's body with one palm and wrist while stroking and restraining it from fleeing with the other hand. At five, Jennifer had had to be shown time and time again, before she could be trusted with the long-suffering animal, but Phyllis had quietly persevered and before long the kitten appeared to be content to be carried.

Arthur lost count of the rooms he was dragged into. He was no longer able to see; only shadowy forms appeared in the greyness that surrounded him as he descended from the white hot euphoric pleasure into a chasm of pain. At times he lay on his back on marble-surfaced floors, at other times he felt downy, satiny bedclothes beneath him. While his mouth, tongue and lips had still functioned, his face had been repeatedly thrust into the wetness at the top of her thighs and once positioned for the maximum effect, those thighs had clamped so tightly on his head that it was impossible for him to breathe. At the same time, other parts of him were constantly being caressed, licked, bitten or stroked.

Now, he was lying on top of her; his head lolling uselessly against her breasts as she lifted him by the hips to provide the endless, rhythmic, thrusting motion she craved. That's me, he thought through the blinding pain, just a ragdoll attached to a giant dildo. Suddenly he was aware of another firm pair of hands on him and he was physically lifted free of Simili. Despite his pain, he could not suppress his laughter as his mind saw a giant electrical plug being pulled from its socket. He knew however, that the snarls he heard were not imagined, nor were the sounds of blows being struck. He heard whimpering sounds behind him as he was tenderly wrapped in something soft, lifted as easily as a baby into strong arms and carried down the stairs.

Chapter Thirty

The sounds of birds singing moved stealthily into the anxiety dreams Arthur was experiencing. He struggled to distinguish reality from the imaginary, and was still sure that he was late for something, that he had failed to prepare properly for some long-ago exam, or that he had forgotten to pay for an item in a store and had set off an alarm at the exit, to be caught by a security guard. He sat up, opened his eyes, and saw the now familiar sight of broken sunlight filtering through the tree outside his bedroom and felt the cool breeze coming in through the open window. He realized he was taking short nervous breaths and lay back down on his bed, trying to regain control of his breathing.

'Are you alright?' he heard someone say softly. He turned his head so that he could see the half-open door. Yetti's anxious face was peering through the opening. 'I thought I heard you say something.'

'I just woke up,' he said, stretching. 'Ahh, that's better. I must have been dreaming.'

'How do you feel?' Yetti asked, sitting on the edge of his bed and reaching over to kiss him on the forehead.

Arthur sat up, stretched again and put one arm around her waist, pulling her closer to him. She was wearing one of the white towelling robes; he assumed she must have stayed the night, but he was no longer surprised by any of the comings and goings of this household. 'Hungry is, I think, the answer to that question.' He leaned over and returned her kiss in the same manner.

She looked at him earnestly, her face inches away and smiled for the first time since entering the room. 'Do you really feel like eating something?'

He yawned, took a deep breath and stretched again. The worrying feeling of something amiss had faded. 'Umh yes, I could definitely eat something. I'm really quite ravenous,' he saw the concerned look come over Yetti's face again. 'It isn't too early is it?'

'I'll just tell Ashri,' Yetti said, rising from the bed. 'She is helping Aszli this morning.'

Arthur pushed the coverlet down and turned as if to follow her, but she put a hand on his shoulder, restraining him. 'No no, stay there. We'll bring you a tray.'

'I don't want to be any trouble,' he protested. 'I'm perfectly capable...' He stopped as his eyes followed hers. His waist was almost covered with large square plasters. He pushed the coverlet further and could see the chequerboard of plasters continued down both thighs. He raised one hand to his neck, as he was suddenly aware of something around his throat and could feel he was covered in one continuous bandage from his chin to halfway down his chest.

'Bites,' Yetti explained, 'you were covered in bite marks. Well, actually, you were covered in blood when Zanli brought you in, but when we washed you off we could see where she had bitten you again and again. A couple of the bites needed stitches.'

Arthur gave an involuntary shudder when he remembered some of the more unpleasant aspects of his encounter with Simili. 'I don't understand how...'

'*Uudontha* root,' Yetti said. It meant nothing to Arthur. 'It was probably in aqui,' she went on, 'did you drink some aqui?'

'Yes,' Arthur tried to remember. 'We both did. I didn't think anything of it.'

'Zanli thought it must have been something like that. She had heard of it, of course, but had never come into contact with it. Rani recognized it straight away. She said your breath stunk of it, and called Noni. That was before they realized you would need stitches, so it was just as well she was already on her way.'

'What is *uudontha* root?' Arthur asked, still puzzled.

'It's banned,' Yetti said, shaking her head, 'it has been for generations. It's a leftover from our darker past. Our foremothers used to use it long ago, when they captured a man. If it was a young man, he would still, how would you say it, fuck himself to death,

240

but it sustained him and made him last longer. He could usually service fifteen or twenty before he expired.'

'But why?'

'There have been times when the surrounding villagers were deathly afraid of us. They would attack us on sight, because they thought we would steal their men. And we did, of course, when we needed daughters. We have made peace with them since we learned to have just one man that could father our daughters, but there are still those who distrust us. These hill villagers are uneducated, superstitious people. I've heard of more than one taking pot-shots at our people on the roads to the valley.'

'Seriously?'

'Oh yes. That is why the couriers who make trips everyday to the surrounding villages dye themselves green. It was an agreement long ago to show that they were on business and that they posed no threat.'

'I thought that was some kind of a joke,' Arthur laughed. 'You know, another wind-up like the girls did on my first day.'

'I'm sorry,' Yetti said, moving towards the door, 'I must be tiring you with my prattle. I'll see if I can hurry Ashri. Will you be alright for a minute or two?'

Before Arthur could reply, Ashri entered carrying a tray laden with breakfast things. It looked to Arthur enough to feed several people. She sat the tray on his bedside table, before turning to him and hugging his head to her bosom. As she rocked him back and forth in her arms, she murmured, 'Oh Arthur, Arthur, how could we have let this happen to you?'

'It's okay,' he managed to articulate through Ashri's overlapping arms, 'I'm alright. There's no permanent damage done.'

Ashri released him from her grasp, only to take his face in both hands and look meaningfully at him with large round concerned eyes. 'Are you sure you're able to eat? I can feed you if you like.'

'Honest, I'm fine, but that breakfast looks great.'

Ashri removed the tray from the bedside table and placed it on the bed in front of Arthur, before sitting down, side-saddle fashion facing him. Yetti took up a mirrored position on the other side of the bed.

'Don't gulp your food if you're that hungry,' Yetti warned, 'take little bites and chew them well'.

'Yes, my little mother,' Arthur teased, forking several of the poffertjes onto his plate and pouring the hot chocolate sauce over them. 'Perhaps I should let you feed me after all.'

'No, it is me that should apologize; I am just so concerned for you,' Yetti stroked his upper arm with one hand, the other poised to stop him if he took too large a mouthful.

'Did you and Simili have the same to eat and drink?' Ashri asked.

'Yes, I think so,' Arthur said through a mouthful of the little pancakes. 'Actually, we didn't have anything to eat, just a drink or two.'

'And Simili had the same as you?'

'Well, perhaps a bit more than I did. She was drinking the aqui as if it was water.'

'The stupid girl,' Yetti said unsympathetically, 'it could have killed her'.

'Shouldn't someone see if she is all right?' Arthur asked, 'I mean if she is in any danger...'

'I can't believe you, Arthur,' Ashri protested. 'She tries to kill you and you're concerned about her health. Rani said she was perfectly okay when she went around there yesterday morning. Her mother was there and they were both quite defiant when Rani announced she would take them to the council.'

'I don't believe she actually meant to kill me,' Arthur said, as he gulped a mouthful of tea. 'She just did something stupid.' He paused as her words sank in. 'Wait, you said Rani went there yesterday? Wasn't I there just yesterday?'

'No,' Yetti joined in. 'You slept all day yesterday.'

'You went to Simili's day before yesterday,' Ashri added, 'you've slept all the time since Zanli brought you home. Or perhaps, it's more accurate to say you were unconscious. Rani said you were covered in blood when Zanli brought you in.'

'I think she said you both were,' Yetti corrected. 'She had been driving with one hand; she had the other arm around you to keep you from falling out of your seat.'

'She hasn't left your side since she brought you home, you know.'

'Well, not until a couple of hours ago, when we persuaded her to get some sleep.'

'She blames herself,' Ashri said. 'You must convince her that she has nothing to feel guilty about.'

'Guilty?' Arthur asked in surprise. 'Why should she feel guilty? From what you've said, it isn't just that she rescued me from a situation that was getting unpleasant. It sounds as if she saved my life.'

'That's what we told her,' Yetti said, 'but she thought she had hesitated for too long. She felt that something was wrong as soon as she left you and instead of coming back here, she parked the jeep nearby and waited.'

'She wasn't supposed to pick you up until the following morning,' Ashri said, 'but after a couple of hours, she had such a strong feeling that you were in danger, she went to investigate...'

'You can imagine how she must have been uneasy...'

'It would have been so embarrassing if she had walked in and the two of you were just having afternoon tea.'

'Two hours?' Arthur asked in surprise, 'Zanli came back after two hours? I thought I must have been there for more like two days. It seemed to go on forever.'

'I thought time was supposed to fly by when you're having fun,' Yetti laughed nervously. 'Are you trying to tell us you weren't?'

'Don't make jokes about it,' Ashri scolded. 'Arthur could have died if Zanli hadn't followed her instincts.'

'I didn't mean to make light of the situation,' Yetti said apologetically, 'I guess I'm just so relieved that you're okay.'

Their voices seemed to fade as Arthur was suddenly overcome with a feeling of nausea

'Excuse me,' he said, urgently trying to push the tray aside.

The food he had eaten seemed to swell up inside him and as he attempted to extricate himself from his position between the two women, a further wave of dizziness overwhelmed him. He only just managed to get to the bathroom in time, before his stomach noisily emptied itself of the food he had consumed. He rinsed his face with cold water and turned back to the door. Rani was standing in the opening with an anxious expression on her face.

'Arthur, you must not try to get up,' she said, putting an arm around him. 'Let me help you back to bed.'

He didn't feel like putting up any kind of argument or trying to explain that his sudden trip was mostly involuntary, but as another wave of light-headedness overcame him, he peaceably allowed her to support him as she guided him back to his bed.

Ashri and Zanli still stood either side of the bed, one holding the remains of his breakfast, but Rani motioned for them to leave. She smoothed his bed linen with one hand and turned him so that he could lie back down, before pulling the light coverlet up.

'I'm going to pull your curtains,' she said, 'I can see you're squinting at the light. And you must try to get some more sleep. Can you think of anything you would like before I go?'

Chapter Thirty-One

Arthur awoke to find himself in almost complete darkness; only a little light from a distant candle came in through the open doorway. How long had he slept, he wondered; it had only been the middle of the morning when Rani had ordered him back to bed.

He started to sit up, but the dizziness struck him again and he winced at the stabbing pain in his head. He heard the rustle of someone arising from a chair and soft footsteps as they left the room. Within minutes the light coming through the doorway grew stronger and a figure entered carrying a candle, its flame shielded from his eyes by their free hand. She sat the candle on his bedside table and leaned over him. He could see it was an elderly woman with white hair, only partially covered by a shawl. She looked familiar, but he couldn't remember where or when he had seen her before. At first, Arthur didn't understand her softly spoken words, but from the intonation, he was sure she was asking him a question. When she repeated, what seemed to him the same phrase, he realized she was merely asking him in German how he felt. His German had never been very good at the best of times and was rusty from long lack of use. All he could think of for a reply was, '*vehr gute*'.

The woman gave a soft chuckle. 'I think you are not very good. Otherwise, you would not be lying here like this.'

Arthur desperately tried to remember enough to more accurately describe his condition. 'My head is... *not* very good,' he at last managed.

She put the back of one hand to his forehead and held it there for a moment. Then, from somewhere within the folds of her sari, produced a large fob watch on a shiny blue ribbon and observed it as she felt for the pulse in his wrist.

'We will make you better,' she said, her eyes shining reassuringly as she leaned over him again. 'Drink this.'

She held out a small, curious-looking cup. It resembled a silver milk jug, but with an overgrown, curved spout that was effectively blended into a funnel, allowing him to drink the contents without raising his head.

He could not suppress a laugh. Suddenly he was a child again; accompanying his father to the petrol station on a Saturday morning for the ritual care of their aging Armstrong Siddley. In those days, when petrol pumps were still attended, Arthur loved watching and breathing in the aroma as the tank was filled with petrol. The tyres were then checked and the snaking hose hissed as the pressures were adjusted. The high point of his morning occurred when the elderly attendant lifted the bonnet, revealing a myriad of caps that had to be unscrewed and the contents examined. Finally, the dipstick was withdrawn, wiped clean with a rag that the old man had produced from somewhere, and re-inserted. The second time it was removed, he would carefully lift it until it almost touched his glasses. Then, peering over the top of those thick lenses, he would say to Arthur, 'I think she's going to need at least a pint.'

No other aspect of his morning, not even patiently waiting to see which lollipop, pack of sweets, or crisps, his father had chosen in the kiosk as his *surprise* held as much suspense for him as waiting, not daring to breathe in case the man failed to add, 'Are you going to help me, little man?'

He would trot alongside as the attendant limped to a wooden shed attached to the kiosk. Within was a stout wooden bench holding three metal barrels, lying on their sides. Above the barrels a shelf with objects hidden under a thick, creamy coloured cloth ran the length of the bench. Rows of shiny black tyres with white sticky labels lined one wall, but they held no interest for Arthur. The attendant would lift the dust cloth to reveal a row of dark green metal jugs, each with a funnel-like extension set at an angle. The jugs were identical except for size, graduating from large to small, evenly spaced and arranged to all point in the same direction, as if soldiers on parade. The appropriate jug was selected, according to the demand of the dipstick, and placed under the tap of one of the barrels. The tap would be slowly turned and a viscous stream of translucent, greeny-gold liquid would begin to flow, picking up the light from the doorway behind them so that it seemed to glow of its own accord as it silently fell into the jug. When the jug was filled, Arthur would accompany his mentor back to the car to watch as the filler cap was removed and the jug tipped slightly, letting its precious contents flow into the engine without ever spilling a drop.

The little jug above him was beautifully proportioned, simply shaped with a curving handle set to one side, and its inside surface of gold caught the light in an almost hypnotic fashion, but as he drifted back to a dreamless sleep, he could only think that its function was the same as those rolled-tin objects of his childhood. Its contents of bitter-sweet tasting aqui had been tipped into his mouth without spilling a drop, and without his having to even lift his head.

***

Arthur struggled to wake again, but his aching head and the discomfort in his arms and legs made him immediately regret it. He thought of trying to regain the relief of sleep, but something was nagging at him. He had been dreaming; dreaming about Phyllis. Why was it that she would force her way into his mind whenever he was least prepared? Without any conscious thought, he let the memories from long ago flood into his present awareness, concentrating on them, letting them help block the pain.

It had been in the second semester of his second year at university. The cheques from home, to help with his daily expenses, had become without warning, fewer and for smaller amounts. He had taken a part-time job, serving in one of the dormitory cafeterias, but it was only enough to help with his meals and left little to pay for any extras. Although his tuition was taken care of by the trust, he still needed to pay for his room, books and regular fees. His parents had originally sent regular amounts that left enough, after the essentials were paid, to see the occasional cinema or *movie* and meet other students in the union for cokes after classes. With the reduced income from home, he was rapidly eating into his small reserves and he reluctantly sought, once again, the advice of Mr Roberts, his student counsellor.

The man was probably only in his early thirties, but gave the appearance of someone much older. Overweight, with a ruddy complexion, a clip-on bow tie and a collar that seemed always to be choking him, he gave the impression to Arthur, of someone who would rather be doing something, perhaps anything, else.

'So, the cafeteria job isn't working out?' he asked, through a mouthful of the sandwich that lay, without benefit of a plate or napkin, on his desk. 'I said you wouldn't get rich.'

'It's okay, I like the work and it means my meals don't cost me anything, now,' Arthur replied, 'but I can't get enough hours to give me more than a few dollars at the end of the week'.

'And that's not enough?' The sandwich dangled indecisively in mid-air, as if trying to fly, then committed suicide between the nicotine-yellowed teeth.

'Well, not really.' Arthur hated to be seen as begging. 'I've got more fees to pay by mid-semester and I'm using up what little cash I've got.'

'I *have* more fees; what little cash I *have*,' Mr Roberts had corrected pedantically. 'We try not to use *got* in this country any more than necessary. Especially after *have*. If you say *I've*, it's a contraction of *I have*. Have got, it sounds dreadful, like some kid from the wrong side of the tracks. Don't they teach you English in England?'

Arthur had overlooked the fact that Mr Roberts was his Composition and Rhetoric lecturer; he just seemed to stumble from one mistake to another.

'Anyway,' Mr Roberts said, laughing at his own little joke and suddenly relaxed now that his outburst of indignation had re-established his superior position, 'you have a social security number, right? And your food handlers permit for the cafeteria job?'

Arthur nodded acquiescence; his interlocutor had been helpful in obtaining the former and fortunately not the latter, which had required the perplexing indignity for Arthur of obtaining a stool sample.

'So,' continued Roberts, 'if you can do more hours, see this guy. I know he's looking for an evening person.'

He tore a piece of paper from the notepad on his desk and carefully wrote a name and address on it. Arthur had glanced at the note as it was handed to him. "Phillips Drug Store" and a telephone number, was written on it in a surprisingly beautiful, almost calligraphic script.

'You know the place?' Roberts had asked. 'Just go up College Avenue to where it meets Main Street, turn left and it's in the second block on your right. He's an okay guy if you treat him right and do the job. And he'll pay you what you're worth, but if you screw up, you'll be out on your ear. I'll give him a bell this afternoon and let him know you're coming. Just turn up after your last classes. Okay?'

'Okay,' Arthur had turned to go.

'One other thing,' Roberts had added, a hint of a smirk on his chubby face. 'It's only a couple of blocks from the High School and the place gets filled up after school with young poontang. Don't be tempted! You get caught putting it to any of that jailbait and I don't mean if somebody sees you, I mean if they run tell daddy, or mama wrings it out of them, you'll go straight to jail. Five years minimum. The laws on statutory are very unforgiving in this state.'

Mr Phillips was tall and though middle-aged, almost athletically lean, with closely cropped, crew-cut, sandy hair that was rapidly going out of fashion. Arthur presumed he was of the right age to have been in the war, but his slightly military bearing seemed out of keeping somehow with the role of a pharmacist and drug store owner. His manner was pleasant however, with an engaging smile and he asked a stream of friendly questions about Arthur, his background, how he fitted in at the university as a foreigner, and his ambitions. His questions were interspersed between bouts of telling Arthur about the various departments within the store. The questions were innocuous enough, but Arthur realized, were ultimately enough to build a comprehensive image if answered truthfully. Arthur also believed that if he had tried to *bullshit* his way through the informal interview, he would have been rapidly caught out. He was grateful he had not been tempted to exaggerate or hide anything.

The store was, Arthur learned later, typical of an American drugstore, with full-length plate glass windows either side of the entrance. A central aisle led past displays of health-related items on one side and greeting cards, magazines, comics and paperbacks, slotted into a rotating wire-framed rack, on the other.

The paperbacks all seemed to be westerns or detective novels, Arthur recognized some of the more popular authors like Mickey Spillane and Zane Grey. Most had lurid covers of well-endowed young women in revealing apparel, torn blouses or gaping dressing robes, being threatened by thuggish, unshaven outlaws or gangsters, while a clean cut cowboy or detective in the background tried to rescue them. Arthur smiled to himself as he realized that the unshaven look no longer signified someone of disreputable character, but was now considered the height of fashion.

The aisle led past a soda fountain with a number of swivelling-seat bar stools and a high counter. Atop the counter was a collection of dispensers; slightly reminiscent of the beer engines common in pubs at home, but chromium instead of brass, and taller with smaller handles. After eighteen months in America, he had seen these used many times to produce sodas and soft drinks, but he still found them fascinating and looked forward to learning their functions. Behind the counter was another chromium machine with rotating shafts that could hold tall stainless steel cups for making milkshakes. Not the thin, watery, artificially flavoured concoctions of his childhood, but thick, freezing cold mixtures of good quality ice cream, usually rich chocolate sauce and milk, that took half an hour to devour. Alongside this machine was a hotplate holding three of the double globe, hourglass shaped glass jugs which Arthur knew were used for making coffee.

Mr Phillips had led him past these arrays of Americana, briefly pointing out certain aspects while continuing to ask Arthur questions about himself. Arthur noticed there were only two customers at the counter, chatting with the young woman serving. If it was always this quiet, he wondered why Mr Phillips seemed so anxious to fill the position. They continued past the serving counter through a wide opening in the partition wall, into an area with two rows of high-backed booths, each easily large enough for four adults. Marks on the floor gave evidence that another booth had once been positioned at the corner, but this had been replaced with a jukebox. Arthur had seen and occasionally used similar machines, there was one in the student union with a comprehensive library of rock and roll music, but was unable to resist stopping to admire this display of polished wood, neon, and shiny metal workings clearly visible through the glass front.

'You may get to hate this machine when you hear the same song being played over and over,' Mr Phillips laughed, 'but I hope that won't put you off'.

'I don't think that's enough to cause me a problem,' Arthur said. 'I quite like music.'

'I'll ask you how you feel about it again in a few weeks, that is, if you decide to take the job. The kids can be a little noisy at times and are always asking to have the volume turned up, but I have the controls locked. I work back there,' Mr Phillips pointed at a raised prescription counter behind the booths, 'so I can help to keep order at the busiest times, but there will only be the two of you for most of the evening'.

It had been that simple. They had agreed upon times when Arthur could work and Mr Phillips had introduced him to Carol, the young woman he had seen at the serving counter. There had been three days a week when Arthur's classes finished in time for him to start work before four o'clock, the time when a deluge of high school students descended upon the drugstore, and all day on Saturdays. Finishing at nine o'clock would leave him only so much time for studying at night, but he thought he could manage with early mornings and studying during his lunchtime.

The first few days of work had been confusing. The workings of the dispensers had been far more complicated than it had looked. Handles pushed or pulled the wrong way would result in ruined drinks and Arthur found it difficult to remember orders taken from the booths amid the shouting of rowdy teenagers. Fortunately, at the busiest times the drink orders were the simplest. The high school students would almost always order one of the two most popular cola drinks. Arthur was completely unable to distinguish between the two, but failure on his part to produce the correct item was almost invariably detected. In an attempted display of sophistication amongst some of the older students, coffee was ordered. Any of the younger students overheard ordering, what was considered by the older ones, to be a childish concoction, would usually be chided with laughter and jeers of; 'Hey everyone, little Bobby wants an *ice cream soda!*' Not many students had ordered sodas or sundaes twice during crowded times.

Arthur had taken an immediate liking to Carol, the young woman he had met at his interview. With long dark hair framing an oval face above a trim figure, she was, he guessed, about ten years his senior and admitted to having worked in the drugstore since leaving high school. Her friendly, positive and energetic manner made her seem capable of much greater things, but she changed the subject and appeared uncomfortable when he voiced the subject. He found her very patient, both when instructing him at the soda fountain and with awkward or elderly customers in the other departments and with her help he had gained some confidence in his own skills within a short time.

Some of the customers proved to be trying; not so much at peak times when they were so busy talking about the day's activities and vying with each other to gain the crowd's attention, but later in the evening when many drifted back in, after having had their evening meals, he assumed.

Girls, some only a couple of years younger than himself, would pretend to swoon when he went to take their orders, or sit up in an exaggerated formal manner and effect a phony English accent – 'Oh, I do thank you so very much' – when he served them. He overheard barely suppressed conversations comparing him to David Niven or James Mason; he found neither particularly flattering, but took it for granted that it was intended to be. He also assumed they were the only English actors the girls had been exposed to with the scarcity of English films available.

Some of the boys were a little more trouble; probably, he thought, due to the attention he was receiving from the girls. Most of it was completely harmless and he forgot just how many times he had heard, 'Oh, I say old bean, pip, pip and all that, old chap', in a similarly feeble attempt to sound English. Who, Arthur wondered, had given Americans the notion that the English had ever said, 'pip, pip'? One young man, with short ginger hair and a heavily freckled face, but taller than Arthur when he stood up, was particularly adversarial and regularly made unfavourable comments. One busy evening he had become unusually vociferous. 'Hey Limey, what's it like living in a country that has to call in the Americans every time they get in trouble?'

Arthur thought for a placatory answer, refusing to take the bait, but before he could reply, a boy from an adjoining booth shouted back. 'What's your problem, Terry? My dad was over there in the war and he said the English, he called them Tommies, were really good fighters.'

'Yeah,' another joined in, 'they had them commandos, didn't they?'

'Well,' Terry went on, 'my uncle was over there in the war and he says it was a shit country. He said it rained all the time, you couldn't get any decent hamburgers, they had warm beer that tasted like piss and the girls would screw you for a pair of stockings.'

Arthur fought to suppress his anger and managed to reply in a steady voice. 'That was during the war. There was a shortage of everything and we had bombs coming through our roofs. You never knew if you were going to be next and I think people could be forgiven if they just wanted to live for the day.'

Mr Phillips had suddenly materialized at Arthur's elbow. Arthur hadn't been aware that he was still in the building. Perhaps he had been taking stock at the front; his usual position at the pharmacy counter, where he could overlook the booths had been empty.

'Terry,' he had addressed the aggressive youth in a quiet voice. 'I expect my staff to be friendly, helpful and respectful towards all our customers. And, I expect our customers to return the favour. If you can't do that, I'll have to ask you to take your custom elsewhere.'

The boy had appeared to shrink into his seat. 'Yes, Mr Phillips,' he had replied quietly. The surrounding booths were completely silent.

'You see,' he had continued, 'I was in England during the war too, up until D-Day, that is. And most of the people I met had it really hard, but they were always friendly and welcoming to us Yanks. So, it makes me a little angry when I hear anyone bad-mouthing them, you know, 'cause in their ignorance, they thought we were somehow superior, or better, just because we had a lot more.'

'Yes, sir.'

'So, I hope we'll see you back again, if you can behave, but if you can't, then I don't want you in here, okay?'

'Yes, sir,' the boy had whiningly repeated, 'I didn't mean to cause any trouble, I was just joking'.

'Sure, son,' Mr Phillips had put a hand on the young man's shoulder and patted it once before turning and walking back towards the front of the store.

The buzz of conversation quickly rose from a few quiet whispers to its usual volume and Arthur remembered what he was doing before the interruption. 'Who was next?' he asked, to be answered by a request for a cherry coke from an attractive dark-haired girl.

One evening as he had been cleaning booths, wiping down the counter and washing the last of the glasses in preparation for closing, a young woman he had not seen before had entered and taken a stool at the counter. She was older than his usual evening crowd of students, wearing a dark suit and white blouse and was encumbered with a heavy-looking briefcase.

'Is it too late,' she had enquired wearily, 'to get a cup of coffee?'

Arthur glanced at the clock behind him. It showed less than ten minutes till closing, but there were still three or four customers in the booths at the back. He knew the glass coffee jug was still half-full, but he had made the last batch nearly two hours earlier.

'I'm afraid it won't be very fresh,' he said apologetically, as he filled a cup with the dark liquid and placed it in front of her, 'but you're welcome to try it. If it isn't fit to drink, you don't have to pay for it.' He remembered that had been Carol's admonition in a similar circumstance.

The young woman had sipped tentatively, after adding milk and stirring in a spoonful of sugar, and then had taken a larger mouthful.

'That's better,' she said appreciatively, before taking a second gulp, 'I don't suppose you have anything left to eat?'

Arthur looked at the clock again; he knew Mr Phillips would

be arriving within minutes to empty the till, but it would take him several minutes to count the day's takings while Arthur evicted the hangers-on in the back and finished the last of the sweeping.

'I can fix you a bowl of soup or chilli.'

'I'll go for the chilli, please. You're sure you don't mind?'

'I can't let anyone starve, can I?' he joked as he opened a tin, placed it in the circular heater that would bring it to a scalding temperature within minutes, then arranged a bowl, spoon and two of the little cellophane wrapped packets of saltines on a tray before resuming his place at the sink. When the timer announced the chilli to be sufficiently heated, he had removed the can with the padded gloves kept for that purpose and carefully emptied it into the bowl he had prepared. As he placed the tray with its steaming contents if front of her, he noticed she had drained her cup.

'It's very hot,' he warned, 'so be careful; there's plenty of time. Would you like a refill on the coffee? It won't cost you anything. I'm about to pitch it if you don't want any more.'

'That's a really great recommendation and it is pretty bad,' she paused to gently blow over a spoonful of the steaming chilli to cool it, 'but it's wet. And I don't think it'll keep me awake tonight.'

She crumbled both packets of saltines into the bowl, turning the soupy concoction into a pasty texture, before tasting another spoonful. Arthur had been appalled when he had first seen someone do this, but had tried it out of curiosity and become an immediate convert.

Mr Phillips had entered the front door, precisely at nine o'clock and slipped the night latch that would allow customers to exit, but prevent anyone else entering.

'Working late again, Phyllis?' he had asked as he slipped behind the counter. His voice was affectionate, empathetic and implied this was more routine than not.

'Sure am, Mr P,' her reply was equally affectionate and the weariness was suddenly replaced with an unforced cheeriness. 'Monthly report has to go out at the end of the week.'

'I'll bet you've had a lot of good help, haven't you?' His slightly ironic tone implied otherwise.

'Well, you know, Mr Gibbs always needs to double check on some of the farmers' acreages,' she laughed, 'and it's always the ones the furthest away that might be fudging a little, so by the time he gets back, it's far too late to come back into the office'.

'That poor man,' Mr Phillips had said mockingly, 'he really works his fingers to the bone'.

It seemed to Arthur to be a regular joke between the two of them.

'Have you met Phyllis?' Mr Phillips had suddenly asked him, pausing in his counting of the change from the till. 'She used to work here when she was still in high school. How long ago was that Phyllis? Four years, now?'

'It's been six years since I graduated.'

'That long? Anyway, Art, she was one of my best.' He resumed deftly sliding the spread out coins into his free hand, five at a time. 'After having her cheery smile around the place for a couple of years, it was a real disappointment to lose her.'

'Thank you, Mr P, I wish I still had you for a boss.' She pushed her emptied cup and bowl towards Arthur. 'I'll get out of your way and let you finish up. And I've got a long walk home.' She bent to retrieve the case she had sat down by her stool.

'Your car in the garage, again?' Mr Phillips had asked.

'Yeah, something wrong with the distributer drive gear, or at least I think that's what Murray said. He's had to order a new one, but it won't be in until the end of the week.'

Arthur looked up as he was emptying the sink of the last of the washing up, to see her straining with the heavy case. He had a sudden impulse to know this person better.

'Excuse me,' he blurted, 'can I walk you home? I could carry your case for you.'

'That's really nice of you,' she had replied, indecisively shifting her weight from one foot to the other, 'but it's a very long walk'.

'All the more reason you should let me carry that for you.' He pointed to the case she had sat back down. 'It'll only take me a couple of minutes to sweep up, if you don't mind waiting.'

'I think I can vouch for him, Phyllis,' Mr Phillips had interrupted, 'and I'd feel better if you weren't walking home on your own'.

'Okay, then,' she had agreed. 'I wasn't looking forward to lugging this all the way home.'

Arthur had checked that there was no one left in the back room, that all the glasses were washed and stacked and that everything was in order for Carol to open up the following morning. He removed his apron and fetched the broom and dustpan from the closet, but as soon as he started to sweep, he had felt a hand on his shoulder.

'It won't hurt me to do this for a change,' Mr Phillips had said. 'Get out of here and don't keep her waiting.'

'You're sure?' Arthur had hesitated for a brief moment, but seeing the nod of agreement added a hasty thanks and grabbed his jacket.

The route Phyllis had taken led towards the less upmarket end of the main street, past automotive spare parts stores, second hand and shoe repair shops, an antique shop that looked older and less cared for than any of its meagre contents and a couple of dingy looking bars. Turning off the main street, they had entered a residential area of modest houses with shallow angled gables and full width front porches facing the street behind stingy little, frequently overgrown and uncared for looking, front lawns. The streetlights were spaced further apart, leaving large areas of near total darkness between the pools of dim yellowish light. The whole area contrasted sharply to the more prosperous looking houses on the university side of town.

As they walked their conversation had been about her work, she was an administrative assistant with a state agricultural office, and about his studies. They discussed films they had recently seen and she seemed curious, if amused, about the differences between his life in England and at the university, but he realized, after saying goodnight in front of one of those modest homes for the blue-collared, that he had learned little of her personal details. He didn't know if she was married – she wasn't wearing any rings he had noticed – if she lived with parents, or friends, or on her own. On the long walk back to his own room, it must have been twice as far as the mile long walk to his work, he resolved to find out more about her.

She had apologized for not asking him in, but at least, he told himself, he had found out she would be working late again the following night and she had promised to stop by the drugstore if she finished before it closed. He had tried to study when he reached his room, but found himself unable to concentrate for thinking about her. She might not be everyone's idea of a raving beauty with film-star looks, but she was rather pretty and had a wonderful laugh. It was obvious she was three or four years older than him and that only seemed to add to the attraction.

Chapter Thirty-Two

Their relationship had grown like a bud about to burst into blossom, over the next few evenings. The following night Phyllis had appeared a little earlier, but without the heavy case and though he was too busy to exchange more than a few words, after he had closed up and walked her home again, she had asked him in.

Her first-floor apartment had the looks of having seen better days, with linoleum covered floors, old-fashioned floral wallpaper and dark brown varnished woodwork fashioned in the curious, to Arthur's eyes, style of short, but wide panels in the doors with round doorknobs, instead of the English manner of four long panels in rows of two, with proper L-shaped handles. There was a small electric cooker, a rather tall refrigerator and a wide sink placed beneath glass-fronted, white-painted, wooden cabinets at one end of the large room that functioned as kitchen, dining and sitting room. At the other end were a couple of wooden chairs, a coffee table complete with ring marks from wet cups or glasses and a sagging couch covered in a pinkish coloured blanket to hide the faded brown, scratchy fabric. Through two partially closed doors he could see what appeared to be a separate bedroom and bathroom.

She had apologized for the apartment's condition, stating that her last place had been much nicer, but that the landlord had frequently intruded upon her privacy and had objected anytime she had brought friends home. Arthur had noted that a vase of fresh flowers had been placed on a side table and despite the worn furnishings, the place was spotlessly clean and tidy. Other little touches had been made to further increase its homeliness, with what were obviously family pictures hanging on the walls.

That night he received his first real kisses and the sensation of her open lips against his, her tongue lightly tracing the shape of his and her body welded against him were overpowering. After returning to his own room, he had lain awake for half the night trying to relive the experience.

The following night had followed a similar pattern, but when he let one hand drop from where it had been cradling her face and it *accidentally* came to rest on one of her breasts, she had made no effort to push it away. He had spent some time examining the shape and feel of them through her blouse and bra, but when he had attempted to find his way past the buttons guarding the opening, she had made a little 'Unh, uh,' sound in her throat and he had let his hands drop to her waist. They seemed to rise of their own accord and caress the soft, beguiling mounds as she kissed him and he returned her kisses with equal passion, but he made no further attempt to bypass the layers of fabric covering them. With her body pressed so tightly against his, he was sure she must be able to feel the reaction she'd had on him, a reaction he was unable to stifle, but she had made no comment.

On the Friday and Saturday nights he knew he would have been very busy until closing time and would have to work for a further thirty or forty minutes cleaning, taking stock and preparing for the following day, so they had arranged to meet on the Sunday evening at a cinema for their first actual date.

All that day he had diligently concentrated on his studies; counting down the remaining hours until he saw her again and trying not to be distracted by the thoughts of what her body had felt like against his. She was waiting for him by the time he arrived at the cinema, and they entered together. They had sat holding hands to begin with, but as he found himself unable to even think about the film being projected in front of them, her knees became the centre of his attention. His hand, seemingly with a mind of its own, wandered further up her inner thighs and as she twisted slightly in her seat to allow him greater access, he found the wonderfully soft skin just above her stocking tops. She had again shifted her position slightly and suddenly his fingers were brushing against the silken material of her underwear.

At a more brightly lit part of the film he could see she was watching him and as their eyes met, she had nodded questioningly at the exit. Together, they arose and threaded their way towards the aisle with many softly whispered 'excuse me's' and 'sorry's'. They had run hand-in-hand, most of the distance to her apartment, sometimes skipping as if they were children. Frequently, their attempts at conversation were accompanied by childlike giggles. By the time they reached Phyllis's apartment, they were completely out of breath.

As soon as the door had shut behind them, they were plastered together in her hallway. Within minutes, she had stopped his fumbling attempts to unfasten her clothing and had disappeared in the direction of her bedroom. He stood uneasily wondering if he should follow, but as she had shut the door behind her, he decided he should wait a minute or two. He had sat down on her couch to try and regain his breath, but before he could come to a decision, she had reappeared, clad only in a light dressing gown, and had sat down beside him. As she had turned towards him, her loosely tied gown had gaped open, giving him his first look at real live breasts.

Of course, he had seen pictures. Among the many magazines for sale in the drugstore, there was one for photography enthusiasts. This regularly contained *artistic* poses of young women in various states of undress and he had occasionally thumbed through the latest issue on a quiet evening as he had tidied the magazine rack. In addition, several of his friends' rooms at the university were adorned with full-colour, centrefold photos of nude models from a stylish 'mans magazine'. But Phyllis's breasts were the first he had seen in the flesh and he was completely intrigued by them. She made no attempt to stop him as he tentatively tried touching them, taking note of their soft resilient nature, the way they fitted so conveniently into the palms of his hands and the way the nipples grew and became firmer as he touched them. He found the urge to bury his face into them, to run his tongue around them and test their firmness with his teeth, irresistible. The excitement and pleasure he found seemed to be reflected by Phyllis as she cradled his face and directed his movements with little accompanying murmurs. He eventually grew bolder and began exploring further with one hand as he continued to alternate between nuzzling her exposed breasts and kissing her lips.

His hand found a smooth, rounded belly, but when he had tried to investigate further her response had been a firm, 'Unh uh, not tonight!' His disappointment in not going further, was only matched by his relief at not having to show his inexperience and he had continued as before until they had eventually parted. Later as he walked home, he had repeatedly replayed the scene in his mind, wondering how much longer he would still be a virgin.

Three nights later when he next worked at the drug store, she had, as they had prearranged, met him when he finished, led him back to her apartment and taken him straight to her bedroom. Wordlessly, but with eyes that never left his, she had undressed him, then indicated that he should lie back on her bed as she slowly and seductively undressed in front of him. Patiently, like a mother teaching a child a new skill, she had positioned herself on top of him, helped him to enter and with her hands on his chest, had set up a slow rhythm that lasted until the expected conclusion. He had felt neither embarrassment nor apprehension about his own performance; only an excruciating pleasure from an experience he hoped would be repeated over and over.

As they lay in each other's arms, she had lit a cigarette while apologizing for refusing to let him make love to her properly at their last meeting. When he had pressed for more information, she had explained that there had been someone else in her life; someone that no longer mattered, as he had been dismissed. Arthur had dreamily rested his face on her chest, falling asleep before she had even finished her cigarette.

Chapter Thirty-Three

The room was silent and totally dark; there was not even a thin slice of light from beneath the door to cleave the darkness. With considerable effort, Arthur could just turn his head slightly from side to side, but was unable to make out anything in the room. He listened for any breathing coming from the chair next to his bed, but after holding his own breath for a short time, he was convinced that he was completely on his own. The pain and itching in his arms and legs seemed to have increased every minute since he had awakened, but he assured himself that it was only the lack of other sensory distraction that made it seem so.

He tried to daydream; a technique he had often used when he couldn't sleep or was in boring situations, such as meetings that had little purpose, or in painful situations as when having a dentist drill on his teeth. His favourite daydream was to simply imagine a pair of breasts; the shape, whether firm and proud or full and pendulous, the texture and colour of the skin, soft, pale and flawless, tanned or freckled, or even rich and dark, the size of the nipples, relaxed or erect, and how they might feel brushed against his face or resting in his hands.

These daydreams though, seemed pale in comparison to the reality of the last few days and he tried concentrating on one of the other tricks he had sometimes used. Attempting to remember the appearance of all the various automobiles he had owned and the feel of their interiors, but that seemed quite dull and he switched to one his other favourites; recreating in his mind the floorplans of all the houses he had lived in.

He had worked his way through the familiar rooms of his childhood and the room he had been allocated at university and was visualizing the linoleum covered wooden floor in the kitchen of his first flat. He had remembered the placement of the little cooker, the antiquated fridge and how the Formica covered table and matching painted chairs looked, but when he moved in his mind to the living room, he knew he was confusing parts of it with the flat that Phyllis had lived in.

He had taken the flat to be close to Phyllis at the end of his second year at university. She was adamant that he was not to move in with her; back then living together was just not socially acceptable. Funny how things can change so quickly, he thought. Ten years later and it was all the rage for young couples to cohabit, rather than to marry too early.

A few days before the school year had ended, he had returned to his room after classes to find a note from Mr Roberts. No explanation was given, just a request to attend his office, late the following morning. When Arthur arrived, he was introduced to a tall, smartly dressed, middle-aged man with immediate gravitas.

'This is Mr Richard Collins,' Roberts said, leaning back in his office chair as Arthur and the stranger shook hands, 'and you want to be nice to him; he's the administrator of your trust fund. I think he even wants to take you to lunch.'

Arthur had protested that he still had classes that afternoon; that he shouldn't be cutting them and was astounded when his councillor had interrupted him. 'I think you have one this afternoon,' he had said confidently. 'I checked. This man's flown all the way from Los Angeles to see you. You'll have plenty of time for lunch with him. And if you miss a class? Well, you've completed your exams, haven't you?'

Their luncheon had gone well. Arthur had taken an immediate liking to his trust fund administrator, there was something vaguely familiar about him, but he was curious why the man had travelled such a distance just to discuss the trust. Before any doubts had even entered his mind, he had been assured that there was nothing to worry about; the man's visit was just to see that everything was going well for Arthur. They had discussed a wide range of topics; Arthur's likes and dislikes, how well he had accustomed himself to the different way of life in America and his ambitions for the future.

The conversation had slowly changed and Arthur found he was being asked whether he planned to return to England for the summer or to look for temporary work locally.

By the time they had completed their meal and had lingered over several cups of coffee, Arthur had received an offer for a summer job in California. He had reluctantly turned the offer down, explaining that his councillor had suggested a local firm of builders who were interested in him because of his architectural studies. Somehow, he didn't think it was appropriate to go into too much detail; that his real reason for wanting to stay locally was very personal.

They had parted after the meal with warm handshakes, firm clasping of shoulders, much direct eye-contact and a promise given, but never kept, that they would meet again. As he had walked back to the campus, Arthur felt that he had learned very little about the nature of his trust fund or the identity of his benefactor. Aside from a letter Arthur received two years later on his graduation, informing him that his trust fund had 'expired' and wishing him well for the future, a letter that was without a return address, he had never heard again from Richard Collins.

The summer passed far too quickly. The offer of the job with the building company arrived, an offer that Arthur had found astoundingly generous, before he had completed the last of his classes. He was initially assigned a place in the workshop; a large, well-lit building on the outskirts of town, filled with woodworking machinery and smelling of sawdust, linseed oil and varnish. Over the first weeks, he was taught to use the drill presses, the table and bandsaws, the sanders and various hand tools. Some of the more complicated machines, the planers, jointers, and thicknessers, the machines with high speed whirring blades, were left for later when he had accumulated more experience. Above each of the powered machines hung a two-foot by four-foot, plywood panel decorated with silhouettes of hands. It was obvious that each of the hands had been simply placed on the wood and a silhouette created by spraying paint around it. Every one of the silhouettes had one thing in common; one or more of the fingers were missing. The dangers implied were additionally emphasized by the hands of the shop foreman, a softly spoken man in his mid-fifties, whose standards for workmanship were very demanding, but matched by his patience in helping Arthur to meet them; hands that had retained only six of their original ten fingers.

After a few weeks in the shop, Arthur had been reassigned to work alongside an experienced carpenter on refurbishment projects. At first, he was unable to tell when his new partner, a mid-thirties father of three with an unpronounceable Polish name, was pulling his leg or actually giving him instructions. Ski, as he was always referred to, had an easy laugh, but was just as apt to tell him a story or ask of him an impossible task with a completely straight face; only bursting into unrestrained laughter, when Arthur accepted the story unquestioningly or attempted to complete the given task.

Despite the frequent windups, Arthur found the work interesting and his days went quickly. The jobs were varied, not just replacing worn or rotted wood, but learning how to chip out cracked plaster, trowel in with new and scraping or sanding to leave a smooth finish. He learned to match paint finishes so that a repair to a wall or ceiling would go undetected, without the entire room having to be repainted.

Ski was just as demanding, and at the same time, just as patient as Arthur had found the shop foreman. Before long, a strong friendship had developed between the two men and they were increasingly spending time together away from their work; stopping for a beer on the way home or going to a movie with Phyllis and Ski's wife, Beth. On the long hot summer evenings they frequently shared a barbecue in Ski's back yard and on weekends, the four of them, along with Ski and Beth's two young daughters, sometimes went for a picnic along the shallow creek that wound around two sides of the town.

His relationship with Phyllis had blossomed. With his increased income, he had been able to give up his job in the drugstore altogether and, if they were not doing something with Ski and Beth, they spent most of their evenings together.

One Sunday, Phyllis had packed a picnic and announced that she was taking him on a grand tour. With her directing him, he drove her aging Chevy out of the town and, after several miles, crossed over the wide river that separated the northern half of the state from the south and into another large town. High on the bluffs alongside the river stood an impressive building that reminded Arthur of the US capital building; pictures of which he had only seen accompanying any television news emanating from Washington DC. Phyllis informed him that it was the state capital building, where her former boyfriend now worked.

The countryside south of the river was drastically different from the flat farmland that surrounded his university town. Great hills, covered with hardwood forests, rose up about them and the road wound its way through them in endless curves instead of going straight as an arrow as it did in the north. At one point, Phyllis instructed him to pull off the road, into to an opening to a narrow, gravelled lane. After some distance of slowly negotiating what was little more than a rough path, they came to an opening in the trees, dominated by a tall, metal, truss-work tower. At the top of the tower there was a platform enclosed by waist-high railings and in the centre, a cabin-like building with the upper halves of its four walls of glass.

'Come on,' Phyllis had shouted excitedly, opening her door before the car had even come to a complete stop, 'you'll love this'.

'It's called a lookout tower,' she added, as she urged him to climb, the metal stairs clonking beneath their feet, 'it's for the forest rangers to watch for forest fires.'

To stay within the confines of the tower, the narrow stairs doubled back upon themselves many times, and soon they were hastily aiming a kiss at each other as they passed. The amorous feat helped Arthur overcome his anxiety of the height; the ground was far, far below them and they were looking over the tops of the highest trees by the time they had reached the base of the cabin.

'I don't think we can get any further,' Phyllis said, looking at the hasp and padlock on the trapdoor above them, 'but we can sit here and admire the view'.

They crowded together on the small turnaround at the foot of the last flight of stairs and looked about. In all directions around them the tree-covered hills stretched as far as they could see. Valleys between the hills were blue with haze, and in the far distance, the faint hills merged with the sky. Two other tiny towers could just be seen on the horizon, their cabins barely projecting above the tree line. The warmth of Phyllis's body, pressed so tightly into his, soon turned Arthur's mind to something other than the view, but she laughed and pushed him away before starting to descend the stairs.

Despite his pain, Arthur could not resist a chuckle in the darkness. Had it been Amy with him at the top of the tower, even with the cramped and uncomfortable position and the possibility of being seen if anyone arrived, it would have been impossible to have descended without having made the most of the situation.

Poor Phyllis, he thought, she was so terrified of becoming pregnant, yet refused to take the newly available pill in fear of the thrombosis rumours and found that condoms irritated her, no matter how much additional lubrication they had used. She could only ever feel safe using her diaphragm, even though it did impose limits on any spontaneity. When he had complained, she had, as a lesson, regaled him with the story of Carol, his friend at the drugstore.

Carol had been a year or two ahead of Phyllis in the high school they had both attended, she'd said. She was popular, bright and had had great things expected of her. She had been homecoming queen two years in a row, voted most likely to succeed, and class vice-president in her senior year. Together with Greg something-or-other, they had been the golden couple. Greg was tall, handsome and the best athlete the school had ever had. Captain of the football team, he was almost undoubtedly going to receive a football scholarship; several universities were enticing him in their direction before he had finished his junior year.

Halfway through their senior year, Carol had discovered she was pregnant. Under normal conditions, couples in similar situations were expected to marry and the school even had a policy of letting the father continue his studies. Girls were, of course expected to drop out; they couldn't be seen at school with a protruding bump in case it was infectious. And there wasn't any great need for them to have a high school diploma anyway if they were to be safely married and didn't require a job.

Greg however, had upset the normal arrangements. Afraid that getting married would jeopardize his chances of a football career, he had refused to marry Carol, even denying that the baby was his. Such a decision had created turmoil amongst the other players and almost evenly split opinions as to who had been to blame. Discord within a team rarely made for good performance, they finished the year at the bottom of their league and the scholarship offers Greg had expected, failed to appear. The last Phyllis had heard of him, she had said, he was working at a tractor factory in an adjoining state. Arthur didn't want that to happen to them, did he?

***

Light flooded into the room as the door was opened. Arthur winced with the pain, but as his eyes adjusted, he realized that it was only a candle shielded with a hand, as before.

'Are you awake?' someone whispered, so softly he could barely hear. He tried to tell them 'yes' and found that he could only grunt in reply. 'I thought I heard you laugh,' it was Zanli. She had raised her voice just enough for him recognize it as she placed the candle on the table, then arranged some object in front of it so that the direct light wouldn't strike his face.

Arthur tried to move his tongue around in his mouth to get some saliva flowing and lick his lips; they were dreadfully dry and every movement was painful. 'I must have been dreaming,' he managed at last.

'Shh, don't try to talk,' she said, before leaning over and kissing him on the forehead, 'just nod your head, yes or no. Are you in much pain?'

He slowly nodded his head up and down. Then something more important struck him, 'could... I... have... some... water?'

'I will be right back,' Zanli whispered, then left the room. Within a few minutes she was back and leaning over him again, holding the little silver jug. 'You can't have any water,' she said, 'but this should refresh you a little. And it will help with the pain.'

She tipped the little jug so that the liquid it contained trickled slowly into his mouth. It was ice cold; Arthur recognized it as the oddly tasting aqui he had had earlier and she allowed him only a few sips before taking it away. The alcohol caused the insides of his cheeks to burn slightly, but it was, as she had promised, almost immediately rejuvenating.

Zanli continued to stand by his bedside for some time after she had given him the aqui, looking at him sympathetically. 'I wish there was something more I could do. I can't stand to see you in pain,' she said, and then added even more softly, 'you know how much I love you'.

Arthur found having Zanli proclaim her love for him, not just her need for him to father her child, very soothing, very reassuring; he was sure things would be better in the morning. He relaxed into the bed, the pain subsiding. 'I love you too, Zanli,' he whispered.

Chapter Thirty-Four

Why could he not stop thinking about Phyllis? Was it a sense of triumph he was feeling? Or a sense of guilt? Either way, he still missed her, even after all these years. He had been dreaming of her, over and over, but the dreams were distorted as dreams usually are, and never reflected reality. Concentrating on their time together helped to take his mind off the pain and might even help him come to terms with what he felt for her.

That summer together was the happiest he had ever known. He probably hadn't even thought about it at the time; he knew that the young often simply accepted the good things without realizing how lucky they are. He didn't suppose he had been any different.

Looking back, it seemed that the sun had shown a little brighter, a little more golden; he almost chuckled, it was he thought, much like film directors trying to depict the fifties by putting yellow filters on their cameras. But it was true; it had been the first summer he had spent in the Midwest, the previous summer he had flown home to be with his parents, and he couldn't stop comparing it to the, more often than not, cool, wet English summers he was accustomed to. Often it was uncomfortably hot; he had regularly removed his shirt if he was working outdoors and would find sweat pouring from him by mid-morning, but his skin had gone brown from the sun and his muscles had hardened from the constant physical work.

He and Ski had finished their refurbishing work and had joined another crew constructing timber frames for a development of houses on the edge of town. Frames started at one side of the lower floor, nailed together like an enormously wide ladder turned on its side, with reinforced holes for the windows and doors. When one side was completed it was raised into a vertical position and the adjoining wall started on. As soon as all the lower walls were in position, joists were lifted to the top of the walls to support the next floor and the process repeated. The work required endless driving of four-inch long spike nails, to join the four-by-two inch timbers together.

At first, Arthur's arm would ache within an hour of starting work and the crew would let him change to sawing the timbers to correct lengths, but he was using the same arm, and for several days his right arm was constantly sore.

'You want to learn to be a switch-hitter,' Ski had said to him one day.

'What's that?' Arthur had inquired.

'It comes from baseball,' Ski had explained. 'Some players can bat either as a southpaw, a left-hander that is, or as a right-hander. You have to pitch differently for different handed batters; the strike zone looks different, you see. It's to try and confuse the pitcher. Watch me.'

It sounded even more confusing to Arthur, but he watched as Ski, holding the hammer in his right hand, drove a spike into place with a few well aimed blows. He had then changed position taking the hammer in his left hand, and drove another spike home as easily.

'Now you try,' he had urged. 'If you can learn to do that, it lets one arm rest at a time.'

Arthur had tried a few tentative swings with his left hand, but it felt odd and the nail had bent double on the third strike.

'No, no, no,' Ski had laughed. 'Look, you have to reverse your whole body. You're trying to use your left hand, but your legs and stance are still in the right-hand position. Look at how you stand or kneel when you're using your right hand. Look at the way you're holding the hammer, and then reverse your whole body as if you're seeing yourself in the mirror.'

Arthur followed the directions he had been given and after a few attempts was able to drive a spike fully home without it bending.

'You might want to choke up on the handle to begin with,' Ski had advised, 'but after you get your eye in, you can grip further back on the handle and let the weight of the head do the work. Don't forget to see the nail as the hammer hits it, like I showed you before. Don't flinch or turn your head away.'

Before the day was over Arthur found he could rest his right arm for considerable periods. How typical of Ski to be so helpful, he thought as he lay there. He wondered if he had ever told him what a good friend he had been.

When their work was finished for the day they would ride home in the back of one of the crew's pickups, the rapidly moving air cooling and drying their tired bodies. Ski and Beth lived only a few blocks from Phyllis's apartment and if they were all doing something together, Arthur usually went straight to her place after Ski had been dropped off. Phyllis would have arrived home a little earlier, but would wait for him so they could shower together and after superficially drying each other, but with still-damp hair, make love before getting dressed to go out for the evening.

Some evenings the whole crew would get together at a local bar, both the other men were married and brought their wives; sometimes he and Phyllis would just go around to Ski and Beth's house for the evening. They would bring the drinks or steaks and leave Ski to tend the barbecue. The two little girls, Jennifer must have been about five and Lily three, were demanding to be played with and roared with laughter as they were chased around the trees in their back garden.

One night a week was card night. After the two little girls had again browbeaten Arthur to play with them until they were completely worn out and had been put to bed with ritual story reading, the four adults would sit around the kitchen table with beers or coffees and a deck of cards. The games became less and less important; they had started by playing pinochle, but it took too much concentration and ruined their conversation. They had changed to progressively simpler games and ended up playing a board game that only consisted of throwing a dice and moving a counter around the board.

All too soon the summer was over and it was time for Arthur to start classes again. On the evening of his last day of work, the entire workforce had gathered at a local restaurant to send him on his way until the following summer; he had already been promised work if he wanted it. As on most such occasions, there was considerable ribaldry, many jokes told, most to the embarrassment of best friends and a considerable quantity of beer consumed. Arthur noticed that

Phyllis was unusually quiet, but assumed that she may have felt out of place with such a rambunctious crowd or, because she had volunteered to drive, and was only drinking soft drinks.

After an endless round of goodbyes, she and Arthur had bundled Ski, who was quite wobbly on his legs, and Beth, into the back of Phyllis's car to drive them home. More slurred goodbyes, wet kisses and promises of continuing their Friday card nights were given before Phyllis drove the remainder of the way to Arthur's apartment.

'Hey, haven't you made a mistake?' Arthur said, 'I thought we were going back to your place first. I can walk home later.'

'I may be making a mistake,' Phyllis said, turning her head slightly away, 'but it wasn't this'.

'I don't understand,' Arthur was suddenly concerned about the sadness in her voice. 'What's the matter?'

'I gathered up the things you had at my place,' she sniffed. 'They're in my suitcase. It's in the trunk. You can let me have it back later.'

'I don't understand,' he repeated. 'What have I done? I thought we loved each other.'

'Oh, I do love you, Arthur,' she was openly crying and wiping at the tears running down her face with the back of her hand. 'You haven't done anything. You're a great guy and one day you'll make some lucky girl a wonderful husband.'

'Is that what you want?' he was still puzzled, and a little addled from the drink he had consumed. 'We can get married. I would have asked you before, but I've two more years before I'll be earning enough to support us. But we can get married now, if that's what you want. I'm sorry, that isn't very romantic is it? And I would have wanted to do it right, you know candle lit dinner, going down on one...'

Phyllis had silenced him with a finger to his lips. 'No, don't, that's not it,' she wiped her nose on the back of her wrist, 'I said I love you and I do, but I love someone more. Do you remember last spring when we first got together? I said that I had finished with another guy. And I thought I had. I'd been seeing him for a couple of years, but he was married and kept putting off getting a divorce. He made excuses, it wasn't the right time, his wife was having health problems, it wouldn't be good for his career, you know.'

'He doesn't sound like a very nice guy,' Arthur was suddenly angry with this man. 'How can you want to be with someone like that?'

'Oh, I probably exaggerated a little,' she was suddenly defensive. 'Anyway, he's split with his wife, she's filing for divorce, and he wants me back.'

'And you're going back to him? Just like that? Don't I get any say in this?'

'I've been fretting about it for a couple of weeks, but I couldn't discuss it with you. It's something I had to decide for myself. I'm so sorry,' she leaned over and kissed him on the cheek. 'Promise you won't hate me.'

Arthur blinked back tears that had suddenly filled his eyes, 'How could I hate you?'

He slowly opened the passenger door, desperately tried to think of something else to say, something, anything that would put it all right, but his mind was blank. He walked to the rear of the car in a daze, opened the boot and removed the suitcase. It felt too light for its size, but of course, he reasoned, there would have been only a spare pair of jeans, a tee shirt or two, some socks and a toothbrush. Blinking back a further wave of tears, he had closed the boot lid, walked back towards the driver's window and waved as she put the car into gear, released the clutch and slowly drove away.

Chapter Thirty-Five

Arthur couldn't remember how long he had been asleep. It must have been days, now. He couldn't remember what was wrong with him or why he was in so much pain. He woke for brief intervals and if he couldn't get back to sleep straight away he tried to concentrate on various things from his past to assist his passage back into that blessed oblivion. Memories kept surfacing to plague him like a recurring dream that wouldn't go away.

For Arthur, his third year at the university he attended, had at first, seemed to have been a blur of opportunities. English music had invaded America and anything to do with England was suddenly worshipped. He was besieged with invitations; a few from girls he knew and might have been interested in at one time, others were from girls he might have been in the same class with, he thought, that when he had first started probably wouldn't have given him the time of day. He was frequently stopped by freshman girls he had never seen before and asked to say something, anything in fact, just so they could listen to his accent.

For a short time he was willing to accept as many of these enticements as he could find time for; he had returned to his evening job at the drug store, but with an apartment to look after instead of a room in a hall of residence, and with some savings from his summer work, he had no longer needed his job in the dormitory cafeteria.

Soon, he came to the conclusion that the girls who seemed so eager to see him, only really wanted to be seen with him. He mostly found them shallow and self-interested. After finding that he couldn't satisfy their curiosity about 'swinging' London, Carnaby Street or musical groups with ridiculous haircuts, they seemed to only ever want to talk about themselves. Arthur tried inventing stories about a London that he was completely unfamiliar with; he couldn't comprehend how it could, by the greatest stretch of imagination, be considered *swinging*, it had always seemed grey and wet, and beyond infrequent trips to the Albert Hall or the Science or Natural History Museums, a thoroughly unwelcoming place. He would not have been able to locate Carnaby Street, even if given a map. He had also quickly learned not to try and describe the school he had attended; the concept seemed to be completely alien to them; even the fact that *public* schools in England were private, confused them. Apparently, every High School in America was labelled 'Such and Such Public School' and he had to agree that logically, if they were open to the public, that was the probably the best thing to call them.

Before the first semester had even ended, he had found himself perfecting excuses not to attend parties and often trying his best to avoid those who had sought his company. He continued to see Ski and Beth occasionally, but without Phyllis their evenings seemed to lack something; it was difficult to find card games that the three of them could play comfortably and they too often had long awkward pauses in their conversations.

At the drugstore he had formed a strong friendship with Carol despite their age difference, and they occasionally saw a movie together or went for an informal meal. She had made it clear from the first that she wasn't interested in a romantic relationship, but she soon appeared to enjoy his company almost as much as he enjoyed hers. After checking with them that it was okay, he had invited her to go along for one of his evenings with Ski and Beth. Arthur had not realized that in a town as small as theirs, and with the three of them being of a similar age, they would probably have attended the same school and would know each other, if only by reputation.

When this became apparent, and remembering the prejudice against unwed mothers that Phyllis had told him of, he felt suddenly awkward on Carol's behalf. His fears were unfounded however, and the evening quickly turned into one of animated conversation and almost continuous laughter. Soon, with Carol's presence, the card games resumed on a regular basis, although they could only take place later in the evening or when neither he nor Carol were working.

His relationship with Carol never went beyond that of a friend; an occasional hug when one of them had made a minor success of something and a regular kiss on the cheek when they parted after an evening of cards with Ski and Beth. Arthur had managed to form liaisons with some of his young women classmates; some of them lasting for several weeks before one or the other tired of the situation, but he was unable to feel for any of them the emotional intensity he had felt for Phyllis.

The school year had passed far too quickly. Suddenly the summer break was on them and Arthur had to decide whether to accept the offer of experience in the drawing office, something he knew would be advantageous for his future career, or to work alongside Ski again on various building projects. The choice was an easy one for him. The thought of being cooped up in an office seemed like an extension of his year of classes. The fresh air, sunshine and easy camaraderie had been far too enticing. His second summer of working with Ski and the familiar crew went by even more quickly.

His last year of studies became one of familiar routine, much like his social life. He had drifted from one girlfriend to another, often without remembering anything significant about them; sometimes even asking out a girl he had dated earlier, without realizing it. The evenings with Ski, Beth and Carol continued and it was only as his final exams approached that he realized how much he would miss them when he graduated. He had already, after a surprisingly low key interview, been offered a position at the building company's head office. The offer was far too generous to turn down, but the office was just outside of Boston, nearly a thousand miles away.

The day after Arthur's final day at the university, his work colleagues held another going away dinner for him at the same restaurant they had blessed with their custom nearly two years earlier. Again drinks flowed, jokes were told on workmates and confidences were betrayed. Carol had accepted his invitation and was unusually affectionate, keeping one arm around him for most of the evening. After the last goodbyes had been said, the promises to keep in touch made and Arthur and Carol were in a taxi, she had invited him back to her home. Arthur thought, in his state of mild inebriation, that at last she was going to relent in her refusal to go any further than a platonic friendship. When the babysitter had been dismissed and she was making coffee in the kitchen, he had crept up behind her, putting his arms around her waist. She had laughingly pushed him away.

'Don't, you'll make me spill this,' she'd said, pouring coffee into two mugs, 'and don't get the wrong idea, I only wanted to talk to you some more. To be with you for a little longer, yes, but I have a little confession to make as well. Promise me that you won't be angry with me.'

'Aww, how could I be angry with you?' Arthur could hear himself slurring slightly; he hoped the coffee would sober him up a little. 'I could never be angry with you, but I do really, really want to go to bed with you.'

'You know that's never going to happen. I love you, but only as a friend. I could never let myself fall in love with you or be used as one of your short-time girlfriends. You're going to be somebody one day, someone that people will admire. I could only hold you back.'

'How can you say that? You would be an... an aspect? I mean an asset, to... to anyone.'

'Thank you for your vote of confidence; that's really nice of you. Just what I've come to expect, but you know I have a reputation, and reputations have a way of following you around.'

'I don't think that matters. Anyway, I'm going to start work in Boston in a couple of weeks. You could come with me. Who's going to know about your past there? Or even care?'

'Someone will always find out. You just can't run away from things. You may as well be honest from the start. I've never tried to hide the fact that I'm an unwed mother and it's not something I'm ashamed of, but I'd never forgive myself for holding you back.'

'You wouldn't,' Arthur protested, 'or I could take you back to England. No one thinks anything about...'

Carol had reached out and put a finger to his lips. 'Shhh. It's not going to happen. For one thing, you're not in love with me. Anyone can see you're still carrying a torch for Phyllis. Have you seen her?'

'What?' Arthur was puzzled by the question. 'You mean since she moved away?'

'No, I mean since she came back.' Carol looked at him as if she already knew the answer, 'didn't you know?'

'No.' The desire for Carol that, in his intoxicated state, had been building in intensity, suddenly waned. 'When?'

'I think she has been back living with her parents for some time. I only ran into her a couple of weeks ago.'

'Does that mean she's broke up with... what's 'is name?'

'Brian? I guess so. She more or less said that she left him when she found out he was sleeping around, but reading between the lines, I think he wanted rid of her when he found out she was pregnant.'

'So, is she getting a divorce, or what?'

'She doesn't need a divorce; they never got married.'

Arthur stared at his almost empty mug, lost in uncertainty as he swirled the cold remains. 'When's the baby due?'

'She has a little girl. She's absolutely gorgeous, nearly ten months old now and just starting to walk. You'd love her.'

'I just don't understand...'

Carol took the mug away from him and put her arms around his waist, pulling him closer to her. 'You should go see her,' she said, her voice barely more than a whisper; her lips only inches from his cheek, 'if you really want to take an unwed mother with you...'

Chapter Thirty-Six

His memories, while he lay awake, alternated with the dreams he'd had while sleeping; sometimes dreams of a very disturbing nature. In one of his dreams he thought he had awakened to find himself surrounded by Rani, Zanli, Ashri, Yetti and the white-haired German speaking woman. One of the heavy curtains used to hold back the light must have fallen to the floor. Ashri and Yetti had rushed to reposition it, to restore the near darkness, but the sudden flood of light had stung his eyes and he seemed completely unable to shut them. He was also unable to shut out the sight of the other women bending over him, removing long strips of his skin, wiping away other bits of his skin that seemed to have fallen off of their own accord and softly applying some sort of balm to sooth the pain in his exposed muscles. It was as if he was being subjected to one of the most terrifying forms of torture known; flaying while still alive. As the curtain had been quickly replaced and the pain in his eyes had subsided, one of them had again held the little jug to his lips as someone else had put a folded cloth over his eyes, to protect them from the light of the single small candle.

When he had later regained some semblance of consciousness, he remembered the dream with a shudder. Despite the cloth covering his eyes and the lack of feeling in any of his limbs, or the inability to even move any part of him, he knew with certainty that it had been just a dream. He may have lain there for several days, but regardless of what was actually wrong with him, he knew definitely that it was not long enough for Ashri, Zanli and Yetti to have reached the advanced state of pregnancy that they'd had in his dream.

He seemed to be floating through the darkness without a care in the world; he had such a reassuring feeling that everything would turn out right. The feeling reminded him that he had been dreaming once again about another dream. The dream he'd had after his night with Zanli, when Rani had been so convinced that he had died. He wondered if his dream would have been a reasonable approximation of reality, had he really died.

Was there such a thing as an afterlife, he wondered? He knew it was impossible to recapture the wonderful emotions he had experienced in the dream, but he could remember that they were beyond anything he had ever experienced before. How would it have been possible to actually experience a brief taste of the afterlife and how could he have remembered it when he returned? No, it just wasn't possible. If our sensations and thoughts are simply the result of some electromagnetic activity in our brain; didn't doctors and researchers attach electrodes to one's head to measure the amount of activity? Of course, electromagnetic waves propagate outward and didn't they, he tried to remember long ago physics lessons, diminish inversely to the square of the distance; wouldn't that mean that they could never actually reach zero? That they would go on to infinity, becoming infinitely small but never disappearing completely. So, if at death one's awareness just shifted from the brain to the stream of waves? No, it was absurd. Radio waves travel at the speed of light, he thought, and in his lifetime his radiation probably wouldn't have left our own galaxy; he wasn't sure how many light years our own galaxy was across, but probably many times more than his age. And he had dreamed that the entire universe, billions and billions of times greater than our galaxy, had dropped out of sight in seconds…

Such thinking made his head hurt and he went back to thinking about Phyllis. Why, he wondered, had he never been unable to summon up, what, a little courage? Some forgiveness for an imagined injustice?

He had left for his new position in Boston without, as Carol had suggested, even trying to see Phyllis again. It had been too painful to think that she had done everything with her old lover that she had refused him. He knew that she had moved in with him and that they were living together, and she had obviously left behind her almost obsessive caution about contraception. He knew it had been an adolescent reaction, but he had felt hurt and at the time it had seemed like some sort of justice if she had to endure the scorn of ending up an unwed mother.

Later, in his new surroundings, when he had had time to reassess his own attitude, he had meant to write to her. He had tried to think of something adequate to say in a letter, but had put it off until it became harder and harder; each day he found it easier to find an excuse not to write. He told himself he would arrange to meet her when he returned to attend homecoming games, but on those occasions he had always ended up staying too long with Ski and Beth, had taken Carol and her son Mark to the football games with him, and had just never found the time.

For four years he had returned each autumn for a long weekend. Initially, he had slept on the couch at Carol's house; the cost of the train fare and the tickets precluded any extravagances, but seeing old friends, wandering around the town and the campus he had so enjoyed, reminded him of just how empty was his new life in Boston. As his income had increased he began staying in a local motel during those weekends. He saw less of Carol, and only once had she ever reminded him that he had never contacted Phyllis. She had refused to give him any more information, saying it was up to him to ask at the source, but each time he had tried to pick up a phone and call Phyllis, something inside had caused him to stop.

On what turned out to be his last planned visit, he was determined to contact Phyllis beforehand, regardless of what her reaction would be. He had spent days trying to think of the best way to approach her. He had agonized on what he would do if she simply told him to "shove off", but he was unwavering in his single-mindedness of seeing her again. He was actually looking at his telephone as it rang and, for a brief second, he unrealistically expected it to be Phyllis on the other end of the line. Instead, it was his father's solicitor calling to tell him that his parents had both been killed in a road accident.

Chapter Thirty-Seven

He had flown back to England for the first time in just over seven years and despite having had a somewhat difficult relationship with his parents, the loss he had felt was strangely unexpected. It was impossible to get accustomed to the idea that he would never see them again. The thought of making funeral arrangements was daunting and he didn't know where to begin, but the solicitor had been very helpful, putting him in touch with a local undertaker, and guiding him through the seemingly endless paperwork of death certificates, wills and contacting authorities.

There had been heaps of sympathy cards inside the front door of his parent's house when he had finally managed to obtain a key, but otherwise the house was eerily in order. His parents had moved from the large home he remembered from his childhood, to a smaller bungalow soon after he had left for university and it seemed odd coming into a strange house. They had been killed while on a touring holiday and he remembered from his childhood his mother saying she 'never wanted to return to a mess', but this unfamiliar house seemed almost sterile.

At the funeral he had been surprised by the number of people in attendance. There were some faces he vaguely remembered from his childhood, but most, although they seemed to know everything about him, were complete strangers to him. Everyone had seemed so kind; he couldn't believe the amount of food that had arrived and after the ceremony at the crematorium, the house had been filled with people, even though he couldn't remember having invited anyone. There had been endless offers of help and when people began drifting away, a few kind souls had stayed behind, clearing away dishes and glasses.

Things had seemingly passed in a blur for several days. Two of his mother's friends, women he had met at the funeral, had volunteered to help with the task of clearing out closets and taking unwanted clothes to charity shops. Arthur had simply let them get on with the difficult job. The thought of wading through his parent's things, many so familiar, so evocative of distant times, was depressing. He pleaded with them, to not be asked to make decisions, but to use their own judgement. When they had finally finished, one of them had brought to his attention stacks of letters tied up in ribbon.

'I found these in a drawer in your mother's dressing table,' she'd said, 'underneath her lingerie. It was all folded so neatly that these were completely hidden. I was sure you wouldn't want them thrown away.'

When the women had left, Arthur examined the stacks of letters. One stack he recognized as letters he had written to his mother from the hated school where he had felt so out of place.

'At least your parents love you enough to make some sacrifices for your benefit,' a school friend had once said to him. 'The fees here only mean that my father has to settle for driving a Bentley instead of a Rolls.'

The stack was embarrassingly small and probably, he thought, contained all of the letters he had ever written to her. He had never been much of a letter writer and the replies from his mother had been as infrequent as his own.

The second stack was much thicker, held together with an ancient rubber band that had perished and disintegrated limply when he started to remove one of the letters. The letters were a mixture of styles and materials; some were simply folded card, decorated with a large green cross that divided the address side into four quarters, a few were folded paper with the outer side serving as the envelope, while others on slightly yellowed paper were in envelopes with various coloured banding. All had stamps bearing the face of the king and official looking warnings on the front. Some included a list of subjects that could not be discussed and most warned that they would be opened and read.

Curious, he opened the first to see it headed Middlesex Yeomanry, followed with a unit number, a serial number and his father's name.

He felt momentarily voyeuristic, as if betraying a confidence, but after only a slight hesitation and realizing that it no longer mattered, started to read the contents. These were letters from his father to his mother; obviously, from the dates handwritten across the front, posted during the war. The letters contained little more than intimate assertions of love, a few joking references about day-to-day incidents and frequent complaints about the years they had spent in the desert. The last letter that Arthur opened told of a rumour going round that there might be home leave, but his father had discounted it as speculation. He turned it over and looked at the front. It was dated the fourth of June, 1943. He knew his father had been in the Western desert during part of the war, but had never been that interested in dates of battles and had never before thought how long he might have been there. He felt a sickening void inside as he compared the date to his own birthday, only four months later.

He pushed the scattered letters to one side before turning his attention to the last stack. These were more uniform in size, pale blue with a broken, darker blue band on the edges and a label proclaiming "Air Mail" on the lower left hand side. The stamps were from the USA and the postmarks, mostly dated from the late 1940s to the mid-1950s, read 'Sacramento'.

He opened one at random, to read a brief note acknowledging the previous letter from his mother and mentioning the cheque that was enclosed. Another was an impersonal discussion about *the boy* and about further provisions for his education.

As Arthur carefully refolded the last letter and pushed it back into its envelope a photograph fell out of the stack and landed face down on the floor. He picked it up and turned it over. The deckle-edged, white-bordered picture in black and white had obviously been taken many years earlier and was of his mother looking impossibly young. Standing next to her was a much younger version of his trust fund administrator in an American serviceman's uniform. Arthur thought he had seen something on the back as he had picked it up and turned the picture over again; he could just make out the faint words, written in pencil and obviously erased at some time, but just visible when held so the light fell at the right angle, 'All my love forever, Richard'.

Chapter Thirty-Eight

Arthur awoke to a faint light creeping in under the cloth that covered his eyes. For a few seconds his eyes rebelled at the unusual condition and he had to blink several times. It must have been days, he thought, since he had seen anything going on around him and he unsuccessfully tried to shake his head in an attempt to remove the cloth.

'Just nod your head gently if you are awake,' he heard Rani say quietly, her voice seeming to come from alongside his ear, 'I'm going to take the bandage away.'

Arthur slowly nodded his head up and down. His neck was stiff and the movement took a surprising amount of effort. He felt her make some adjustments to the material at the side of his head and she continued softly, 'You should probably keep your eyes shut for a while, or the light may be painful.'

The bandage covering his eyes was slowly peeled away and even through his closed lids the increase in illumination was almost overwhelming. He tentatively tried opening one eyelid and at first it seemed very bright, but within seconds he was able to withstand it and tried squinting through the other eye as well. He could just make out that a thin curtain was still covering the window, but from the dancing shadows of leaves he could tell that the sun was shining outside.

With some effort he managed to turn his head towards Rani. In the gloom that managed to filter through the curtains he could see her standing at the side of his bed, looking down at him. Her smile was one he couldn't quite identify, almost of pride; not in something that she had accomplished, more like that of a young mother smiling proudly at an offspring, a toddler who had suddenly made an unexpected leap in its abilities.

'Does the light hurt?' she asked. 'Do you want me to pull the blind back down?'

'Nnn,' he could only croak; he had wanted to tell her that he felt fine, but his voice didn't seem to be working. With some effort he managed a feeble cough in an attempt to clear his throat.

'Try this,' she said, putting a hand behind his head and lifting, while holding a small glass of water to his lips. He wondered what had happened to the little jug with the curved spout, but forgot it completely when, at the first sip, he realized how thirsty he was and greedily tried to swallow the remaining amount in one gulp. Rani laughed as she mopped at his chin. 'Not too much at one go, I'll give you some more in a moment.'

'I... I think the light's okay,' Arthur managed to say. 'It hurt to begin with though. Could I have some more water?'

He heard her pouring water into the glass from a larger jug, before holding it to his lips again. The water was so refreshing, he thought, it was as if he had been lost in a desert. He concentrated on trying to drink more carefully this time,

'Do you think we could have a little more light?' he said when she had sat the glass on the bedside table. 'I can barely see you.'

'We can try making a small adjustment,' Rani said, crossing to the window and opening the curtain a tiny amount, 'but if it hurts your eyes, tell me immediately. We don't want to tire them. Are you hungry?'

Arthur hadn't noticed it before, but he was suddenly ravenous. After all, he thought, it had been several days since he had eaten. 'Oh yes, I could eat a horse.'

Rani laughed. It seemed a very long time since he had heard her musical laughter. 'I don't think we have any horse on the menu. You may have to settle for a little broth.'

She moved slowly out of his sight and he tried unsuccessfully to turn his head enough to follow her movement, but his neck was too stiff. He heard a whispered exchange of words near the door before Rani reappeared carrying a tray with a bowl and spoon. Someone must have been waiting just outside, he thought. The other voice he had heard was too faint for him recognize, but he assumed it was Aszli's. Rani set the tray down.

'I'm going to see if you can sit up a bit,' she said, grasping his shoulders. 'Do you think you can help a little?'

Arthur pushed down with his arms with as much strength as he could muster and struggled to raise his head. He was pleasantly surprised by the lack of pain in his body. Stiffness yes, and some parts were a still little numb, but everything seemed to work properly. With Rani pushing and propping up his back with pillows, they managed to get him into a reclining position, if not quite sitting upright.

Rani pulled a chair into position, sat the tray on his bed and tucked a napkin under his chin before proceeding to spoon the warm clear liquid into his mouth. The taste was not what Arthur had expected when Rani had mentioned broth. It was nothing like the salty but weak, chicken-flavoured concoction his mother had fed him as a child. She should have described this as nectar, Arthur thought. It tasted wonderful and he was unable to stifle the little appreciative 'umms' that escaped his lips with each sip. Long before his hunger was sated, Rani was scraping the bottom of the bowl to scoop up the last drops.

'Do you think I could have some more?' Arthur asked as Rani picked up the tray.

'Not just yet,' Rani said. 'I'll bring you something in another hour. I don't want to wear you out; you should try to get some rest now.'

'I've been resting for days now,' Arthur protested, licking his lips. 'Please? I really am very hungry.'

'Perhaps a few extra spoonfuls wouldn't be too much for you. I'll get Aszli to put a little more in your bowl. I'll be right back.'

'I don't think I'm going anywhere,' Arthur tried to laugh, but the effort made his chest hurt slightly. It reminded him of the nights when he had awakened in pain.

He looked around the room as much as his stiff neck would allow when Rani had disappeared; the stiffness was starting to ease, but he still wasn't able to turn enough to see much more than what was in front of him. He was relieved though to see that, even in the dim light, his room appeared to be just the same as it had always been. There were no signs of tubes running to his arms or bottles hanging from, whatever it was they hung bottles from. He shuddered as he remembered an earlier scene; perhaps it really had just been a bad dream.

Rani came back into the room, carrying only the bowl and spoon. As she sat down Arthur wondered what had happened to the tray, but as she held the bowl in front of him, he was disappointed to see that she had not exaggerated; there really were only a few spoonfuls in the bottom. When he had finished, he felt suddenly tired.

'That was absolutely wonderful,' he said, sleepily, 'but I think you may be right. Perhaps I should have a little rest.'

Rani leaned over and kissed him on the forehead. He noticed guiltily that she appeared as tired as he felt. There was even the slightest suggestion of bags under her eyes. How much extra work had his illness caused her, he wondered guiltily, as he drifted off to sleep.

***

When Arthur awoke again the sun was still shining beyond the curtains. He could tell from the angle of the shadows however, that it was much later in the day. Far too many of the last few days seemed to have been spent either asleep or lost in thought in darkness. Now that his body was not weighed down with pain, he resolved to get out of his bed as quickly as possible.

With some effort he managed to pull both arms from beneath the coverlet and tried to sit up by himself. Twisting his trunk back and forth and pushing down with his elbows as hard as he could, let him resume the near sitting position he had achieved earlier with Rani's help, but the exertion left him breathless. As he relaxed into the pillows still heaped behind him, he heard the door opened and soft footsteps approach.

'Are you okay?' Ashri asked anxiously, when she had entered far enough for Arthur to see her, 'I thought I heard you moving about.'

'I was just trying to sit up.' Arthur said, 'but it took a little more effort than I had anticipated'.

'You mustn't try to do too much, too soon,' Ashri said, putting the back of her hand to Arthur's forehead. 'You have rather been, through the wars, as they say.'

'I'm starting to feel so much better, but I'm terribly weak.'

Ashri took her hand from his forehead and used it to affectionately stroke the top of Arthur's head, as if petting a small animal.

'You don't have any fever now, she said, 'and you're starting to look quite normal. I shouldn't think it will be any time at all before you're back on your feet.'

'Do you think you could hand me my glass of water?' Arthur asked, 'I can't quite reach it. I seem to have a terrible thirst again. And I could stand a little more light, if you don't mind opening the curtain some more. The sun is nearly down, now.'

Ashri obediently handed Arthur his glass, after first making sure he was able to hold it by himself, then moved to the far side of the room and opened the curtain further. As she turned to re-join him, he nearly dropped the glass of water. In the increased light it was obvious that Ashri was hugely pregnant.

Chapter Thirty-Nine

It was a scene straight from some fantastical dream, but Arthur was being regularly reassured that he was not dreaming. He was surrounded by what had become the four dearest people to him in the entire world. Each one was gently rubbing one of his arms or legs; encouraging the circulation, they later explained. It had been a daily ritual for many days, even before he had awakened they told him, ever since the new skin had been strong enough to withstand it.

Ashri, Zanli and Yetti were each so enlarged from their pregnancies it seemed there was hardly room for them all in the same room, let alone crowded around his bedside. Only Rani appeared as Arthur remembered her. The look of tiredness Arthur had noticed earlier, or was it yesterday – he kept losing track of time – was absent.

From time to time the massage was interrupted with a cry from one of the three younger ones. 'Oh Arthur, your daughter is kicking me. Quick, feel here, just here,' and a rounded belly was presented to him; a hand guided his to the correct location and he could indeed, feel the new life within. Each movement brought tears to his eyes. He had never before felt such love, such protectiveness or such responsibility to another being. Looking at the three, each one so happy in their present state, he could not help feeling uncomfortable. The passion he had discovered with each, now seemed somehow wrong. They felt more like daughters to him; the act in retrospect struck him almost of incest and he could not but help feeling disgusted with himself.

Rani had tried to explain to him that his emotions might be distorted. She had sat at his bedside that morning telling him that the months of darkness and sedation had been necessary; he had undergone, what they called "the metamorphosis".

'And I haven't turned into a gigantic beetle?' he had quipped weakly, trying to make a joke of the situation.

'No Gregor, but for a few days you may have a similar problem rolling over,' she had replied with a smile. 'Seriously though, it is not uncommon for those of us from the valley to undergo such a change as we approach old age, but we have the strength, or perhaps the stamina, I'm not sure which is technically correct, to withstand the process. When it occurs to outsiders, the process has in the past been usually fatal.'

'What causes it?' Arthur asked, verging on exasperation, and before she could reply, 'Is it something I caught from one of you? God, how many other ways do you have to kill us?'

'It is probably a virus or something.' Rani said, patiently. 'I cannot give you a scientific explanation; you will have to ask Neanthi for that. As far as I know, she is the only one who has made a study of the problem.'

'Neanthi. She's the older, white-haired woman? Speaks German? Is that Zanli's grandmother?'

'Yes... yes... and yes again,' Rani said, quite seriously, but with hidden laughter in her eyes, 'and I think perhaps, in that very order'.

Arthur was unable to suppress a laugh; he suddenly remembered how much he loved this woman.

'Neanthi practiced, and taught, medicine in Germany for many, many years,' Rani continued, 'and when she returned to our valley, she was able to do research in, well, in things that are peculiar to us'.

'I see.'

'So, it is thanks to her that you have survived.'

'Remind me to thank her when I see her again.'

'I'm sure you won't have to be reminded,' Rani smiled, 'and as far as the other ways we have of killing you, the list is far too long for me to enumerate.'

She bent over and kissed Arthur's forehead, then abruptly left the room. Arthur had only just started thinking how much he hoped she was joking when she returned carrying a mirror set in a slender wooden frame. She had placed the mirror glass side down on the bed before going to the window and pulling the curtains wide open.

Arthur blinked with the increase in light, but it no longer hurt his eyes. When she returned to his bedside, she lifted one of his arms from under the coverlet and held it where he could see it.

'Arthur, look at yourself,' she commanded. 'Can you not see a change?'

He looked at the arm she was holding; the skin was pale, almost too pale, a hint of babyish pink just stopped it looking deathly white. It was covered, not with the generous growth of hair, mostly turned grey, that he was accustomed to seeing, but with a short, soft, dark fuzz, like the incipient beard of a teenager.

His gaze moved to his hand. The veins that had wandered across the back, like the trail of a navigationally-challenged mole, were no longer visible. The lines across knuckles and the network of parched-earth-like, tiny furrows had similarly disappeared. Instead of sagging and wrinkled, his skin was taut; true, it was the same pale colour as his arm, but his fingers were firmly fleshy. He turned his hand over, flexed his fingers and admired them in the light from the window. They seemed to have very little strength, but perhaps that wasn't too surprising; they appeared to be the fingers of a child. His mind struggled with how this had come about and what it might mean to him.

Rani had picked up the mirror and held it so that he could see his own face. The top of his head was covered with, an only slightly longer version of, the soft fuzzy hair on his arm; dark brown, almost black hair. The bushy, white tipped eyebrows he had had to trim so regularly were now a thin line of the same hair. Pale whitish skin, like that on his arm, covered his face; a face devoid of bags under the eyes or of hollows in his cheeks. Superficially, he was the same person. It was his own face staring back at him; the same nose and chin, the configuration was still the same, but his eyes were much brighter, and the look of approaching old age was gone.

'Don't worry,' Rani said, soothingly. 'When we've had you out in the sun for a few days you'll get your colouring back.'

'I don't understand,' Arthur said. 'What has happened to me? And please, don't give me that "metamorphosis" stuff, I need to know in simple terms.'

'In simple terms? Your body has regenerated itself. Effectively, you've shed your old skin and grown new, along with most of the muscle tissue. It's more complicated than that, of course, but when everything has settled down you will be, umh, much as you would have been... twenty, perhaps twenty-five years ago.'

Rani's explanation only served to raise more questions in Arthur's already spinning head. 'Does that mean I'll have an extra twenty years, you know, that I'll live longer?' Before Rani could answer, he suddenly felt his desire for this beautiful woman again; the implication was frightening. 'But... but, if I'm younger, does that mean I can't make love to you? You know, what you said about being fatal to younger men, not just you of course, all of you and your attraction to older men and everything...'

'Shhh, shhh,' Rani said quietly, she had taken his head gently between her two hands and turned it so that her eyes were only inches away from his, 'Arthur, Arthur, don't worry. It'll be alright. Believe me, it is a good thing that has happened to you.'

'But, but...'

'We do find old men beautiful. Well, because they are, of course, but because we don't suffer from guilt by causing their deaths. We will still find you beautiful. Even if you do look much younger. And truthfully, much more handsome.'

'That still doesn't...'

'And,' Rani was gently stroking his head, it was to Arthur, almost hypnotic, 'you mustn't worry. I promise you will be able to make love to us. To me, as soon as you are strong enough. And to lots of us. For a very long time. We won't have to worry now about your being "used up", unless you were to do something really silly.'

***

The warmth in his arms and legs from the blissful massage seemed to Arthur a sign that his strength was also returning. He found that he could lift an arm without difficulty, or hold a hand to a quivering belly when commanded to do so. Rani and Zanli each had a foot in one hand and were alternately pushing against it until his knee was raised and the leg bent to nearly ninety degrees. He was then being told to push against them until the leg was nearly straight again. The rhythmic calls of 'push, push', and the alternating movement of his legs combined to give a comical impression of lying down and pedalling a bicycle at the same time.

Why the thought of cycling should suddenly remind him he couldn't fathom, but he was suddenly filled with panic. His lack of thought was inexplicable and at the same time unforgivable. He had been awake for, how long now, receiving explanations, assurances and loving care, but not once had thoughts of her crossed his mind. He pulled an arm free from Yetti and clapped his hand to his mouth.

Rani looked up with concern, from her task of manipulating his leg 'what is it Arthur?'

'Ester?'

Chapter Forty

'I think you girls should leave us alone for a few minutes,' Rani said quietly, 'Arthur's had enough exercise for now.'

The three filed out obediently, after each giving Arthur a kiss on the cheek or forehead and telling him that they would see him later. When they were out of earshot Arthur turned to Rani. 'How long did you say I had been like this? Over six months?'

'Just under seven.'

'I feel so stupid, so selfish. I was so wound up with what was happening with me; I never gave a thought to Ester. Have you managed to contact her? To tell her I'll be all right?'

Rani pulled a chair up to his bed again and took one of his hands in hers. She looked him directly in the eyes, hers wide with sincerity. 'Arthur, you must understand; you could never have gone home again.'

'But,' he blurted, 'I was only supposed to be here for a fortnight. She'll be worried sick. What do you mean? Never gone home?'

'I'm sorry, it may be difficult for you,' Rani replied, 'I had hoped to get you to volunteer to stay here. I think you would have, if your condition hadn't come on so quickly. I could happily shoot that bloody girl.'

Arthur had not heard Rani swear before. Her vociferousness surprised him; reminded him of an uncomfortable episode; distracted him from their present conversation for a moment.

'It's going to be okay,' she continued, softly stroking his head with her free hand. 'You have seen what we are, how we live, how different we are from you. Surely you know in your heart, that we could never have let you gone back to the outside world with that knowledge.'

'I thought you loved me. Do you mean you would...' he was reluctant to say the word, '...kill me? I wouldn't have told anyone about you. No one would ever believe me, anyway.'

'Of course we wouldn't have killed you. And I do love you; more than you can imagine. We would just never have shown you the way out. You would never have been able to find the way on your own.'

'That isn't what I meant though; did you find a way to contact Ester? Even if it was only to tell her that I wouldn't be coming back?'

'She has been informed by the authorities,' Rani shrugged. 'She thinks you are dead, Arthur. Some things of yours were found; your shoulder bag with your passport and driving license inside. It was badly chewed and mauled, but recognizable and covered in your blood. The car you had hired was found abandoned in the tiger reserve you went to visit. Your guide said you insisted on venturing alone into areas that he was too frightened to go into. He was very convincing, seemed very ashamed and blamed himself for not stopping you. You have been formally declared dead.'

'That's ridiculous,' Arthur was almost shouting. 'How could that have happened? I didn't hire a car and I haven't been near a tiger reserve. Well, not on this trip.'

'I know Arthur, I know,' Rani continued to stroke his head as if soothing a small animal. 'But don't you think that way is easier on Ester? Don't you think she would be hurt if she thought you had abandoned her for another woman? Let alone an entire valley of young women queuing up for your attention,' Rani allowed herself a small laugh, 'I really don't think she would understand, do you? Isn't it better to have you declared dead? She can collect your insurance, she will not be left in limbo and she can remarry if she finds someone suitable. Let's hope she doesn't settle for that dreadful friend of hers, though.'

Arthur was nearly devastated by the amount of information coming at him all at once. The thought that the headaches he had suffered might return worried him for a moment, but within seconds he realized that Rani was right; had he been asked to stay, he would have gladly agreed. It had been resolved without any effort on his part; nor was there any reason to feel guilt, it was all beyond his control. An almost palpable peacefulness descended upon him, leaving him only feeling curious.

'How did you manage to arrange all that?' he asked, 'I mean with the bag and the hire car and all.'

'It was very easy, Arthur. We are surrounded with a very poor country. And in such a country, bribery is still a way of life.'

'Was it really that easy?'

'Perhaps I oversimplified it a little; there was a more to it than that, but it is fairly easy to get people to do or say what you want them to with a little money and we do have useful contacts.'

Something in Rani's argument was nagging at Arthur's brain. 'What did you mean by Ester settling for *that dreadful friend of hers*? Are you suggesting there is someone else?'

'Oh Arthur, are you really so naïve?' Rani gave a slight snort through her nose as she stifled a laugh. 'You must know, or at least suspect, there is someone else. From the little you told me of Ester, I can't believe for a moment that she wasn't having an affair. And I'm sure that deep down you must think the same thing yourself.'

'Well, I can't believe she would have an affair,' Arthur replied, angrily pushing Rani's hand away as he forced himself to an upright position. 'And I can't remember what I might have said that makes you think I suspect her of having one, but if she did, I'm sure it wouldn't be anything more than a spur of the moment thing. You seem to think I know who it would be with, but I can't think of any of her friends that I would describe as *dreadful*.'

'I'm sorry Arthur,' Rani said soothingly, 'let's hope that I'm wrong. Perhaps I just put two and two together...'

'No, maybe it's best if you are right,' Arthur said, settling back into the pillows, his anger spent as quickly as it had flared, 'I'd hate to think of Ester grieving for me; she's strong in some ways, but she shouldn't be on her own. That may be why I couldn't decide to stay here when I really wanted to. I knew that I'd feel so guilty that it would spoil everything.'

Chapter Forty-One

Over the next few weeks Arthur made, what he thought of as, astonishing progress. Each step towards his full recovery seemed to be a major accomplishment. The day following his argument with Rani, he had taken his first steps since being bedridden. Accompanied by Yetti and Zanli, actually he admitted later, supported between Yetti and Zanli, he walked as far as the bathroom. He had rebelled when one of them had approached with a bedpan and had pleaded with them to let him try walking. He was exhausted by the time he had returned to his bed, but was filled with a feeling of pride.

He had seen his reflection in the large mirror and pulled his robe open to have a better view of the changes. The smooth white skin covering his body and the almost formless flesh gave him an appearance he could only think of as a slug-like. He shuddered with repugnance and hastily pulled his robe around himself again.

'Don't worry,' said Zanli, putting an arm around his shoulders and pulling him firmly against her. 'You will get your colour back when we can get you out in the sun.'

'And your muscle tone will quickly improve,' added Yetti from his other side, 'just as soon as you are able to start doing some exercise'.

'But look,' Zanli added, patting his buttocks as she took the robe from him and helped him back into his bed, 'that bottom is no longer sagging'.

'Not to mention,' Yetti giggled, as she stroked his stomach with one hand, before pulling his coverlet up, 'your little pot belly. It isn't there now; you will soon have a nice flat tummy again.'

'I didn't have a pot belly,' Arthur protested, not sure if they were teasing or serious, 'and I wasn't aware that my bottom sagged. Is that what you really thought of me?'

'Oh yes you did,' Yetti went on. 'You held it in very well when you thought about it, but when you relaxed,' she patted his stomach again, 'it often popped out over your belt'.

Both girls laughed. Zanli stroked the soft downy hair on his head and gave him a loving look; from the other side of his bed Yetti softly ran a finger down his cheek and smiled at him. Together they leaned over and kissed him on the cheeks from either side.

'Your bottom was only a little saggy,' Zanli said softly, as they turned to leave the room. 'Actually it was pretty good for your age.'

The very next day Arthur insisted on having his meals in the dining room. Despite returning to his room completely exhausted and needing a nap after each meal, he refused to be fed any more meals in his room. Within days though, he was spending most of his time in the sunny little courtyard behind the kitchen.

Instead of returning to his room after a meal, he would first stop in Rani's library to select a book, before wandering into the kitchen. After a short conversation with Aszli which usually left him feeling unnerved, he would continue to the courtyard and position one of the old-fashioned, wood and canvas deck chairs in the sunniest corner. On his first venture there, Ashri had shown him the path of the shadows from the overhanging vines and placed him in a position that would be in shade within an hour.

At first he was accompanied everywhere he went; usually by either Ashri, Zanli or Yetti, but sometimes by two or even all three. He no longer knew what to think of them as; true, he loved each one deeply, but to think of them as lovers didn't seem quite right. He felt absurdly protective about them, especially in their present awkward state and, never having had children, wondered if this was how a father felt about his daughters. The thought that he was responsible for their present state, again made him feel uncomfortable, even though he constantly reminded himself that, in spite of his paternal feelings, they were not related to him and he had no reason to feel guilty about the joy they had shared.

If he wanted to read, his consort for the day would also select a book; if he felt like talking or asking questions that troubled him, they would quickly put their book aside and engage in conversation;

if he felt tired and only wanted to fall asleep in the sun, he usually awoke to find them napping as well. He started to feel guilty about such deference and spoke to Rani about it one evening after dinner.

'I don't think you quite realize,' Rani said confidentially, 'just how highly you are now regarded. Since your survival of the metamorphosis, you've attained an almost god-like position in this valley. There are literally hundreds of young women vying to be the first to mate with you. In being the only three that have "produced" before your metamorphosis, Ashri, Zanli and Yetti have also been awarded great status. They will always be thought of as your protectors, your permanent consorts.'

'I hadn't realized,' Arthur said pensively; it seemed suddenly an enormous responsibility.

'The love they feel for you is beyond description.'

'You must know that I feel the same for them,' he paused, 'but it isn't the same as I feel for you. It's more a… platonic… a fatherly love, I guess you could say. What I feel for you is so different. When you walk into the room, I suppose I shouldn't tell you this, but I find it difficult to breath; I can't take my eyes off you, I forget what I was thinking about…'

'That's just lust,' Rani interrupted; the twinkle had returned to her eyes. The tired look she displayed too often disappeared for a moment, 'and I feel exactly the same about you. I told you once, that you would be able to make love to me soon, but your change came about too quickly. It has been far too long for me. I promise as soon as you are strong enough, we will be together.'

'It's more than just lust,' Arthur laughed. 'And to think that I'm going to be able to stay with you… perhaps for the rest of my life,' he paused again, 'it's too good to be true'.

Rani moved to the other side of the table and pulled a chair around so that she could sit beside him. He put one arm around her shoulders and she leaned against his chest. They sat that way for a long time.

***

Days went by. As his strength returned Arthur began to feel restless and with someone always to accompany him, started taking afternoon walks around the neighbourhood. He expressed concern about the effect that too much exertion might have on any of the three who were pregnant, so Aszli was given the responsibility of being in attendance when his walks grew longer. Spending more time with her, he lost most of the uneasiness that he had formerly felt in her presence, but he still felt that she was in some way controlling him, especially when he had returned from a long walk in the countryside, but could remember little of what had taken place or where they had been.

One afternoon when Rani had suggested they went for a drive, he asked her to stop. In a nearby field a small group of women were carrying bundles of hay from where they had been cut and tied into shocks, to a rapidly growing stack. Arthur remembered his summer of working in the open air and felt an irresistible desire to help them.

'Do you think they would mind?' he asked Rani.

'I'm sure they would love you to help them,' she said with a grin. 'Just don't wear yourself out.'

'They won't...'

'No, I'll move the jeep over into the shade under that tree,' she gesticulated, 'and sit there and read. I brought a book in case you wanted to rest for a while.'

The women were a mixture of ages and several crowded around him in excitement when Arthur walked across the field to where they were working. He steeled himself for a reaction similar to those he had had on his first few days in the valley, but the women kept a respectful distance. Their excitement turned to bemusement when he started gathering a few of the shocks together, hoisted them onto his shoulders and carried them to the foot of the growing stack. When he dropped the bundle in front of a woman with a pitchfork, as he had seen the others doing, she gave him a wide grin, wordlessly stabbed at the bundles of hay with her fork and heaved them upwards where two other women were strategically placing them around the perimeter of the stack. The other women resumed their work of gathering the shocks into bundles, but Arthur could hear murmured comments spreading amongst them.

The sun, which had seemed warm when he first started work, soon felt very hot and he considered removing the light cotton *kurti* he was

310

wearing. From the days of sunbathing in Rani's courtyard his normal colouring had returned and from the exercises that Neathili had prescribed, his muscle tone had vastly improved, but remembering the first glimpse he had had of himself in his new form, he still felt momentarily reluctant to bare his chest. The heat rapidly drove him to a corner of the field where the women had left extra clothing, bottles of water and what he assumed was the remains of their lunches. He removed his jacket and folded it neatly before placing it alongside the piles of belongings, then returned to the working area.

Picking up his next bundle of shocks, he realized the mistake he had made. The scratchy bundles of hay clawed at his neck and shoulders without the protection of his jacket. He was about to return for the garment despite the heat, when he noticed one of the older women beckoning to him. As he approached her she began unwinding some of the material tied around her waist. She gestured for him to sit in front of her and carefully wound much of the length of material around his head into an approximation of a turban. The remainder she positioned at the back of his neck, then tied the ends around his shoulders.

The makeshift cape gave far better protection from the sharp ends of the hay than his jacket had afforded and he was determined to work with the women as long as he was able. He could not fail to notice some teasing of the Good Samaritan but it always seemed to be good-natured and she seemed to wear a perpetual grin when he looked her way.

As dusk approached, the last few shocks were gathered and stacked. There were now three large haystacks in the corner of the field and Arthur felt he had contributed a noticeable amount. He was surrounded by the women as they all made their way back to the corner where their belongings had been left, but he could only sense a quiet respect and nothing of the ribaldry he had experienced in his first few days. He shared one of the water bottles that were passed round and, with a little effort, managed to unwind the caped turban before returning it to his benefactor with a slight bow. She took it from him with a giggle then, as if it was an afterthought, grabbed his hand and kissed it.

Arthur found Rani sitting sideways in her jeep, the picnic rug that seemed to live in the vehicle propped against her back and her legs resting on the passenger seat. The book she had been reading was turned pages down on her lap and she at first appeared to be sleeping. As he grew closer it became obvious her head was turned down and away, not in sleep, but in an attempt to suppress her laughter.

'That seemed to go well,' she said when she had regained her composure. 'Have you completely tired yourself out?'

'Ye-es,' he said with a stretch and a yawn, 'but it feels so good to be working my body. Or, perhaps it's just being able to do the work. But, I'm really looking forward to a hot shower when we get home.'

'You will probably be full of aches tomorrow,' she said, repositioning herself behind the wheel as he climbed into the other side. 'Would you be happy if we went for a sail on the lake again?'

Chapter Forty-Two

'I hope you aren't unhappy with me,' Rani said, 'you were very quiet last night.'

They were sitting on Rani's little boat, the remains of their picnic resting on the engine cover. They had headed towards the centre of the lake, until the whiteness of the rising mist again surrounded them and had obscured their view of the distant shoreline. Rani had cut the engine and the boat had coasted to a stop. Arthur had expected the excursion to be a repeat of their earlier trip onto the lake and had started to unbutton his shirt in anticipation of a swim, but Rani had immediately started to unpack their lunch.

'I suppose I was tired from my work in the field yesterday,' Arthur replied. 'I'm certainly not unhappy with you. Why would I be?'

'I don't know; I have rather forced you to stay here. You're sure you don't have regrets? You're not missing Ester?'

'Do you know?' he thought for a moment, 'it's such a relief. I should, of course, but I don't miss her at all. Quite the opposite, in fact.'

'Promise me, you're not just saying that.'

'Absolutely. For the last few years, even before I retired and spent more time around the house, it seemed that everything I did annoyed Ester. She criticized me constantly. I simply couldn't do anything right, or at least, not in her eyes.' Despite himself, his voice rose as he remembered various incidents. 'If I washed up, as I usually did, and forgot to wring the little sponge we used completely dry, I would get a ten-minute lecture about how it would smell if it wasn't dried properly. If I vacuumed before dusting, I would get a lecture about doing it wrong. It was such bloody, trivial, sh...' he stopped himself, aware he was almost shouting, 'stuff!'

Rani put a hand on his shoulder. 'It sounds as if you've been bottling up things for quite a while.'

'You know,' he resumed in a more even tone, 'she tried to do some lovely things. When I retired, she even bought me an expensive set of golf clubs and a membership in a prestige club.'

'I think that sounds very nice of her.'

'I would have thought the same thing if I hadn't said so many times how much I disliked golf. I had tried it when I was younger, but to me it just seemed pointless and I didn't like the competitive blustering of some people when they got on a golf course or the jokey, blokey banter in the clubhouse afterwards.'

'So you didn't appreciate her gift?'

'I honestly tried to take up the game up again; took some of my friends that were golfers as guests, but ultimately just stopped going.'

'Wasn't Ester disappointed that you didn't appreciate her gift?'

'I never told her. For a while, I had tried playing one day a week, Thursdays, and when I stopped playing I just didn't mention it to Ester. I went to the library instead.'

Rani laughed. 'I can't decide if that is completely underhand or admirably altruistic.'

'Oh, it was completely underhand,' Arthur joined in her laughter, 'you see, if I started to read a book in the daytime, and I really do enjoy reading, Ester would always find something that was *more important*. Something that urgently needed to be done. The lawn needed mowing. Her car was in desperate need of cleaning. Couldn't I repair that, something or other that was in dire need of repair?'

'Was it really that bad?'

Arthur wasn't completely sure if Rani was sympathizing, or questioning his ability to present the situation without prejudice. 'Probably not, but by spending the day, or at least an afternoon, in the library I could indulge my own interests and at the same time, not hurt her feelings. I thought it would give her a little time in the house alone. I'd read that some women who had grown accustomed to having a house to themselves, felt encroached upon when they had to share it with a retired husband. I'd actually overheard complaints from a friend's wife, when he had retired, about suddenly having a husband under her feet all the time.'

'I can assure you that no one will ever ask you to play golf here.'

'And I can assure you that I miss nothing of my past. To me, it's as if I've been here only a few days, but I know that I'm happy to spend the rest of my days here with you.'

Rani leaned forward and put her arms around Arthur, kissed him on the cheek, then let her head rest on his shoulder. They sat like that for a few minutes, then her voice little more than a whisper, Rani said, 'Could we sit together like we did last time? Could you just hold me for a while?'

Arthur rearranged the cushions so that he could lean back against the transom with his arms around Rani as she in turn reclined against him. For some time the only sound was from the lapping of little waves against the hull. He could feel her body relax against his and just as he was beginning to think Rani had fallen asleep, she turned her head enough for him to hear her whisper, 'I think it will be tonight.'

***

To Arthur, making love to Rani was like coming home to the smells of freshly baked loaves of bread, coffee gently bubbling in a percolator, gingerbread cooling on racks and a fire blazing away on the hearth. It was the fulfilment of longings for things that had always been absent from his existence. Things that he had imagined were commonplace to those around him, but were denied to him, despite any amount of requests. It was as if he could palpably feel the warmth of Rani's love for him, the unquestioning acceptance of his faults and the forgiveness of all of his transgressions.

Her arms had enveloped him and her kisses, though initially as painful as her predecessors, took him to unprecedented heights of ecstasy. When they joined, it was like two great rivers merging, the Mosel flowing into the Rhine, the Missouri meeting the Mississippi; each retaining their own identity for only a brief period before becoming one magnificent force. Nothing existed outside of their

315

mutual indescribable bliss. Finally after what could have been hours, but may have been minutes or even seconds, time had become an almost incomprehensible irrelevance, they exploded like some supernova amongst lesser stars.

To Arthur, the overwhelming feeling of peace, of completion, of achievement, that accompanied the floating weightlessness which followed, was as much a part of the experience as the passion that had preceded it. There was no need for conversation; there were no words which could add to their enjoyment. He felt himself drifting off to sleep, aware only of this wonderful creature lying in his arms.

Chapter Forty-Three

Arthur awoke to the feeling of pins and needles in one arm. Rani was still lying with her back to him, her head resting on his outstretched arm. The smell of her hair, so close to his face, brought an aura of excitement and he wondered what the new day would bring. Would there be a repeat of the previous day's performance?

Finally, he could withstand the pain no longer. He kissed Rani's bare shoulder and with his free hand lifted her head enough to pull his protesting arm free. She made no indication that he had disturbed her and he softly lowered her head back onto the pillow. Her shoulder had felt cold when he kissed it so he pulled up the light coverlet that had been pushed aside in the night, tucked it around her and patted her shoulder. Still she made no response. Was she just pretending to be sleeping so deeply? Would she suddenly leap up like a child playing a joke? He leaned over to look at her face. Her eyes were closed, but she wore a contented smile as if she were enjoying the most delightful dream. He trailed his fingers lightly down her cheek; it felt as cold as her shoulder.

Arthur suddenly felt a wave of panic, something was very wrong. He put one hand on Rani's shoulder and shook her firmly, but there was still no response. He knelt beside her and pulled her upright against himself. Her head lolled to one side and her arms fell limply. Her entire upper body felt as cold as her shoulder.

'No,' he screamed, as the realization struck home, 'no, no, no-o-o....'

He held her in his arms and rocked back and forth, tears streaming down his face. He remembered her having held him in the very same manner, calling him back from somewhere very distant.

'Rani,' he cried out, 'Rani... Rani... come back, please come back'.

He felt a gentle hand on his shoulder. 'It is no use,' he heard Ashri say, 'you must let her go. She wouldn't want to come back; you must not distress yourself.'

'I don't understand,' he sobbed, continuing to hold Rani's limp body to his chest, supporting her head, stroking her hair. 'How can you say she wouldn't want to come back? We've only begun.'

'Arthur, I told you that *oolontha* was called the gift. It can also be a gift of release,' her hand continued to slowly stroke his shoulder and the back of his neck, 'a gift of freedom from pain. A gift of a new beginning. A beginning that you so briefly experienced. Would you deny that to her? You must let her go, Arthur.'

Barely able to see through the tears, Arthur gently lowered Rani's body to the bed, placed her in a comfortable-looking position and arranged the coverlet to hide her nakedness. As he straightened, he felt Ashri's arms envelope him; her enlarged breasts and belly pressing firmly into his back.

'Rani was afraid that you would be distressed by her choice,' she said, kissing the back of his head. 'She made us promise not to let on, not to give you the slightest hint of her intentions.'

'You mean you knew?' he twisted to look her in the eyes. 'How could you let her do such a thing?'

Ashri lowered her eyes. Yetti and Zanli had entered the room and both moved to his side, reaching out to touch him, to stroke a shoulder or his head.

'You must not blame Ashri,' Zanli said quietly. 'We all knew of Rani's wish for release.'

'But why,' he asked, blinking at the tears, 'just when we could be together?'

'She was dying,' Yetti said, her eyes also full of tears. 'She had waited as long as she could. Her pain must have been almost unendurable at times.'

'If it had been possible,' Zanli added, 'she would have left us months ago'.

'There were a few times,' Ashri said as she continued to stroke his shoulders, 'when she didn't think she could wait for you to emerge from your metamorphosis. I found her crying in her office more than once; afraid she would be unable to give you her goodbye.'

Chapter Forty-Four

To try and distract himself from the confused noises around them, and quite unable to hear anything she was saying, Arthur concentrated on the construction of the litter Yetti was carried in. He presumed that litter was the nearest descriptive name in English; he hadn't been able to understand the word Yetti had used for it. The seats, foot and backrests were of a heavy woven fabric and the frame, that gave it the look of a director's chair with long poles protruding to the front and rear, was made of polished wood. The whole assembly was like an open sedan chair and was carried by four women on either side.

Just in front of them Ashri and Zanli were also being carried in the same fashion, but Arthur avoided looking in their direction. When he forgot to avert his eyes, he couldn't help but see the larger version of a litter that Rani was carried upon. The four poles supporting the central platform ran laterally instead of longitudinally and each pole had four women on either side, carrying the entire affair on their shoulders. The platform Rani was resting on was covered with flowers and her body was draped in a rich looking, deep red fabric. Only her face was visible and if Arthur forgot and looked in her direction she appeared to be smiling upwards at the sky. In some places the road or pathway was too narrow for eight women abreast and the outer columns would stand to one side or run forward and re-join when there was more room.

He had made a remark, as they were getting ready for their journey into the mountains, that thirty-two seemed an excessive amount of pallbearers, but Yetti explained that such was the esteem in which Rani was held, hundreds more had volunteered for the honour. Everyone around them seemed to be dressed in their finest costumes, bright and colourful, almost garish costumes; costumes more resembling those he had seen in pictures of African ceremonies, with elaborate, turban-like headdresses and long flowing gowns.

Near the front of the cortege, just behind the dancers and the musicians, strode Rani's two daughters, Zetla and Yantha. The previous day, only hours after his discovery of Rani's "departure", he had been dumbfounded when he had met them. Ashri had introduced Zetla as her mother and Yantha as her aunt, but each held such a physical resemblance to Rani, even to Zetla appearing to be at least as old as Rani, that Arthur couldn't help but thinking it was some kind of cruel joke. He had found them to be mere images of Rani and was grateful that, except for brief periods as they rounded bends or climbed steep gradients, he was unable to see them from his position next to Yetti.

His mind had rejected the explanations of plans made and last visits scheduled. He couldn't make up his mind about how he had felt, being denied the knowledge of Rani's impending death

Ashri had warned that any display of grief would be frowned upon; the procession was to be a celebration of Rani's life, of the joys her existence had brought to those around her and of the wonders of her new state.

'Grief,' she had explained, 'is seen here as selfishness. As simply feeling sorry for oneself. You will not hear anyone asking, "What about me? How am I to go about my life without her?"

Her words had not however, quite warned him of the gaiety that would be displayed. All around them there were songs being stridently sung, there was riotous laughter in response to what Arthur assumed were jokes or anecdotes being told.

When he looked back, at times he could see the parade extended for what looked like miles. They had passed through two other villages, before turning towards the mountains and Arthur assumed they were taking the same route as the procession he and Zanli had witnessed on their day together, but this one was many times larger. And the size of it had grown enormously as they went along. In the villages and lowlands their path had been lined with many others standing alongside, either unable or unwilling to join them, but still cheering and shouting their approval.

Yetti reached out a hand to him and pulled him closer, until he was nearly rubbing against the supporting poles of her litter as he walked alongside.

'It isn't too much for you,' she shouted above the din, 'is it?'

Arthur shook his head.

'Perhaps I can translate some of the stories for you,' she continued, 'it might help you understand'.

'Yes, please,' Arthur shouted back, between noisy bursts of laughter.

'That woman was telling of something Rani had said to her, after one of her visits to your country. You mustn't be offended.'

Arthur shook his head again.

'She said that in travelling about, she had come across many places where the road was being resurfaced. And, although it was clearly evident that the old surface had been scraped away or that fresh new tarmac had been laid, invariably there would be a large red sign, prominently displayed, advising of *Road Markings Removed.* "Wouldn't it have been better," she had asked, "if the sign had been printed in Braille?"'

Arthur smiled to himself; it did indeed sound very much like some of the observations he had heard Rani make on their long journey across India.

Yetti waited for another wave of laughter to subside. 'That woman was telling of Rani's dislike for men westerners like to call *alpha males.* She had never seen it as something to be aspired to and had usually found them quite loathsome. She had said that those who thought of themselves as such, were never good at anything except bellowing and beating their own chests. Shouting down any good suggestions at the meetings she attended and trying to substitute their own ridiculous ideas; for instance, like wasting money on redundant signs, warning of *Road Markings Removed.*'

Arthur suddenly thought of his last afternoon on the boat with Rani. It was the only time she had ever spoken sharply to him. He had jokingly suggested that if he was to remain in the valley, to father the valley's daughters, he would be the new "alpha male".

'Arthur,' she had responded angrily, 'you could never be an alpha male!'

He had, at the time, taken it as an affront; as a dig at his masculinity, or his age or his lack of drive, but he now realized she had meant it as a compliment and he smiled once again.

Far behind them, just barely able to be heard over the laughter and contrasting to the rhythmic drums, flutes, cymbals and singers at the front of the procession, was a song being sung that Arthur recognized from many years ago. It grew louder as more and more of the women trailing behind them joined in and eventually the musicians at the front changed their beat to match that of the singers. Although the tune was familiar, Arthur could not remember what it was about or understand the words being sung until some of the closer women started singing the chorus in English. The song was one about the majority who cannot see much of life about them compared to the one who could see the overall picture.

Before long it seemed as if the entire cortege was singing the song, over and over. Arthur turned to look at Yetti; their eyes met and although she was smiling, he could see that she was trying just as hard as he, to hold back the tears.

After another hour of slowly climbing, the route grew more and more narrow. Vertical cliffs rose to one side and a sheer drop of hundreds of feet overlooked a small river to the other. In answer to Arthur's unspoken query how they were to get Rani's litter through this narrow passage, he saw the lateral poles angled so that they almost ran fore and aft. Most of the women pallbearers stood aside as the remaining few carefully negotiated the narrow passage. Zanli's litter bearers, who had been walking alongside those of Ashri's, stood still as hers continued on, falling in behind only after Ashri's had passed through. Arthur started to release Yetti's hand, but she gripped it even tighter, pulling him so close that they were able to squeeze through the passage together.

On the other side, the pathway led into a wide, bowl-shaped area overlooking the river below. Those carrying Rani's remains approached a mound of what appeared to be white gravel, near the sheer drop and lowered the litter to the ground at one side. The musicians and dancers had already filed past the mound as Zetla and Yantha took up a place at the far end. The women carrying Ashri,

Zanli and Yetti also lowered their litters to the ground, allowing them to walk the last few paces. Yetti, still holding tightly to Arthur's hand, followed them to a position at the opposite end of the mound. Arthur watched as the hundreds of women, suddenly silent, streamed through the narrow passage and slowly filled the entire area. When he turned back he could not help but see that Rani's body had been placed atop the mound, still clad in the mound of red material and surrounded by the bundles of flowers.

'Is there to be a funeral pyre?' he wondered to himself. 'But if so, where are the stacks of wood that would be required? Surely, they were not just going to pitch her body into the river below.'

A low chant started amongst the most distant of the crowd, spread to the entire assembly and was joined by the percussion instruments, increasing in volume until the entire area reverberated with its intensity. It continued for several minutes until, like a radio being unexpectedly turned off in mid-song, it stopped abruptly and the gathered women started filing past the mound, before passing out through the narrow entrance. At the rate of their solemn parade, Arthur knew it would take many minutes, perhaps an hour or more, before the entire crowd had left and was grateful when Yetti released his hand, before putting her arm around his waist and pulling him towards her. Together they supported each other in silence until Arthur noticed Yetti was scrunching up her shoulders as if in pain. He moved her to one side so that he could rub her shoulders and back, but in turning he noticed one woman amongst the crowd, clad completely in black, her face partially hidden by the black shawl covering her head.

'Someone forgot to tell her that mourning was forbidden,' he whispered in Yetti's ear, nodding in the woman's direction.

'She isn't mourning for Rani,' Yetti whispered back, 'she is mourning for her daughter. Or rather, the daughters she will never have. That's Simili. She has been made to wear that garb as one who has been convicted of a dreadful crime.'

'Why won't she have a daughter?' Arthur asked. 'The three of you became pregnant after only one... uh.'

'Yes, I know,' Yetti smiled at his embarrassment. 'She was made to give up the foetus; it was aborted. Now, she will never be allowed to mate.'

323

'That's terrible.'

'She was very lucky not to have been put to death for what she did to you. If you had died, she would have been. Tragically, it has resulted in another line of our people that will not continue. Do you see why I am so in favour of changing many of our rules?'

Arthur watched fascinated as Simili grew closer. Their eyes met briefly as she drew abreast, but she lowered hers immediately. The look of contrition on her face was like a stab in the heart to Arthur. He suddenly felt guilty; more the cause for her predicament than the victim of their encounter; he had an urge to run to her, to take her in his arms in front of everyone and tell her she was forgiven.

As if sensing his intention, Yetti squeezed his hand even tighter and put her other arm back around his waist. Reluctantly, he realized that this was Rani's day; that to follow his urges might divert the obvious adulation of this crowd for her. He followed Simili with his eyes and saw her turn to look back at him over her shoulder, just before she disappeared into the narrow passageway. He smiled and nodded in her direction, trying to reassure her that he was aware of his obligation.

Yetti's squeezing and releasing of his hand brought him back to his surroundings; she was being loaded back into her litter, as was Ashri and Zanli. Zetla and Yantha had already passed by, as had the musicians and all but four of Rani's pallbearers. They turned as one to begin their long journey back and as Ashri's litter passed him, she leaned over and told him firmly that he was not to look back.

'No, whatever you do,' Yetti echoed, 'you mustn't'.

Their admonitions only strengthened his curiosity and his momentary glance was enough to see that the last women had removed and folded the crimson cloth covering Rani's body. She lay there, still surrounded by flowers, but naked, vulnerable and completely exposed to the elements. His distraction with Simili had made him oblivious of the dark shapes that had gathered and were circling in the sky above them. The first of these was still back-pedalling its huge wings to halt its descent as it hopped the last few paces towards the mound, its scrawny neck and hooked beak outstretched in anticipation.

Chapter Forty-Five

Yetti had tried her best to console Arthur. She had asked her bearers to let her dismount and had taken Arthur in her arms, holding him tightly to her swollen body. He had managed somehow to negotiate the narrow passage, his vision distorted by tears, but as he emerged onto the wider path, he had given way to the sadness inside and fallen to his knees, his body shaking uncontrollably. Yetti held him tightly as she stroked his back and whispered soothing words to him.

'How can you do such a thing?' he had asked in bewilderment between sobs. 'It's barbaric.'

'Is it such a bad thing?' Yetti asked softly. 'Is it worse than burying someone in the ground, to let their body rot or be consumed by worms? Is it worse than burning them, reducing their body to ash? Are not two of our greatest fears, that of being buried alive, to be confined under the soil, unable to breathe or of being painfully burned in a fire?'

'I know, I know,' he whispered, 'but those creatures are so horrible'.

'We believe that every creature serves a purpose, including vultures. We are all part of the whole, are we not?'

'I know I've read of something similar, are they called Parsis that practice this? Or, perhaps I should ask, are you Parsis here?'

'No, we are not Parsis, but we may have come to India at the same time and we may have adopted some of their practices, or they ours. Parsi means Persian and their religion is that of Zoroaster. We all came to India fleeing from religious persecution. Our belief is called Oneism, as I said, we are all part of the whole. Every atom, every worm, every insect, every grain of sand and every being. The whole may be the universe, the cosmos, everything. You might think of it as God, we just call it One.'

With Yetti's help, Arthur regained his feet and in turn helped her back into her litter. The hand that had clasped his so tightly on the outward journey held it just as firmly for the entire return.

***

Aszli had prepared a meal for him and volunteered to keep him company for the evening. Everyone else would be attending the gathering. Zanli had warned that over the entire valley, the evening's gatherings were to be further celebrations of Rani's life. The celebrations would be unusually riotous, filled with storytelling, dancing and singing. Enormous quantities of aqui would be consumed, even by those whose condition should preclude such activities and those returning to Rani's house would probably arrive as morning approached, much the worse for wear.

Arthur could not decide if it had been his own idea or if it was the influence of Aszli's hypnotic eyes, but he had persuaded her to join the others. He would, he insisted, be perfectly content to be left on his own.

The meal looked to be as appetizing as the best of Ashri's offers, but he could not bring himself to even try it. Instead, he merely sipped at the cold white wine and that too seemed to be without appeal. He sat the glass down and wandered into the little courtyard. It was still light out, but he knew the sun would soon be setting and he was no longer surprised by how quickly darkness could envelope the world here. He could already hear the sound of music, of drums, of flutes and of singing from the distant gathering. At times the music paused, but he could still hear a clamour of shouts and of laughter that penetrated the stillness of the evening.

He was perplexed that in the happy celebrations of her life, in the recounting of her many achievements, no one had spoken of missing Rani. How could no one else feel the emptiness that ate away at him? He tried desperately to concentrate on the joys in store for him; holding in his arms the baby daughters that were soon to be born. He thought of the love he felt for their mothers and of the multitude of similar young women of whom he might feel the same way. His old life was behind him and there was little of it he missed, but he could not escape from the guilt he felt for his treatment of Ester. He thought of the punishment that had been meted out to Simili; was he not partly responsible? Should he not have made more of an attempt to resist her demands on him and slow down her impulses?

He remembered the glass of wine he had left behind in the dining room. It suddenly appealed and he retraced his steps, lighting candles in the kitchen and hallway. The wine had lost its chill, but not its subtle flavour and he took a large gulp instead of his usual sip, nearly draining the glass. On his way back through the kitchen he found the opened bottle, residing in a niche in the large refrigerator, and refilled the glass, before returning to the delicate wrought iron chair in the courtyard.

Everything he saw reminded him of Rani. This was Rani's house, her own creation, and he could not look at a single object without being reminded of her. The way she looked when descending the stairs or sitting at the little table in her library, her legs elegantly crossed and ankles neatly tucked under her chair. The way she concentrated when she sat at her computer, surrounded by the purposeful chaos on her desk. He could not stop thinking of her large turquoise eyes, her soft full lips or the fragrant smell of her when he had held her close.

The nearly full moon was rising, only slightly obscured by the trees. It reminded Arthur of his first afternoon with Rani on the lake and the mad moonlit dash she had made through the many villages on their way back. He suddenly remembered the way she had called him back from his 'dream' and inevitably, the utter peacefulness he had experienced during it.

Was that what Rani was feeling now? Would her memories of him, of her daughters, of her entire life vanish as quickly as his had? Would they be replaced by the indescribable joy of mingling with countless other souls? If he were to follow her, would they fail to recognize each other? The thought of being with her, even if they were to never remember what they had shared or felt for each other, suddenly offered a release from his despondency.

He drained the last of his wine, sat the empty glass back on the table and stood up. In the distance the sounds of the gathering had risen to a new pitch, but he knew the presence of his adopted family would frustrate his purpose. Both outward and return journeys to the mountains had again taken them through Village Number Three and he was sure he could find the shortcut Zanli and he had used when they had cycled there.

Out on the now familiar street, the appearance was unchanged, but the flickering, sconce-held torches reminded him of his first night when he had arrived with Rani and his feeling of loss increased, knowing she would never guide him along this route again. At the edge of the village the light from the lit streets diminished, but the moonlight was almost as bright as daylight and within minutes he found the lane that led through the fields. The sounds of the gathering at Village Number One faded before he had even found his second wind, but was soon replaced by the faint, more distant sounds of celebrations from another gathering. A gathering that he assumed would be less inhibited. He was suddenly aware of the pounding in his ears of his own heartbeat. The tempo of his footsteps increased and he smiled at the thought of his own liberation.

Chapter Forty-Six

Ester sat in the cheery little waiting room, staring without comprehension at the glossy celebrity magazine on her lap. The cup of coffee on the table beside her had gone untouched and now was too cold to drink. How many hours, she wondered, had she spent here? How many magazines had she glanced at and how many cups of coffee had she let go to waste?

She was grateful for the advice from the nice young nurse, the one that seemed to understand and always had time to explain things to her, that it would be more pleasant to wait in here, in these quiet surroundings, where the coffee was free and the people going in and out were so much more relaxed than those agitated souls in the corridor-like room with its uncomfortable plastic chairs outside the intensive care unit. The same nurse had had a word with the receptionist on her first visit; this waiting room for the physiotherapy department in the private wing was only just around the corner and convenient for the intensive care unit.

If she came too early there always seemed to be a crowd inside and often overflowing into the corridor outside the door to Arthur's room. Sometimes it appeared to be an annual general meeting of the hospital, there were so many involved. There were often more nurses than could be imagined; the anaesthetist who seemed to be in charge, another man she thought was an orthopaedic surgeon, perhaps the one that had put his broken bones together and others she didn't recognize and seemed to change daily, did it really take so many?

Even after she was allowed into his room, she was often ushered out while "adjustments" were made. Tubes would be removed from one place and would reappear, protruding from somewhere else on his body. For a few days he had been turned on to his front, his neck at an awkward looking angle and then turned onto his back again when it was found he hadn't "progressed" as had been expected. The gruesome-looking pipe secured with tape and nearly filling his wide-open mouth had, for a time, been replaced with a mask that nearly covered his face. Within days, the convoluted pipe had returned as the mask had "presented complications".

The medical dramas she had so often seen on television simply had not prepared her for the actuality of watching someone you love in such a situation. She had found it dreadfully distressing to see Arthur's bloated face, his wildly rolling eyes and his struggles, as he appeared to be frightened by his carers. She had expected, as was usually depicted, for him to merely lie there serenely, with perhaps a bleeping sound from the watchful electronics indicating that everything was going according to plan. Instead, the too frequent emergencies; his breathing tube regularly filling with mucus and having to be noisily emptied or any of the other problems where she was asked to leave the room as they were corrected, she had found equally upsetting. And if someone tried to explain to her what they were doing or why, in terms that were too technical, like the superior-mannered doctor's details about needles clotting over and pumps giving "surges" resulting in too little or too much pain-killing drugs, her mind seemed to glaze over, leaving her in a state of fuzzy helplessness.

She had been prepared for the bandages, after all the police had told her he had been knocked down by a hit-and-run driver, but then at the hospital she had been told that his injuries were almost insignificant when compared to the pneumonia-like infection he had gained lying in a frosty ditch all night.

The accident had obviously occurred when he was walking back from the once weekly visits to his favourite pub. How many times had she begged him not to use that dark, narrow twisting lane as a short-cut and to stick to the main well-lit streets? With the care he was receiving and the apparent capability of his medical team, she had expected a quick recovery, for there to be fresh signs of progress daily, to be told good news each day as she arrived, but this business of their being optimistic one day and being told of further complications the next was, after nearly three weeks, getting her down.

What would she do, she thought, if he failed to improve, if it came to the worst and he simply failed to recover? They had warned her that he might at first suffer from personality changes after so long in a coma and after so much sedation, but then they reassured her that in time he should be himself. She was prepared to cope with this, but what would she do if he actually died?

She knew that she still loved him; surely there couldn't be any doubt in anyone's mind about that. After nearly twenty-five years together, although they no longer shared feelings of great passion, perhaps they never had, and she had convinced him that she could no longer muster any kind of sexual desire, there was still an affinity. No something greater than an affinity, a real bond between them.

Not only that, and she felt completely selfish just thinking about it, there were all the little things he did for her each day. The breakfasts every morning, she had missed them since he had been away, plus the cleaning and the other chores he did around the house. Her friends were continually telling her how lucky she was to have a husband that actually enjoyed housework, who wasn't afraid to empty the rubbish bins or push a vacuum around the house, and who could even put an enjoyable meal together.

It wasn't just the things he could do for her that she missed, though. She thought about the amount of time they had spent just discussing everyday events, watching television or taking walks together. After so many years together, there were the funny little things that they both noticed almost every day, that reminded them of a previous occurrence and that after little more than a glance at each other, could provoke instant laughter. Admittedly, they had always had more time for each other than most of their friends, they hadn't had to spend all their spare time chasing around after children, taking them to their various activities and scrimping on things in order to pay for school fees, but somehow she felt that it would never have been a problem for them. Arthur would have simply found the time, she was sure.

Of course, it probably hadn't been fair for her to let him think the reason for their inability to have children had been his fault, or to have dissuaded him from pursuing tests to determine the reason, by telling him that she simply didn't want them. Perhaps it was true; she had been told after the complications of the abortion that she would never be able to conceive and after that she had put the idea of having children completely out of her mind.

'Were you finished with this?'

Ester looked up. A cleaner stood in front of her indicating the cold cup of coffee. She nodded and watched as the tired-looking woman with ankles swollen from carrying her excessive weight, wordlessly emptied the cup into the container on her trolley, before pushing it to the table next to the drinks machine, already covered with empty cups. Ester continued to watch her as she slowly stacked them onto the trolley, made a token gesture of wiping the table's surface with a damp cloth and waddled out behind the squeaking trolley.

Momentarily, she felt a twinge of guilt as she thought about the draining board at home covered with dirty dishes, the confusion of clean and dirty things in the dishwasher and the heaps of old newspapers and empty takeaway containers in the sitting room. This time, she promised herself, she really would tidy up the house before Arthur came home. She could not bear to watch him again, quietly going about the house putting things in order as he had so many times before, after a long overnight flight when he'd been away on business for a few days. Nor did she want to see the look of resignation on his face as he quietly listened to her improbable excuses about the creative and their incompatibility with tidiness.

'Yes dear,' she had heard him say so many times. 'One day, you'll write that novel you keep talking about, or perhaps do some more painting.'

He had always made those remarks or similar, without a hint of derision and had explained long ago, after one of their early arguments, that if it was his need for order, and his alone, then he should be prepared to create it. She remembered she had once accused him of obsessiveness and had protested that it wasn't natural for a man to want things to be so orderly, but he had simply said that as a child, he had found it the only way to be compared favourably to his older brother.

It was funny when she thought back; at the time it seemed the most horrible thing she would ever have to endure. She had resented her father's stipulations, but she could not bear to see that look of disgust on his face ever again and had agreed to his demands. Charles had been sent away, never again to creep late at night into her room. Never again to take advantage of the passion she had felt for her older brother.

She had not been remotely in love with Arthur, nor did she ever expect to love him as she came to, but he had been her father's choice. Max had thought that his stability would be good for her, had encouraged her to see him and had made subtle arrangements for occasions when they could meet. When the inevitable happened and Arthur succumbed to her charms, Max had welcomed him into the family as he had Charles' new wife.

Ester looked at her watch; it was still a quarter of an hour until the time the nurses had told her Arthur would be ready for another visit. She wondered what changes they would have had to make overnight; he had seemed to be improving yesterday and they had spoken optimistically that he might be able to come off the respirator. Perhaps this would be the day that she actually received some positive news.

Whatever happened she knew it would be necessary to make some changes. She was determined that she would tackle the chaos at home. She would try to tidy her wardrobe and dressing room, and find a way to organize the cupboards and freezer, throwing out the surplus of overbuying. It seemed an insurmountable task, but Arthur had always told her it was simply like laying bricks. That to build a brick wall, or a building, might appear to be too big a job for any one person, but they all went up one brick at a time. She might at last even resort to hiring a cleaner; why should she worry about disapproving looks from someone she was paying?

And of course, Hugh would have to go. She felt a little twinge of excitement just thinking of him. Or was it amusement? She had nearly laughed out loud at his absurd attempts at power dressing on their first meeting. He had arrived early to pick up Elizabeth from their bridge club and without an invitation, he had pulled his chair alongside his wife's, but with one of his wide spread legs brushing against Ester's thigh.

Why she had mentioned that Arthur was away on business, or why she had let her free hand drop to surreptitiously stroke his leg, she never knew, but he had arrived at her house by eleven the next morning. She had opened the door still clad in her dressing gown and although she had expressed complete surprise, the gown had been discarded before they even entered the living room. The strength of his attention had been so intoxicating, it was as if he could easily see the dissolute side she had tried so hard to hide; it was like some of her wildest fantasies of being ravished, and she had been a willing and an encouraging participant.

But she was also aware of his complete lack of fiscal responsibility. Too often poor Elizabeth had spoken of his failed 'projects,' of his boasts about his next big venture, and of the many times she had bailed him out of trouble with her dwindling inheritance. It was not only in his sexual habits that he was so like Charles; she simply could not let him destroy her life.

'Mrs Howard?' She had been so deep in thought that she had not heard the nurse enter the room; it was the stern, seemingly unsympathetic one. 'Would you like to come back to the "quiet room" with me?'

Ester winced at the sound. The "quiet room" was just the beyond the intensive care unit, where they sometimes took relatives to explain procedures or more often, to give bad news. Ester followed the woman's purposeful stride, trying unsuccessfully to keep up with her, until she turned the corner and held the door open to let Ester enter.

'Please, have a seat; Mr Morgan will be with you in a minute.'

Thankfully, the woman had decided against waiting with her and had pulled the door closed as she left. Ester tried to remember which one was Mr Morgan. She had little time to wonder, he was suddenly in the room, taking one of her hands in both of his. The look of sympathy on his face demolished any hope she had this discussion was merely to explain some new procedure. Why had she let Arthur go off to see his old friends when their last words together had been so heated?

She listened without hearing to the meaningless platitudes and the talk of unexpected changes, staring only at the huge picture behind him of the whale's dripping tail about to strike the surrounding water. What was he saying now? Something about tigers, for God's sake.

'What?' she asked completely bewildered. 'Could you repeat that?'

'I only asked you if there was something significant about tigers, if it meant anything to you.'

'I... I... tigers? No, I don't think so. Why?'

'It's just that; early this morning, before his condition started deteriorating, he was able to say a few words. It seemed terribly important to him, but of course, he might have been still feeling the effects of the sedation. He was very faint; the nurse had to put her ear almost to his mouth, but she said she could hear him quite plainly.'

'So,' Ester was rapidly losing her patience, 'what was it that he said?'

'The nurse said that he repeated your name several times. She thought for a minute that he had mistaken her for you, until she realized that he was saying, "Tell Ester..." When she asked him what he wanted her to tell you, he said to tell you that it wasn't the tigers. He said it two or three times. She said it seemed terribly important to him.'

'And that was it? He didn't say anything more?'

'She was too busy getting help to listen any longer. All of his levels had suddenly started dropping. They put him back on the respirator as quickly as possible, but it was as if someone had turned off a switch. I'm so very sorry.'

'I really can't think what he could have meant about tigers,' the man's face was suddenly blurred as she reached for the offered tissue. 'Maybe it will come to me in time.'

The End

Lightning Source UK Ltd.
Milton Keynes UK
UKHW041339060622
403994UK00001BA/122